D1367030

# GRIEVANCES

## A novel

# Mark Ethridge

NEWSOUTH BOOKS
Montgomery | Louisville

NewSouth Books
P.O. Box 1588
Montgomery, AL 36102


Copyright © 2006 by Mark Ethridge
All rights reserved under International and Pan-American Copyright
Conventions. Published in the United States by NewSouth Books, a
division of NewSouth, Inc., Montgomery, Alabama.

Library of Congress Cataloging-in-Publication Data

Ethridge, Mark.
Grievances / Mark Ethridge.
p. cm.
Novel.
ISBN-13: 978-1-58838-192-7
ISBN-10: 1-58838-192-7
I. Title.
PS3605.T47G75 2005
813'.6—dc22
2005031245


Design by Brian Seidman
Printed in the United States of America

*To my family*

# Acknowledgments

Thanks to Liz Holt, Margaret Lucas and Doug Marlette for providing early encouragement for this book and to Gerry Hostetler for letting me use her quote; to Jeff Kellogg of the Stuart Agency for his brilliant editing and for keeping the faith; and to Randall Williams, Suzanne La Rosa, and Brian Seidman at NewSouth Books for believing enough in *Grievances* to make it happen.

# GRIEVANCES

# Chapter One

There's something about a newsroom that attracts people with grievances. After five years in the business, I've seen my share of people convinced that the government is bugging their house, that aliens are controlling their brains, that a partner has cheated them out of a fortune, or that an ex-spouse is illegally denying them contact with their kids.

Because I work nights with no regular beat, I'm often assigned to talk to these nut cases and I've developed a talent for quickly identifying them. Reams of documents or long chronologies written in capital letters are dead giveaways. But I also think I have a genetic gift, passed on by my journalism family. My father, Lucas Harper Jr., was the beloved editor at *The Detroit Free Press* and his father was the crusading publisher of *The New York Sun*. They must have been good at spotting nut cases. In this business, you don't get far unless you can.

But snap decisions can be wrong. Everyone in the business remembers the city editor who dismissed anonymous accusations about sexual escapades and the theft of millions by a TV evangelist. The tipster contacted another newspaper, which won the Pulitzer Prize for the Jim and Tammy Faye Bakker scandal. And my father's newspaper had won a Pulitzer Prize after it pursued a crazy, anonymous tip that a 1972 vice presidential candidate had received electroshock therapy and kept it hidden. No one wanted to be the editor or reporter who failed to take the next PTL club or Thomas Eagleton call.

I was running late when I reached my cubicle in the *Charlotte Times* newsroom. Walker Burns, my boss and the managing editor, sprawled in my chair, his feet on my desk. The sight stopped me short and sank my stomach like a blue light in the rearview mirror.

"Matt, what a dang treat!" he said, springing up to pump my hand like I was a long-lost friend. "Thank you sooooo much for coming in today." At six foot four to my five foot ten, Walker towered over me. I felt like Romper Room's youngest, smallest student being welcomed by Miss Francis.

"Sorry, Walker."

"No problem, pardner. But a bunch of us have gotten together and decided we're gonna try to put out a newspaper." His smile loomed over the silver and turquoise slide of his Texas string tie. "I was beginnin' to worry we were gonna have to saddle up and ride off without you."

"Sorry, Walker."

"Well, now that we're all ready to go, there's some ol' boy at the reception desk who's showed up with a yarn to spin. Spend some time with him. See if he's got anything."

"That's the only thing we got going?"

"I could always round you up an obit . . ."

Obituaries were Walker's ultimate bad assignment threat. "That's okay," I said. "Has he been drinking?"

"Doesn't appear so."

"Is he wacky?"

"Well, pardner, your job is to figure that out," he said as he headed back to the city desk. "But I don't think we're lookin' at another Colonel Sanders."

Colonel Sanders was a deranged but harmless man who had visited the newsroom regularly for several years. He told anyone who would listen that he'd been a colonel in Korea and that he'd been captured by the Communists who had inserted a transmitter in his brain. The VA, he said, had turned down his disability claims because they were all part of the same conspiracy, as were a number of Congressmen to whom he had also written without result. Reporters new to the story were shown the correspondence.

When Colonel Sanders died a pauper and with no known relatives, the newspaper did a story and Walker Burns took up a collection to give him a proper burial. Because a portion of the fund was diverted for election-night pizzas, there was only enough for cremation and a simple urn, which, along with Colonel Sanders's ashes, was delivered back to Walker, whose name was on the forms from the funeral home.

Colonel Sanders still sat on a corner of Walker's cluttered city desk, next to the police scanner. Over the years, a baseball cap had been placed on top of the urn and a cigar stuck out from under the lid. Colonel Sanders no longer talked, but in the heat of deadline, he was talked to a lot.

I draped my blue blazer over the back of my chair, loosened my tie, and motioned to the receptionist to send the man over.

He wore a tweed jacket with leather elbow patches, open-at-the-collar Oxford blue shirt, gray slacks, and brown walking shoes. He was narrow-shouldered, trim, and a little pale. He moved delicately through the newsroom. He could have passed as a teacher at a boarding school. I judged him to be in his mid-thirties, just a bit older than me.

He reached the cubicle and extended his hand. "I'm Bradford Hall."

"Matt Harper." We shook hands.

"Thank you for agreeing to see me."

"It's what I get paid for." I didn't say it in a mean way, but it was important to establish distance. I was there to collect information, not become an advocate. There's usually a point where you have to tell people like Hall that the paper won't be covering their story.

"Oh, thank you," he said, reaching inside his coat pocket for his wallet. "I wasn't sure how it worked. How much?"

"No. No. No. It's not like that. The newspaper pays me. You don't have to pay me unless you're buying an ad or a subscription in which case you've come to the wrong guy. What brings you to the *Times?*" I was thinking I might be done with Mr. Hall in a hurry. Obits, here we come.

He glanced around the newsroom. "Is there a, uh, better place we can talk?"

It was late in the afternoon. The time for planning tomorrow morning's edition was past and the actual work of writing, editing, and laying out the paper was picking up, the pace marked by the muted machine-gun tapping from several dozen keyboards. The desks were full. The conference rooms were empty. I selected the one with the fewest coffee stains on the carpet and some framed *Charlotte Times* Famous Front Pages (Man Walks on Moon; Billy Graham at White House; Kennedy Shot) on the wall. I slouched into a well-worn brown couch; Bradford Hall sat on the edge of a matching easy chair. He wasted no time.

"I am here because your newspaper has a reputation for being concerned about justice. I've read about what the *Charlotte Times* has done in the past. You led the way on civil rights. The *Times* supported the sit-ins and school busing. The *Times* was about the only Southern newspaper to say something nice about Dr. King."

"True," I said with some pride.

"Well, I'm in the middle of something—something that has to do with justice and with civil rights. I think it might be a story."

I looked hard at Bradford Hall. On the surface, there was nothing to identify him as crazy. No impossibly smeared eyeglasses or overcoat in summer or sheaves of clippings and "affidavits" spilling out of a battered briefcase.

"Go on."

"First off, I'm not from here."

"I could tell."

He laughed. "I'm told I haven't lost my Yankee accent. But, these days I live mostly in South Carolina at our family plantation along the Savannah River, although from the rest of the family's point of view, I've become not very welcome."

"What happened?"

"They feel I ask too many questions."

Something about how he said it got my attention. Nothing gets a journalist going like someone telling him that he's asking too many questions. We get paid to ask the questions, however rude. We will decide, not the people we are questioning, when there are too many of them. I didn't even know Bradford Hall. And he wasn't a journalist. But I knew

I didn't like anyone telling him he was asking too many questions. I sat up straight on the couch.

"About what?

"A shooting. A murder, really. In Hirtsboro, a tiny little town by our plantation. The victim was a thirteen-year-old black kid named Wallace Sampson."

"When did this happen?"

"Almost twenty years ago." He sat back in his chair. "After some civil unrest."

I took out my reporter's notebook. "What was his name, again?"

"Wallace Sampson. He was shot in the head with a deer rifle shortly after midnight. He was in the black part of town. They took him to the medical school at Charleston but he was already dead. No one was ever charged. I don't know if anybody even investigated."

"But you have been."

"Yes, I guess I have."

"Why?"

Bradford Hall eased back into the brown chair and it seemed to swallow him up. "You know," he said after a while, "my father asks me that. My wife asks me that. Sometimes, *I* even ask me that. The only way I can explain is if I start at the beginning."

For the next two hours I watched through the thin slits of the conference room windows as the sun set, the sky flushed pink, then darkened to deep blue and black. In the newsroom, dayside reporters packed up and went home. Copy carriers shuttled between the news desk and the back shop, carrying the early proofs of the next day's pages. My colleagues on the night shift busied themselves with their assignments, trips to the coffee pot, and the occasional detour to catch a careful nonchalant peek inside the conference room. Reporters are paid to know what's going on. Closed doors make them nervous.

He talked. I mostly listened. Because for Bradford Hall, starting at the beginning meant starting more than three hundred and fifty years ago when his family came over on the Mayflower. In succeeding generations, he said, Bradfords had served as governors and senators and preachers and philanthropists. His great-great-grandfather had started New England's biggest bank. Another started Bradford College. And, of course, along the way, the family acquired some fabulous property—an estate in Boston; one in Westchester County, New York; a summer compound on Martha's Vineyard; a winter home in Florida; and in South Carolina's Low Country, a plantation known as Windrow.

"I was there several months ago working in the potting shed when I overheard two of the help talking. Mary Pell runs everything and she was talking to Willie Snow, our caretaker, and she said, 'Do you think Mrs. Sampson will ever find peace?' And Willie Snow said, 'Not until there's justice.'

"I don't think they knew I was there until I asked her who Mrs. Sampson was. And she said, 'Just some momma that lost her baby a long time ago. Nothing you need to fret about.' I didn't fret about it but I didn't forget about it. A few days later, I asked her again. She didn't want to discuss it. That got me even more interested."

I sympathized. "I hate it when people tell me something's not my business. I'll be the judge of whether it's my business."

"Me, too. I guess I've always had a curious streak," Bradford continued. "I studied botany at Harvard. I've made it a life goal to identify every plant species at Windrow. It drives me crazy when there's a plant I don't know. I wanted to know more about Mrs. Sampson, so I started poking around."

"So why do you care about this?"

"It bothers me that it was never investigated. It bothers me that no one wants to talk about it. Plus, it's an intellectual challenge. Solving the murder of Wallace Sampson is like trying to find the name of a plant I can't identify. I really can't stop until I do."

Over the years, the building that houses the *Times* had settled and some of the floors had become uneven. The problem was particularly pronounced on the fifth floor, where the newsroom shared space with the library, and it was at its worst in the corner where the conference room was located. As a result, the walls shook and the Famous Front Pages rattled when someone approached. Certain staffers had very distinct walks and I could tell from the nature of the rattle who was coming before they got there.

Walker Burns was on his way. He knocked, opened the door part way, and stuck his head in.

"Can I borrow you for a moment, Matt?"

Bradford stood. "I'm sorry, I've really taken too much time."

"Sit down," I told him. "I'll be right back." I followed Walker out of the conference room.

"Are we comfy in there?" he whispered. "Can I get you anything? Coffee? A donut?"

"Sorry, Walker."

"What's this loco want anyway?"

"I'm finding that out."

He opened his eyes wide in mock disbelief. "You don't know yet? In the amount of time you've already spent with that guy I could have written *War and Peace!*"

I rolled my eyes.

"Wrap it up and get your hide out here! The publisher just came by with a tip about some fatcat downtown friend of his who died. He wants an obit for tomorrow morning."

"Why can't Ronnie Bullock do it? He's the obit writer."

"If you've got some journalism more worthwhile to do, then *you* ask him to do it." Walker headed back to the city desk.

I returned to the conference room.

"I hope I didn't get you in trouble," said Bradford. He started to stand again. I motioned him back down.

"I'm going to have to wrap it up," I said. "This investigation of yours is all very interesting, but what is it that you expect us to do?"

Bradford Hall sat so far forward on the edge of his chair that he was practically kneeling. "When it comes to finding out about plants, I know where to look. There are books and periodicals and drawings and texts. When it comes to a killing, I don't know where to start. I was hoping you or someone here could help me. You could even stay at my place. I once saw a newspaper series about unsolved crimes. Maybe the *Times* could look into this. Maybe somebody wrote about it at the time. Maybe somebody remembers."

My job is night general assignment reporter. I come in late in the afternoon. By the time I arrive, the creative stories, the ones where you can really write or really investigate, have already been given to the dayside reporters the big editors favor. Those of us on the nightside get the obits, the stories from the cop shop, and night general assignment. Whatever's left. That's generally not going to include any time spent writing about a years-old unsolved killing on the edge of our circulation area.

But before I told Hall that, I wanted to do a little checking. I thanked him for thinking of the *Charlotte Times*, told him I would get back to him, and ushered him out of the newsroom.

On my way back to my cubicle, I passed Bullock. "Ronnie," I asked, "Any way you can handle this obit for me? I've got to get back to the library and pull some clips on this nut case."

"Sure thing," he said. "We wouldn't want to have to burden the progeny of Lucas Harper with the unseemly task of writing obits."

Bullock could be lazy, not to mention a jerk. I've never used being a Harper to get ahead. If I had, would I be a general assignment reporter working nights at a mid-sized daily in North Carolina? The truth of it is, in terms of journalism, neither my father nor grandfather taught me anything. Lucas Sr. was dead before I arrived and Lucas Jr. might as well have been.

"Forget it," I told Bullock. "I'll do it myself."

It was the end of the shift before I could get to the newsroom library. Nancy Atkinson, the librarian, peered at me over her glasses. "Almost twenty years ago? You're waaaay before newsroom computers, honey. In fact, you're before microfiche. You'll be looking for clippings."

Assassinations, wars, scandals—Miss Nancy had catalogued it all. I couldn't recall her ever getting excited about much of anything. But Miss Nancy actually hurried past the library's computers and the film readers and deep into a maze of shoulder-high Army-green filing cabinets. I could sense her delight.

"It's so nice to retrieve real stories from real newspapers," she sighed.

"Even microfiche is okay. But computers and these files make news stories seem so artificial. Anyway, there's no proof anything was really ever printed. No proof at all."

Miss Nancy bent down in front of one of the cabinets and pulled out a drawer, releasing the unmistakable musty smell of aging newsprint. She fingered through a row of brown envelopes and pulled one labeled *Murders–South Carolina*.

Inside were maybe a hundred clippings, most a paragraph or two long. They were arranged by date so it didn't take me long to find the one I was looking for. It was yellowed but didn't look like it had been touched since it had been put in the morgue. The four-paragraph clip had been stamped in red with the date it ran in the *Times*. It read in its entirety:

### South Carolina Youth Shot, Dies

Hirtsboro, S.C. (AP) A 13-year-old boy was shot in the head shortly after midnight here Friday night.

Wallace Sampson was taken by Hirtsboro Ambulance to the Medical University of South Carolina in Charleston where a spokesman said he was pronounced dead.

Police said they were investigating.

The shooting followed several nights of racial unrest.

I scanned the rest of the clips. There were plenty of other briefs on stabbings and shootings and one longer piece about a Spartanburg preacher who'd been poisoned by his wife. But there had been no follow-up stories about the Sampson incident. I made a copy of the clip and returned the file to Miss Nancy.

"Are you on to something, Matt?"

"I don't know," I said, which was true. Most of these things never went anywhere.

I headed back to the newsroom deep in thought. Some of Bradford Hall's story checked out but that didn't mean much. I knew nothing about him beyond what he'd told me. But I liked what I saw in him—curiosity, honesty, a willingness to pursue something, even against opposition, that he could have ignored. And of all the people with grievances I'd ever met, he was one of the most unusual: a Yankee blueblood investigating an unsolved South Carolina civil rights murder of almost twenty years ago.

I slid into my cubicle and lost myself in a photograph I keep on my desk, one my father took of my late brother Luke and me in our swimming suits standing on a platform floating in the middle of a lake. We're tanned, wet, and smiling. Luke, a head taller, has his right arm around my shoulder. Cradled in his left arm is a football, its leather soaked black from a game of catch that quickly escalated to spectacular diving grabs made while leaping into the lake from the platform.

I was still in the picture when a stack of letters, held together with rubber bands, hit my desk with a thud. The top letter was addressed to "The Racist Reporter" with the name and address of the *Charlotte Times*. I thumbed through the others. More of the same.

I looked up at the receptionist, who had known exactly for whom the letters were intended. "It's such a shame, Matt. They've got you all wrong."

I shrugged. "I understand where they're coming from."

"At least the demonstrators in front of the building are gone," she said hopefully. "Did they ever find out where you lived?"

Walker Burns has a saying: "If your mother says she loves you, check it out." This seemed like a very good weekend to spend some time checking out Hirtsboro and Bradford Hall.

# Chapter Two

The northbound traffic on the interstate faced me three-wide and stretched as far as I could see as I headed south toward Hirtsboro. The sprawl of south Charlotte spilled seamlessly into York County, South Carolina, and, except for billboards touting fireworks, video poker, and subdivisions with lower South Carolina taxes, there was little to indicate that life fundamentally changes once you cross the border to the Palmetto state.

But it does. South Carolina was the last of the original thirteen colonies to join the union, the first state to leave the union after the start of the Civil War in Charleston, and the last to rejoin the country after the South had lost. South Carolina has always operated by a slightly different set of rules.

Whenever things got slow on the city desk, Walker Burns would send a reporter to troll around South Carolina for a few days. Inevitably, that would produce a fantastic story along the lines of: blacks who weren't being allowed to vote in a Low Country town that hadn't yet gotten the word; a funeral home that kept as an advertisement in its front window the embalmed body of an Italian carnival worker (known locally as "Spaghetti") who had died and been left behind when the show moved on; two NASCAR fans who wounded each other after staging an old-fashioned pistol duel over the question of which was a better race car—Ford or Chevrolet. (Technically, the duel had been written about previously. The new angle uncovered by Walker's South Carolina bureau chief related to the claim by local officials that taxes should have been paid on the $1,725 in tickets sold to attend the duel.)

Walker says that for every mile you go deeper into South Carolina, you go another year back in time. By his reckoning, by the time I got to Hirtsboro I'd be in the antebellum South.

As I cleared Rock Hill, the subdivisions gave way to peach orchards and rolling hills of red clay. I turned off the interstate near Columbia where the land flattened and the soil turned sandy. In the fields, tufts of picked-over cotton clung to dead, stripped black stalks like tiny flags of surrender.

South of Bamberg, I pulled off the asphalt and onto the hard-packed sand that served as the driveway for a white-painted cinderblock Gulf station, next to the Orange Blossom Motel and Tourist Cabins. I pumped gas and went inside, where a wizened old man whose shirt identified him as "Shorty" smoked on a stool behind the cash register and watched the store, the driveway, and an evangelist on a small black and white television. I picked out a six-ounce glass bottle of Coke and a postcard that had a picture of black field workers piling cotton bales on a truck and the words "Every Yankee Tourist is Worth a Bale of Cotton and Much Easier to Pick."

"Be anything else now?" Shorty asked, grinding the butt of an unfiltered Camel into an overflowing ashtray.

"I need a pen. Do you have a pen?"

"Do what?"

"A pen."

"I don't believe we carry no pea-uns. I mean we used to carry 'em—diaper pea-uns and such but folks don't hardly use 'em no more. I wanna say we don't have any." He lit another cigarette and returned to the TV.

"I mean a pen."

"That's what I said. Pea-un."

"Like you write with."

"Oh, you mean pin. No, we don't have none of those neither."

An hour and fifteen minutes later, I arrived at the entrance to

Windrow. Two brick columns and a simple black iron gate marked a dirt road that left the paved highway and went laser-straight through a thick forest of slash pines.

The road was wide and well-maintained and in a few minutes I'd emerged from the pines. The road took a hard left and skirted a flat field of corn stubble that stretched to the horizon. Ahead, on a slight rise, stood the plantation home of Bradford Hall. He had described it as "modern." What it was was a modern architectural wonder—stark, soaring walls, vast windows of tinted glass, angular porches. About the only thing it had in common with the columned antebellum Scarlett O'Hara plantation mansion of my imagination was its color—white.

Two golden retrievers bounded out the front door and ran up to meet the Honda. They were followed by Hall.

"I can't tell you how pleased I am that you've come," he said. The dogs sniffed my legs and eagerly wagged their tails. "Tasha and Maybelle agree. I'm sorry my wife Lindsay McDaniel isn't with me to greet you but she'll arrive from New York tomorrow. Let me help you with your things."

He showed me into the house. Its core was a massive two-story living room with a glass wall overlooking the rocky shallows of the Savannah River. A stone fireplace and hearth had been built into the wall but with no chimney to interrupt the view. Instead, Bradford explained, a hidden fan sucked the fireplace smoke down, out, and away. My room was off one of two spiral staircases that flanked the entrance to the living room. From my bedroom, a sliding glass door led to a triangle-shaped porch that jutted out, like a ship's prow.

We walked out to the porch and looked over the river. "Nice view," I said.

"Thank you. It does what I intended. The magic of Windrow is the river, the animals, the plants. I wanted to live outside, but inside. I wanted to bring the outside in. There are no curtains. It makes Lindsay rather uncomfortable but the fact is, you don't need them. We're pretty much alone here. My father's place is a couple miles away, at a different bend in the river, but it might as well be a couple of states away."

He pointed to a battered Ford pickup in the driveway. "We're on our own until Lindsay arrives tomorrow. Lemme show you around."

A box of plastic bags, a safari hat, and a well-worn copy of *South Carolina Wildflowers* sat in the passenger seat. I tossed them on the floor and climbed in.

"My plant-hunting gear," Bradford said. He wheeled the pickup down the driveway and out toward the main road. "General Sherman came right through here," he said, sweeping his arm out the window and gesturing across a rolling cornfield that stretched to the horizon. "An English planter started Windrow in the early 1820s as a freshwater rice and indigo plantation. Confederate General Beauregard used the main house as a field headquarters for a while. But when the Yankees came through, they pretty much left the place alone."

"Why?"

"In a hurry to get to the sea, I suppose. Anyway, it was lucky. My great-grandfather and his brothers bought it years ago for bird-hunting. They had their own railroad line from Augusta and they'd haul everything in—food, supplies, servants, guides and guests—entertain for the season and then return to Massachusetts and New York. My grandfather built a year-round place that my father lives in now. I spent my early years up North and went to school there but Windrow is where I really grew up."

We turned off the road and cut across the dry corn stubble, kicking up dust as we bounced to the top of a rise. In the distance the Savannah River stretched to the horizon like a piece of silver string. We returned to the road and had been driving about twenty minutes when I asked, "How big's the plantation?"

"We're still on it."

"Oh."

He pulled to the side of the road and turned off the engine. "I have to tell you, I find it very embarrassing. The size. The houses. The help. The lifestyle. It's how I was brought up. It's who I am and I'm proud of what my forebears accomplished. But when you see how people live here, the disparity is appalling. It's not fair. But that's not a very popular position in my family."

"Did you develop this concern for social justice at Harvard?"

"Didn't have a chance," he laughed. "Got thrown out after my sophomore year. The administration took exception to some of the plants I was cultivating in the botany lab."

I laughed.

"It was the times," he shrugged. "Anyway, I'd already finished all the good botany courses. Let's head into town and I'll give you a look at Hirtsboro."

Bradford started the pickup and did a U-turn. We stayed in the shade cast by the long shadows of the pines as we headed back down the road. A heavy sweetness filled the cab.

"*Daphne odora*," he said.

"What?"

"That sweet smell is from *Daphne odora*. Botanists identify lots of things by smell. It's an ornamental shrub from the Mezereum family. In Greek myth, Daphne was a nymph who changed into a shrub to avoid Apollo's advances. Her scent lingers, very fragrant as you can tell. *Daphne odora* is a very difficult plant. Short lifespan and nurseries don't like to stock it. But at Windrow, it grows wild."

"It's intoxicating."

"I understand she was quite an alluring nymph."

"Bradford, how'd you get into botany?"

"Call me Brad. Not many kids to play with at Windrow, at least not many kids my parents deemed 'up to Hall standards.' So I made friends with the plantation animals, became a vegetarian when I figured out some of them were ending up on my dinner plate, and I started getting interested in Windrow's plants."

"It seems like a good place to do it."

"It is. Botanically, Windrow is in a marvelous part of the world. It's in a region that's the northernmost subtropical point in the United

States. I have in mind to do a coffeetable book devoted entirely to the botany of Windrow. You have pine trees and palm trees—more plant species than you could ever imagine. The frustrating thing is when you come across something that just doesn't seem to have a name. Tracking down the facts becomes an obsession."

"I know the feeling."

It was mid-afternoon when we arrived in Hirtsboro. The sun scorched with the intensity of a heat lamp, glinting off railroad tracks that bisected the town and split treeless Jefferson Davis Boulevard, a lane on each side. Two blocks of one- and two-story storefronts faced each other across the boulevard. I took out my notebook and wrote down the signs as we drove by: Farmers & Mechanics Insurance Agency; the Great Southern Auto Supply and Appliance Store; International Feed & Seed; a consignment store called Second Time Around; Classen's Clothes (Come to Classen's for Classy Clothes!); the First Bank of Hirtsboro (open Monday, Wednesday and Friday) and, in gold letters in old English type, *The Hirtsboro Reporter.*

"This town looks like the model train set my brother Luke and I had as kids," I said.

Brad turned off Jefferson Davis and we cruised slowly through the neighborhoods behind the storefronts. Unlike with the train set, there was a right side and wrong side of the tracks. On one side, a few blocks behind the storefronts, fine old homes sprawled on large lots with sidewalks and landscaped yards adorned with huge, spreading magnolias and carefully attended azaleas. In the neighborhoods on the other side of the tracks, peeling-paint shotgun houses sat on small sun-baked yards. There were no sidewalks. The streets were sandy, narrow, and unpaved.

"Savannah County is ninety percent black and always has been," Brad said. "The land's good for plantation crops like cotton, rice, and indigo. If you were white, you were a planter or maybe an overseer. If you were black, you were a slave. There wasn't much else. After Emancipation, people who were here just stayed and there's never been reason for anybody else to come. The white people, by and large, are descendants of the planters and overseers. The blacks are descendants of the slaves. It hasn't been that long."

We returned to the center of town where the diagonal lines of parking spaces angled out from the railroad track like bones from a fish spine. Brad parked his pickup with its bumper sticker reading "Meat is Dead" next to a souped-up Chevelle with a bumper sticker reading "I Have a Dream"—along with a picture of the Confederate flag flying over the U.S. Capitol.

"Let's stop in at the paper," Brad said. "I want you to meet the editor."

A young man with a large waist and green visor stood as we entered. Brad introduced me as a *Charlotte Times* reporter to Glenn Hudson and told him, "I've talked Matt into coming down here to look into the story."

"Great newspaper," Hudson said. "If I can help in any way, let me know."

Out the plate glass window, I watched a boy about seven or eight years old struggle to push a bent and broken bicycle across Jefferson Davis Boulevard. As he got closer, I could see he was crying.

The red bike's front wheel was folded over into a crescent. Snapped spokes splayed out in all directions. The handlebars were twisted, the seat turned sideways. The bike's white sidewall tires were flat. Struts of the frame intruded into the misshapen rear wheel so that it would not turn. The chain dragged on the ground.

Halfway across the street the boy gently lowered the bike and used his sleeve to wipe his eyes. Hudson shoved by me, ran into the street and scooped the boy up.

"My bi-i-i-ke," the boy sobbed.

The boy clasped his father's neck and buried his head in his shoulder. The man stroked his son's hair and kissed him on the cheek.

"What happened, son?"

"I rode my bike over to Michael and Chris's to play and they broke it. They had concrete blocks and they knocked it down and they just kept throwing them." The little boy wriggled out of his father's arms, hugged the bike's broken frame and broke into a new round of sobs. "They said their dad told them to because you're a nigger-lover."

Hudson picked up Jimmy with his right hand and slung him over his shoulder. With his left hand he picked up the bike and carried them both to the sidewalk. "C'mon, Jimmy," he said. "We're going shopping."

Brad and I watched them disappear into the Great Southern Auto Supply and Appliance store. They emerged a few minutes later, Jimmy riding a new red bike in circles around his father.

When they got back to the newspaper office Hudson took several copies of that week's edition of *The Hirtsboro Reporter* and tucked them into his belt so that they covered his stomach. Then he showed Jimmy how to make a fist.

"Don't wrap your fingers around your thumb, you'll break it that way," he said. "Put your thumb on the outside. Now, hit me in the stomach, as hard as you can."

Jimmy poked at the newspapers.

"You won't hurt me. That what the papers are for."

Jimmy hit a little harder.

"I said hard!"

"Why?"

"Because nobody's going to do that to your bike again."

It took a few more times and a bit more encouragement, but eventually Jimmy hit his father as hard as he could.

I wanted to cry. I know some of it was because I had been moved by what I had just seen—by Hudson's love for his son, his instinct to do whatever it took to protect him, and by Jimmy's need for his father. My father never would have done that for me.

But mostly it was because I was angry. I was angry at parents who encourage hate. I was angry at the cruelty kids inflict on each other. I was angry that an innocent boy named Jimmy had to be hurt for something he had nothing to do with. I was angry that he had to be taught to make a fist so that he could defend himself.

Before we left, Brad took out his wallet, peeled off some twenty-dollar bills and offered them to Hudson. "For the bike. I should never have gotten you into this."

Hudson waved the money aside. "Cowardly bastards. One damn editorial. I'm gonna get 'em back."

On the drive back to Windrow, I asked Brad what Hudson had written.

"Something outlandish and radical," he said. "He wrote that Hirtsboro should try to solve the murder of Wallace Sampson."

# Chapter Three

The next morning, a blast of humidity and the high whine of cicadas greeted Brad and me as we left the house and crunched across the gravel to the pickup for the drive back into Hirtsboro.

"If there are any Sampson family members around, they'll be at church," Brad said as we parked near the fountain. "And if they're not there themselves, someone at church will know where they are."

On the right side of the tracks, a bell began to toll, slowly at first and then with increasing vigor as it summoned the white population to services. From the wrong side of the tracks, the breeze carried the strong chords of a piano.

We followed the music, drawn to a large white wooden-frame building with a simple steeple at the corner of two sandy streets. The church sagged from age but the exterior was freshly painted and the lawn neatly mowed. A sign identified it as the Mt. Moriah House of Prayer, pastored by the Reverend Clifford Grace. The front door was open and we could see the backs of the people in the congregation and, up front, two high-backed altar chairs covered in red velvet. Behind the chairs on risers fourteen members of the purple-robed choir—men and women, young and old, black—swayed as they sang "Precious Lord, Take My Hand."

I had seen this scene before, but only in my mind. When I was little, my family would drive from Detroit to Florida for a week at the beach and on Sunday we would leave at the crack of dawn to drive home. Dad would fiddle with the radio as he drove, discovering each year that on

Sunday mornings in the South, church was the only thing broadcast. With pianos, electric guitars, and singers and preachers that sounded like they meant it, black church services were much more entertaining than white. I would close my eyes as we listened, trying to picture the small country churches, their preachers, and their choirs.

By the time the choir finished with "Home is Over Jordan," *I* was home, in the station wagon with Mom and Dad in the front and Luke and me in the back, rolling northward as we listened to gospel music, the car filled with the smell of Thermos coffee and smoke from unfiltered Chesterfields.

Brad and I walked in quietly and slid into a back pew. A few members of the congregation turned our way and nodded—an old women in a lavender dress and an ornate flowered hat; a teenage boy in a bright blue athletic warm-up suit; a teenage girl with a gravity-defying swirl of hair; a man in a suit; a farmer in a threadbare jacket and boots.

I picked up a Popsicle-stick fan with a picture of a radiant brown-haired, blue-eyed Jesus on one side and the words "Courtesy of Short & Sons Mortuary" emblazoned on the back. Except for Jesus, Brad and I were the only white people in the place. A tall, lanky man in purple liturgical robes rose from one of the altar chairs, partially blocking my view.

"Thank you and praise Jesus for the magnificent choir," he boomed, leading the congregation in applause. When the clapping died, he said, "Before we end today we'll follow our custom of sharing our joys and concerns. Joys and Concerns, brothers and sisters." He stroked his salt-and-pepper beard and motioned to someone I couldn't see.

"My joy is that I'd like to ask our church youth basketball team to stand up because they won the league championship last Saturday up at Bamberg," said a woman. A round of applause and I saw the teenager in the athletic suit stand shyly.

A middle-aged woman near the front stood. "My concern is for my great aunt in Cincinnati who is in the hospital with surgery. I ask that the church pray for her." She sat.

The preacher pointed to a woman in the congregation. "I ask your prayers for my daughter Delicia and her kids in New York and that things get worked out with her boyfriend," she said.

A man in a blue suit stood. "I praise Jesus that the Men's Association chicken dinner raised six hundred fifty-eight dollars last Saturday night for new robes for the choir."

And so it went. A joy about a son's promotion in the Army; a concern about an ill parent; a joy about a new baby; a concern about a nephew in jail; a joy that Reverend Jesse Jackson was running for president; a concern about "the way things are up in Columbia." And then one that caused my heart to race: "I ask your prayers to give me strength to find justice for my loving son Wallace."

"Amen!" the congregation resounded.

When the service was over, the minister greeted us at the door. If he was surprised to see two white men among his worshipers, he didn't show it. He smiled a huge smile and extended his hand. "Welcome to a day the Lord hath made," he said. "I am the Reverend Clifford Grace."

"I'm Brad Hall. This is Matt Harper. I don't believe we've met but I live at Windrow. My family—"

"I know who you are, Mr. Hall," Rev. Grace interrupted.

"Reverend, I'm sure it's a surprise for you to see us here." Grace didn't react. Brad continued, "We've come because we could use your help."

"On Wallace Sampson," Grace said.

"How'd you know?"

Grace laughed. "Mary Pell is a member here."

"I'm surprised she brought it up," Brad said.

"Word gets around. Mr. Hall, it's been years since Wallace was killed. Rumors get started. People make guesses about who did it. And every Sunday, Etta Mae Sampson reminds us of a mother's pain. It's a poison in Hirtsboro, a devil that won't be exorcised. So, it's not a surprise when black people want to know who killed Wallace Sampson. But when a white man does, especially a Hall, that's something different."

"Were you here when it happened?" I asked.

"I was."

"Would you tell me about it?"

"Later." Reverend Grace glanced at his watch. "Right now, I've got to get on over to the county jail." He smiled. "Services for the prisoners."

As we left, Reverend Grace pointed out Etta Mae Sampson's white-frame house a block away.

For reporters, going to see the family of someone who has died comes with the territory. I have had to do it maybe half a dozen times. Once you're there, it often ends up being not as bad as it sounds. For one thing, survivors and family members usually want to talk. It helps them remember the dead and process their own grief. The other thing is that whatever you're asking them to do is a lot easier than what they've just been through. After you've actually lost a parent or a spouse or a child, how bad can talking about it really be?

Somehow all that logic never makes it any easier, though, and I was nervous as we knocked on the door of Etta Mae Sampson's house. Potted red geraniums were positioned on either side of the front door. A woman in her fifties, her dark hair pulled into a neat bun, came to the door but stayed behind the screen. Mrs. Sampson was still dressed for church in her purple dress and matching shoes.

"Mrs. Sampson, I'm Brad Hall and this is Matt Harper. I live at Windrow and Matt is a newspaper reporter up in Charlotte. I'm sorry to intrude. Mrs. Sampson, I'm wondering if we could ask you about Wallace."

"My Wallace?"

"Yes, ma'am."

"Did someone send you?"

"No, ma'am. We're here on our own. Matt is writing a story about what happened."

*Not so fast*, I thought, but kept quiet.

"Mary Pell works for you," she said to Brad.

"Yes, ma'am."

"I know who you are."

She turned to me. I was prepared to produce my press card but Mrs. Sampson didn't ask. Instead, she said, "I don't understand. Why now? What kind of story?"

I could have told her that Brad's explanation that I was doing a story wasn't exactly right, that Brad was the driving force and, at this point, I was still along for the ride, just taking a sniff, as those in the investigative reporting trade say. It's a Cardinal Rule that you never promise anybody there will be a story. There's just too much that can go wrong—from leads that don't pan out, to fresh news breaking, to production mistakes, to idiot editors. Every reporter has had the experience of going home at night with every assurance his story was going to appear and maybe even on the front page only to search through the next day's edition in disbelief because the story never ran.

But telling Mrs. Sampson that there might never be a story would have been like saying, "Mrs. Sampson, I'm not sure your dead son is worth writing about." So instead I said, "As I understand it, it's an unsolved murder and it's never really been investigated."

"It never was investigated but it isn't unsolved," she said matter-of-factly.

She invited us in and offered us some iced tea. We sat in her living room—Brad on an old upholstered chair with a lace doily, me uncomfortably on the edge of a rocker, and Mrs. Sampson on a dark red velvet settee. A small television sat in one corner, a simple kerosene heater in another. Three photographs hung on the wall: two eight-by-ten color pictures, unframed but protected by Saran Wrap, of Martin Luther King Jr. and of JFK, and a cardboard-framed school picture of a brightly smiling boy of twelve or thirteen in a red and white striped polo shirt, clearly the child of the woman to whom we were talking, despite his lighter skin.

If I ended up writing Wallace Sampson's story for the *Charlotte Times*, I knew that Walker Burns would want that photo. I had learned that lesson when I'd neglected to get a photo for a front-page Sunday story about a teenager who'd accidentally been electrocuted at the state prison.

"Oh, don't worry about a picture," Walker had said sarcastically. "We'll just let the readers imagine what the kid might have looked like." A breakneck four-hundred-mile, six-hour roundtrip drive to the boy's parents' house in Morehead City produced the photo just in time for deadline. I've never forgotten the lesson.

"Wallace was twelve when that picture was made," Mrs. Sampson said as she caught me staring at the photo. "I think about what he would look like now. Would he be tall, like his father? He was already pretty tall. He played on the church basketball team. Sometimes, I imagine that he's all grown up and sometimes I see him in heaven and he's my baby, with little angel wings. But every day, I think about what it would be like if none of this had ever happened and I came home and he was there, sitting there where you are, looking just like he is in that picture."

"Do you have other children?" Brad asked.

"The twins. Praise and Rejoice. They'd grown up and both moved to D.C. by the time Wallace was born."

Sometimes I think that what I get paid for is to ask the rude questions, the ones everyone else wants to ask but finds too difficult. "Mrs. Sampson," I said, "tell me about the day that it happened."

She closed her eyes, rocked back, and sat a long time before she spoke. "I told him not to be out late. There'd been trouble—a bunch of young hotheads in town. Wallace wasn't part of that crowd. He was over visiting his girlfriend. It was Friday night and I said, 'You be home before too late.' He said, 'Yes, ma'am.' That was the last thing he ever said to me, 'Yes, ma'am.'

"I stayed in bed waiting up for him, waiting for him to come home. It wasn't like Wallace to be late. And then someone knocked on the door and I knew it wasn't Wallace because he would never knock. I got my robe on and it was Reverend Grace and he told me Wallace had been shot." She wrung her hands, exhaled, and leaned forward. "They took him to Charleston, to the university, but he had already passed. I never got to see him. By the time Reverend Grace and I got there, they had done an autopsy. I didn't want them to but they said they had to and they'd already done it. They said because of where he was shot, in the head, that I wouldn't want to see him. But I wanted to. No matter what. He was still my Wallace, even if someone put a hole in his head. He was still my baby."

Softly, Wallace Sampson's mother began to weep and I began to wonder what I loved so much about reporting.

"He didn't have a suit," she continued. "He was only thirteen. So I gave Mr. Short at the mortuary his best school pants and that shirt in the picture to bury him in. All his school friends came. They wanted to see him one last time. But we couldn't have an open casket."

She composed herself. "He's buried up at the cemetery. You can go there. I go there every day."

"Why do you think Wallace was killed?" Brad asked.

"Meanness," she said, as if that explained everything. "The world is filled with so much meanness."

"Mrs. Sampson," I said, "when we first arrived you said Wallace's killing wasn't unsolved. I thought no one had ever been charged."

"That doesn't mean no one knows who did it. There are at least two who know for sure who did it."

"Which two?"

"Whoever shot him. They know they did it. And God. I believe Wallace was God's gift to me. God knows who killed Wallace. And God will make sure there is justice. Maybe not in my life. Maybe not on this earth. But God knows and He will have justice."

"I, for one, would prefer to see justice now, on this earth, and not wait for God," said Brad.

Mrs. Sampson looked him in the eye. "I know black folk that talk crazy like that. You're the first white."

"It's not crazy and there are other people, black and white, who feel the same way."

"Mary Pell said you were crazy. You got that article in *The Reporter* written, didn't you?"

"Yes, ma'am."

"And him down here?" She nodded at me.

"Yes."

"Well, you all do what you want," she said. "It don't matter to me. God will deliver the final judgment."

I asked to see Wallace's room. Two pairs of pants and two shirts hung on nails. A baseball bat, its broken handle nailed and taped back together, sat in a corner. A lump formed in my throat when I saw a basketball trophy inscribed "Wallace Sampson–Mr. Rebound" on the bedside table. A picture of twin girls was tucked into a corner of a small mirror above a dresser. A tiny school picture of another girl was pinned to the wall along with a poster of Hank Aaron.

"That's his girlfriend, Vanessa Brown," she said, pointing to the little picture. "I never changed anything in here since the night he didn't come home."

I picked up a framed picture of a younger Mrs. Sampson holding hands with a black man in an Army uniform. "My late husband," she said. He didn't look all that tall to me.

Mrs. Sampson sat on the edge of her dead son's bed. "I'm okay during the day. But I have trouble at night. Sometimes I awake from my dreams and I am scared that I will forget him. So I come to this room and I lie on his bed and I pick up his shirt and I can smell him in it. Each child has their own smell. Did you know that? And my worst time is when I become afraid that I will forget what he looked like and what he smelled like. I think that no one will remember him. So I look at his picture and I smell his shirt and I hold the trophy and I think to myself, I am holding the very thing that he held. And then I am only just that far away from him. And I tell him, 'You will never, ever, ever be forgotten.'"

As we said our good-byes I told Mrs. Sampson, "I'm sorry for your loss. I'm sorry to have to make you relive it."

"Mr. Harper, I relive it every day. You can't hurt me. I have already been hurt the worst that there is."

We left, having dredged up a mother's grief with no assurance that anything good would ever result from it. And without one of the things that we had come for. Because even though she had been hurt all she could, I just couldn't bring myself to ask Mrs. Sampson for her dead son's picture.

WE MET REVEREND GRACE later that afternoon after he returned from his jail ministry. He told us about the Friday night before the shooting when a group of about twenty young men threw stones at the Hirtsboro town police car near the wrong side of the tracks.

"The mayor called me down there to see what I could do," Reverend Grace recalled. "I knew most of the crowd. Mostly they were boys. A few of them were troublemakers but most were good kids. Some had been drinking and they were full of themselves. There was all this stuff going on all over the country—protests at black colleges, marches in the streets—and people were facing down authority. There was this feeling of power, like nothing anyone from Hirtsboro had ever felt before. I tried to calm them down but they didn't want to listen." It ended with the arrival of six sheriff's cruisers and twenty-four deputies.

"And that's all there was to it," Reverend Grace said. "The next night, Wallace Sampson got killed."

"Reverend Grace, do you know why Wallace Sampson was shot?" Brad asked.

Grace paused. "I only know what people say."

"Can you tell us?" I asked. "The truth shall make you free."

Grace gave me a rueful smile. "Not in Hirtsboro, South Carolina."

Being a reporter is all about trust. To get Reverend Grace to talk about what he really knew, he would need to trust me. It worked the other way, too. For me to evaluate what Reverend Grace said, I would need to know how much I could trust him.

"Reverend Grace, what brought you to Hirtsboro?"

"I believe it was the grace of God. I was assigned to this church right out of seminary. It was the posting they all laughed about through school—the poorest town, the meanest whites, the sorriest blacks. But it was the right posting for a four-hundred-fifty pound twenty-four-year-old who was last in his class, stuttered, and jiggled like jelly with every step."

Brad and I exchanged quick glances and stared in disbelief at the fit man before us. "I came here miserable and it only got worse. And one day I begged God to just take back my body and let me die. He didn't let me die but he did what I prayed for. He took control of my body. And with God in control, my weight began to drop. Because of my miracle I knew for certain that salvation was possible. And I began to understand that I had been called here for a purpose."

"What purpose is that?" I asked.

"To get beyond the cross."

Reverend Grace led us into the darkened sanctuary. He walked behind the purple-draped altar and stood below a large rough-hewn wooden cross that hung on the wall.

"In 1932, the Klan lynched a black teenager who was accused of raping a white Hirtsboro girl. There were no charges, no trial. They just hung him in a big oak tree, right outside of town. Later, the boy's daddy cut the tree down and hauled the trunk home. He cut it into planks and made this cross and gave it to the church. You see, he could deal with what had happened if he thought of his son dying on a cross."

Brad approached the altar and touched the cross. "Why do you want to get beyond it?" he asked.

"These people have lived under slavery since their ancestors were forced onto ships in Africa. The label changes but this is still slavery. The ones who can, leave town. Young people like Praise and Rejoice Sampson. The rest stay with only one thing to hang on: the salvation that comes in the next life. In Hirtsboro, justice is a gift from God and won't happen in this world. But in the next life there will be justice and we will all live in glory. Meanwhile, the comfort of Jesus helps us ease the pain while we're on this mortal earth. That's what this cross means to them.

"But to me, that cross is still a lynching tree. Every Sunday my congregation looks at a symbol that killings go unpunished, that there is no hope for justice in this life. I hate that cross. We have got to move beyond it."

"Reverend Grace," Brad asked, "If God can perform a miracle on a four-hundred-fifty-pound young man, can't the people of Hirtsboro believe that justice is possible now, on this earth and in our time?"

"I haven't given up. But it's a lot easier to believe in heaven than it is to believe that things will change for people in Hirtsboro in my lifetime."

I saw an opening. "We can help them change, if you'll tell us what you've heard."

"Even if I believed that, communication between priest and parishioner is sacred, a trust that cannot be violated."

"Like a reporter and a confidential source," Brad interjected unhelpfully.

Reverend Grace took my hands in his and looked into my eyes. "I can't violate my parishioner's confidences," he said. "I can't tell you what I've been told. But maybe I can give you a sort of roadmap. I tell you where to look, but I just don't tell you what you're going to find when you get there. I might be able to do that. I'll pray on it."

"Please do," I told him.


AN ATTRACTIVE WOMAN waved to us from the deck as Brad and I arrived back at his home that evening,

"She's arrived," Brad said happily. My impression of Lindsay McDaniel Hall was Newport Yacht Club—straight blonde bob, bright blue eyes, flawless skin, angular features and teeth that had paid for an orthodontist's sports car. She wore white Keds, blue jeans, a simple white T-shirt, and minimal makeup. Brad Hall had married within his class.

She smiled when we were introduced. "I hope you can stay for dinner."

I said I needed to be getting back.

"Nonsense. We're due at Brad's father's in half an hour. I'll tell Mary Pell to add another setting."

"I thought we'd eat here," Brad said, retrieving the book, the hat, and the plastic bags from the pickup's floor.

"It's Sunday night."

"I know it is." He slammed the pickup door. "I thought we'd eat here."

She smiled uneasily. "Sunday night supper at Windrow is always at Dad's, Brad."

I began looking for a place to hide.

"We've had Sunday supper with my father almost every week of our married lives. I believe we can miss once."

In my experience, we were one cross word away from an argument.

"Brad, we have almost nothing in the house. I'm sorry. If I'd known . . ."

"Father can be such a boor," Brad said with a forced smile. "But if there's nothing in our house, then Father's it is." And without much strain, the Halls pulled back from the brink.

That would never have happened with Delana and me, I thought. I could never pull back. One word spoken with the slightest edge or hint of anger would take us down the path of poisonous words and hurt. I admired how Brad and Lindsay Hall did it.

The sun was setting over the Savannah when we arrived at what was called, without irony, "the Big House," the plantation home where Brad's father spent much of the year. As Brad had explained it, his father lived alone except for the regular presence of Mary Pell, the housemaid, and a trickle of Yankee visitors who became a stream when bird-shooting season arrived on Labor Day.

Everett Hall was tall, silver-haired, and his tanned, creased face gave him the look of an outdoorsman—a look confirmed by the tweed shooting jacket he wore when he greeted us, holding a glass of red wine. I straightened my tie as he gave his daughter-in-law a kiss on the cheek and his son a handshake. Then he turned to me.

"This is Matthew Harper with the *Charlotte Times*," Brad said. "Matt, this is my father, Everett Hall."

"A reporter? Well, we're delighted to have you here anyway," Everett Hall said in a way that left unclear whether he meant it as a joke. "Drink?"

He refilled his glass. I accepted a glass of wine and followed him out to the veranda where the four of us watched the sun sinking over the Savannah and into the Georgia hills beyond. A great blue heron cruised up the river and lit on a branch overhanging an eddy. "He fishes there every night," Everett Hall said. And soon the bird speared a wriggling flash of silver in his rapier-like beak and deftly slid it down its throat.

"Touché," Brad Hall said quietly.

"Survival of the fittest," said his father.

Dinner was served at an enormous table in a dark-paneled dining room with high-backed red leather chairs. Old portraits of Halls, Bradfords, and Everetts lined the walls. A small, stooped gray-haired black woman in a lavender maid's uniform and white apron served cold vichyssoise as the first course. I hadn't lifted my first spoonful when Everett Hall said, "Tell me, Mr. Harper, about what you do."

"Well, I'm a general assignment reporter. Basically I show up in the afternoon and work on whatever stories I'm assigned. Could be anything."

"Does it pay well?"

"Not at all."

"Then what attracts you to it?"

"The opportunity to write, to be creative. Also, to make a difference."

"How so?"

"Well, you can expose wrongs, crusade. Reveal information that others want hidden. H. L. Mencken said the role of the press is to comfort the afflicted and afflict the comfortable. I like doing that." I had quoted that line many times and I said it then without thinking about my audience—the entirely comfortable. I knew it was a mistake even before Everett Hall's already ruddy face deepened.

He drank from his glass of wine. "Why does the press make so many errors?"

"Errors, sir?"

"Mistakes of fact and of bias. I hardly read a story that I know something about where there isn't an error."

I felt myself flush but I admit I've often observed the same thing. "There're thousands of facts in the paper each day and almost all of them are right. It's an imperfect craft. We get it as right as we can within the confines of deadlines and space."

"Well, you do a poor job of it."

There isn't a journalist alive who hasn't had to withstand an assault on his or her profession, whether from grandstanding politicians, crazed conspiracy theorists, or even readers legitimately upset about an error in a story or, even more often, an inaccurate headline. But I hadn't expected vitriol with the vichyssoise. My surprise must have showed because Brad jumped in to deflect the tension.

"Father, I wasn't aware that you even read the Charlotte paper."

"I don't have to. *New York Times. Washington Post. Charlotte Times. CBS.* It's all the same. A liberal bias infects the whole media. You heard Mr. Harper say it himself. He wants to afflict the comfortable. People like us." He took another swallow. "And comfort the afflicted. Whom do you mean by that?"

"The poor. The powerless. The exploited." I was rising to the debate.

The elderly black woman picked that moment to enter from the kitchen and quietly began refilling the water goblets. Before I could answer his question, Everett Hall turned to her. "Mary Pell, do you feel afflicted?"

"Pardon, sir?" She stood back from the table, holding the silver pitcher.

"Mary Pell, this is Mr. Harper," Everett Hall said.

I stood up. Mary Pell nodded but said nothing. "Mr. Harper is a reporter. He likes to comfort the afflicted. Are you among the afflicted?"

"I got my aches and pains, Mr. Everett, but the Lord's blessed me."

Everett Hall bored in. "Mary Pell, are you exploited at Windrow?"

"Father!" Brad said, but his father paid no attention. I sat down.

"Do we exploit you, Mary Pell?" Everett Hall demanded.

"I'm very happy at Windrow, Mr. Everett. You know that. Very happy." Mary Pell smiled uneasily and retreated to the safety of the kitchen. I saw Brad mouth "I told you so" to his wife, who looked embarrassed and stared at her lap.

Everett was getting drunker and I knew there was no percentage in arguing. I tried to humor him, hoping to get us on lighter ground.

"Wait a minute? Afflict the comfortable? I don't believe I said that. I've been misquoted! The press is always getting it wrong!" I said. Brad and Lindsay laughed. Mr. Hall didn't.

"You said your business is creative. I understand that, because you make things up."

I felt my face redden.

"I don't and I don't know of any journalist who does."

"Your bias shows in what you select to cover. You look for bad things because there's no story if they are good."

"Correct. If things work the way they are supposed to, that's not news. It's news when they don't. We play no favorites. Republicans and Democrats, liberals and conservatives, blacks and whites, men and women. Everybody's fair game."

"Afflicting the comfortable and comforting the afflicted isn't playing favorites? You ever see a newspaper crusade on behalf of some business-man getting harassed by the federal government even though he's risked his own money and created jobs? It'd be okay for a white man to get screwed but stop the presses if it's some poor black."

Tell that to those *Times* readers who are sure I'm a racist, I thought to myself.

"You think the press would have gone after Nixon if he'd been a Democrat?"

"Without question."

"The press gave Kennedy a pass."

"Journalistic standards were different then."

He bolted down his wine. "Standards? You have no standards. Do you have to get a license to be a journalist? Do you have to pass some test? Is there a body of knowledge you have to master? No. You need a license to cut hair and give a manicure. But anyone can be a journalist." Mr. Hall finished his salad. "That was delicious."

Finally, we had found something we could all agree on and I took the opportunity to chime in. "Wonderful. What kind of greens were they?"

"Lion's Tooth," Brad said. "Genus *taraxacum. Dent de lion.* Otherwise known as dandelions."

But Everett Hall wasn't about to quit the battle. He resumed as Mary Pell cleared our plates. "Watergate was the worst thing that ever happened to your business. It made every youngster in journalism school decide to go out and look for a coonskin to nail to the wall. Well, there weren't that many coons out there that needed skinning. So people got it whether they deserved it or not. Politicians. Businessmen. Everybody. You said it yourself. Everybody's fair game."

"Those who got it deserved it," I said. "And that's exactly our function—to keep everybody else honest, to make sure the people know the people's business. It's why the First Amendment is first. We're a watchdog, a fourth branch of government—beholden to nothing but the truth."

"Fourth branch of government? And who elected you?"

"Our readers, every day. If we don't pass their test, if we're not accurate and honest, we're out of business."

"Which explains why the *National Enquirer* sells so many copies." Mr. Hall raised his glass signaling a temporary end to the conversation and, I'm sure in his mind, victory. Brad shrugged and gave me an apologetic look.

Mr. Hall pressed a hidden button under the table. I heard a faint buzzer in the kitchen and Mary Pell emerged to serve the main course—dove and quail bagged during a recent shoot. For the vegetarian Brad, she served something she called Brad's Rice, which turned out to be a delicious wild rice hybrid he had developed and planted on several acres of Windrow that he had returned to cultivation. And, of course, there was more wine. A crisp white, this time. The conversation turned more pleasant and certainly more mundane, with me asking a lot of questions.

I have heard it said that people become reporters because they're shy. They want to know everything about other people but, in the guise of objectivity, never have to reveal anything about themselves. They are afraid of involvement. They don't want to participate in the action, they want to observe it. That may be true. But all I was trying to do was keep the conversation going in non-controversial directions. So I asked Brad about the process that had led to the rice. And his father about the quail and dove season and whether the river was low. And then about the stock market. Lindsay went on and on about Tasha and Maybelle, intuiting the dogs' likes and dislikes and generally talking about them the way parents talk about their children.

I was beginning to think the interrogation hadn't been so bad—a lively debate, although maybe a bit confrontational—but in the end, no more outrageous than behavior I'd observed in other tipsy, aging parents, including mine. But as Mary Pell, accompanied by a black man I assumed was Willie Snow, moved silently about the dining room clearing the main course, Everett Hall went after his son.

"Bradford, let me guess. You've induced Mr. Harper to come down here to help in your little wild goose chase."

"I wouldn't call it a goose chase."

"I would. You propose to solve a killing that was thoroughly investigated twenty years ago."

"If there was an investigation, it wasn't good enough to find the killer."

Everett Hall sighed. "Son, you're stirring up things that don't need to be stirred up. That editorial in *The Reporter* was stupid and naïve. It's an embarrassment and everyone in town knows you're behind it. How do you even know the kid was murdered?"

"For God's sake, father! He was shot in the head with a deer rifle!"

"Probably by his own kind," Everett Hall said, as Willie Snow swept up the crumbs that were left on the table. "Most killings of blacks are by blacks. Black-on-black crime. They keep killing each other off."

Mr. Hall paused for emphasis, then, looking squarely at me and paying absolutely no heed to the fact that two black people bustled around his dinner table, added, "Which is just fine with me."

"Father!" Brad and Lindsay said in horror.

"What? Nothing against the blacks. It's just natural selection. People generally get what they deserve. The strong live and the weak die. It's true of any race. Ain't that right, Willie Snow?" Mercifully, the man had disappeared.

Mr. Hall did not let up.

"The kid probably deserved it. Probably a troublemaker."

"Not based on what we learned at his house."

"You went to his goddam *house?*" Mr. Hall asked. "In niggertown?"

"I wish you wouldn't say that word. It's an embarrassment."

Everett Hall stared at his son. "Bradford, it's your actions that are the embarrassment. I forbid you to continue. I will not have my son poking around niggertown and getting everybody riled up over some dead nigger kid. Except for you, no one cares."

In the course of a short evening, Everett Hall had insulted me, my profession, black people, and his own son. I thought about the promise I had made to myself in junior high when a bully teased a black girl about her kinky hair and I had said nothing. As the girl cried in front of her locker and tried desperately to brush her hair straight, my brother Luke had tracked down the bully and made him apologize. "Nothing is funny when it's at someone else's expense," Luke had explained. I had promised myself then that I would never stay silent again.

"I'll tell you who cares," I interjected, my anger rising. "Wallace Sampson was a thirteen-year-old kid. He had friends. They care. He had parents and sisters. I'm sure they care. And you know who else cares? Every black person in this town ought to care whether or not they ever knew Wallace Sampson. Because if the murder of Wallace Sampson doesn't matter, then we're still in a time and a place where the killing of any black person doesn't matter."

I caught my breath and added, "And if you were anything other than a blueblood fatcat who was born on third base and thinks he hit a triple, you might care, too."

I detected a faint smile from Brad but his father was stunned. The room fell silent. Mary Pell and Willie Snow were nowhere to be seen but parfait glasses of blueberries and heavy cream had found their way to our places. I got the feeling that no one had ever spoken to Everett Hall this way before, especially not at Windrow where he was the lord and master.

"Enough," Mr. Hall commanded, pushing himself away from the table. "This discussion is done."

"Well," Lindsay said brightly, as if it were just another meeting of her book club. "This has certainly been a lively evening. Such good conversation."

Good-byes were awkward—compliments to the shooter of the birds and to the chef but no mention of the dinner-table controversy. As Brad

drove us back to their house in the Volvo, Lindsay searched for some
common ground that would bridge the gap between her husband and
her father-in-law.

"Brad, I know you feel strongly about this. I admire what you and
Matt are doing, but aren't there people who deal with these things? The
FBI or the state police or something?"

"There's no federal crime for the FBI to be involved in."

"It just seems like you shouldn't do it on your own. You need some
investigative expertise."

"That's why Matt is along."

"You have so many other important things to keep you busy, like
the Windrow plant book."

"More important than finding a killer?"

"Well, it's just not something we should be associated with. It's such
a local issue. It really should be handled by the local community."

I wanted to say, "Do you think it matters to Mrs. Sampson who
solves her son's murder?" But I kept quiet on the grounds that I had
staked myself out far enough for one evening. And besides, Brad had a
better answer.

"Honey," he said, "we *are* the locals."

"Not in the same way they are. Look, Brad, we have a good thing
here. A good life. You're going to mess it up."

"What's messed up is that a thirteen-year-old was murdered and no
one cares."

Lindsay tried a new tack. "What about your relationship with your
father?"

"What are your worried about, the inheritance?"

"That's so crass!" she said. "Your father loves you. You are a Hall.
You have a heritage to live up to. Don't ruin that."

We had arrived at the house. Brad turned off the engine but remained in the driver's seat thinking. "The Halls used to have a heritage.
My forebears took risks, crossed the seas over principles. But the genes
have gotten weak. I don't think my father or his brothers would cross

the *street* for a principle. Honey, there's no heritage to live up to. There *is* one to restore."

I lay in bed listening to Brad and Lindsay sparring in the bedroom and realized Walker Burns was right. Even if we hadn't traveled all the way back to the antebellum South, we weren't far off. My dad was the editor of *The Detroit Free Press* during the Detroit riots of 1967. I'd heard the gunfire downtown from my bed in the suburbs. After the riots, the National Commission on Civil Disorders warned that America was moving toward two societies, one black, one white. Hirtsboro wasn't moving that way. Hirtsboro had started out that way and almost two hundred years later, jerks like Everett Hall and even Lindsay were making sure nothing changed. They and the rest of their kind needed to be set straight.

# Chapter Four

**W**alker Burns was waiting for me when I returned from Windrow. "I got a good one for you today, Big Shooter," he drawled, true to his Texas roots. Walker called all reporters Big Shooter when he was in a good mood, which is to say when news had broken out. "I guarantee you it's a 'Holy Shit, Mabel.'"

A "Holy Shit, Mabel" story was, by Walker's definition, a story good enough that it would theoretically cause a woman to lean over her fence and say to her neighbor, "Holy shit, Mabel, did you see that story in the *Charlotte Times* today?"

I had intended to bring up the Wallace Sampson story with Walker first thing. I needed time—company time—to go back down and really investigate. I had spent the drive back from Windrow thinking how to get Walker to buy into the idea. Convincing him wasn't going to be easy. I had a few lingering doubts myself.

Hirtsboro was a long way away, Wallace Sampson had been killed years ago and the only thing we had to go on was a rich guy's suspicion and a vague promise of help from a local preacher. I had prepared a pretty good argument that, at worst, we could get a feature on an unsolved killing and a rich Yankee's unlikely quest. In the very best case, I would argue, the *Charlotte Times* could solve a murder. And a newspaper which published either one could hardly be portrayed as racist. But for now, the Wallace Sampson story pitch would have to wait.

When news breaks out, the newsroom is my favorite place in the world. It is a place where the job changes in an instant, where a plane crash or a press conference or a document hidden in city hall determines what you do that day—and you seldom know in advance what that's going to be. It's a place where you get information before anyone else and then get paid to tell everyone. But more than anything, it's a place of fascinating people—writers, a few of them tortured; photographers, many of them off-the-wall; graphic designers, including the artistically temperamental; and copy editors, stern custodians of the purity of the Mother Tongue, some of them zealots.

As the managing editor, Walker is the ringmaster of our little circus. He has several assistants, but at the end of the day it is Walker who decides what stories will be covered and who will cover them. It is Walker who, as the final editor, ultimately determines how the stories will read when they finally go to press. His desk sits smack in the middle of the newsroom, police scanners on one side, radios to communicate with reporters and photographers in the field on the other, a bank of phone lines in the middle, and, of course, Colonel Sanders. But Walker spends much of his time moving from reporter's desk to reporter's desk in the newsroom assigning, cajoling, joking and editing.

"Let's hear it," I said to him.

"Last night, a commercial jet on a flight from New York to Charlotte comes in so low at the airport that it hits a telephone pole short of the runway. The pilot pulls up in a hurry, makes a safe landing and doesn't tell anyone. Just moseys along to the hotel and hopes no one notices."

"Holy shit!"

"Exactly."

"How'd we find out?"

"Maintenance guy is getting the plane ready this morning and notices there's a hole in one of the wings. He happens to bunk with a local flight attendant who came in on the plane. She tells him there was a huge bang on board, that there's no way the pilot couldn't have known what happened. The maintenance guy doesn't fully trust the airline or the FAA. So he calls us. I got Jeffries chasing the airline. Keating in the Washington bureau is thrashing through the bureaucracy at the FAA. Bullock's working the phones trying to find passengers—one hundred twenty-one of them, plus crew. I need you to find the pole. Take a photographer and get a picture of it. How tall is it? What's it look like? We got an artist working on a re-creation. I want to know exactly how high that plane was and how far away it was from the end of the runway."

"Got it." I hesitated. Bringing up the Sampson case now, even indirectly, had its risks. Approached at the wrong time, when his mind was elsewhere, Walker was likely to shoot down, at least in the short-term, any idea, no matter how good. But I decided to plunge ahead. "Walker, after deadline, I need to talk to you about something."

"I know. You want a raise."

"Yeah, but that's not it. It's about a story."

"Fine. Now grab Drake and get going. I need you back by seven o' clock."

Within minutes, photographer Fred Drake and I were headed for the airport. Coming from New York, I figured the plane had landed from the north to the south on Runway 36. We parked at a chain link fence a quarter mile off the end of the runway and started walking in a straight line away from the airport through the low brush, counting steps and avoiding broken beer bottles as we went. We found the telephone pole fifteen minutes later, next to an aircraft radio beacon installation. It was shorter than normal, leaning to the side and shattered at the top. Splinters littered the ground and on some of them I could see gray paint. I had taken five hundred twenty-five steps. I figured my stride averaged thirty inches. That meant we were a quarter of a mile from where we'd parked and that the pole was just a half-mile from the end of the runway.

Drake scrambled around the site like a monkey, shooting close-ups of the splinters on the ground; then telephoto shots of the top of the pole; then wide-angle shots of the whole scene, which showed the relationship of the pole to its surroundings. He extracted a tape measure that he used for precise focusing of studio shots, shimmied up the pole to the top and dangled the fully extended tape.

I was imagining a 737 roaring over, its unknowing passengers only a few feet above my ahead with another half mile to go before touchdown, when a voice commanded, "Hold it right there! Hands in the air!"

My first thought was that we were being robbed. There were some tough neighborhoods not far from the Charlotte airport. But I looked up to see a county policeman walking through the brush toward us.

"Who are you and what are you doing here?" he demanded.

"We're from the *Times*," I said. "I'm Matt Harper. This is Fred Drake. We're on a story."

"You need to get outta here now or I'm going to arrest both your asses." The officer grabbed me by the elbow. Drake shimmied down the pole, raised his camera and snapped a picture.

Infuriated, the cop charged Drake and grabbed for the camera.

"Hands off the equipment, officer!" Drake yelled, whirling away. The camera flew from his hand, smashed into the concrete slab that supported the airport beacon and popped open, exposing the film in the back.

The cop smirked. "It looks like I don't need that camera after all."

I thought of telling him how airports belong to the citizens and not to the government. That as long as we weren't a danger to aviation, no one should be hassling us because no harm can come from the people simply knowing the facts. But I kept quiet. An argument with a cop over the public's right to know wasn't an argument I was likely to win. Accompanied by the officer, Drake and I made our way back to the car. We were back in the newsroom, as instructed, by 7:00 p.m.

Walker Burns sat at a computer keyboard flanked by reporters Ronnie Bullock, Rich Keating and Julie Jeffries, the *Times*'s newest staffer and the first recruited from a television station. I joined the huddle over Walker's shoulder. The reporters had typed their notes into the system and Walker was crafting them into a story. The first-edition deadline was looming.

"Was it one hundred twenty-one passengers including crew or one hundred twenty-one passengers plus crew?" he demanded of Jeffries.

She flipped her perfect brown hair from her face, consulted her notes and answered crisply, "One hundred twenty-one total. Five crew and one hundred sixteen other passengers." With her pouty mouth, bedroom eyes, and gym-honed body, Jeffries was TV-gorgeous. Rumors that she'd been hired on orders from the publisher were certainly plausible. But I had to admit she knew what she was doing.

Walker banged out a few more paragraphs. "What's the FAA say?"

Keating read him the agency's boilerplate response and Walker typed it.

"The FAA. What horseshit. Bullock, give me your best quote from a passenger."

"I got a lady from Rock Hill who says it was as if an occult hand reached down and . . ."

"Cut the shit," Walker barked. It was a time-honored *Charlotte Times* tradition that Walker would give you the day off if you could manage to get the phrase "it was as if an occult hand had . . ." into the newspaper. Walker had to pay off so infrequently that reporters had taken to asking questions this way (as in the case of a tornado): "Would you say it was as if an occult hand had reached down and tore through the trailer park?" Sometimes the puzzled interviewee would say, "Yeah, I guess so," and the quote would be written up and submitted, only to be caught and edited out by Walker.

"Bullock, what I'm looking for is something that says there's no way the pilot could have not known that he hit something. There's two great angles here: that the plane hit something close to the ground and that the pilot covered it up."

"Use this," said Bullock. "It's from a Charlotte businessman. He said, "It was a very loud thump and the plane shuddered. The only way anyone wouldn't have felt it is if they were dead.""

"Perfect," Walker said. "Harper, how high was he? How much of the pole is left?"

"Twenty feet, nine inches."

Walker looked up from his computer. "How do you know?"

"We measured it with a tape measure."

"Excellent. How thick was the pole?"

"The same as a normal telephone pole, I assume." I regretted saying it as soon as it left my lips. "Actually," I admitted, "we didn't check. You didn't mention you needed to know how thick it was."

"Pardner, do I have to tell you every question to ask or can you think for yourself? Now get your ass back out there and find out how thick it

was. We'll leave it for the first edition and fill in the hole in the second."
He removed his glasses, cocked his left eyebrow and stared at me. It was
a familiar gesture and I grimaced. "Now, hustle."

I grabbed Drake's tape, jumped in the staff car and beat it back to
the airport. When I got to where we had parked, my heart sank. The area
between the road and the pole had been cordoned off with yellow police
tape. Where there had been one cop, now there were at least a dozen.

I spotted the officer we had encountered earlier and hoped he wouldn't
hold Drake against me. "Sir, I'm sorry to have to bother you but I need
to get back in there just for thirty seconds."

"You ain't goin' nowhere. Feds are here now."

"I just need to measure the pole."

He walked away.

They say nothing focuses the attention like an impending execution
and maybe that's what suddenly inspired me. I approached two crew-cut
men sitting in a dark sedan with government plates and a seal on the
door that said Federal Aviation Administration.

"Excuse me, sir," I said to the driver. "I'm Matt Harper from the
*Charlotte Times*. I'm hoping you can help me. I need to get into the site.
I'm doing a story about what happened."

"Comment has to come from Washington." He turned away.

"I don't need comment," I persisted. "I just need to get to the pole
that got hit."

"Why?"

"To measure how thick it is."

"How thick? You mean how tall."

"No, I mean thick." I wasn't going to tell them I already knew how
tall and get into a whole controversy about how I'd been trespassing
earlier.

For the first time the FAA guys looked interested, as if I had some
theory about the incident that they hadn't thought of, a theory that
somehow related to the pole's thickness. "Why?" he asked.

"To tell you the truth, I really don't know," I confessed. "My editor
wants it in the story we got going in the morning. He wants to know

something, my job is to find it out. You ever have a boss that asks you to do stupid stuff you don't understand?" I was trust-building. After all, these were government workers and knew about stupid bosses. "You know how for a while you fight it and then you figure out the path of least resistance is best because in the end, you're gonna end up doing it anyway?"

"Every day," the driver said.

"Every day," his colleague agreed.

"That's what this is."

"Hop in," the driver said.

I jumped in the back seat. As we drove through the security perimeter, I gave a thumbs-up to the cop who had threatened to arrest us. When it comes to freedom of information prevailing, I am not exactly a gracious winner.

When I returned to the newsroom, Walker was still at the terminal. The first edition hadn't yet gone to press but Walker was already hard at work doing a rewrite for the second edition.

"It was right at forty inches around," I reported.

"What was?" he said without looking up

"The pole."

"The pole. Oh, good," he said it as if the information were no longer relevant. "How do you know?"

"I measured it."

"Good. So that makes it how thick—about a foot?"

"Using sixth grade math, which is as far as I got, yes."

"About like a normal telephone pole," Walker concluded.

"That's what I first said."

"Yeah, but you didn't know. There's a difference between what you think and what you know. Now you know."

Walker returned to the terminal and I returned to my desk. Sometimes one of the most frustrating parts of being a reporter is waiting on all the people who have to work with your copy. After Walker, there's the editor for the part of the paper where the story is headed—local or front page. Then it's off to those sticklers on the copy desk who feel compelled to justify their professional existence by asking irrelevant questions and suggesting inelegant changes. If it's big enough, the top editor will read the story and maybe even the publisher. All the while, the reporter waits with two things in mind—be available in case there's a need to answer questions; be vigilant in case idiots fresh from journalism school start trying to butcher the copy or write an off-base headline. Two things are guaranteed: if you stick around, no one will have questions and no one will mess too much with your copy. If you don't, there will be questions and changes galore.

Walker kept writing and editing. I knew he would have to be done soon because final deadline was approaching. Except for me, Walker, and a front page editor to handle the last edition airplane story rewrite, the rest of the newsroom had headed home. Except for sports. Because sports got the latest deadlines to accommodate news of West Coast night games, it was still fully staffed.

But no one in sports or anywhere else, including me, even looked up when the sound of human suffering, an anguished, frustrated scream, erupted from the middle of that department. "You pathetic mess!"

The sound came from Henry Garrows, one of the greatest sports writers in the history of the newspaper. Garrows attended sporting events but he didn't write about games. Instead, he wrote about universal human themes like struggle and sacrifice and failure. Sports writing was cerebral for Garrows. It was creative and imaginative. Garrows wrote to make people see and he believed every story could be a masterpiece, every insight or turn of phrase a work of art. And Garrows was every bit the tortured artist.

As deadline approached, Garrows would prepare to create art by placing a liter bottle of diet cola just to the left of the computer screen, donning yellow noise-canceling headphones, belting himself to his chair and draping a large black shroud over the computer terminal and his head to create a light-proof tunnel between his eyes and the screen. Eliminating distraction and creating focus, Garrows believed, was the only way all of his genius could emerge in the short period of writing time mandated by covering sports news for newspapers on deadline.

The system was not foolproof, however, and Garrows, increasingly anguished as deadline closed in, would resort to verbal self-abuse, as in "you pathetic mess" and much worse. It happened frequently enough that no one commented or even looked up anymore. Staffers would, however, look up when the abuse escalated to include the physical. "You piece of worthless shit!" Garrows would howl and then pop himself in the jaw, hard, with his own clenched first. "You total screw-up!" Once, still belted to the chair, he knocked himself over and struggled like a turtle flipped on its back for several minutes before remembering to unlatch himself from the chair.

But tonight the muse was kinder and "you pathetic mess" apparently got the job done. There were no more explosions from Garrows.

Finally, Walker summoned me. "I think we're ready to roll." I scanned the story on the screen. It included lots of the detail I had gathered in pretty much the form I had given it to Walker.

"A pilot neglected to notify authorities that his airliner hit a telephone pole a half mile short of a Charlotte airport runway Tuesday night, bringing 121 people 20 feet from near-certain death," the lead said. It was classic Walker: the story was good; an attempted cover-up was even better.

Walker hit the "send" button on the computer and the story went to the front-page editor on its way to the copy desk and then production. At this stage in the evening, this close to deadline, there would be no questions.

"Let's get out of here," he said.

"I need to talk to you about that other story."

"Sure," he said with an enthusiasm that surprised me. It had been a long day for him. I hadn't come in until afternoon. He started at 9:30 every morning, which meant he was due back at his desk in nine hours. But Walker loved a story. And if you had one, he wanted to know about it. I followed him to the conference room with the Famous Front Pages. Walker slouched in an easy chair with his feet on the coffee table. He leaned his head back against the pillows, balanced a Ticonderoga #2 pencil between his lip and his nose and closed his eyes.

"So watcha got?" he said, straining not to move his upper lip and upset the pencil.

I told him about Bradford Hall showing up in the newsroom, a reminder that the whole situation started with me just doing my normal nightshift job. I explained the basics of the Wallace Sampson story: a thirteen-year-old boy shot in the head with a deer rifle shortly after midnight following minor civil unrest, a murder apparently uninvestigated and unsolved despite widespread suspicions in the black community; a crusade by a wealthy Yankee plantation owner to solve the killing which had aroused opposition in his family.

What I didn't get into is the personal commitment I had begun to feel. Some think reporters are supposed to be objective, to chronicle the events of life and not get involved in them. There is no question reporters can and must be fair and that a reporter has to take pains to ensure that all sides in a story are conveyed completely and accurately. That is a standard of the profession. But objectivity is impossible. Everyone, journalists included, has an opinion. Everyone is a product of their past.

"Walker," I said, "the uninvestigated murder and Bradford Hall's search for justice is the minimum we get. That in itself is a helluva story. And the maximum story we get is that we solve the murder."

Walker sat upright. The Ticonderoga went flying. "Here's what we need to do," he said. "We'll get all the great investigative reporters and line them up at the South Carolina border and we'll have them ride high in the saddle through the state from the mountains to the sea. They'll write stories they flush out as they go. It'll be like hunters flushing out birds. My God! There'll be Holy Shit, Mabel story after Holy Shit, Mabel story. Pulitzer Prize after Pulitzer Prize. There's probably a million Sampson cases down there."

"Let's just start with this one."

Walker sighed. "It *is* a good story. There's just one problem. Hirtsboro isn't in our circulation area. There are a lot of good stories out there. A lot of them. The Middle East. That's a good story. The ferry crash in the Phillipines. That's a good story. But we won't be staffing them either because they are not in our circulation area."

It was true. The *Charlotte Times* billed itself as the newspaper that covered the Carolinas from the Appalachians to the Atlantic and at one time that had been the case. But over the years, maintaining outlying circulation proved expensive. Charlotte-area advertisers had been reluctant to pay for distribution to people who would seldom travel to Charlotte to shop in their stores. So distribution to far-flung areas of the Carolinas like Hirtsboro had been cut back, at first restricted to single copy sales from racks and then eliminated entirely.

"Maybe there's a local angle," I pressed. "We won't know unless we investigate."

"What kind of local angle? Bradford Hall passes through Charlotte on the way to the plantation?"

"Walker, sometimes you have to do a story because it's a good story. Hirtsboro isn't in our circulation area but it isn't in anyone else's either. If we won't do it, it won't get done."

"I'm not worried about stories in Hirtsboro not getting done. I'm worried about stories not getting done in Charlotte. Matt, in case you hadn't noticed, we have six empty desks in the newsroom. Six reporting jobs I can't fill. Why? Because the publisher has decided we're in a hiring freeze. No hires until ad lineage improves and circulation starts going up again."

"Uh, maybe we could improve the circulation numbers by not cutting back in places like Hirtsboro."

Walker laughed. We both knew the newspaper's business and marketing policies were suicidal. Cut back distribution, reduce the number of reporters and thereby stories in the paper, and then wring your hands wondering why fewer people are reading. Go figure. As managing editor, it was Walker's job to represent management to the journalists. But Walker was enough of a journalist himself that he couldn't pretend to defend top management's decision-making when it was so obviously indefensible.

I felt an advantage and pressed ahead. "Walker, this is the kind of story that gets people reading wherever they live. It's a Holy Shit, Mabel story. And it's a story only a newspaper can give them, not TV or radio. It's why we exist, for God's sake."

Walker closed his eyes and sighed. "Matt, it's a tough time to argue that. I'm gonna have to bite the bullet and tell you something I was hopin' I wouldn't have to. The Jeffries hire kinda put us in the hole. The publisher's makin' noises about cullin' the herd even more to make up for it."

It took me a moment before I understood him. "You talking layoffs? To pay for Jeffries?"

"Pardner, it's worse than that. You're on his list."

I was stunned and hot. "It's not all about Jeffries, is it? The son of a bitch is gonna cave! He's gonna sacrifice me because of the heat we're taking!"

"It hasn't been a fun time," Walker admitted.

He was right about that. For the last two weeks the *Charlotte Times* had been the subject of vocal protests from some in the black community over a minor story I'd uncovered about supervisors in the Department of Public Works using city workers for their private projects like driveway paving and roof repairs. It ran on the front page of the local section along with photos of four of the seven supervisors. The problem came because the pictured supervisors happened to be black and the ones whose photos were not used happened to be white. An unfortunate headline referred to taxpayer money going to a "black hole."

The *Charlotte Times* hit the streets, as always, by dawn. The first press conference to denounce the newspaper for racism occurred by noon. The local caucus of black officials—led by a city councilman running for mayor—threatened a subscriber boycott. Members of the black clergy denounced the newspaper from the pulpit, encouraged picketing of the *Charlotte Times* building and organized a letter-writing campaign. Because few in the public understood that the reporter doesn't write the headlines or choose the photos that go with a story, the protesters focused their anger not just on the *Charlotte Times* but on the reporter who had produced the story—me. I'd received more than one hundred letters, some addressed by name, many addressed simply to "The Racist Reporter."

A handful had come to my home. Picketers marched for two days until the publisher agreed to their demands for a meeting and apologized for the newspaper's unthinking mistake, as he should have.

"Walker, none of that's my fault," I argued. "The story was fair. It was the news desk that screwed it up. You know I'm no racist."

Walker gave me a weak smile. "Of course. All along I've been thinking this is probably like a summer Texas thunderstorm—lots of dark clouds and lightning but no rain. And it still has a chance of blowin' right by. But you have to figure that if the publisher's lookin' to make sure the posse has given up the chase, shootin' you is one way to do it."

"Walker, you can't let him get away with that."

Walker leaned forward. "Pardner, you need to know it ain't the only ammo he's got. He did a count of every reporter's bylines for the last year. You didn't rank so high. And no blockbusters, either."

"Of course not. I spend most of my goddam time doing roundups and local inserts. To get a blockbuster, you need a real story." I thought a moment. "Where'd I rank?"

"They way he tells it, dead last. Matt, here's the deal. The publisher wants more obits in the paper and I can barely get Bullock to crank out one each night. I got six reporters in the newsroom who come to work every day disguised as empty desks and just as much newshole as ever to fill. The publisher's lookin' to cut even more to make up for Jeffries. You're already on his Most Wanted list because of the public works story. This ain't the time for you to be checkin' on some long-shot investigation. Besides, the trail has been dead for years. People forget. People move on."

"Not in Hirtsboro. In Hirtsboro, nothing changes."

"Matt, you're a good journalist. Someday, you might even be a great one. As good as your daddy or your granddaddy. But you've never done a big investigation before. I don't know that you're ready."

"Walker, I've already done some work. I've been down there. If it's there, I can get it."

"You don't seem to appreciate that we're both *already* in hot water. You screw up and the publisher's gonna nail your hide to the wall for sure. And I'm not all that inclined to break a habit I've gotten used to in order to save you. It's called eating. Developed it as a kid." He slouched back in the chair and rebalanced the Ticonderoga on his upper lip.

"Give me two weeks," I pleaded. "Two weeks to go down, take a proper sniff. And then I'll come back, we'll look at what I've got and make a decision then."

"If we have nothing, we stop."

"Then, we stop," I agreed.

He closed his eyes and I knew what he was thinking. Positives: good story, remote chance of a great one. Negatives: old story out of the circulation area, staff shortage, and crap from the publisher. "It's risky, Matt," he said. "Your career can't take a failure."

"Walker, two weeks."

"I'll think about it, Big Shooter."

"*Please.* I *need* this story."

# Chapter Five

I showed up for work the next day desperate for a byline and with my stomach churning over Walker Burns's pending decision. The notice that the newsroom Discipline Committee needed to convene put an immediate dent in the byline hopes, although the meeting did have Live Toad potential.

The Live Toad Theory, developed by Walker, held that if you did something terrible the first thing every day, like swallow a live toad, the rest of the day would invariably go better. There was no way it was going to get worse.

At one time the *Charlotte Times* disciplined newsroom employees like everybody else: management decided who screwed up and what the consequences should be. Bowing to staff complaints that the process was inconsistent and favored some groups of employees over others, management established an employee-run Discipline Committee to hear evidence in disciplinary cases and make recommendations as to the appropriate outcome. While the recommendations weren't binding and management retained the right to do whatever it wanted, it seldom overruled the committee. Staffers rotated on and off the committee and, as it happened, this month I was in the barrel along with three others. The process was often petty and humiliating and, if nothing else, it was time away from what we were paid to do: report, edit, take pictures, or design pages. Given my standing in The Great Byline Count, it was time I couldn't afford to lose.

"Who is it *now?*" I asked Walker.

"Bullock," he said with a shrug.

We gathered after first edition deadline in the dark-paneled board-room beside the publisher's office on the third floor, away from the prying eyes of the newsroom where there were reporters who could read lips through glass conference room walls. The lighting was low and indirect. I sat at a long conference table, swallowed up in a huge, black, high-backed chair. I felt small, as if I were a kid playing executive.

The other members of the committee were already seated and Walker had just taken his place at the head of the table when Ronnie Bullock walked in dressed, as usual, in khaki pants and a khaki shirt. He looked like a cop. His creased, ruddy face, big hands, and stocky frame gave the appearance of someone who worked outside. He was sixty and although his forehead had expanded a little, he still kept a thick head of reddish-brown hair. I thought of him as a short John Wayne. Newsroom lore said he carried a gun. Bullock nodded to members of the committee and took a chair.

John Hafer, the company's director of human resources, entered. Always smiling and attentive, Hafer did his best to come across to all employees like he was their understanding advocate and friend. But everyone, including Hafer, knew that the publisher signed his paycheck. I was surprised to see him and I could tell my colleagues were, too.

"John's here because he is the one who's ringing the fire bell," Walker said quickly. Walker was not part of the committee but served as the moderator. "John, let's get to it."

"As you know, this involves Ronnie," he said, nodding at Bullock.

"Again," huffed Carmela Cruz, the *Times*' s diminutive front-page editor known equally for her page-design skills and her general contempt for local news and sexist behavior. No one followed up. The black-haired, black-eyed Carmela was mercurial and most found it best not to engage her.

Hafer knew it, too, and quickly plowed ahead. "It happened yesterday and I felt it best to report it to Walker. It seems we have a new assistant librarian who is, uh . . . ." Hafer's face twisted as he struggled for the right word. "She is, uh . . . She's very . . ."

"She has a nice ass," Bullock interrupted helpfully.

"Ronnie, you can't say that stuff," Walker said calmly.

"Why not?" said Bullock. "It's verifiably true. Look at her. How can you not be allowed to say something that's true?"

"You can think it," Walker said. "You just can't say it." He turned to the committee. "I think what John's trying to say is that Ronnie found the new assistant librarian very appealing. Would that be a good way to put it?"

"Yeah," said Hafer, relieved at finding a way to avoid expressing a personal value judgment based on appearance.

"Bullock would find mud appealing if it had breasts," Carmela hissed. The assistant sports editor chuckled. Carmela shot him a dagger glance and he smothered the laugh into a cough.

"Save the commentary," Walker sighed. "Go on, John."

"Well, apparently she was walking through the newsroom yesterday delivering some clip files and she caught Ronnie's eye. He picked up the phone and called my office and asked me a question which is so offensive I'm not sure I can repeat it."

"We can handle it, John," Walker advised.

Bullock interrupted. "Hell, I just asked him a question about my pension."

Hafer took a deep breath. "Ronnie said he understood that he would certainly be fired if he got up out of his chair and attached his mouth to the left breast of the new assistant librarian. His question to me, as the director of human relations, was whether it would affect his pension."

The assistant sports editor cackled madly. Walker howled and I even detected a smile from Elaine Heitman, the editor of the *Times*'s editorial pages.

"I am outraged," fumed Carmela, a red flush starting from her neck and moving up to her face. "Absolutely outraged. There is no room for that kind of behavior at the *Charlotte Times* and I will not stand for it. This needs to be a newspaper of the highest standards."

"I agree. We cannot have our employees subject to that kind of verbal treatment," Hafer said.

"Ronnie, did you actually say anything to the young woman?" asked

Heitman. A sensible question, I thought.

Bullock had taken a penknife from his pocket, opened the blade and was examining it closely. "No," he said, looking up from the knife. "Maybe I just should have asked directly instead of calling HR."

Heitman ignored his sarcasm and turned to Hafer. "So there is no allegation that he was verbally abusive or engaged in any kind of sexist behavior directly to her?"

"I don't know of any."

"That doesn't matter," interjected Carmela. "What matters is his state of mind. Women do not need to be subject to this kind of mental leering. It has gone on forever and it must stop."

"She's just jealous I saw her first." Bullock smirked. "There's more dykes in her department than there are on the goddam Mississippi!" He began trimming his fingernails with the scissors on his knife.

The assistant sports editor howled.

"This is preposterous!" Carmela shrieked.

"It's true. You should see her staring at the managing editor's secretary's breasts. She sits in a chair beside her desk pretending to have a conversation about personnel issues but she never takes her eyes off 'em."

"This is libelous!" Carmela shouted, rising out of her chair. "I am not on trial here. I will not be subject to this!"

Walker struggled to get the meeting back under control. "I feel like I'm tryin' to herd chickens. Let's stick to the grievance."

"You can't punish someone for having bad thoughts or even asking rude questions," I said. "What Ronnie did was stupid. But who got hurt?"

Heitman took off her glasses and cleared her throat. "John, employees regularly come to you with questions about company benefits and policies." She said it as statement for him to confirm, a little like a cross-examining lawyer. "And Ronnie's question was about his pension, correct? Whether he would lose it if he got fired for what would be considered sexual assault or sexual harassment?"

"Well, ostensibly," Hafer said cautiously. "But I don't think he was looking for a serious answer."

Heitman charged ahead. "In the human relations department, are employee matters confidential? You have records about pay, medical claims that sort of thing."

"Of course. All confidential."

"If I asked you whether our health insurance covered a particular medical procedure, would that be confidential?"

"Of course."

"Or how much my pension will be when I retire. Would that be confidential?"

Hafer's face fell. He could see where this was heading. Bullock could see it, too, and he began to smile.

"Yes. But this is completely different. This wasn't a serious benefit inquiry. This was a joke!"

"Likely, it was a joke," said Heitman. "A bad joke, but still a joke. Either that, or it was a serious inquiry to the human relations department which is protected by confidentiality. Like Matt said, who got hurt? Frankly, I don't see why we are even here."

Hafer's face turned beet red. "It was crude and offensive."

"Does the young woman, the assistant librarian, feel sexually harassed?" Heitman asked.

"Of course not," Hafer answered. "She doesn't even know."

"Do you feel sexually harassed, John? Did Bullock's remark create a hostile work environment for you?" she probed.

If it was possible, Hafer blushed even deeper. "No, of course not. But Ronnie Bullock was way out of line and this isn't the first time."

"He offended you. It seems to be the normal thing would be for you to tell him that and ask for an apology. Have you done that?"

"No. I thought it was a matter for the Discipline Committee."

"Next time, why don't you try asking for an apology?" she said sweetly.

Walker asked Bullock if he had anything to add.

"I don't think there's much dispute about the facts," he said. "I only have one question. When did we decide we were going to start policing thoughts and not just actions?"

Bullock and Hafer were dismissed from the meeting and for the next half hour the discussion plowed old ground. I was reminded of a conclusion I'd come to before: for people in the communications business, we're pretty lousy communicators. One person gets offended and instead of just bringing it up with the individual who committed the alleged offense, a whole committee has to get involved.

Carmela put up a fight but in the end, Heitman's view prevailed. The committee recommended to management that Ronnie Bullock apologize for expressing an offensive thought and be reminded to avoid sexist language and behavior in the future. There would be no official discipline and nothing would go in his permanent record.

Carmela had her own methods of retribution. "I cannot believe we are going to turn aside our eyes to this indignity! I can tell you that in the future we will have a very difficult time finding room for Ronnie Bullock stories on the front page . . . not that I would expect any in the first place."

Typical Carmela. But it could have been worse. The whole thing had taken less than two hours. A rough justice had been achieved. As far as Live Toads go, the Ronnie Bullock discipline committee meeting hadn't been that hard to swallow.

My luck held when a beat reporter called in sick and I was assigned a school board meeting that ended in a fistfight and a front-page byline for me. I had put the finishing touches on it when I looked up to see Walker Burns approaching my cubicle with an expression like the proverbial cat that swallowed the canary.

"Well, Big Shooter," he said, sitting down and propping his feet on my desk, "you get your wish. Two weeks on Wallace Sampson. No other assignments. Unless the plane crashes." "Unless the plane crashes" was Walker's usual qualifier when doling out a project that would take a reporter out of the mainstream of the flow of news for a while. It meant you had freedom to pursue your project exclusively, except in the case of some overwhelming news event like a plane crash.

It was the best news I could have heard. Certainly it was the first good news I'd had in a long while. At least for two weeks, I could leave behind the world of discipline committees, hate mail, daily deadlines, and one-day wonders and count myself among the true big shooters. At least for a while, I had been given the opportunity to do real investigative reporting.

But I was also scared. Brad Hall was taking a chance on me. Walker was taking a chance on me. *I* was taking a chance on me. My career was dead if this didn't work out and truth is, my gut was less confident than my mouth. I tried to be cool, like this was an everyday thing, but my throat went dry and I could only croak, "Thanks, man."

But Walker wasn't done. "I want to double-team this one. I'm putting you and another reporter on the story, at least for the two weeks."

I was puzzled. It wasn't unusual to put two reporters on a story but I knew we were short-staffed and, anyway, this was one story I had developed on my own.

"We'll cover twice as much ground with two of you," Walker explained. "And in terms of investigative reporting, you're a rookie. I want you to have some help."

"Who?"

"Bullock."

I couldn't believe my ears. "Bullock? That's crazy. We're dealing with black people down there. Bullock's a redneck. No one will talk to us."

"Ronnie Bullock might be able to teach you something. He was a damn fine reporter once."

"Once," I said sullenly. "Why not someone from the projects team?"

"Because we barely have enough reporters to cover the city council meeting much less some years-old killing in a place far, far away. You tell me this could be a good story and my gut tells me you're right and I get paid because someone decided that my gut instincts were the ones to listen to. So we're going to do it. At least, we're going to take the sniff. That's all I'm committing to. But whatever we do, we have to fly below the radar. The publisher can't know we're putting even one staffer, especially you, on this story, much less two. If I take one of the big boys from the projects team, he'll notice in a heartbeat."

Walker paused. "Plus, I've got two other reasons."

"What are they?"

"With the disciplinary crap with Ronnie and all this protest stuff with you, I need to get you both out of the newsroom for a while."

"What's the other?"

"This place is drivin' me loco. I've had it with the publisher. I need a new ranch to ride. I'm lookin' for the story that'll punch my ticket outta here."

Lots of us were. But it was still a shock to hear Walker say it. I couldn't imagine working at the *Times* without him, but that was a discussion for another time.

There's no question I would have preferred to go to Hirtsboro alone. And if I did need to have a partner, Ronnie Bullock wouldn't have made the top ten on my list. But at the end of the day I'd gotten what I'd wanted.

And so was created the unlikely team that would investigate the years-old murder of Wallace Sampson: a rich Yankee blueblood with a social conscience, an occasionally embarrassing redneck reporter throwback, and me.

# Chapter Six

It was the next week before shifts were rearranged and news stopped breaking out sufficiently so that Walker felt comfortable springing Bullock and me to go to Hirtsboro.

It took less time than that for us to butt heads.

"We're taking my Dodge," Bullock informed me as we planned over coffee in the newspaper cafeteria, a place that perpetually smelled of Lysol and green beans cooked to death. "That rice-burner you drive is an insult to the American working man and it sure as hell will look out of place in Hirtsboro, South Carolina. Besides, the Dodge has an engine. We might need it."

Light from the window created a thin rainbow of film that floated on top of Bullock's coffee, like gasoline on water. He stirred four heaping teaspoons of sugar and several ounces of milk into the Styrofoam cup. The coffee barely lightened. "God, this stuff is nasty," he marveled. "I wonder how they make it so bad."

"Get off it, Ronnie. When's the last time a reporter was involved in a high-speed chase?"

"It could happen. You need to remember who's got the experience here. You've never done this before. Tell the truth, I'm a little irritated about having to take you with me."

"*You're* irritated! *I'm* irritated! This is my story. I don't want you blowing it with some racist attitude."

He pushed his chair back and shook his head, as if he's seen it all. "You wet-behind-the-ears jerks with journalism school degrees piss me off. Racist? I'll tell you what's racist. The newspaper's Black History Month.

That's racist. The paper has to have at least one story a day about black history during Black History Month. I ask, 'When are we gonna have White History Month?' Oh, they say, we would never do that. People wouldn't stand for it. Besides, I believe you're the one they refer to as 'the racist.' And here's another thing,"—he was warming to his rant—"the amazing killer editors haul me in and tell me I need to make my stories, quote, more accessible to busy mothers and other women who are joining the workforce in increasing numbers and have less time to read the newspaper, unquote.

"You know what I say to that? I say my job is to find out about things people don't know about. I write them and put them in the newspaper. It's called news. I don't worry if it's for rich people or poor people or blacks or whites or men or women. It's just news. And if mothers don't have time to read it, maybe they should quit their jobs and stay home and take care of the families." He took a gulp of coffee. "God, this is bad. If women are gonna work, at least they ought to make good coffee."

"In case you haven't noticed, Ronnie, the caveman approach hasn't exactly endeared you to women in the newsroom."

"If you mean Carmela Cruz, who cares? I can't figure if she's the woman or the man in the relationship anyway."

"Well, it so happens that Cruz has a lot to do with whether our story gets on the front page. And I care more about writing page-one stories than I do about political correctness. So forget that J-school crap, okay? I've been here five years. I do the same thing you do. I earned this. Without me, you wouldn't be on the story. Without me, there wouldn't even *be* a story."

Trust. Always it's about trust. Not just with your sources, but also with your colleagues. Getting Ronnie Bullock to trust me was going to take some work. Trusting him wasn't going to be any easier.

I called Brad to let him know we were coming. In the spirit of harmony, I agreed we'd take Bullock's car.

THE SMOG FROM CHARLOTTE's one hundred thousand commuters reduced the mid-morning sun to a pale disc and diluted the Carolina sky to a weak blue as we headed south on the interstate. Bullock wore his characteristic khaki uniform, cowboy boots, and mirrored aviator sunglasses.

"We need to make a list of the most important things to get done," I said. "Two weeks seems like a long time. But when you're trying to track down people who don't know you're coming, it's not."

"We need to see where it happened," Bullock said. "And did you already check the police records?"

"Naw. We need to do that. Plus, I want to interview Wallace Sampson's girlfriend. She was the last one to see him before he was killed."

"Get this stuff down," Bullock commanded. "There's a pen in the glove box."

I opened the glove box and a gun rolled out, bouncing off my kneecap and dropping to the floor.

"Damn!" I shrieked. "It's a gun!"

"It's a .38 police special. It'll stop a bad guy."

I felt heat from my neck. "That thing could have gone off!"

"No way. Safety's on. Put it back, will you?"

I gently picked up the gun, afraid it was going to fire. It was the first time I had ever held one. I was surprised by its weight. I laid it back in the glove box and snapped the door closed.

"So, it's true. You *do* carry a gun."

"For this trip, we've got three. The .38 in the glove box. A 30.06 in the trunk. And in case of emergencies, this." He kept his foot on the gas while hoisting his right pants leg over his boot. Strapped around his calf was a garter-sized holster and in it, a tiny pistol. He pulled it out and cradled it in his right palm for me to see. "A single shot derringer. For when all else fails."

A few miles later, the traffic thinned and the interstate stretched flat and straight to the horizon. Without a word Bullock punched the accelerator and we rocketed ahead. We hit one hundred miles an hour before he eased off the gas.

"What happens if we get pulled over with all these weapons on us?" I asked. "Aren't there laws about transporting firearms across state lines? What about the ATF?"

"We're in South Carolina, boy. Down here, Alcohol, Tobacco and Firearms ain't a government agency, it's a damn shopping list." He gunned the engine and the Dodge zoomed around a truck hauling chickens and snowing feathers.

"Look, Ronnie, that cowboy shit is past. I don't care if it *is* South Carolina. I'm not spending time in some jail on weapons charges."

"Relax, Harper," he said. "I've been doing this a long time. Amazing motor isn't it? It's a 383 with quad Holley carbs. If we had to, we could outrun anyone but Richard Petty."

I said nothing. There were only two alternatives, neither of them good. Either we were undertaking an assignment that would involve fast cars and gunplay or we had a nut-case situation. And the nut case wasn't Brad Hall, it was my partner, Ronnie Bullock.

South of Columbia, Bullock announced that he was hungry. I suggested we wait until Windrow. "The Halls will have something waiting. Civilization is pretty scarce around here."

"Nonsense," said Bullock. "Every place has got fast food."

Every place, it turns out, except most places in South Carolina.

The sun was high by the time we reached Edgewood, a small town about the size of Hirtsboro, but with the railroad tracks on the outskirts, by the cotton gins, not in the center of town. A gas station. An abandoned motel. A feed and seed. An auto supply store. A place selling discounted recliners. No fast food. Ahead on the left loomed the First Baptist Church and its cemetery. In the middle of the road in front of the church stood a policeman, his hand raised for us to stop. When we did, he waved and a funeral procession began to file out of the parking lot.

"Hot damn!" said Bullock.

When the last of the cars had left the lot, the cop waved us on and Bullock eased the Dodge behind the procession. We continued down the main road toward the outskirts of town. The procession turned left down a leafy residential street. Bullock followed and when the car ahead of us parked, Bullock pulled to the curb, too.

"Let's go," he said. "Look bereaved."

I started to protest. But before I knew it we were following an old couple up the wooden steps into a very nice home, apparently of the recently deceased. The scent of flowers and fried chicken suffused the air.

Bullock removed his mirrored sunglasses with a practiced snap and grasped the hand of the elderly woman who stood at the door, receiving guests. "I'm Ronald Bullock. This is my associate Mr. Harper. We're so sorry."

"Thank you for coming," she said with a sad smile. "How did you know Sidney?"

"Business," Bullock said quickly. I smiled and nodded.

"That's remarkable. What did Sidney have to do with your business?"

"He was a great friend of the business," Bullock said.

"Sidney was my sister."

"Of course," Bullock laughed. "Slip of the tongue. She was a great friend of the business."

"Mercy," said the woman. "I never knew."

Before she could say more Bullock grabbed my elbow and steered me into the next room where, in the great tradition of Southern funerals, mourners helped themselves to mountains of food. Fried chicken. Baked beans. Lima beans. Green beans. Field peas. Black-eyed peas. Six different kinds of potato salad. Four different kinds of Jello salad. Cole slaw. Biscuits. Cornbread. Lemonade. Sweet tea. The smells made me ravenous and we ate until we were bursting, smiling and nodding at the other mourners and saying nothing.

When we returned to the car, Bullock marveled, "Chicken from one end of the house to the other and when we got out to the back porch, dessert! You jump on any of that strawberry shortcake?"

"Ronnie, that was despicable," I said as we got back on the road.

"I'd say it was damned good."

"You know what I mean. We shouldn't have done it."

"Why?" he questioned. "We hurt nobody and we got fed. And now Sidney's sister thinks she had even more friends than she really did. We did that poor woman a favor."

We stopped for gas outside Hirtsboro. Bullock pumped and when he went in to pay, I went with him. A forty-something woman with bleached blonde hair, lots of gold necklaces, and extremely tight shorts sat on a stool behind the cash register, smoking. She wore a small white T-shirt, which accentuated her impressive chest.

"How are you today?" Bullock asked, fumbling for his wallet and never taking his eyes off her chest.

The cashier cupped her hands below her breasts, thrust them out and said in a high, squeaky voice: "Oh, we're fine! How are you?"

Bullock was unfazed. I bought a drink, paid for it separately and pretended I didn't know him. In less than four hours, Bullock had managed to insult blacks, women, gays, break the speed limit, transport guns across state lines, impersonate a mourner, and commit visual sexual harassment. It was going to be a long two weeks.

"Ronnie, you need to cut it out," I scolded when we got back to the car.

"They don't wear 'em like that if they don't want you to look," he growled. "Hell, she probably hears it six times a day and loves it. Did you catch those shorts? They were so tight she had a dime in her back pocket and I could read the date."

"Would you just rein it in? When it's just you, I don't care what you do. But we're a team and I'll be damned if I'm going to have you screw things up right out of the gate."

"Okay," he agreed. "I'll watch it. Hell with 'em if they can't take a joke, though."

But it was too late. Less than a mile after we left the store, I heard the brief whoop of a police siren and saw blue lights out the back window. Bullock pulled the car to the shoulder, raising a cloud of choking red dust. When it cleared, I saw from the markings on the black and white patrol car that we had been stopped by the Hirtsboro police. An officer emerged from the car and began walking toward us.

Oh, Jesus, I thought. The guns.

"I hope he's not the husband of that clerk," Bullock said.

"Maybe her son."

The policeman, no more than twenty years old, pimply-faced, pale, and skinny, seemed to float inside his uniform. Looking more like a cop than the cop, Bullock snapped off his sunglasses and rolled down the window. "Afternoon, officer. What seems to be the trouble?"

The young policeman bent over and stuck his face almost inside the car. A silver nameplate identified him as O. Pennegar.

"May I see your license and registration, sir?" he asked formally.

Bullock removed his wallet from his back pocket.

"Just the license. Not the wallet."

Bullock handed over the license and the officer studied it for a long time. I felt like he was trying to recall the police academy procedure for what happens next.

"What's the problem, officer?" I asked.

"Speeding," said Pennegar. "Twenty miles over. It's a one hundred dollar fine. You can pay me or we can head into town and visit the magistrate if you request a hearing."

"We were going no more than fifty-five!" I protested.

"I'll handle this!" Bullock snapped. He turned to Pennegar and said politely, "Officer, I thought we were obeying the limit."

"It's thirty-five miles an hour, sir," Pennegar said formally.

"Since when?" I interrupted.

"Since the Hirtsboro town limit a mile back."

"I didn't see any town limit sign." I was indignant.

"There isn't one. Someone shot it up. But that don't matter. Speed limit's thirty-five in town and everybody knows where the town limit is."

"Well, we're not from around here," I said. "We're reporters down here on a story."

Bullock whacked me on the thigh with the back of his hand. "Stow it, dammit!"

"What's the fine again, officer?" he said, turning to Pennegar.

"One hundred dollars. Pay me or we can go see the magistrate."

"Go ahead and pay him," I told Bullock. "But pay him two hundred.

Because the next time we come back through here, we're gonna be doing the same damn speed."

"Can it!" said Bullock.

Pennegar stepped away from the window. He glanced at the license. "I believe I've heard enough from your friend. Now hand me the registration."

Without thinking, I opened the glove box. The .38 tumbled out again.

Pennegar's eyes widened. They darted from side to side. "Freeze!" he commanded, drawing his gun. "Keep your hands where I can see 'em."

Bullock slumped in his seat and stared at me. "You stupid jerk." Then he turned to the policeman. "Officer Pennegar, at this point I must inform you about all the weapons in the vehicle. In addition to the .38 police special, there is a 30.06 in the trunk."

"Step out and away from the car," Pennegar said. As we climbed out, Pennegar leveled a trembling gun at Bullock and unhooked a set of handcuffs from his belt.

"Hands behind your back," he shouted. I obeyed. He snapped the cuffs so tightly around my wrists that they pinched.

"Officer, we're not a threat," Bullock protested. "The weapons are—"

"Quiet," Pennegar ordered. He retrieved another set of handcuffs from his patrol car and cuffed Bullock, leaving his hands in the front. He locked us both in the back of the patrol car and searched the Dodge for the weapons.

"Just keep your mouth shut," Bullock told me. The patrol car doors were closed. The engine and air conditioning were off. The heat was stifling. My heart was pounding. I started to feel clammy. I couldn't get my breath. I felt dizzy, queasy.

"You all right? Bullock asked.

But before I could answer I retched, hurling the funeral lunch over the floor of the car.

"Nice," said Bullock. With the heat, the smell and the embarrassment, it was a miserable ten minutes until Pennegar returned.

"Jesus, what's this?" he said with a shudder.

"Kid puked."

"I hope he didn't pee his pants, too."

We rode back to Hirtsboro with the air conditioner on and the windows open and parked in front of the town hall, a one-story, flat-roofed, white cinderblock building on Jefferson Davis Boulevard, two blocks away from the town's business district. Pennegar jerked me out of the patrol car and led us into the municipal offices. A fifty-ish woman sitting behind a huge desk with a nameplate that read "Patty Paysinger, Town Clerk" looked up from some paperwork, removed her glasses and let them hang from their chain. "Watcha got, Olen?"

"Speeding and concealed weapons."

She eyed us the way my mother did Luke and me when she was sure we had done something wrong.

I could no longer contain myself. "Ma'am, I'm Matt Harper. This is Ronald Bullock. We're reporters for the *Charlotte Times*. We're *not* dangerous. *We're* the ones who told him we had guns."

"I think you can take their handcuffs off, Olen," she said gently.

"Yes, ma'am. The magistrate around?" He unlocked the cuffs. I massaged the marks out of my wrists and looked around the room—a wall of metal file cabinets, a restroom, a windowless office, a large closet with a latch on the door. Patty Paysinger motioned us to a couple of chairs at a rectangular table and we sat down. A window-mounted air conditioner rattled noisily. The cool settled my stomach and dried the perspiration that had soaked through my shirt.

"He's at home. You go fetch him, Olen, and we'll see what he wants to do about these two."

"Uh, there's a problem with the patrol car. One of 'em threw up in the back seat."

"You can clean it up later," she said, tossing him her keys. "Take my car. Now, hop."

"I think he oughta clean it up himself."

"Olen, do as you are told. Now, which one of you was sick?"

I raised my hand like a grade-school kid.

"Oh, you poor dear! Let me get you a wet wash cloth." She disappeared into another room. Pennegar left, slamming the door.

"The magistrate will be here in a few minutes," she said when she returned.

"Thank you, ma'am," I said. "Who is the magistrate?"

"Rutledge Buchan. Been the magistrate in Hirtsboro for years."

Rutledge Buchan entered the building as if he had been waiting for the town clerk to announce him. He wore jodhpurs, a western shirt, and brown riding boots which reported every step with a thud. He was tall, maybe sixty-five years old, and carried himself with a haughty, military bearing. His thin nose and chin and deep-set eyes gave him a hawkish appearance. In his left hand, he held a leather crop. His air of authority was such that Bullock and I immediately stood.

"Well, well," he said, with a thick drawl. "What do we have heah?" He smacked the crop in his hand. I felt like fresh meat.

"Two boys from Charlotte. Reporters," said Patty Paysinger.

Officer Pennegar had followed the magistrate into the room and interrupted. "Like I told you, sir. I caught 'em for speeding out on the highway. Fifty-five in a thirty-five. When I searched the car, I found the guns."

"I volunteered that we had the guns," Bullock said calmly. "I did it for your own protection and so that you wouldn't get the idea that we had something to hide. It's the preferred approach under such circumstances."

"Hold on. Hold on," the magistrate said. "Let's get comfortable heah." He motioned for us to sit back down and he started to pace.

The magistrate turned to Bullock. "Carryin' a concealed weapon is a violation of the South Carolina Criminal Code."

"It would be, sir," Bullock said politely. "But I have permits."

Bullock reached into his wallet, extracted two folded pieces of paper and handed them to the magistrate. Buchan examined them and handed them to Pennegar who inspected them closely and passed them back.

"Signed by the po-lice chief up in Charlotte, I see," Buchan observed. I was as surprised as the magistrate.

Buchan swung a chair around and straddled it so he could face us. "So you boys are reporters from Charlotte?" He said it like "re-po-tuhs." "What brings you all the way down heah?"

Well, I thought, this was just as good a time as any to start the investigation of the killing of Wallace Sampson.

"We're here," I said, "to do a story on a killing that happened almost twenty years ago. Victim was a boy named Wallace Sampson. Do you remember anything about it?"

"'Course I do," Buchan said. "I was magistrate when it happened. Terrible thing. Shot, if I remember correctly. Never caught anyone."

"That's right."

Buchan tipped forward in the chair. "Bradford Hall get you down heah?"

"Yeah," I said. "How'd you know?"

"Hirtsboro's a small place."

Olen Pennegar interrupted. "What about the speeding? Fifty-five in a thirty-five?"

"Where'd you get 'em?" Buchan asked. "Usual place?"

"Just inside the *missing* city limit sign," I pointed out.

Buchan rocked the chair back and laughed. "You know, we were gonna get that sign replaced until we realized we couldn't afford it."

"To get the sign replaced? How much could that cost?"

"Ain't the cost of the sign. It's all the revenue we'd lose because we'd be writin' half as many tickets!" He winked at Patty Paysinger and they laughed as if it was the funniest thing they'd ever heard. "Patty, how's the treasury this month?"

"Not too good. Olen's still a rookie. He'll get the hang of it. But he's not bringing it in like we've been used to."

The magistrate turned to us. "I'm gonna have to find you guilty of speedin' fifty-five in a thirty-five. That's a one hundred dollar fine and one hundred dollars for costs." He stood up from his chair.

"It was one hundred dollars and no costs when we were out on the highway," I said.

"That's right," Buchan said. "It was. But you chose a hearin' so you pay the court costs, too."

Bullock stood up, took two hundred dollars cash from his wallet and handed it to the magistrate. Buchan peeled off five twenties and gave them to Patty Paysinger. "For the town," he said. He split the remaining one hundred dollars between himself and Pennegar, who stuffed the bills into his breast pocket.

"You keep the court costs?" I asked. "Seems like a conflict of interest."

Buchan smiled. "Olen had to bring you in. I had to leave the house and come on down here. Ain't no conflict with *our* interest."

We left the building together. Buchan waited until Pennegar was out of earshot then motioned Bullock and me closer. "I'm sorry about that," he said, his hawk-like features softening. "Those two make sure I treat everybody the same."

"Thanks," Bullock said. "I understand."

Buchan pulled closer. "I've known Brad Hall and his family since Moses was in diapers," he said. "He's a good boy and, bless his heart, I know he means well. But I don't believe he's ever had a job in his life and like my daddy used to say, too much money and not enough to do ain't a good combination. I would hate to see you boys waste your time."

Olen Pennegar dropped us off at the car and pulled away.

"Jesus," Bullock sputtered, "you almost blew it. What the hell were you thinking?"

"*I* almost blew it?"

"Yeah. The only reason we had any trouble is that you decided to be a smart ass and lip off to the cop about the sign. Rule number one if you ever get caught doing anything you shouldn't: Never complain, never explain."

"Ronnie, we haven't even been gone a day and you've already broken the speeding laws, spent time in custody, and almost been busted for concealed weapons. All this fast cars and guns macho bullshit. I've never been closer to getting shot or jailed than I have been today. You kept quiet about the derringer! What if they'd searched you?"

"Hell, they weren't gonna search me. I'd already admitted to bigger guns than that. Besides, the whole point of a derringer is surprise."

"It was an unnecessary risk that jeopardized the story."

We didn't speak until after we had arrived at Windrow where Brad was waiting.

As the dogs Maybelle and Tasha pranced excitedly, he showed us to our room, apologized for Lindsay's absence and told us to meet him on the back deck when we had unpacked. When I got there, Brad and Bullock were already deep in conversation. An open bottle of Rebel Yell sat on a table and Bullock was fiddling with the scope on the 30.06.

"Join us, won't you?" Brad raised his tumbler. "Mr. Bullock is introducing me to the pleasure of a true Southern bourbon."

"I believe I will."

We jumped at the loud crack of the 30.06. "Damn," Bullock said. "Still off." He resumed fiddling with the adjusting screws on the scope.

The deck overlooked the Savannah River and off in a low-lying area to the left a swamp of cypress and Spanish moss.

"You see that Bald Cypress down there in the swamp, Ronnie? The one by Tupelo Gum?" Brad asked.

"The big one?"

"Yeah, furthest to the left. See if you can pick off that clump of epiphyte hanging from the branch."

"Say what?"

"The gray stuff."

"That Spanish moss?"

"That's it, although it's wrongly named. It's an epiphyte, not a moss. Part of the pineapple family. Very spongy. Henry Ford used it for seat padding in the Model T."

Bullock raised the rifle and fired. A piece of the clump drifted to the ground.

"Not bad from one hundred yards," Brad said. "Lemme see the

rifle." Bullock handed it over. Brad aimed at the swamp, fired, and the rest of the clump dropped.

Bullock whistled. "Where'd you learn to shoot?"

"You get pretty good if you grow up on a bird-hunting plantation. I could have been on the shooting team at Harvard but I prefer fencing to guns. More sport if both sides are equally armed." He refilled everyone's tumbler.

"So you support the right to arm bears," Bullock said.

Brad laughed. "Where're you from, Ronnie?"

"Outside of Charlotte." Bullock removed the scope from the rifle and polished its lens with a cotton cloth. "Place called Mallard Creek. Mama's great-great-granddaddy came to North Carolina in the 1700s and kept walking until he found some land he liked. He claimed it, married a local woman, and it went on from there. Bullocks lived off the land—raised cattle, farmed and ran a little moonshine. 'Course the whole thing went to hell when Uncle Horton ran off with a waitress and Aunt Martha got the land." Bullock poured himself another glass of Rebel Yell. "She sold out to developers for a pot-full and they built one of those Yankee Containment Facilities."

"A what?"

"Yankee Containment Facility. Big development with a golf course, gates, huge expensive houses, and a fancy name. No one local ever lives in those places. Just Yankees who move down south, drive to work, drive home to their trophy wives, play golf on the weekends and never even have to feel like they've left Cleveland. Come to think of it, maybe ol' Aunt Martha did us all a service. I've met some of those people. They need to be locked up."

"Those places have funny names," I said. "Sometimes they're not even words."

"The one they built on Aunt Martha's land is called Byrn Brook. What in hell is a Byrn?"

"Byrn Brook. I think that's where the publisher lives."

"What a jerk," Bullock said.

"Well, Ronnie," I said, "We see eye-to-eye on something."

Bullock tried to fill my glass but I was done. "Tell you what," he said. "Let's make a deal. I can act like a gentleman if you can act like you've done this before, okay?"

"Deal," I said. We shook hands. It wasn't the mutual admiration society yet, but it was a start.

"How long have you been at the *Times*?" Brad asked Bullock.

Bullock sighed as his memory rewound to the days just after World War II when he had joined the *Times* after writing press releases in the Army's Signal Corps. His first job was writing obits, the same job he had now. "Great days," he said. "Back before the paper was taken over by a corporate chain. Green eyeshades. Rolled-up-shirtsleeves. Gin in the bottom desk drawer. Hello, sweetheart, get me rewrite. The other thing is, we worked hard to write with style."

It sounded like a jab. "I try to write with style."

"There's no point," Bullock said. "They'll edit the life out of it anyway. Anyway, after obits, I moved to cops and stayed there twenty years. Even had my own office at the cop shop."

"How'd you end up back on obits?" Brad asked.

"My goose was cooked once the *Times* got sold to the chain. Bunch of Ivy League jerks with journalism school degrees took over. They don't care about news. They edit the paper by survey research. They're more worried about political correctness than content."

Bullock shook his head in resignation. "Anyway, I held 'em off for a bunch of years but they finally got me. I got moved from day cops and courts to night cops. Then to night rewrite. Now, my main job is satisfying the publisher's fixation with having obituaries in the paper."

"What do you think this obit fixation is?" It was something I had always wondered.

"I think he's getting old." Bullock said. "Likes to read about his friends." We both laughed about a common enemy.

Bullock fired off another shot and drank one, too. "Don't think I don't care about blacks or about what happened to Wallace Sampson," he said. "I do. But with this story, I've got something else to prove."

# Chapter Seven

The next morning, I watched from my bed with one eye as Ronnie Bullock, up at the crack of dawn, gathered his weapons for battle. Khaki uniform. Tape recorder disguised as a pack of cigarettes. A device for attaching the recorder to a telephone handset. A miniature camera. A small, extendable telescope. Hunting knife. Derringer.

"Jesus, Ronnie, we're not breaking into the Kremlin!"

"Be prepared. Though I don't imagine a communist like you was ever a Boy Scout."

A light rain fell and the Dodge's tires hissed on the pavement as we headed into Hirtsboro, Bullock and Brad in the front seat, me in the back.

Bullock suggested we start with the crime scene. Brad directed us to a street two blocks off Jefferson Davis Boulevard, on the edge of the wrong side of the tracks. We cruised slowly, past a cyclone-fenced field of rusting cars, past a sagging mobile home, a faded Big Wheel the only feature of its stark front yard, past a sandy lot, vacant except for broken beer bottles and patches of scrubby grass.

"There it is," Brad said, pointing to a one-story wooden structure close to the road, behind two Sky Chief and Super Sky Chief gas pumps. Most of the white paint had flaked from the building and the siding had weathered to a light gray. The tin roof was the same color—except for the streaks of red rust which leaked from nail holes like blood from a dozen wounds. The peaked roof extended beyond the storefront, providing a sheltered drive-thru between the pumps and the store entrance. A simple rectangular sign, its letters pale and chalky from twenty years of sun and rain, hung above the pumps. "De Sto" it read in faded green, next to the red Coca-Cola bottle cap logo.

Gravel popping beneath our tires, we eased up the semicircular driveway and parked by the pumps. Brad and Bullock got out and peered through the store's dirty window. I tried the door. The screen door opened easily, but the main door was locked. Through the window, I saw shelves, empty except for a few boxes. A floor-to-ceiling cooler stood along the left wall.

"I got a lock picker," Bullock said, heading back to the car.

"Ronnie!"

He stopped. "What? It's abandoned."

"*Somebody* owns it," I said. "Brad?"

"It's been closed a long time. Anyway, nothing happened in there. Wallace Sampson was shot outside, in the next lot over, near the street."

"Where was the boy when he was hit?" Bullock asked.

"I don't know exactly. The police report might tell us."

I looked out at the street and calculated angles of fire. There were a dozen places the shooter could have hidden. I took out my reporter's notebook and sketched a rough diagram of the area.

"Not much here." Bullock checked his watch. "I'm hungry. What do you say we grab some grub?"

We ate in a Formica-topped booth at the Hungry Tummy Cafe on Jefferson Davis Boulevard. When we had finished, Bullock lit a cigarette.

I looked around. "You sure this is a smoking section?"

"It is now. I allow myself one a day and I enjoy every damn puff."

"Where to now?" Brad asked.

"Let's swing by Mrs. Sampson's." I was still worried that we hadn't gotten her son's picture. "Then we can pick up a copy of the police report."

We drove slowly down the sandy streets of the all-black neighborhood, past the peeling-paint shotgun houses and the Mt. Moriah House of Prayer, attracting the stares of the curious, the old who lounged on porches, the young who played in the streets. Mrs. Sampson wasn't home. But I remembered something she had told me.

"Where's the black cemetery?" I asked Brad.

The rain slacked as we reached the outskirts of town. We turned off the main highway and followed a single set of tire tracks up the wet, sandy drive that led through the white-painted metal arch entrance to Elmwood Cemetery. The road wove through the field of the dead and terminated at the top of a hill in a parking area shaded by a grove of Spanish moss-draped live oaks. We spotted Mrs. Sampson as we drove up, a lone figure with a pink umbrella standing in the drizzle. We parked nearby. Brad and Bullock waited in the car.

"I thought I might find you here," I said as I approached.

"Did you come to see his grave?"

"Yes, ma'am."

She led me to a white slab marker set flush to the ground. A brass vase of fresh-cut zinnias sat below it.

"Here's my little boy," she said.

I looked at the dates on the marker. "He was about ready to turn fourteen."

"Three days. I already had his birthday present. *Charlotte's Web*. His favorite book. I put it in his coffin. We used to borrow it but I got him his own copy. Now, he has it with him."

I was surprised because it had been my favorite book as a child, the one Mom always read to Luke and me. I pictured a brightly wrapped package within the coffin. Inside, a child's favorite book, an ultimately comforting story about the cycle of life and death. The body of a boy, three days short of fourteen, his head blown away by a slug from a deer rifle, with no closure or comfort at all. The rain resumed, God's tears.

Mrs. Sampson knelt at her son's grave. She closed her umbrella and lifted her face to the stinging drops. "Take care of my baby, God." She patted the white marble slab. "See you tomorrow, Wallace."

Mrs. Sampson opened her pink umbrella and shielded me from the rain as we returned to the car.

"Mrs. Sampson, is there any way I could borrow that picture of Wallace on your living room wall? We'd like to use it if we write a story."

"It's the only one I have. I couldn't afford to order."

"You'd get it back."

"How long would I be without it?"

"Couple of days, at most. We'd copy it and send it back."

"I'm sorry. I can't," she looked at me pleadingly. "It's the only one I have."

I couldn't imagine how I was going to explain this to Walker. Best to bring Bullock into it, I figured, so I wasn't the only one taking the blame.

"Not a problem," Bullock said when I got back into the car. He pulled the small camera I'd seen that morning out of the Dodge's door pocket. "We'll take a picture of the picture."

Back at the Sampson house, Mrs. Sampson said, "You can have Wallace's picture, if you want. I have to have it back. But if it will help make sure he's not forgotten . . ."

I knew the original picture would work better. A picture of a picture is one more generation removed from the original. But I also knew it wasn't beyond the *Charlotte Times* production department to damage a photo or lose it entirely. The newspaper's interest had to take a back seat to the interests of Mrs. Sampson. I told her a photo of the photo would do just fine.

Bullock got a small tripod from the trunk of the Dodge while I positioned the photo. "Helps steady the 30.06 firing from the prone position," he explained. "Also fits the camera."

Ten minutes later, we were headed back to Windrow in the Dodge. "Looks to me like ol' Thomas Jefferson musta visited around these parts," Bullock said.

"I don't think he did."

"Well, then, Strom Thurmond or some other white man with a taste for black women. There's some white in Wallace, judging from his picture."

"Ronnie," I sighed. "Try to stay on track."

In one day, we had explored the site of the shooting, visited the grave, got Wallace Sampson's picture, and developed exactly no new information about the killing.

We needed to do better. Walker's clock was ticking.

The next morning we returned to town hall, the scene of our conviction for speeding. The glass door marked Municipal Offices wouldn't open. Inside, we could see Patty Paysinger, the town clerk, at her desk. Bullock rapped on the glass.

"We're closed," she mouthed. She pointed to the right of the door where, for the first time, I saw a sign: *Hours: Monday–Thursday, 1:30–5 p.m. Closed Friday.*

"What kind of backwater is this?" Bullock snarled. "The damn government's open only half the time?" He peered through the glass door. Patty Paysinger shrugged her shoulders and smiled sweetly, as if it were all out of her control.

"I forgot," Brad said. "Sorry."

We returned at 1:30 p.m., having killed half a day with nothing to show for it. Patty let us in. "Sorry you had to wait. I'd love to be full time but poor ol' Hirtsboro just can't afford it, bless its heart."

I remembered my manners. "Mrs. Paysinger, thank you for taking care of me yesterday."

"I hope you're feeling better."

"Yes, ma'am. Mrs. Paysinger, you remember how we're down here to do a story about the killing of Wallace Sampson?"

"I know you said that and I know that Mr. Hall was down here a while back asking about the same thing."

"Well, we need you to find us the police report from the incident itself."

"I can't do that. I'm sorry."

Olen Pennegar walked in. I ignored him. "This is public information," I protested. "Any taxpayer is entitled to look at it."

"Mr. Harper, I'm not talking about the public's right to know. I'm saying I don't have time to drop everything and look for a twenty-year-old police report. Hirtsboro has one full-time employee. That's Olen Pennegar and he's just a pup." Pennegar turned bright red. "The magistrate, the mayor and I are part-time and I'm the only one who gets regular pay. I got a dozen things to do and I'm sorry, but helpin' you boys out just isn't one of 'em."

"Make time. The law says you have to give it to us." I tried to smile but felt my face get hot.

Bullock put his hand on my shoulder. "Easy, Matt." I pushed his hand away.

"We'll sue their damn asses if we have to. Ronnie, we're talking about the people's right to know."

Pennegar stepped forward. "Cursing in the town limits is only a misdemeanor. But we can fine you again."

Mrs. Paysinger turned to me. "I don't how they do it up in Charlotte but I'm sure your momma didn't allow talk like that."

I winced and said I was sorry. Patty Paysinger softened. She told Bullock it was okay if he looked through the files himself, as long as he didn't make a mess.

Bullock motioned Brad and me over to the corner. "I'll stay here and plow through the police reports. You guys see if you can find Wallace Sampson's girlfriend. I ought be able to find this thing in an hour or two."

"I don't like being told I can't look at the records," I said. "Where's she get off deciding who can look and who can't?"

"Will you get off it? Take 'yes' for an answer and keep your ego out of it."

"It's not ego. It's principle. Public records are open to everybody, not just the people the government likes."

"Save it for the Supreme Court. We've got work to do."

Brad and I found a phone book, bloated by the effects of the weather, hanging by a chain from the drive-up payphone perched on a pole in the parking lot. There were dozens of Browns, too many to call.

"Plus, there's no guarantee that she's still Vanessa Brown," Brad pointed out. "She could have married."

"Or moved."

I dialed Reverend Grace's church. If anyone would know the whereabouts of Vanessa Brown, he would. As the phone in the church began to ring Olen Pennegar pulled up in the Hirtsboro town patrol car.

I removed the phone from my ear, cupped my hand over the mouthpiece and looked at Pennegar.

"Something I can help you with?" I asked.

"Nope." He got out of the patrol car and leaned on the front fender, as if he had nothing in the world better to do.

"We'd like to have a conversation here," Brad said.

"Nothing stopping you."

Fine, I thought. We'll play above board. Let Pennegar be the jerk.

"Reverend Grace, it's Matt Harper of the *Charlotte Times*," I said. "I called because I'm trying to track down Wallace Sampson's girlfriend." There was no reaction from Pennegar.

When I got off the phone I told Brad, "She works at the Hungry Tummy."

We walked the four blocks from town hall to the diner past sun-baked brown yards, sand, and bleached gray buildings. Even the leaves of the live oaks straddling the streets seemed pale and washed out.

At the Hungry Tummy, the air conditioner mounted over the door ran loud and hard, dripping water onto the sidewalk, baptizing patrons who hesitated. Brad and I dodged a drip and entered. Heat from the kitchen and the grill swept across the eight-stool counter, aided by a large ceiling fan. The air felt thick and smelled of greasy hamburgers and frying bacon. The air conditioner was fighting a losing battle.

We took the same booth we'd sat in the day before and the same blonde, heavy-hipped waitress took our order.

Brad asked, "Does a Vanessa Brown work here?"

The waitress gave us a guarded look. "Who's asking?"

We introduced ourselves and told her we were working on a story.

"Good Lord Almighty! You wanna interview Vanessa Brown? For the paper?"

"Yes, ma'am," I answered.

"You sure you got the right Vanessa Brown?"

"Girlfriend of a young man who got shot here twenty years ago."

"Don't know nothing about that."

"Reverend Grace told us she washes dishes here."

"That's right. Tried her at waitressing but you have to be able to write. That or remember the order. She can't do neither."

Wonderful. An ideal witness.

"Could we talk to her?"

"Sure," she said. "Soon as the lunch rush is over."

After we had eaten, we went outside and waited under a big umbrella at a picnic table near the back door of the restaurant. It was clear from the saucers of overflowing cigarettes butts that this was where the staff came to smoke.

A short time later Vanessa Brown emerged dressed in jeans and a red T-shirt that said Brown Family Reunion. Her hair was straight, pulled back from her face and, except for a ribbon that stuck out the back, hidden under a blue bandana. She was five foot four, maybe one hundred thirty-five pounds and wore large black glasses. We stood up as she approached the picnic table. I got out my pen and reporter's notebook.

"Vanessa Brown?" Brad asked.

She stared at the ground. "Yes, sir."

"Miss Brown, I'm Bradford Hall. I live out at Windrow. This is my friend Matthew Harper. He's a reporter. I wonder if we might ask you about Wallace Sampson."

She kicked a pebble and looked up.

"Maybe there's a better time to talk," I said. "When do you get a break?"

"Don't get no break."

"We'll wait until you get off."

"Why you care 'bout what happened to Wallace?"

A complicated question. Because Bradford Hall was trying to reclaim the heritage of his family? Because Ronnie Bullock wanted to prove he wasn't washed up? Because I needed this story to save my job? Because Walker Burns wanted a Pulitzer Prize and a ticket to a different newspaper? "We're trying to help out Mrs. Sampson," I said.

Vanessa Brown looked up for the first time. "Mrs. Sampson asked you to do this?"

"No," Brad said. "We volunteered. But she knows what we're doing."

Vanessa Brown took a seat at the picnic table and I knew we had made a breakthrough. I started with the questions that seemed the easiest: how she and Wallace had met ("I'd been knowing him all my life"); what kind of boy he was ("Real sweet"); how long they'd been dating ("Since sixth grade"); what they did on their dates ("Mess around"). When I felt I had her confidence, I moved to the night of the killing.

"He came to my house. We sat on the swing and held hands. At midnight, Momma made him go home." She lowered her head and picked at a splinter on the table. "I watched him walk down the road. Then he got shot."

"Did you hear the shot?" I asked.

"Yes, sir."

"Do you know where it came from?"

"No, sir."

"Did you see Wallace fall?"

"He spun around first."

I made notes.

"How could you see him if it was late at night?"

"Lights from De Sto. It was closed. But lights was always on inside."

"What did you do when Wallace spun around?"

"Ran up to him. His eyes was open but part of his head was gone. I ran home and told Momma and she called the police."

"Did you see anything else just before or after the shooting?" Brad asked.

"I didn't see nothin', 'cept Wallace fall."

"Has anyone ever asked you before about the killing?" I asked.

"My friends."

"The police? Sheriff?"

"No, sir."

"Do you have any idea who might have wanted to kill Wallace Sampson?" I asked.

She shook her head and picked at the bench with bitten-down nails.

"Is there anything else we should know?" Brad asked.

Vanessa Brown looked at my notebook. "No," she said. "That's it."

I asked for her phone number in case we needed to follow up. She gave us the number to her party line. I gave her my card with Brad's number written on the back. It was getting close to 5:00 p.m.—time for Patty Paysinger to evict Bullock. Brad and I headed back toward the Town Hall.

"I think she knows more than she's saying," Brad said. "Seemed like she was holding back."

"Probably scared. She barely looked at us."

"In the old days they weren't supposed to."

"She has a party line. Maybe it's still the old days."

My eye caught three black girls—I judged them to be about ten years old—holding hands as they skipped down the street dressed in T-shirts, flip-flop sandals and shorts. As if a starting gun had been fired at a track meet, the girls broke into a sprint and raced, laughing, toward a drinking fountain planted on the sidewalk in front of the thick glass doors that marked the entrance to Classen's.

A girl in pink shorts surged quickly to the lead and didn't let up until she broke through an imaginary finish line between the store and the fountain. Bent over with her hands on her knees, she was still laughing and trying to catch her breath when her companions flailed to a stop beside her.

The girl stumbled to the fountain and began to drink.

The other two girls shouted "Keisha" as the door to Classen's flew open and a blue-haired white woman exploded from the entrance.

"Stop that!" the woman commanded. She began to swat the girl with a balsa yardstick. "Go on! Get away!" The girl warded off the blows but stayed frozen at the fountain until one of her friends, in red shorts, pulled her away.

"She's sorry," the girl in red shorts said. "She's not from here."

"She needs to learn her place," the woman said.

"Yes, ma'am," the girl said. Her eyes never left the ground. As the woman watched, the girl in the red shorts took the hand of the girl who had been drinking and led her across the street to a spot near the railroad tracks where a rusty spigot emerged from a tangle of a weeds, gravel and broken glass. "Colored water's here," she said. "That other's white."

"I don't want colored water," the girl said, bewildered. "I want plain old white water, just like we have at Atlanta."

The girl in the red shorts turned on the spigot. "Same water. White folks drink there. Black folk drink here."

The woman straightened her hair and returned to Classen's.

I was stunned. "Jesus. Segregated public facilities? How can this be?"

"They took the actual 'White' and 'Colored' signs down years ago," Brad sighed. "But no one has to be told what their place is. Unless you're not from around here."

# Chapter Eight

The next morning I wanted to visit Reverend Grace while Bullock resumed his search for the police report on the Sampson shooting. Bullock had other ideas.

"It's a damned train wreck in there," he said as we ate breakfast with Brad Hall at the Hungry Tummy. "Dozens of file cabinets—three doors high and green. You know the kind. The police reports are there but there's no pattern. We're gonna have to go through every damn one. It's gonna take days. Maybe weeks."

The grill sizzled with strips of bacon and country ham. A steamy pot of grits mingled with the smell of fresh-baked biscuits. The air conditioner above the door was already running at full blast. I groaned.

"Why don't we *all* look?" Brad said. "We'll work around the clock until we finish."

"One problem," I pointed out. "The place is only open half a day."

"And Friday," Bullock remembered, "we can't work at all."

From time to time I've worked on the speech I'd give if my father ever asked me to lecture to one of his journalism classes. Reporting is a lot like academic research, I'd tell the students, and a newspaper story is a lot like a thesis. In academic research, you might poke around old books and documents in the musty corner of a library. In reporting, the documents are in a musty corner of a city hall. In a thesis, you say what you're trying to prove at the beginning and spend the rest of the paper marshalling the argument and providing the proof. Same thing with a newspaper story—only with shorter words and no footnotes.

Over the next few days Brad Hall, Ronnie Bullock, and I joined Patty Paysinger as regular inhabitants of the Hirtsboro town hall. She seemed to enjoy the company. After their first half day, she and Bullock were already on a first-name basis.

"The easiest thing to do is look for the date," Bullock advised. "May 4, 5, or 6. It's in the top right of the page of the report so you don't have to pull each one all the way out of the file."

But occasionally curiosity got the better of me and I could not resist pulling an entire report from the stack and reading the hand-written accounts of Hirtsboro's high crimes, misdemeanors, and cows in the roadway.

"Hey, look at this, Ronnie," I said, sliding a report across the table. "Someone stole fifty pounds of barbecue from the Hungry Tummy back in '78. Broke in through a ventilation shaft. The local pig was all over that one."

Bullock frowned. "Hilarious. Now how 'bout you quit wasting time."

There were twenty-two file cabinets—sixty-six drawers. In a half day, Bullock had been through two of the drawers. At the end of the first day together, each of us had made similar progress. Only fifty-eight more drawers to go. If Hirtsboro's lone officer wrote four reports a day over twenty years, we were going to be examining forty thousand documents. Even if we could average one document every fifteen seconds, it would take fifty-five hours per person. We didn't have that kind of time.

"We've got to be able to work more than part-time on this," Brad said that night. "Any chance Miss Patty'd let us work when she's not there?"

"None," Bullock replied. "But I've got an idea."

In the days ahead, we developed a pattern: arrive with Patty Paysinger, work as hard as we could while Town Hall was open and, whenever Patty went to the bathroom or left the office, smuggle drawers of the unexamined police reports to the car and spend the next morning sifting through them at the Hall dining room table before returning to town with the files, smuggling them back in and repeating the process over again.

During all this, town business went on uninterrupted—a parade of residents paying water bills and property taxes or asking that the town gravel truck fill the potholes on their road. Olen Pennegar made irregular appearances, stopping to talk quietly with Patty. He rarely acknowledged us. We never saw Magistrate J. Rutledge Buchan.

It was late in the day Tuesday of our second week when Brad held up a single-page police report and said casually, "Here's something interesting. The day before Wallace Sampson was shot, someone threw a firebomb at De Sto."

"That old store, across from where the shooting occurred?" Bullock said. "What happened?"

Brad scanned the report. "Apparently, it scorched the side but there wasn't any structural damage. But here's what's strange. The officer who investigated the incident was Olen Pennegar."

"Can't be," I said.

"See for yourself." Brad pointed to the signature. It was as plain as day.

"Patty, let me ask you something," Bullock called. "How come Olen Pennegar's name is on a police report that's almost as old as he is?"

"That's his daddy," she laughed. "Olen Pennegar Sr."

A second later, Brad exclaimed, "I've got it! I've got the report on the Wallace Sampson shooting!"

All of us, including Patty Paysinger, rushed over to Brad's side of the table. The first thing I noticed is that the handwriting was the same as on the report about the firebombing of De Sto. The report had been written by Olen Pennegar Sr.

Beyond that, it contained little helpful information. No reporting persons. No suspects. No motive. No detail. Just a hand-written, single paragraph that read, "Subject was laying in the street w/head wound that appears to have been caused by a gunshot. Subject transported to USCMC/Charleston. No witnesses located. No weapons found."

Bullock asked, "Patty, is Olen Pennegar Sr. still around?"

"He took disability about fifteen years ago. Lives out in the country in a trailer next to his son. But he ain't all there. Had a case of the nerves. Just wasn't safe for him to carry a gun."

"So his son took over for him?"

"Heavens, no. Olen Jr. was just a boy. We had several other officers between them. But he does wear his daddy's nameplate and he carries his daddy's gun."

We used the town copying machine to make copies of the reports about the shooting of Wallace Sampson and the firebombing of De Sto and said our good-byes to Patty Paysinger.

"We appreciate your kindness," said Brad.

She smiled. "Certainly. It was nice to have someone else around. I'm going to miss the company."

She turned to Bullock and me. "I need two things before you leave for Charlotte. You made four copies on the town machine and Hirtsboro needs to be reimbursed. It's fifteen cents a copy so the total is sixty cents."

Bullock searched his pants pocket and came up with two quarters and two nickels. He handed them to Paysinger who put them into a box in her desk and wrote out a receipt.

"What's the other thing?" he asked.

"Make sure those drawers of reports you've been loading in the trunk of your car when you thought I wasn't looking are all back in here. They're town property. I will not have them disappearing."

Bullock flushed like a six-year-old caught with his hand in the cookie jar.

"Yes, ma'am," he stammered.

"And drive safely."

"Damn," he said when we got back to the car. "She must have eyes in the back of her head."

"Before we drive back to Windrow, I want to get another look at De Sto," Brad said. We drove over and parked in the circular gravel drive.

"The place doesn't look like it was firebombed," I said.

"The police report said it didn't do much damage," Brad answered.

"Let's see if we can find where it hit," said Bullock.

We walked around to the right and there it was—an unmistakable spot at the base of the building where scorch marks leeched through faded white paint. Bullock knelt down and ran his fingers across it. "The paint's bubbled, but the wood never caught. The pattern is very characteristic of a fire from an accelerant," he pronounced.

"You mean gasoline," I said.

"Or kerosene. Or lighter fluid. Could be any number of things." Bullock stood up.

"So we know that on night one, there was civil unrest including a firebomb tossed here by someone," I said. "And we know that shortly after midnight on night two, Wallace Sampson was shot, supposedly as he walked past the store."

"Correct," said Brad.

Bullock crashed through wet kudzu vines which had swallowed the back of the building, muting its edges but leaving an outline, like a fish in the gullet of a heron. The broken kudzu smelled of grape.

"*Pueraria lobata*. Pea family," Brad said. "Named for the famous Swiss botanist, M. W. Puerari. The government imported it from the Orient for erosion control during the Depression. The good thing is, nothing kills it. The bad thing is, nothing kills it."

We came to a rear entrance. The doorknob turned when Bullock twisted it. Bullock looked at me. I nodded. He looked at Brad. Brad nodded. Bullock pushed the door and kicked its base and we were greeted by an escape of musty air and mildew.

Bullock went first. "Jesus," he said, emerging. "I can't see a thing." He unclipped a penlight from his khaki shirt pocket and flicked it on. He ducked back through the door and waved us inside.

There were no windows, no natural light except from the door. It took my eyes a while to adjust as Bullock played the tight beam around the room. A sink. A table with a couple of empty liquor bottles. A mattress on the floor. A shower curtain dividing the small room. Another mattress on the other side of the curtain. Cigarette butts ground out on the wooden floor.

The rain began to fall, so hard it sounded like radio static as it peppered the tin roof.

Bullock swept his light across the walls. A mirror. A dresser. A string of Christmas lights.

"Someone musta lived back here," Bullock said. "Maybe it was an apartment or something." The beam probed the wall between the room and the front of the store. "It doesn't look like there's any door between this room and the store."

I was beginning to feel uneasy about the trespass when Brad said, "Let's move on."

"Agreed," I said, relieved that we were getting out of there and also that I hadn't been the one to suggest it. "One run-in with Olen Pennegar and the Hirtsboro legal system is enough for me."

We crunched through the kudzu to the front of the building. "Well, speak of the devil," Bullock said.

There, cruising slowly in his squad car, was Olen Pennegar Jr. He gave a two-fingered wave, nodded and kept going.

BACK AT WINDROW that evening, a delicious odor of sizzling soy filled the kitchen as Brad made noodles and stir-fry vegetables.

"Ooooooohhhhh, those poor little babies," Bullock wailed when Brad sliced baby carrots. "Cut down before they even got to the prime of their life."

But even Bullock, who said he had been expecting fruits and nuts, conceded the meal was delicious and, as had become our habit, after dinner we ended up on the deck with three short glasses and the dwindling bottle of Rebel Yell bourbon.

Bullock consulted a copy of the police reports. "The firebomb was reported when the guy who ran the store—a Mr. Raeford Watson—arrived for work and saw the scorch marks. The report says he told Pennegar the marks hadn't been there when he'd closed up the night before. There's nothing in the report about who might have thrown the firebomb or why. There are no witnesses. The next night, Wallace Sampson is shot in the head with a deer rifle as he walks by the store. Again, no witnesses."

"In each case, Olen Pennegar Sr. is the investigator," I pointed out.

"Because he's the only cop," Bullock said.

"We need to talk to Pennegar," said Brad.

Bullock speculated that Wallace Sampson had thrown the firebomb one night, had come back the next night to try again and had been shot by Watson who'd stayed to protect his store.

"I don't think he was the type of kid to be throwing firebombs," Brad said. "And if he was, why wouldn't the store owner just say what happened? It would clearly be a case of self-defense."

"Wallace Sampson didn't have a firebomb when he was shot," I pointed out. "There's no reason to think the firebombing and the killing were even connected."

Before we went to bed, we agreed we'd go see Pennegar the next day and try to track down Watson, although we had no idea where to start since it was clear the store had been closed a while. Brad suggested we also talk with Mary Pell.

Three leads. Three days left.

The next morning Brad and I found Mary Pell on the back porch off the kitchen of the Big House, hunched over a game table next to a brown wicker basket of shotgunned doves. Their small, limp bodies showed surprisingly little blood.

"Mornin', Mary Pell," Brad said with an uncharacteristic hint of a drawl.

"Mornin', Mr. Brad." She wiped her hands on her apron and nodded at the basket of doves. "Your daddy and his guests had a big day yesterday."

"So I see."

Brad told her we were trying to track down some information about when Wallace Sampson was killed and specifically if she could tell us about Raeford Watson, the man who ran De Sto.

Mary Pell turned to the table and picked a dove out of the basket. With quick fingers she tore the feathers from the carcass and tossed it on the table. "De Sto was a bad place," she said. "Raeford Watson was a bad man."

"What do you mean?" I asked.

"Gouged people. De Sto was the onliest place people from the community who didn't have a car could shop. He could charge whatever he wanted. Then he'd let you run credit and charge on top of that and folks could never get out of hock." She picked up another dove, stripped it in seconds and tossed it beside the first.

"Is that why De Sto was firebombed?"

She paused for a moment. "Don't know nothin' about any of that."

"Mary Pell, where can we find Mr. Watson?" Brad asked.

"Burnin' with the devil, I imagine. He passed on probably five or six years ago."

This was certainly a setback. "Mary Pell, could Raeford Watson have shot Wallace Sampson?"

"I'll tell you this. A lot of folk have wondered the same thing."

Back at Brad's house, I called the *Charlotte Times* library and asked Miss Nancy to search the clips for anything on Raeford Watson. Then we hashed over the morning with Bullock. While we spent time with Mary Pell, he had tracked down the location of the residence of Olen Pennegar Sr.

"It's on Brown's Ferry Road," he told Brad. "You know where that is?"

"About ten miles from here," Brad said.

We left town on the main highway, headed toward the Savannah River under the scorching South Carolina sun. The road cut through stands of slash pine alternating with plots of cleared land that had been planted in soybeans, milo, and one house trailer per plot. Of the crops, only stubble remained and a gusting wind kicked up dust devils that danced through the parched, dead stalks and merged into the cloud of dust that trailed the Dodge.

"It should be on the right," Brad said, consulting his notes. "Just up ahead. This is it." A dirt driveway led up to two house trailers that sat in a field of soybean stubble—a single-wide with a picture window on one end and a small deck built onto the front and, maybe fifty feet directly behind it, a faded white model with a quilted aluminum skirt that sagged and rose like an uneven hemline.

By the mailbox, where the driveway met the road, an old man in a floppy straw hat and overalls sat in a lawn chair, his right hand raised in what seemed to be a greeting.

"Afternoon, sir," Brad said out the window when the Dodge had come to a stop. "We're looking for the Pennegar home."

The man made noise that sounded like "unh."

We got out of the car and I looked more closely at the old man. Large wire-framed glasses magnified bright blue eyes that stared without ceasing. The left side of his face drooped and a trail of spit curled from the left side of his mouth. His left arm dangled limply at his side, possibly the result of a stroke. He kept his right hand raised, like a Boy Scout taking his oath. We introduced ourselves and I asked him if he remembered the killing of Wallace Sampson.

"Unh."

"I don't think he's going to be much help," Bullock said.

I asked the old man if he could speak.

"Unh-unh."

"I can't tell if he's saying yes or if he's saying no," Brad said in frustration.

"I think 'unh' is yes and 'unh-unh' is no," I said. "Is that right, Mr. Pennegar?"

"Unh," he said.

I asked if he had considered Raeford Watson a suspect or had interviewed him about the shooting. Each time, he indicated he hadn't. I pulled out my reporter's notebook and began taking notes.

"Uh-oh," Bullock interrupted. "Here comes trouble." The Hirtsboro town patrol car sped down Brown's Ferry Road trailing a cloud of dust. It skidded to a stop and Olen Pennegar Jr. jumped out and shouted, "Just what in hell do you think you're doing?" Without waiting for an answer, he hurried to his father and wiped the drool from his lips. "Papa," he asked, "are you okay?"

"Unh," Olen Pennegar Sr. said.

"What's this about?" his son demanded.

"We were interviewing him about the Wallace Sampson case," I said.

"For God's sake, he's a sick old man. He can't even talk."

"I'm sorry," Brad said. "We didn't know that."

"What gives you the right anyway?" he demanded. "Look what you've done to him." Olen Pennegar Sr. had begun to cry.

"I'm sorry, but it's the public's right," I said. "Your father was working for the people. You are, too."

"Ain't working for you. You're not even from around here." He spat in the dirt.

"The only reason we're down here is that your police department didn't get the job done. No one's ever solved Wallace Sampson's murder. Not your father. Not anybody else since. And not you."

Olen Pennegar Jr. lunged at me with a right cross. I bobbed back and he hit me square on he neck, right on the jugular. I saw stars. Bullock grabbed Pennegar. Brad grabbed me.

"Get off our property!" Olen Pennegar Jr. screamed.

I broke free of Brad and took two steps back onto the shoulder of Brown's Ferry Road. "I'm not on your damn property. I'm on a public right-of-way."

"Take it easy, Matt," Bullock said.

I shoved my reporter's notebook into my back pocket. "Don't think we're gonna stop," I shouted. "The public has a right to know."

"And you don't give a damn about hurting an old man while you do it," he shouted back.

The truth shouldn't hurt, I was about to respond, before Bullock said, "It's time to go." Reluctantly, I got into the Dodge.

"Uffing," I heard Olen Pennegar Sr. say.

Bullock pulled a U-turn on Brown's Ferry Road and we headed for home.

# Chapter Nine

On the antique game table in the front hall, we found a message from Nancy Atkinson, the newsroom librarian. We called her from the kitchen as Mary Pell busied herself cutting tender shoots of bamboo.

"Looks like we're eatin' panda food again," Bullock whispered as he dialed. "I'm for goin' out tonight . . . Hey, Miss Nancy. It's Ronnie and Matt Harper. Anything turn up?"

Bullock waved frantically and made a writing motion. I handed him my pad and a pen. He flipped to a blank page and began taking notes as he talked. "Holy shit," he said softly. "That's right. Watson. When? How long?"

I struggled to make sense of his scrawl. I could read dates but that's all. He flipped the page and kept scribbling.

"Where? Where's that? Okay."

"Ronnie, what is it?"

"Holy shit. Holy shit. Holyyyyyyyyyyyyy shit!"

"What is it?" I was practically jumping up and down. "What the hell is it?"

Bullock made more notes. "Is that it?" he asked. "If it's the same guy, it's just what we're looking for. Do me a favor and keep the clips out. We're coming right back. Better yet, take them over to the newsroom and put them in my top desk drawer." A pause.

"OF COURSE I'LL BRING THEM BACK!" he yelled.

Bullock hung up and turned to Brad and me with a smug smile. "Raeford Watson once did time for clubbing a civil rights marcher nearly to death in Columbia. He was one of the Grand Dragons in the South Carolina Ku Klux Klan."

"Holy shit," said Brad.

"Holy shit," I chimed in.

"Anybody around here could have told you that," said Mary Pell. "I said De Sto was a bad place."

In an hour, Bullock and I had packed our things, said good-bye to Brad, Mary Pell, Tasha, and Maybelle, and were speeding back to Charlotte. Brad would continue searching the police reports at Town Hall for any sign of a follow-up investigation while Bullock and I worked on the background of Raeford Watson, starting with the clips.

"We got lucky," Bullock said when we hit the interstate.

"I can't believe she found Raeford Watson in the clips."

"That, too. But I'm talking about getting out of Windrow before dinner. Who the hell eats bamboo?" He shuddered. "What say we stop for a thick juicy steak once we get to Rock Hill?"

"Done."

Bullock reached over the sun visor, extracted a cigarette and lit it. "Okay," he said, exhaling a stream of smoke that took a sharp left turn at the steering wheel and rushed out the driver's side window. "So what do we know?"

I uncapped my pen, flipped to a new page in my reporter's notebook and made notes as we reviewed what we had learned so far. When we finished Bullock flicked the cigarette out the window and his eyes narrowed to slits. I could see his mind churning.

"Okay," he said. "There's racial unrest in Hirtsboro. Lots of milling around. De Sto's a target because the owner gouges the community. Not only that, it's known that he's big in the Klan. Somebody firebombs De Sto. It doesn't go off but Wason isn't taking any chances. He decides to spend the next night at De Sto."

"In that room out in the back." I could see where Bullock was going with this.

"Sometime after midnight the next night, Wallace Sampson walks by. Maybe he actually threw the firebomb the night before and he's coming back for a second shot. Or maybe he's just a thirteen-year-old kid coming home from a date who happens to be in the wrong place at the wrong time. Doesn't matter. Watson decides to shoot first and ask questions later. Wallace Sampson goes down."

"Which explains why Vanessa Brown didn't see anyone leaving the scene."

It all came together, no question. The firebomb gave Raeford Watson motive. Being the operator of the store probably gave him opportunity. And the Klan connection and beating of the civil rights marcher showed he was capable and had a history.

"There's just one problem," I said. "Raeford Watson's dead. We can't interrogate him. We have no witnesses. It's all circumstantial unless we find someone that places Raeford Watson at the scene with a gun. And even then, we'll never know his motive. Maybe he's a killer Klansman. But maybe he's just a scared store owner trying to protect his property."

"By killing an unarmed thirteen-year-old? Gimme a break." Bullock was silent for a while. He grabbed another cigarette from the sun visor.

"That's your second cigarette of the day. You said you limited yourself to one. This is your second."

"Yeah, but I gotta think now. I think better when I smoke." Bullock took a deep drag. "The reason we'll never know about Raeford Watson was that no one ever asked him, right? The shooting wasn't investigated."

"That's what Hall says. Obviously, no one ever got charged. So far, there's no evidence of any follow-up investigation."

"What did Pennegar say?"

I flipped back a few pages in my notebook and reread my notes. "I don't think we actually asked him how much he investigated." I said. "We did ask him if he'd ever interviewed Raeford Watson about the killing."

"What'd he say?"

"He said 'no.' Actually, he said, 'unh-unh.' But it was 'no.'"

We both thought it at the same time but Bullock said it first. "That's the story!"

"Right. It's not a story about who killed Wallace Sampson. It's a story about how authorities didn't adequately investigate the killing. A story about official accountability. It's our back door into this thing."

I started writing in my notebook and talking at the same time. "Police didn't . . . scratch that . . . never . . . Okay, here's the lede. Police investigating the killing of a thirteen-year-old never questioned a Ku Klux Klan member who operated a store near the shooting."

"Failed to question," Bullock interrupted. "Make it failed. Failed is stronger than never."

"Okay," I said. "Police investigating the killing of a thirteen-year-old *failed* to question a Ku Klux member who operated a store near the shooting, the *Charlotte Times* has learned. How's that?"

"Almost," Bullock said. "We need to mention that the store had been firebombed the night before and we need to get in that the store owner had been convicted of racial violence in a separate case."

"And we need to say the kid was black," I added.

"The lede's gonna be fifty words long," Bullock moaned. "Walker's gonna go crazy."

I didn't answer because I was already reworking the lede in my notebook.

"Texas Roadhouse is eight miles ahead," Bullock said reading from an interstate billboard. "Great steaks."

My hunger had disappeared, suppressed by the adrenaline that raced through me as I wrote. "Let's wait until Charlotte," I said. "I'm on a roll."

By the time Bullock pulled into the newspaper's parking lot, I had it. We sat under the yellow glow of the vapor lights as I consulted my notebook.

"Okay, here it is. The lede's gonna take two sentences but it works. Dateline Hirtsboro, South Carolina. By Matt Harper and Ronald L. Bullock."

"I want top billing," said Bullock.

"Forget it, Ronnie."

"Alphabetical. I'll settle for alphabetical."

"Dateline Hirtsboro, South Carolina. By Matt Harper and Ronald

L. Bullock. Police investigating the killing of a black teenager following civil rights protests here failed to question a Ku Klux Klan member who operated a store near where the shooting happened. Paragraph. The store had been firebombed during the protests. The owner had been convicted of beating a black civil rights marcher in another incident."

"Son," Bullock said with a grin. "I think we got us a news story. Now let's go get that steak."

THE NEXT MORNING, Bullock and I, temporary members of the dayside staff, rolled into the newsroom ready to write.

The newsroom is a different place in the day, more crowded, more normal. Executives and their assistants come and go on regular schedules, untethered to the whims of the news. Every newsroom department is fully staffed and bustling, including Features, the home of the garden writer. I knew better than to look. When Brad had shown me Venus flytraps at Windrow, I recognized her immediately—a cute little man-eating carnivore luring the unwary with her come-hither beauty.

"Damn, even the coffee's better dayside," Bullock said as we sat in my cubicle in front of my computer. I was at the keyboard and Bullock was to my left—just the way I wanted it. Bullock could report but it was well known that writing wasn't his strength. Walker used to say that every Ronald L. Bullock byline should carry the addendum "as told to Walker Burns."

Our goal was to get a first draft to Walker well before 4:00 p.m. when he went into a meeting where the content of the big Sunday paper would begin to be shaped. The front page is the most valuable real estate for any story and we wanted a piece of it.

Bullock looked at the notes we had made in the restaurant and winced. "You know, I'm not sure we improved things at all during dinner."

He was right. I began typing, starting with the original lede.

"I think the next graf ought to go back to the beginning," Bullock said. "Something like 'Wallace Sampson was shot with a deer rifle shortly after midnight on May 5. The shooting followed several nights of civil unrest in Hirtsboro . . .'"

For most of the next four hours, I sat glued to my chair and the keyboard, the yellowed newspaper clippings detailing Raeford Watson's past piled to my left, my own notes to my right. Bullock stayed with me—verbally editing as I wrote and patrolling the perimeter of my cubicle like a nervous Marine, protecting me from nosy members of the projects team who cruised by to see what we were working on, and from the newsroom's story-tellers, wandering reporter minstrels who stroll from desk to desk in search of an audience while they await the arrival of The Muse or the next assignment from Walker Burns. Occasionally Bullock would eject me from the chair and slam out a few grafs himself. In the interest of our partnership, I tried to preserve his phrasing even as I trashed his paragraphs.

Instinctively and without effort I stuck to the three basic rules of journalism that seemed to be part of my genetic code, stuff my father and every other professor of journalism drilled into first-year students.

1) Don't make any sentence longer than thirty words. (Supposedly, thirty words is all the average newspaper reader can digest at one time.)

2) Don't make any paragraph longer than three sentences. (Long paragraphs of dense gray type are not easy on the eye. Creating white space is more important than following the rules of grammar.)

3) Get the key stuff up high. (When a story comes out longer than an editor has planned for, the people in production don't read the stories to carefully edit the material to fit. They cut from the bottom.)

Plus, I adhered to two rules I developed on my own: 1) Use exclamation points sparingly. 2) Adverbs are not your friend.

At 3:00 p.m., the first page read:

**By Matt Harper and Ronald L. Bullock**
*Charlotte Times* Staff Writers

Hirtsboro, SC—Police investigating the killing of a black teenager following civil unrest here failed to question a Ku Klux Klan member who operated a store near where the shooting occurred.

The store had been firebombed during the protests. The operator had been convicted of beating a black civil rights marcher in another incident.

Wallace Sampson was shot in the head shortly after midnight on May 5 almost 20 years ago. He was taken by Hirtsboro ambulance to the Medical University of South Carolina in Charleston where he was pronounced dead.

No one has ever been charged in the shooting.

The shooting happened near a grocery store that had been firebombed the previous night. Store operator Raeford Watson, a former Grand Dragon of the South Carolina Ku Klux Kan, was convicted and served time in prison in a separate case where he was accused of beating and severely injuring a civil rights marcher following a protest in Columbia.

During a two-week investigation, *Charlotte Times* reporters reviewed police records and interviewed people in Hirtsboro familiar with the case. Among the people the *Times* interviewed was Olen Pennegar Sr., the Hirtsboro policeman who responded to the killing.

Pennegar, now retired, confirmed he did not interview Raeford Watson about the case, even though Watson had a prior civil rights conviction and operated a neighborhood store, called De Sto, which had been the target of the firebomb attack the previous night.

Watson has since died. De Sto is closed.

The story went on from there.

"Okay," Bullock said. "Let's show it to Walker."

It was 3:00 p.m. The press start for the first edition was just seven hours off and the newsroom was starting to come alive. Reporters and their editors huddled around terminals, haggling loudly about words and deadlines. In the aisles, editors from different sections bartered over the placement of stories and pictures. In the middle of it all, the assistant managing editors, the merchants of the newsroom's most valuable commodity—space in the paper—held council amidst much waving and shouting. It was a big day in national news, I heard. More pages would need to be allocated there. Features was slow. They could give up some pages. The whole scene reminded me of a Middle Eastern bazaar.

Yellow legal pad in hand, Walker Burns floated from cluster to cluster, a trail of supplicants in his wake, all begging for a moment of his time. He slipped into my cubicle and Bullock stood guard.

"Let's see how you two cowboys have been spendin' the stockholders' money," he said as he settled into my chair and hunched over the terminal. "The byline's good."

"Very funny," Bullock said. "Just read the damn thing." We hovered over Walker's shoulder, reading silently along with him. I read to the bottom three times waiting for Walker to say something.

"Whatcha think?" I finally demanded.

"Pardner, I ain't done yet," Walker said in frustration. "I gotta move my lips when I read." He put a little asterisk at the end of the second paragraph.

"What's that about?" Bullock asked.

"I'll tell ya' when I'm done." Walker made another mark at the end of the paragraph about Pennegar failing to question Raeford Watson.

After what seemed like forever, Walker pushed back from the screen. "Well," he said, "I ain't exactly bookin' my ticket to the Pulitzer Prize awards ceremony yet, but it's a start."

Coming from Walker, that was high praise. Bullock and I beamed.

"So we're on for the weekend?" I asked.

"We got some ground to cover. But if we saddle up and ride hard, yeah. I believe we can get there."

Bullock's face fell. "What do you mean we got some ground to cover? The story's good. It's all there."

"Fix the lede," Walker said. "Make it 'never bothered to investigate' instead of 'failed to question.' It's longer but it's stronger."

Everyone who edits a story feels like he or she needs to change something but in this case, Walker was right. "Okay," I said.

"Your fourth paragraph is weak," Walker continued. "You got all the facts but there's no outrage. A thirteen-year-old kid is dead, for God's sake. The cops don't care. We're *upset* about it. We're *pissed off*."

He turned to the computer and killed our sentence that began, "No one has ever been charged in the shooting." He substituted: "Almost twenty years later, the killing remains uninvestigated, unsolved, and unpunished."

He pushed back from the screen, looking pleased. "Not bad, if I say so myself. Couple more questions. Did the store that got firebombed burn up or what? Clarify that."

I made a note in my notebook.

"The other thing is, you really point the finger at this Raeford Watson fella. It sounds like he's the killer but I don't know if we can be that strong. I mean the ol' boy's not around to defend himself."

"Or to sue for libel," Bullock pointed out.

"Yeah," Walker mused. "But I'm not sure it's fair."

"Why not?" Bullock argued. "He had motivation and he was in the Klan. We know this guy was no angel."

"Did the police ever consider him a suspect?" Walker asked. "It would be even better to say in the lede that police never bothered to interview a suspect who was a Klansman with a history of racial violence."

"We don't know," I admitted. "The old cop could barely talk. Wasn't much of an interview."

"We can say he was a possible suspect," Bullock pointed out. "I mean, he'd have to be."

"Have we tried to talk to any of his relatives?" Walker asked. "His widow or his kids? We need something in this story that defends this guy."

I was beginning to see his point. "Something like I don't believe my husband would have done such a thing?" I offered.

"That's it," Walker said. "We've got a good story about the failure of police to investigate. But it needs an edit and there are still a few holes. Plus, we may have a good idea who done it, but we ain't solved the murder. And we need to keep on the trail until we do."

"We ought to be able to find out when Watson died," Bullock said. "His obituary should give us survivors. We got all Friday to chase it down."

"We can fix the store thing in a heartbeat," I said.

Walker started toward his desk. "Plug the holes and we're golden. It doesn't solve the murder but it's a good story. And with any luck, it will shake loose some more leads."

"Are you gonna pitch it in the front-page weekend meeting?" I asked.

"Hell, yes. The *top* of the front page."

The Sunday paper is the biggest of the week by every measure that counts and the perfect place to showcase stories like the one Bullock and I were set to deliver. During the week, the *Charlotte Times* sells maybe two hundred thirty thousand copies a day. On Sunday, that figure zooms to more than three hundred thousand, boosted by readers who want the color comics, the TV Book, and once-a-week features like the Book section. More readers mean more advertisers and that means more sections and more pages. More pages mean more space for stories—necessary for showcasing investigations like the Wallace Sampson story. Plus, on Sundays, the theory goes, readers have more time to spend reading.

Even the corporate bean-counters liked Sunday blockbusters. They sold papers—at one dollar instead of the usual twenty-five cents—and the best ones, the "Holy Shit, Mabel" ones, could convert occasional readers into everyday readers.

Because of the Sunday paper's importance, the Thursday afternoon meeting where the Sunday front page was planned was one of the only occasions when members of the news side and the business side of the *Charlotte Times* met to talk about content. The pressroom needed to know how many pages and copies to print. That couldn't be determined until the circulation department estimated how many single copies it might sell. And the circulation department wouldn't estimate single copy sales until it knew something about the front-page content.

Today, the meeting was scheduled for one of the corner conference rooms. From his desk, Bullock and I could see Walker spreading photos on the conference table. "Why is the E.B. in there?" Bullock asked.

"The E.B.?"

"That new chick they hired from the TV station. She's one eager beaver."

"She's in there?" I struggled to see but front-page editor Carmela

Cruz shooed in late arrivals like a mother hen with chicks and closed the door.

That night, nervous excitement kept me awake. The next day was Friday, the last day of our two-week sniff, and the first Wallace Sampson story was in the bag. A major investigative story, headed for the front page. No question, it would buy us more time to pursue our reporting. Over and over in my mind I polished the lede and rearranged the paragraphs until I fell into a fitful sleep. When I awoke, I couldn't wait to get to work.

When I arrived Bullock was already in his cubicle tracking down the relatives of Raeford Watson for comment, a mini tape recorder attached to the handset with a suction cup. He crooked his thick, sunburned neck to hold the receiver and his stubby fingers pushed the buttons fast and hard, as if force would make the electric impulses move even faster. I snapped on my computer and settled down to polish our prose and input Walker's changes.

By late morning, Bullock had located a phone number for Raeford Watson's widow in Sumter and had left a message on her answering machine. I had finished the rewrite, the top three paragraphs of which now read:

**By Matt Harper and Ronald L. Bullock**
*Charlotte Times* Staff Writers

Hirtsboro, SC—Police investigating the killing of a black teenager following racial unrest here never bothered to investigate a potential suspect—a Ku Klux Klan official who had been convicted of beating a black civil rights marcher.

The shooting happened near a store operated by the Klan official. The store had been subject to firebomb attack during the unrest.

Wallace Sampson was shot in the head shortly after midnight on May 5. He was taken by Hirtsboro ambulance to the Medical University of South Carolina in Charleston where he was pronounced dead.

Almost 20 years later, the murder remains uninvestigated, unsolved and unpunished.

"Wow. That's strong," Bullock said when he had read it. "Some of that Lucas Harper talent found its way to you after all."

We went through the story line by line, leaving a spot for a comment from Raeford Watson's widow. If we didn't get one, we'd simply add a line that said she couldn't be reached.

It was after lunch before Walker came by to give the story a final edit. Bullock paced and I was killing time talking to the receptionist when the publisher pushed through the double doors and into the newsroom. My stomach dropped.

The best publishers are ones that come out of the editorial side but ours didn't. Warren Reich had made his name in advertising. Even though he was now head of the whole enterprise, he was still all about revenue and profit. Nothing could be further from the thoughts of journalists. Having a publisher in the newsroom was seldom good.

If your name is on his cut list, it's even worse. *Please*, I prayed, *just let it be a request to do an obit on another fatcat businessman.*

Reich spotted Walker in my cubicle and headed for him. I followed, my heart pounding.

"Hirtsboro, South Caro-fucking-lina? Where the hell is that?" Reich stood with his arms folded. Walker had gotten out of my chair to face him. Our story glowed on the screen.

"Down by the Savannah River," Walker answered calmly. "It used to be in our circulation area."

"Well, it's not now. Jesus, I couldn't believe it when I saw the rack card. The name of the newspaper is the *Charlotte Times*," Reich steamed, emphasizing "Charlotte." "Not South Carolina. Charlotte. How long did we spend on this thing?"

"Not long. A couple weeks."

Reich stared at the screen. "Both reporters? Two weeks each?" He looked at me. "Piss-poor productivity."

"It's a helluva story," Walker said. "It's gonna make some waves. It'll sell newspapers."

"Sure," Reich said. "In places none of our advertisers care about. Two weeks at what? Six hundred dollars per week each."

Actually, it was a bit more than that but Walker said, "Yeah."

"Plus, hotel, food, mileage," Reich groaned. "Hell, this is going to be a two thousand dollar story."

"We stayed for free," I interrupted. Walker and Reich turned around. "We hardly spent a dime." I made a mental note not to expense the strolling violinists from our celebratory dinner.

Reich tried a different tack, as if we were all now on the same side. He leaned close to Walker and said loud enough for me to hear, "Look, I know better than to mix business and editorial but the governor called to warn me about this story."

Walker was startled. "The South Carolina governor?"

Reich looked around conspiratorially. "I contributed to his campaign. You three aren't the only guys with sources. The governor says your guy Bradford Hall is a fruitcake. The governor shoots birds with his old man. Stand-up guy, apparently, but the kid's another story."

I winced.

"So the governor called you," Walker said.

"Given the problems with the public works story, he said he didn't want us to look bad again. Said he owed the newspaper because we endorsed him last time around. Sounds to me like you need to double check your sources."

"We have no sources," Walker pointed out. "Everything we have, we have directly. We've seen the police report, we interviewed the officer, and we're relying on our own stories for the background on Raeford Watson."

He looked at me and I nodded. "Besides, we know all about the problems between Brad Hall and his father. The issue isn't all Brad, believe me."

Reich was smart enough not to antagonize a reporter and an editor in the middle of the newsroom. "What's done is done," he pronounced. "But you damn well better be right." He looked directly at me. "I will not have this newspaper embarrassed again."

Reich started to leave. "From now on, let's stick to stories that have something to do with the lives of our readers."

"That's what we try to do," Walker said softly. By then Reich was twenty feet away. He stopped in his path.

"You can put that South Carolina story on the front page for the early editions," he called back over his shoulder. "But see if you can find something closer to home to replace it later. I want something local for the city edition."

Walker watched him until he disappeared through the swinging doors. "You know what the sad part is? If this paper ever did get noticed for an investigation, that asshole would be the first one to take the credit."

By 5:00 p.m., Bullock hadn't heard from Mrs. Watson and we felt safe in packing it in. We agreed to try her again tomorrow, but beyond that, we were done. I was exhausted but already looking forward to coming to work Monday morning to receive pats on the back from my colleagues and even some new leads that the story might generate.

The Sampson story was a big investigative piece and even if it wasn't exactly a home run, at least we were on base. Walker had assured me that Reich was just having a bad day and that we'd get more time to pursue the investigation. And with luck, I'd soon be off the Cut List and maybe even on the projects team full-time.

I considered calling Mrs. Sampson but rejected the idea. Better to wait until the story had hit and then keep the ball rolling with a follow-up story on her reaction. Without knowing exactly why, I dialed Delana Calhoun, the one person I could trust enough to violate my own Cardinal Rule: Don't tell anyone a story is going to be in the paper until the press actually starts. There was no answer so I left a message. "Buy the Sunday paper," I said, then joked, "When we win the Pulitzer Prize, you can say you knew me when."

Before I left I phoned Brad. I knew he'd be as excited as I was.

"It's good you called," he said. "I went back to Town Hall on Thursday to go through the last of the files. I found one more of interest."

"What's that?" I asked uneasily.

"Not long after he reported the firebomb, Raeford Watson suffered a heart attack at De Sto. Olen Pennegar drove Watson to the hospital in Charleston."

I felt my stomach sink. The implications of Raeford Watson suffering a heart attack and being taken to the hospital only hours before the shooting of Wallace Sampson threatened to torpedo our story which suggested he should have been regarded as a suspect. Watson would have had to have been one helluva marksman to shoot Wallace Sampson from his hospital bed in Charleston one hundred miles away. I entertained the hope that possibly Watson had been diagnosed only with indigestion, had been released and, still seething at the attack on his property, had returned to Hirtsboro.

My theory was dashed when a glum-faced Bullock stumbled into my cubicle.

"We're screwed," he said. "Mrs. Watson called back. She says she remembers the day well. Her husband was so upset by the firebomb attack that he suffered a heart attack."

"I know," I said. "Brad found the police report."

"Watson was in the hospital the night Wallace Sampson was shot. And for two weeks after. Air-tight alibi."

"So Pennegar had no reason to question him." I took a deep breath and felt a little dizzy. "Shit."

I stumbled out of my cubicle. I could see Walker in a meeting in the corner conference room but I could not spare the time to wait for him to finish. I slouched to Carmela's desk.

"We're going to need to hold the Wallace Sampson story," I said. "There are a few loose ends."

Carmela sighed, called the circulation department and told them they'd need to adjust their expectations for Sunday sales.

By the time I got back to my desk, word had spread through the newsroom that the weekend's big investigative package—my story, my way out of the publisher's crosshairs—was dead.

# Chapter Ten

Sunday morning I stayed in bed too depressed to retrieve the newspaper from my doorstep, even if it did have a big story on Cyprus and a feature on single-sex math classes.

The phone finally roused me from my bed. It was Delana, and I was sure I knew why she was calling.

"Sorry about the message," I said. "The story got held."

"I wondered. But that's not why I called. Matt, your dad has cancer. He phoned me yesterday when he couldn't reach you."

I collapsed into a chair, a hole in my stomach, a weakness in my limbs, a lightness in my brain. I was reeling, outside myself, as I struggled to absorb what Delana had been able to learn. Multiple myeloma, a cancer of the blood. No known cause. Treatable but not curable. Maybe one year. Maybe ten.

"Matt, we need to see him," she said.

"I'll be there in an hour." I hung up and stared dumbly at the blinking light on my answering machine. I'd deliberately ignored it, unwilling to be distracted from the Sampson story. I pushed the button, picked up the model car I keep on my desk, and listened to my dad saying he had some news and that I should call.

Some people keep family pictures on their desks. On mine, I keep a set of vise grips and a miniature model of a green two-seat Triumph TR3 sports car like the one my father drove when I was growing up.

I had some of the best times in my life in that car. I can close my eyes and summon the smell of its oil-rich exhaust and worn black leather upholstery. I can hear the winding engine and the delighted screams of my brother Luke, scrunched sidewise in the tiny space behind the seats, as Dad took turns low and fast. Unbuckled in the front, I can feel myself pressed back as Dad accelerated through the gears and then, during turns, tossed between the door and the handbrake.

Saturdays, Dad worked, "holding down a desk" as he put it, overseeing production of the big Sunday paper. Little League, Scouts, family trips to the park were out. But, sometimes, late Saturday afternoon Luke and I would be playing when he'd pull into the driveway. He'd put the TR's top down, lift Luke and me in and we'd be off, cruising all over town. As the editor of the paper, Dad knew everyone and everyone knew him.

"Evening, Mr. Harper," cops would say from their patrol cars as we idled at the lights.

"Put me in the paper, Mr. Harper," my friends would beg when he'd drop me off to meet them at the movies. "Take a picture of me in your car."

In the TR3, Dad never seemed happier. I keep a model on my desk because I want one just like it.

I use the vise grips to hold down papers. I like to twist the adjusting screw while I'm talking on the phone. Sometimes, I try to get the grip to just the right tolerance so I can pick up a brand new *Charlotte Times* #2 Ticonderoga pencil without cracking its yellow paint.

I have had them since the day I turned thirteen. Among the bright packages of T-shirts, shorts and music tapes at my birthday party was a heavy package wrapped in brown paper and string and a tag that said "Happy Birthday, Dad." It felt heavy enough to be something really good. I kept thinking—what? a radio, maybe? I pulled away the paper and felt the metal, cool and slippery, lightly coated in mineral oil to prevent rust. I held the vise grips and looked at Mom and Dad.

I searched their eyes for a clue. Was this some kind of gag? Maybe there had been a mistake. But it was no mistake. Now that I was beginning to enter adulthood, my father explained, it was time that I began thinking about a career. It should be something that involved working with my hands, he thought. It was time I start building a collection of tools.

I had tried to smile and say thank you and maybe I did. I tried not to hurt but I couldn't. There is not a single person, including my mother and father, who knows who I am, I remember thinking. I am alone in this world.

Now, the feeling came again.

I DROVE IN A DAZE to The Farmlet, Delana's weathered farmhouse and pottery studio outside of town. I found her in the kitchen looking sexier than I wanted. She wore jeans, a sports bra, and no shirt. Her dark hair caressed her smooth shoulders as she turned her head to greet me, her hands in the sink.

"I'm making him a blackberry crisp," she said. "Sorry." She hunched her shoulders to indicate her bareness. "These things stain like crazy. I didn't want to dress until I was finished." She returned to work at the sink. "I'll have this in the oven in a minute."

I sat by the window at the small breakfast table, the one where we used to start the mornings with the paper and coffee. Behind me, a cobalt blue pottery vase full of lavender, red, and pink zinnias stood in stark contrast to the black wood-burning stove on which it sat. The old ceiling fan turned lazily, giving off a familiar click on each rotation. I was surprised to see the picture we'd had taken of us together at sunset at our favorite place, the aging dock at The Farmlet's secluded pond, still on the shelf. For a moment I felt as if I had never left.

I have known Delana Calhoun half my life, since we were fifteen and my father used to drive us on our first dates. She is gorgeous. She is smart. She is sexy. We'll always be friends. If I were a better man, it might have been more.

Delana busied herself at the counter, mixing the berries, oatmeal, brown sugar, butter, and flour. She opened jars of cinnamon and nutmeg, sprinkled them into her bowl and began spooning the mixture into a glass pan. When she had finished, she washed her hands, shook them out over the sink and hugged me.

"Matt," she said, "it's so awful about your dad. I'm so sorry."

"He's a tough old bird. He'll fight it."

She laughed. "I remember the first time I met him. He bowed and kissed my hand. He was so mannerly. So cultured and polite. You were like that, too. That's one of the first things that attracted me to you."

"I used to be better at it." It was true.

"You're better than you think." She smiled and squeezed my hand hard.

She bit her lip and her chin quivered. For the first time since I got the news, I could not hold back.

"I'm glad I didn't put on my mascara," she sniffed as she pushed away. She slid the glass pan into the oven and had to kick the door shut. "Twenty-five minutes and we'll be ready to go."

"Smells good," I said.

She smiled. "Must be genetic. It's always been your father's favorite."

I caught myself staring. "I'm starting to get distracted," I said. "You need to put your shirt on."

"Put it on?" she laughed. "That's a switch."

I laughed, too, but it didn't take. I missed her too much. I had assumed that by now I could be easy and breezy about our past—just two one-time lovers who'd grown up and moved on but could look back fondly on the times that had been. But it still hurt. I remembered my father and my heart was stabbed again.

The sweet, syrupy smell of baking blackberries and brown sugar filled the room as I read the paper and killed time. I wondered whether my father had ever had one of his stories crash and burn. I wondered if he'd ever been fired.

I spotted a piece of Delana's pottery I hadn't seen before—a spectacular blue-glazed tray impressed with natural items from North Carolina, a pine cone, a dogwood bloom, a magnolia leaf, that Delana was using as a mail holder. Her new stuff had moved well beyond functional pottery. It was art.

A letter from a New York gallery lay open in the mail tray. My reporter's genes made me read it. The curator had enjoyed his recent trip to North Carolina, the letter said, and wanted to make sure Delana understood his offer. The gallery was eager to represent Delana's art, was prepared to buy twenty-five thousand dollars-worth of pottery up-front and would launch a month-long exhibition if only she'd say "Yes." The letter was dated two weeks earlier.

The timer on the stove announced the completion of the crisp and of Delana's dressing routine, which I could not bear to watch. But I saw it anyway because I knew it by heart.

Delana covered the hot crisp with foil and placed it in a picnic basket. She packed the basket with hot pads to secure the crisp and keep it warm. An hour later, I could still sense its warmth as it rode on the floor of the back seat on our way to visit my father.

I asked about the letter from the gallery as we drove.

"Who can figure the New York art world?" She shrugged her shoulders. "For years they wouldn't look at me and now they won't leave me alone."

"Congratulations. You're finally getting the recognition you deserve. Twenty-five thousand bucks and your own show."

"The Farmlet could use the money," she said ruefully, "but I'm not going to do it. The work isn't quite where it should be yet."

I was stunned. "The gallery obviously thinks it is."

"But I don't. Besides, they'll still be there when I'm ready."

Before long we were almost there. Like a kid on the high dive with a line of impatient swimmers waiting, I knew I had to jump. "Delana," I said, "I've got to tell you something. I've never told Dad about what happened."

"What do you mean?"

"I mean I haven't told him yet that we aren't getting married."

Incredulous, she swiveled toward me. "Why not? This is a *big* thing in people's lives. This is your father! How does this not come up?"

Beyond her disbelief, I could feel her hurt, as if our breakup meant so little that it didn't even merit family mention. But that wasn't it at all. I had so many good reasons for not telling my father about what happened with Delana that I didn't know where to start. How about shame? How about denial? How about because not talking is the nature of father's and my relationship? In the Harper family, I've learned that if I need a shoulder to cry on, mine is the shoulder I turn to.

"He doesn't need to hear bad news right now," I said, skipping to where I knew the conversation was headed.

But I had already uncapped the well of her anger. "Well, maybe you should have thought of that before you decided to fertilize the hot little tomato," she said. "That bitch."

I flashed to the morning the *Times* garden writer and I were awakened by the clanging of trashcans. Peering out from the slits in the blinds of her bedroom window, the bed sheets pulled around our necks, we watched Delana dump can after can of garbage on the garden writer's neatly manicured lawn.

"It wasn't her fault," I said weakly.

"I wouldn't call her blameless. I'll never understand what you saw in her."

She stared out the side window, chin in hand. I tried to lighten things up. "Besides," I said, "I probably did you a favor. My story's dead and my career's even deader."

"That's crap and you know it, Matt. The story's not done and you're not done. Quit feeling sorry for yourself."

We rode the rest of the way in silence.

Dad's habit was to spend Sunday afternoon at his office. I planned to pick him up there while Delana waited at his townhouse with the blackberry crisp.

"So what are we going to do about telling him about us?" she asked when I dropped her off on a leafy side street not far from campus.

"I don't know."

I haven't seen my dad all that much—maybe two or three times a year, less than that after Mom died and he quit the newspaper to take the teaching job. But I knew where to look: in his office at the School of Communications on the second floor of Lowell Hall. Head down, he graded papers at his desk, the walls behind him adorned with the record of his splendid newspapering past—awards, citations and photos with the famous. For a long time I watched him silently from the doorway, as a parent might a sleeping child.

The fortunate among us outlive our parents and therefore experience their deaths. But as I watched him, fortunate is not how I felt. I was scared for him. I didn't want him to hurt and I didn't want him to die unhappy. I was scared for me. If it was his turn now, it might be my turn next. As Walker Burns once put it, "When your parent dies, it means the lemming right in front of you just went over the cliff." Mostly, I was sad for both of us. I've always wanted my father and me to be closer. I used to think we had years, but we were running out of time.

Every kid wants to envision his dad a hero. Lucas Harper Jr., had a lot of material to work with. He is the son of a crusading newspaperman who became one himself. His passion for human rights and commitment to social justice found expression daily on his editorial pages and in our lives at home. At the university, his ferocious memory and piercing wit are legendary among the next generation of journalists and crusaders.

On Labor Day 1962, civil rights protesters marched through our all-white suburb. Mom, Dad, Luke, and I joined the neighbors at the curb. Dad hoisted me to his shoulders. The marchers were well-dressed, peaceful, and carried signs bearing slogans like "Integration Now" and "End Discrimination." But as the marchers passed, I saw faces twisted in anger. People began to boo.

Then suddenly my father stepped forward, off the curb and into the street, me on his shoulders and Luke and Mom beside us. The Whites, our next-door neighbors, followed. Soon others from the curb began to fall in and before long the streets were filled. Only now do I understand the impact of my father's step and the courage it required for him to take it.

At home, it was Dad who set the standards. We said "sir" and "ma'am" on all occasions. Mom might let a lapse slide but any failure within earshot would be immediately addressed by Dad removing his eyeglasses, staring at the offender, arching a left eyebrow menacingly, and demanding, "What did you say?"

"I mean 'sir,' sir," we'd quickly scramble.

"That's better." That was the script. Every time.

We were to rise when any woman or any adult entered the room. We were not to speak unless spoken to. We were to be seen and not heard.

High standards applied to life, school, and work, not just social occasions. If something was worth doing, it was worth doing well. The greatest sin was a failure to think. Perfection was the point.

In fifth grade I came home excited because I'd learned that Robbie Schroder's parents paid for grades—fifty cents for each B and one dollar for each A. My ten As and two Bs added up to eleven dollars, I had already calculated.

"Young man, we do not pay for good grades in the Harper family," my father informed me. "We expect good grades. Excellence is not the exception. It is the rule. Now, get cracking on those Bs."

At home, there were no free rides. We had a duty to contribute to the household, Dad would explain, as if it were a lesson in ethics and economics. A suitable contribution became defined as two hours of chores every Saturday during the school year and two hours a day, Monday through Friday, during summer vacation. An allowance wasn't a gift. It was money earned.

One day, Luke had had enough. "None of my friends has to do what we have to do," he told me. "Johnny Doyle's mom does everything for him and he gets five dollars a week. I'm going on strike."

I knew what a strike was. Dad's newspaper had to stop publishing once because the pressmen's union had walked out. I knew it meant you refused to work and I knew it was serious. I was delighted that Luke was testing the limits but I intended to lay back and see how it all turned out. Luke was principled, uncompromising, and stubborn. So was Dad. It was going to be interesting.

"I'm on strike," he told Dad. "I'm not working. And you still have to feed me and buy me clothes. The law says so."

"The law doesn't say I have to feed you hot dogs and hamburgers," Dad shot back. "I can feed you tomatoes." Luke and I hated tomatoes in any form except ketchup.

"Then I'd starve to death and you'd go to jail."

"You'd have to not eat for thirty or forty days to starve yourself to death."

"Well, I'm not working and if all I get is tomatoes, I'm not eating."

And so Luke's strike commenced. It had started conceptually as a labor strike but also took the form of a hunger strike, at least for the first day. When Mom served dinner the first night, Luke sat silently and left his plate untouched. Luke wasn't going to work but he wasn't going to take any family food, either. Dinner finished with the controversy never addressed.

By the next day, the strike had been modified to allow the consumption of food from non-home sources such as Johnny Doyle's mom and the Good Humor man. By the day after that, the terms had been modified to allow consumption of food from our home as long as Mom and Dad didn't know about it. And by the fourth day, the strike was over, the issues that sparked it still unaddressed and unresolved.

All this attention to obligation and standards came from Dad's conviction that much is expected from those to whom much is given. Lucas Harper Jr. had grown up with a good education and a father with an important job. So would Luke and I. Dad made clear to us that Harper family members had been given the gifts of education and good fortune and we were to use them to make the world a better place.

So I worked hard. No hunger strikes. Good grades, even with no pay. A reasonable approximation of the required weekly chore hours. And I followed him into the profession.

The father of my boyhood was small, but strong and wiry, able to lash a golf ball farther than any man his size. Over the years, he'd developed a slight belly, but, beyond that, when I'd seen him six months ago he looked fit. There was no reason to think he wouldn't live forever.

He looked better than I had expected. But I could see the illness was already taking its toll. He was thinner. He had just begun to lose his hair in patches. He was already wasting away.

"Dad?"

"Son!" he said with genuine delight. He got up and put his left hand on my right shoulder and weakly shook my hand. "Where's Delana?"

"Back at your place. I'll give you a lift over there. How are you?"

He waved his hand. "Later." He motioned me to a chair. We sat, his desk between us. "I'm good. I had a transfusion, a temporary fix. Red blood cells were down to nothing. But now I feel a lot better. How about you?"

"Okay. Worried about you."

"I'm going to be fine," he said dismissively. "I've already started chemo. Gonna need to get a wig, though."

"How long do you have to do chemo for?"

"You mean, 'For how long do you have to do chemo?' Ending a sentence with a preposition is a practice up with which I will not put, to paraphrase Winston Churchill."

"Thank you, Professor Harper. For how long do you have to do chemo?"

"Six weeks. It's a new kind of chemo. If it's working, we'll keep going. If it's not, they'll try something else. It turns out the best guy in the business is here at the university hospital. They'll throw whatever they have at it."

We moved on to his journalism law course and the recent Supreme Court rulings about freedom of the press. ("There's a reason the First Amendment is first," Dad groused. "Those reactionaries out there haven't figured that out yet.") We talked about what it was like to teach. ("It's like performing for a parade," Dad said. "The parade stops in front of you, you give your performance and the parade moves on. When the parade stops again, you give another performance.") We talked about the current crop of students and the ones who might make good interns for the *Charlotte Times*. ("There's a junior, Lulu Sharpe. I like her energy. On a dare she once bit me on the ass at a J-school party. I like that.")

I was feeling better. There was life in the old boy yet. It was reassuring to talk about normal things, about journalism and interns and the Supreme Court.

But I wanted more. Dad and I were just skipping across the surface. It was a conversation that could have occurred between any two people who had just met. I wanted something more fundamental, a meaningful talk between father and son. A discussion of death could be avoided today, but it was still the elephant in the room that wasn't being talked about. We were running out of time.

Walker Burns has a saying about what a reporter needs to do when confronted with a distasteful task. "Stick your hand into the wound," he would say, meaning don't shy away, no matter how unpleasant or difficult. Confront the worst. That's what I wanted. I wanted our conversation to be real. I wanted it to be about the important things. I wanted to stick my hand into the wound.

"Dad, how do you feel about the multiple myeloma?"

"Well, it makes me feel tired, like it's hard to get my breath."

"No, I mean how do you feel about having it. What do you think about it?"

"Think about it?" Dad shifted and cleared his throat. "What do I think about it?"

I sighed. I don't know why my family became reporters and writers. My grandfather was once quoted as saying, "It beats plowing." Maybe it was genetic, but whatever the reason, a lot of us had turned out to be pretty good reporters and writers. What we didn't do much of, my mother used to say, was communicate.

I heard the squeak of the wooden floor in the hallway, followed by a quick knock on my father's open office door. A young brunette breezed in wearing tight jeans and a too-small T-shirt. She feigned surprise.

"Oh, Professor Harper. I didn't know I was interrupting."

"Not at all," Dad replied sweetly. *Not at all* indeed, I thought to myself. In my day it would have been, "Young man, you're interrupting." At minimum.

"Professor Harper, I have my paper. I know it was due last week. I'm sorry it's late." She literally batted her eyes.

"That's okay," he smiled. "The most important thing is that it's good."

I couldn't believe my ears. This was the man who used to say that anyone could do a good job if they took all the time in the world. The true measure of excellence, he would insist, was getting the job done in the time allotted for it. Or in less.

"Oh, it's good." As if to assure him she grabbed his hand and drew it close to her body. "It's five pages. I know you wanted ten but I ran out of time. It's a good five."

"I'm sure it is," Dad answered gently. And then, remembering that I was there, he said, "I'm sorry, Darla. I should have introduced you. This is Matt Harper, my son. Darla Clark." No mention of the fact that I was in the profession.

"Pleased to meet you," I said.

"I'm so pleased to meet *you*," she gushed. "You are *so* lucky. Your father is the sweetest nicest most understanding man in the *whole* world."

"I can see why you feel that way."

She kissed my father on the cheek, said her good-byes and whirled out of the room.

When she had gone I asked, "So does everyone get that kind of break from Professor Harper or just the cute coeds?"

He smiled. "So young. So pretty. And a head so completely filled with air."

"I can't believe you let her get away with it," I said. "The thing was late and half the assigned length. You would have scalped us for that as kids."

"You would have deserved it."

"She didn't?"

"There's a difference. She's paying, or her parents are. If she doesn't take advantage, it's her loss. She's a supposedly responsible adult. It doesn't reflect on me."

"Whereas, we did."

"Whereas, you did."

I decided to plunge the hand into the wound. "Dad, are you happy about the way I turned out?" It was a long-shot opportunity to get him to open up but it was worth trying.

"Reasonably so."

No score.

"Before she came in, we were talking about the multiple myeloma. You were telling me how you feel about having it."

"Displeased. But there's not much I can do about it."

"Why you?"

He put his hands behind his neck, elbows out and leaned back in his chair. "I understand that's a common reaction but I don't look at it that way. We're all going to die of something. I'm always amused by these Centers for Disease Control statistics—how we've pushed down the mortality rate for this disease or that. For Chrissakes, it's a zero sum game. Push down the death rate for cancer and guess what? The rate goes up for something else. No one gets out of life alive. Multiple myeloma may get me. But you know what? Maybe it will be something else."

"Well, I'm not worried about it," I lied. "You're going to be around for a good long time."

"I intend to be. But I've been reading the obituaries for a long time and I've noticed that most people who die are between forty years old and eighty. I'm right in the middle."

I felt myself growing angry. "I don't see how you can be so philosophical about this."

"Here's what I've asked myself since I was old enough to think about it: if I died today, how would my obituary read? Would there be a picture? Would the story be long or short? Would it be on the inside or the section front? Or possibly on the front page? Or would there even be a story?

"Right now, I think it would make a pretty good obit. Son of a famous newspaper man who become a pretty fair country editor himself, then a tenured professor. The Pulitzer Prize might even move it to the front page. I probably ought to make sure there's an updated mugshot." He chuckled at the thought and made a note in the reporter's notebook he kept in his inside jacket pocket.

"Fine for you, but what about me?" I said angrily. "You may be okay with it, but I'm pissed off. I'm pissed off that you're sick and I'm pissed off that you don't even care how I feel about it."

My father got up and went to the window. He clasped his hands behind his back and rocked back on his heels, watching the empty courtyard.

"Let's go see Delana," he said finally.

As we walked to the car, Dad looked even thinner, gaunt, a little stooped. His eyes blazed bright blue. An effect of the chemo, I wondered, or just the contrast with the pale parchment of his skin? He was starting to resemble the late-in-life pictures I have seen of my grandfather, his father.

At the townhouse, he greeted Delana with a kiss on the cheek and a hug. "How are you, cutie?" he asked.

"I brought you this," Delana said, holding the picnic basket.

"I'll bet I already know what it is."

"You're limping a little," I said.

"Hip," he said. "Apparently, the disease starts to work on the bone." He pointed to a cane in the corner. "They gave me one of those, but I don't use it."

"Dad," I said, "why didn't you tell us about this before?"

My father ignored the question, opened up the picnic basket, carefully unloaded the crisp and peeled back the aluminum foil that covered it, releasing its sweet scent.

He breathed deep and exhaled. "Magnificent!"

"Now, you all sit down," Delana commanded. "Colonel, do you have any vanilla ice cream?"

He smiled at being called Colonel, the name she had invented for him. It honored his Kentucky heritage but it was also a good way to deal with the problem of what to call your prospective father-in-law.

She served us at the kitchen table. Dad ate slowly, with precision, savoring every bite. He closed his eyes as he chewed and I imagined that he was capturing the taste and sensation, mentally recording every nuance, thinking that this crisp was likely to be one of his last.

"Takes me back to summers in the blackberry patch down by the creek, catching crawdads, skinny-dipping, and eating blackberries. I'd get a whippin' when I got home because I'd spoiled my dinner." He chuckled at the memory.

Delana served him a second helping and for the next hour we talked—about the university and the prospects for the college basketball team, about the stupidity of academic administration, about news—everything, of course, but about his disease.

I was flabbergasted. "Dad," I asked again, "why didn't you tell me about the cancer sooner?"

"I've got a pipeline straight into the circulation system," he said, unbuttoning his shirt to show us the implanted port in his sternum. "The chemo goes right in there. No need for needle pricks. Pretty neat, huh?"

I frowned. There was nothing neat about it.

"Matt, you always worried too much. Your mother, too."

Delana steered us from the rocks. "How does the chemo make you feel?"

"Okay. I've got it worked out pretty well. It's every couple of weeks and I have it done on Friday. By Monday, I'm ready to teach a class."

It struck me that he had it backwards. "So let me get this straight," I said. "You schedule this so you can feel bad on your own private time at home and can be well on university time when you have to work?"

"Home life's overrated," he said.

It was a throw-away line. In another context, another time, I would have let it go. Or maybe even laughed. But what came to my mind was the image of my mother struggling to keep dinner warm, looking at her watch, and doing her best to preserve a family meal despite the vagaries of the news, defending Dad and his tardiness while Luke and I complained. I thought of Luke who lived each night for the sound of the Triumph roaring up our street and into our driveway and for my mom to call out, "Daddy's home."

And I thought of all the times Dad had ignored me—times I'd waited until bedtime for him to emerge from his study, the fortress into which he locked himself nightly after the ritual two shots of bourbon. On the day I won the eighth-grade writing award, desperate to have him read my short story that had won it, I cried myself to sleep outside the locked study door when he wouldn't respond to my knocks. When I awoke my father was gone. But he had written a single comment on my prize-winning paper. "It's 'lie' down," he had written in the margin, "not 'lay.'"

"Was family life always overrated?" I asked.

Dad looked surprised.

I felt a kick from Delana under the table but I didn't care. I should have been used to it but he'd pushed me over the edge. For as long as I have known him the man who has so much compassion for people in general has shown zero to his family. Not once during our visit had he acknowledged my hurt. Whatever he felt, it was always all about him. Despite that, I should have done what Delana would have done. I should have told him that I understood. I should have decided that no matter what, from then until the day he died, I would show him all the love I could in all the ways I could show it. But I didn't.

"No, that explains a lot," I said. "Maybe if you'd cared as much about us as you did about the world, we'd still be a family."

I braced for the withering fire that I knew would come in response. Dad loved a debate and didn't care if it was personal. Words were his weapons and he was a master.

But it didn't come.

Instead, he just sat there looking small, sick, and weak. This was no time to tell him about Delana and me.

"I'm sorry," I said. "I shouldn't have said anything."

"Don't worry about it."

"I know you've had a lot on your mind."

We sat there until Delana broke the ice. "Matt," she said, "tell the Colonel about the story you've been working on."

And so I told him about Wallace Sampson, about our trips to Hirtsboro, our work at the Town Hall and our interviews with Olen Pennegar Sr., Mrs. Sampson, and Wallace's girlfriend, Vanessa Brown.

"So where's the story?" he asked when I was finished.

I told him about the last-minute development that had made us pull it.

"So, really, you're nowhere closer to solving the murder than you were when you started," he concluded.

"Yeah," I said. "We're no closer than when we started."

We talked for a while more and then we said our good-byes. Dad escorted us to the door.

"Thanks for coming," he said and shook my hand.

I stuck to my pledge not to tell him that I loved him until he told me first. "I enjoyed it," I said.

He turned to Delana. "Thank you for the crisp. You have learned the way to my heart."

Jesus, I thought to myself. And to think that all I had to do was learn how to make a damn crisp.

Delana scolded me when we got to the car. "What you did in there was terrible. I can't believe you're more worried about your feelings than his. I can't believe you talked that way to a dying man."

"Dying doesn't get you off the hook from being a decent human being."

"He's a wonderful man. A wonderful, very sick man."

My hands tightened on the steering wheel. "Let me tell you something about him, godammit," I snapped, unleashing the wrath on Delana that I had held back from my father. "If he has *ever* directly said, 'I love you,' I don't remember it."

"I don't believe you."

"I am *not* kidding. I play this game where I try to get him to say the words, 'I love you.' I've *never* won."

"What is it they say in your business? It's better to show than to tell?"

"He showed his love all right. He showed it by closing the door on his family every chance he got."

Delana sat quietly and I didn't feel like talking either. We kept to ourselves the rest of the way home.

The sun was setting over The Farmlet's front pasture as we rolled up the driveway and parked in front of the house. We watched it disappear into the longleaf pines and then behind the rusted tin roof of the neighbors' barn.

"It's all related," Delana said finally, breaking the long silence.

"What is?"

"The garden writer. The thing with your dad. How uptight you are about the story."

"What do you mean uptight?" I bristled.

"You know what I mean. Look at the pattern. You crave your father's approval and are angry when you don't get it. You need to reassure yourself by seeing if you can pluck some hot little tomato. You've never believed in yourself, Matt. It's all about what you need to feel secure."

"You're way off base."

"Let me ask you something. Why do you want this Sampson story? So you can measure up to your father and grandfather? So you can prove that you can play on the same team as the newspaper's big boys? So you can put some rednecks in their place?"

"Something wrong with that?"

"When are you going to learn that you don't need your dad's okay or anybody else's? Matt, it's not about you. Someone killed Wallace Sampson and is getting away with murder. That's what matters. Sometimes you just have to do the right thing and all else be damned."

She got out, shut the car door and walked toward the house. At the stone bench by the front door, she turned around, and marched back toward the car. She stuck her head into the window just inches in my face.

"And the thing with the garden writer? It wasn't about me and you know it. It was about you running away. But you can't run from yourself, Matt. Sometimes it's all you have to hold on to. One day maybe you'll figure that out."

# Chapter Eleven

By noon Monday everyone in the newsroom knew about the highly touted investigative piece that had fallen through—at great expense and inconvenience to the paper.

I kept my head down and tried to pretend the whole thing never happened. Walker had been burned pretty badly and I wanted to let as much time pass as possible before bringing up the subject of Wallace Sampson again.

I covered the school board meeting because the regular education writer was on vacation. The second night I ended up on the front page with six paragraphs on a Pineville farmer's pumpkin that looked like Elvis, provided that you squinted and sort of tilted your head sideways. It was my first front-pager in more than a month.

But the Sampson story was on my mind and on the third day back, I brought it up with Bullock.

We were alone in the cafeteria except for a janitor and the cloying smell of disinfectant and hard-boiled coffee. "Ronnie, we need to find a way to get back down there. Another couple of days is all we need. Maybe a week."

He rolled his eyes.

"We were rushed."

"You asked for two weeks. You got two weeks."

"Two weeks was a guess. We had no idea it would take as long as it did to get the police report." I was rehearsing the argument I would use on Walker. "There's stuff we still need to do. We never went back to Reverend Grace. And there's got to be a way to get to Olen Pennegar.

Even if he can't talk, he understands. Both of them were around when it happened. We need to ask Walker for another week."

Bullock tore the tops from four packages of artificial creamer and emptied them into his coffee. "God, this stuff has all the appeal of number two grade crude." He took a sip and sighed. "You could be right. But I don't see Walker buying it. Our credibility isn't exactly at a high point."

We shuffled back upstairs to the newsroom where a copy carrier was busy placing the latest edition of *Saints & Sinners* on all the newsroom desks. *S&S*, as it was known, was Carmela Cruz's weekly in-house two-page newsletter critique of the previous week's content. It was picky: "We said in a sports story that Monroe is twenty miles from Charlotte. It is eighteen," she wrote. It was provocative: "Of the thirty-five photographs in the Business Section last week, thirty-five were white males in ties." And it was well-read: On days when *S&S* hit the newsroom desks, work didn't start until reporters, editors and photographers had had a chance to see if their work had earned bouquets or brickbats or, the usual case, had attracted no attention at all.

No one had elected Carmela the arbiter of newsroom quality. She had started *S&S* on her own and everyone understood that many of its items carried an underlying theme: heroic copy editors (who worked, of course, for Carmela) were responsible for all that was good in the *Charlotte Times* as they worked miracles with poorly executed metro stories while producing clever, insightful headlines and weighty national and international stories that delighted readers.

Knowing all that going in, I was still stunned when I got to the item in *S&S* titled "Never Send a Boy . . .": "The Wallace Sampson story debacle was a failure of concept and a failure of execution from which the metro desk would do well to learn," the item read. "The first question is: Of all the stories in the world, why would the *Charlotte Times* elect to go after one with no apparent relevance to our readers? And, second, if it were such an important story, it would have been well to select reporters experienced in dealing with such an assignment. These decisions were quite costly and would have been more so, had the story run. Fortunately, readers were spared—and instead were treated to the National Desk's excellent package on Cyprus."

My ears burned and I flung the copy of S&S out of my cubicle where it fluttered to the floor.

"Bitch," I swore to no one in particular.

Ronnie Bullock arrived at my cubicle with his neck muscles bulging and twisting a copy of S&S like he was trying to strangle it. "What a bitch. Where the hell does she get off? She's never been out of the office. Never reported a damned story in her life. She's probably never written anything more complicated than a grocery list. And she probably leaves *that* to the woman in the family."

I wouldn't have said it myself. But I was angry enough that I didn't mind when he did. And I knew then and there that no matter what I was not going to give up on the Wallace Sampson story.

"I'm gonna trash those things," Bullock announced. He began going from desk to desk, collecting the just-distributed copies of *Saints & Sinners*. "This stuff is complete bullshit."

"Ronnie, I don't think you ought to do that."

"It's trash. It belongs in the trash."

"It looks like censorship."

"She *needs* to be censored. Walker's gonna go crazy when he sees this. We'll never be able to talk him into letting us go back down there."

"Maybe there's another way. Walker's probably never going to be able take another chance on us. But who says we need his permission?"

Bullock looked at me like I was nuts.

"I'm serious. We don't have that much to do. We could do it in a series of day trips. It's good that we work nights. We could leave early, before dawn and get to Hirtsboro first thing in the morning. If we head back right after lunch, we could be in the newsroom in time to work our regular shifts."

"You're crazy."

"Why? We just go down there every morning and come back every afternoon until we get what we need. Then we spring it. It'll be too late for anyone to tell us no."

He looked across the newsroom at the rows of desks and the copies of *Saints & Sinners* on each.

"I'll pick you up at 5:00 a.m.," he said.

EVEN ON A SLOW NIGHT, it takes me two hours to wind down once I get home from the office. On a high adrenaline night, or if I've been drinking a lot of coffee, it can take longer. It was 3:00 a.m. before I fell asleep and only ninety minutes later when the alarm went off. But I was ready when Bullock arrived, with military precision, at 5:00 a.m.

The sky had not yet begun to lighten and a crescent moon hung low on the eastern horizon as we sped south, too drowsy to talk. Bullock tuned in WWL from New Orleans and we listened to country music and the weather forecasts for the interstate highways system from Oregon to Florida, programming aimed at truckers, our brother travelers through the night. When we turned off the interstate and away from the lights of the city, the sky grew thick with stars.

The highway through rural upstate South Carolina was straight and empty. Bullock set the cruise control at seventy-five miles per hour. The Dodge whooshed smoothly through the cool night air. With a series of clicks, Bullock notched the cruise control higher and soon the speedometer read 80, then 85. Then 87, 89, 91.

"Better take it easy, Ronnie. We don't need another ticket."

"Would you relax? Every minute we save coming and going is another minute we can spend reporting."

I shut my eyes and let him go. The radio switched from an upbeat country song to a report from Nashville about the goings-on of various country music personalities including two that had announced their engagement. Before long, I was asleep and dreaming a strange dream in which Delana and my father were in the University Chapel getting married while my dead brother Luke served as best man. I watched from the choir box, unable to make myself seen or heard.

The sensation of falling snapped me awake. It took me a moment to get my bearings. WWL had turned to static. The sky was lightening in the east. Fog clung to the ground like clouds that had descended to earth in the night and had failed to rise before dawn. The sun popped over the horizon and I felt the heat on my cheek. I glanced at the speedometer. The needle nicked 95.

Bullock caught me looking. "This is why we have the Dodge instead of your old beater," he said.

Ten minutes later and without slowing down, we followed the highway into the swamp. Sunlight filtered through the high tree canopy and illuminated the remnants of fog that created a gauzy, dreamy quality, like we were driving through a fairy tale.

In my peripheral vision I caught the blur of a doe and three fawns standing by the edge of the swamp. I was thinking we were lucky they hadn't bolted across the road when Bullock swore and swerved. The Dodge fishtailed into a three-sixty. I caught the huge scared eyes of a giant buck right outside my window as we spun down the highway in a slow-motion pirouette. The glove box popped open and the .38 slammed into my knee again. My reporter's notebook went flying across the backseat. Bullock gripped the steering wheel, hit the gas and kept his foot off the brake. Miraculously the car straightened. Bullock braked to a stop in the middle of the highway. The buck, the doe, and the fawns were gone.

We sat there breathing heavily, our hearts slamming in our chests. After a minute, Bullock slipped the Dodge into gear and pulled over to the side of the road. Moments later, a school bus passed in the opposite direction, its driver and passengers oblivious to what had occurred.

"Close call," I said.

"Yeah," he said. "Good thing I spotted him. Those things will about take out a car."

We drove the rest of the way at the speed limit. It seemed like we were crawling but we reached Hirtsboro by 8:00 a.m. Just in time for breakfast.

Bullock parked by the tracks on Jefferson Davis Boulevard. "We don't have time for the Hungry Tummy. I'll call Brad and let him know we're in town. You go over to the Feed & Seed and get us a couple of Moon Pies and RC Colas. Then we'll go see your buddy, the Reverend Grace."

We got out of the car. The sun had climbed higher in the sky. Bullock unbuttoned the pocket of his khaki shirt, extracted his aviator sunglasses, slipped them on and went in search of a phone.

Just over the tree line, where Hirtsboro stopped and fields started, a crop duster roared past, swooped high, made a sharp turn and descended for another long low pass over the surrounding furrows. On the street in front of me, a tractor chugged by pulling a trailer. Twelve black men in floppy straw hats sat on the edges of the flatbed, their legs dangling off the sides, workers on their way to the fields. I crossed the street to the Feed & Seed just as the rig pulled to a stop in front.

"Ya'll be quick about it," commanded the driver, a deeply tanned white man in a John Deere cap. "We're already late." The workers slid off the flatbed and ambled to the store. I followed.

I plunged my hand into the icy water of the open cooler by the front and pulled out two RCs. I found the Moon Pies at the checkout counter. The men on the flatbed were already there, waiting to pay for individual cigarettes sold from a glass jar with a hand-lettered sign that read, "SMOKES—10 CENT EA."

The tractor driver came into the store, pulled two six packs of beer from the cooler, grabbed a bag of ice, and got in line behind me. "Don't be botherin' me for it 'til quittin' time," he said to the workers.

I paid for the RCs and Moon Pies and met Bullock back at the car.

"Brad'll meet us at the church."

At the Mt. Moriah House of Prayer shrieks of laughter could be heard as two dozen young children chased each other and tumbled on the church grounds as three older women watched. The smell of fried chicken and cooked vegetables wafted from an open window along with the sounds of laughter and the banging of pots and pans from the church kitchen. We found Reverend Grace bent over a small desk in his office, writing.

"Lord have mercy! You scared me," he said, unfolding his lanky frame and jumping up quickly when I stuck my head inside the door. "I heard you'd given up and gone home."

I had forgotten how tall he was. The top of my head reached his clerical collar. I had to look up to look him in the eye. "No, sir. Just a little setback. We're still on it." I remembered he hadn't met Ronnie Bullock and I introduced them.

Bullock, apparently seeing the dark pants, black shirt and clerical collar as a uniform, stepped forward, shook hands firmly, took a crisp step back, and said, "How are you, sir?"

"Ronnie and I are double-teaming this thing," I explained.

"Triple-teaming it," said Brad Hall, walking into the office. "Good to see you again, Reverend. Matt. Ronnie." We shook hands.

"Three wise men," Reverend Grace said. "Seeking what?"

"Road map information," I answered. "What we talked about. What you said."

Reverend Grace closed the door to his small study, walked to the window and silently watched the children playing outside. Finally, he spoke. "The church in Hirtsboro exists to ease the burdens of its members. We take care of the young. We feed the poor. We mourn the dead. I counsel them about their sins and their fears. There is not much we don't know about the lives of our people. But I cannot give you information I have learned in confidence."

"I understand your vows," I said impatiently. "I understand confidentiality. Just tell us where to look."

Grace turned to Brad. "How well do you know the people who work for you? Do you know their names? Their last names, not just their first names? Do you know what comes after Miss Mary? Or Mr. Jim? Do you know the names of their children? Their grandchildren? Do you know what they think about Strom Thurmond? Or Jesse Jackson? How *well* do you know them?"

"I've known them all my life," Brad said. "Look, don't start on me about where I'm coming from. I'm the guy who got this whole Wallace Sampson investigation going."

Grace pressed his palms together as if he were praying. "Have you talked to Mary Pell?"

"I don't see . . ." Brad said and stopped. "Mary Pell?" he said incredulously.

"In the church, we can tell people how to get to heaven. We can show them the path. But we don't know exactly what they're going to find when they get there."

Outside the church, Bullock glanced at his watch and said, "Oh-ten-hundred hours. Do we have time to talk to Mary Pell today or should we head back?"

"She'll be at the Big House," Brad said.

"Half hour to Windrow. Maybe three and a half hours drive back," I calculated. "Let's go for it."

We caravanned to Windrow, Bullock and me in the Dodge trailing Brad in his pickup. We found Mary Pell at the Big House, just as Brad had said. She was in the kitchen, on the phone.

"Now, Charles, don't be sending me any of those bent cans this time. You sent ten cans of soup up here last week and three of the cans were bent. Mr. Hall doesn't want bent cans so don't try to send any more of them up here."

The cord on the wall phone was long and Mary Pell paced back and forth as she talked. She wore her lavender maid's uniform, trimmed in white at the collar and hem. She was small and wizened, her salt-and-pepper hair pulled back in a bun. Brad said she was sixty-five but she looked older. As she paced, she favored her right hip.

"She's on the phone to the market," Brad whispered. "She phones in the order every day to the grocery and they bring it out. She knows everyone who works in the place or ever has so she tends to get her way."

"Make sure that beef is lean, Charles," Mary Pell was saying. "You pick me out a good one, y'hear?"

"I swear those boys think I just fell off the turnip truck," Mary Pell said when she hung up. "Mr. Matt, I didn't know you'd be comin' back. I don't believe I have your beds made up."

"We're not staying. As a matter of fact, we have to head back after we talk to you."

She looked surprised. "Why do you need to talk to me again?"

"Mary Pell, we've been talking to a lot of people," Brad said. "You know how long I've been working on this. Matt and Ronnie have, too. We want to solve this killing. You were around then. Someone told us we should talk to you about De Sto and the firebombing, that you might be able to help."

"Who told you that?"

"Can't tell you," I said. "We promised. Besides, it doesn't matter."

"What do you mean you can't tell me who told you?" she asked archly.

"We made a promise of confidentiality," I said. "We promised the person we wouldn't tell. Sometimes people will tell reporters information only if we promise not to put their names in the paper. We made that promise."

"You can break it."

"We wouldn't do that," I said. "Reporters have gone to jail to protect that privilege even when they've been ordered to talk by a court."

"So you believe in civil disobedience."

"I never thought about it that way, but in this case, yes."

"Would you make that promise to me?"

I looked at Bullock who nodded his head. "Yes," I said. "But it's conditional on one thing."

"What?"

"You can't lie," Bullock said.

Mary Pell took off her apron and laid it on the counter. She hung up a dishtowel that was lying by the sink, went into the pantry and began stacking jelly jars. She emerged from the pantry a moment later. "I like what you said to Mr. Hall, the way you stood up to him that night at dinner. Willie Snow and I laughed about it all night. I knew I could trust you then." She turned to Brad. "Your father can be stuck in the past."

"No one knows it better than me," he replied.

We followed her down a flight of stairs and into the basement. Two bare light bulbs hung from the ceiling. A washer, dryer and commercial clothes press sat in the corner next to a laundry sink. A toilet stood in the open. A copy of *Ebony* magazine rested on the tank. I wondered if

Mary Pell was not comfortable using the toilets in the main part of the house or if it was not permitted. Mary Pell's purse sat on a laundry table. She rummaged around in it and pulled out a small tin.

She led us to a corner where an old couch and several stuffed chairs sat around a hooked rug. She snapped on a table lamp, sat down, opened the tin of snuff and popped in a pinch.

"My sanctuary," she announced and motioned for us to sit.

"You were the one who told us that De Sto was a bad place, that Raeford Watson was a mean man," Bullock began. "We know he was in the Klan. We know that he gouged the community and we found a police report about how De Sto was firebombed the night before Wallace was shot. We wonder if the shooting might be related."

"Why?"

"Maybe retaliation. Possibly even self-defense."

"Wasn't no self-defense. The boy had no weapon."

"We also know that Wallace was not shot by Raeford Watson. He was in the hospital at the time. So if he wasn't there either to protect the store or to avenge the firebombing, who was? Who would have cared?"

Mary Pell spat into an empty soup can on the floor beside her chair. "I don't know nothin' about the shooting. But you're wrong about the firebombing of De Sto." She took another dip of snuff. "Everyone knew Raeford Watson was a Kluxer. He gouged, that's for sure. But that ain't why De Sto was firebombed. If it was, it'd happened long before."

"Then what was it?"

She eyed me carefully. "What went on in back. There's another room in the building, behind the part where the store is."

"We saw that," Bullock said. "We went in there."

She looked surprised and sat forward. "What'd it look like?"

"Like somebody lived there," Bullock said. "It had beds, a sink. It was decorated."

Mary Pell considered that for a moment and then asked, "Do you know what jumpers are?"

"Paratroopers," Bullock said.

"Workers at the bomb plant."

"The Savannah River Nuclear Plant up at Barnwell," Brad explained. "They call it the bomb plant because the government makes plutonium there."

"They started runnin' girls out De Sto," Mary Pell said. "Black girls. Worked out of that room you saw in the back. I always wondered what it looked like. Jumpers was the main customers." She spat into the can. "De Sto gouged the community, but I 'spect jumpers is where the real money came from."

Brad was stunned. "I never knew."

"The community knew. We'd see the cars show up with license plates from all over and we'd know it was pay day down at the bomb plant."

"So someone tried to firebomb it," I said. "It was an affront to the community."

"I don't know if it was that. But it hurt to know what was going on."

"Did Raeford Watson run both operations?" Bullock asked.

"He was the one that collected the money and paid the girls."

"Mary Pell, how do you know?" Brad asked. "We need to know how you know."

Mary Pell looked at me. "You promise you won't use my name? Not in the newspaper and not to anybody, even the police?"

"Yes, ma'am."

She closed her eyes and was quiet for a long time. "My daughter worked over there," she said after a while. "She was an addict. She did it to support her habit. She did it for two years."

"I'm so sorry," Brad said.

"Don't matter. She's dead now."

Brad slumped back as if he'd been hit in the chest with a rocket. "Mary Pell, when did that happen? Why didn't you tell me? How could you not say anything about this?"

"About five years ago. And I ain't in the habit of talking 'bout my family with the boss man. Plus, she was already grown."

I thought back to our conversation with Reverend Grace.

Bullock changed the subject. "Mary Pell, did Raeford Watson work with anyone or have a partner? Is there anyone else who would have wanted to retaliate for the firebomb?"

"I don't know anything about the shooting."

"Then who threw the firebomb?"

"It don't make no never mind," she said. She got up from the stuffed chair. "Now I need to get back to work. I've told you everything I can that could help you."

I thought about pressing harder but we had made some progress. We'd be returning to Hirtsboro tomorrow anyway to try to talk to Olen Pennegar and we could always come back to Mary Pell.

"One more question," I said. "Why do they call them jumpers?"

"The government has rules about how much radiation nuclear workers can absorb," Brad answered. "Some of these guys absorb their annual limit in a month or six weeks and they're done. No more work. They can't make the same money doing anything else so they jump to another nuclear facility, get a job under a new name and start again. Jumpers."

I pulled out my notebook and dashed a reminder to tell Walker Burns about another potential South Carolina prize-winner.

"Come on," Bullock said impatiently. "We have three and a half hours to get back."

THREE HOURS and forty-five minutes later—fifteen minutes late and out of breath—we burst through the newsroom door.

My first break came when Walker didn't notice my late arrival. My second came when I learned there was no news.

"It's as dead as an armadillo on the exit ramp to a truck stop," Walker advised when he finally swung by my desk. "I got a feelin' we're gonna get stuck roundin' up local inserts tonight, so just hang out and be ready to make some phoners."

Ordinarily, I would have groaned. Writing local inserts meant chasing down information that could be added to a national or international story to make it more relevant to the local community. They were unglamorous and unrewarding. They were often stupid. One reporter had been asked to produce a paragraph on the likelihood of a volcanic explosion in the Carolinas for insertion in a story about an eruption in the Philippines. Even worse, local inserts produced no byline that could be counted when reporter productivity was measured. And those were bylines I desperately needed.

But today chasing local inserts was perfect. I'd been up since 4:00 a.m. and was operating on two hours sleep. My heart was in Hirtsboro, not in the newsroom. All I wanted was to coast through the evening, maybe get out a little early and slide into bed. Then get up at 4:00 a.m. and do it all over again.

I was almost dozing at my desk when one of Walker assistants came by with word that a man in a trailer park had taken a hostage. Police had him surrounded, TV cameras were already live from the scene, and I needed to be on my way.

The park was six miles away in a tough part of town. I pushed the Honda as fast as I dared but by the time I arrived, the reporters were packing up. The man had passed out, a cop told me, and his wife—the hostage—was unsure if she wanted to press charges. I phoned in a couple of paragraphs for the briefs column and headed for home.

# Chapter Twelve

It seemed like only seconds went by before I was awakened by the bleating of the horn on Bullock's Dodge. "Your turn to drive," he said, flicking away a cigarette. "I'm whipped."

"You're whipped? What about me?"

"You're young."

"Since when did you consider that an advantage?"

"Since now. I'll drive this afternoon. You can sleep then."

I didn't really mind. There are times when I am my own best company.

Bullock eased his seat back and turned on his side. His left pants leg hitched up and I could see the glint of the derringer by the dashboard light. I kept the radio off and the windows up as we sliced through the dark hours before South Carolina's dawn. In moments, he was snoring.

We were running out of strings to pull, by my way of thinking. We needed to take another run at Olen Pennegar Sr. He had to know about what went on in the back of De Sto. And we needed to go back by the town hall, only this time to look at the real estate records instead of police reports. Watson operated the business but did he own the building? Today and one more day of reporting, I figured. After that, we'd either have more leads or we'd be out of luck.

Fatigue pushed my chin to my chest. My mind played tricks and I kept imagining deer darting from the shadows by the side of the road. I struggled to keep my eyes open and the Dodge between the white lines. I felt my eyelids close. My mind started to drift until fear shocked me awake. I clenched the steering wheel. When we arrived on the outskirts of Hirtsboro at 8:30 a.m., I was so tired it hurt.

"Brad's gonna meet us at Town Hall," Bullock said, emerging from his cobwebs. "We should find out who owned the store building before we go see OP senior."

"Let's hope the property records are in better shape than the police reports."

Lights gleamed inside the cinderblock building but the parking lot was empty except for our Dodge. The doors were open but inside, the clerk's desk was empty.

"Miss Patty?" Bullock yelled. Then louder. "Anybody home?"

"I am." I whirled around to see Brad Hall. "What are you guys doing here? It's Friday. Town Hall's supposed to be closed."

That's right, I thought. I'd forgotten. "But the door was open," I said. "The lights were on."

Brad shrugged.

Bullock eyed Brad, who wore hiking boots, shorts, floppy hat and had a knapsack slung over his right shoulder. "What the hell are you dressed for, a geriatric nature walk?"

"I've been collecting specimens," he said.

Bullock yawned. "Exciting."

"It *can* be." Brad unslung his backpack, unzipped a pocket and pulled out a plastic baggie, which he held to the light. From it he carefully extracted a leafy green vegetable matter attached to a long root. "*Cnidoscolus stimulosus,*" he said proudly. A natural aphrodisiac that grows in the woods here. Country people call it the Courage Plant."

"What's it do?" Bullock wondered.

"Makes you feel like a teenager. Twenty minutes later, you're ready to go again. So I hear."

"Lemme see that," Bullock grabbed for the plant.

"Careful. The leaves are covered with little hairs that will sting you. The magic is in the root."

Bullock took notes as Brad explained the identification and proper processing of the Courage Plant but my attention drifted. I strolled around the room studying the paper trail of a tiny town's bureaucracy—faded faxes

about federal mandates, three-by-five cards with the new garbage pickup
schedule, and the maintenance bill for the Hirtsboro police car.

I noticed a set of file cabinets apart from the ones containing the
police reports and started pulling the file drawers. I didn't think about it.
It's just something I do. Closed doors make me nervous. Closed drawers
make me curious. The files were in alphabetical order. I skipped to the
Ps and began thumbing through them. Payroll. Pension, Personnel, and
then the one I was looking for: Property Taxes.

The youthful voice of Olen Pennegar Jr. sent my stomach to the floor
and stopped me cold. "Freeze!" he shouted. "Hold it right there!"

I started to turn around.

"I SAID FREEZE," he shouted. "PUT YOUR HANDS OUT TO
YOUR SIDES WHERE I CAN SEE THEM."

I did as I was told.

"Now turn around."

Slowly I turned and realized Olen Pennegar Jr. wasn't talking just to
me. Bullock and Brad stood with their hands in the air. Pennegar swung
his gun back and forth between the two of them and me. He was taller
than I remembered. He might be a rookie cop, I thought to myself, but
he looks pretty comfortable with a gun. For a while, we were all too
shocked to speak.

"Just what the hell are you doing in here?" Pennegar demanded.

"We just came by to say hey to Miss Patty," Bullock said. "But no
one was home. Jeez, put the gun down." He dropped his hands and took
a step toward Pennegar.

Pennegar pointed the gun at Bullock's head. "Hold it right there!
You're all under arrest." Bullock stopped in his tracks. "Patty don't work
Fridays. Town Hall is closed. You knew that."

"The door was unlocked," Bullock said.

"I doubt it but it don't matter. It's Friday. You're not allowed here."

"So what's the charge? Some big crime like trespassing on public
property?" I avoided looking at Bullock and Brad, whom I knew would
disapprove of my sarcasm.

Pennegar's face boiled. "Attempted theft of government property, pal.

A felony. Get over here and spread 'em. Hands on the wall."

"Theft!" Bullock protested. "That's bullshit."

"I saw him going through files," Penneger said, meaning me. "You were attempting to steal something."

I put my hands on the wall and assumed the "get frisked" position, just like I'd seen on the TV shows. I couldn't read the young cop to tell if he was just jerking us around or if he really believed we'd come to commit a crime. "This is crazy. I wasn't stealing. I was trying to figure out where some real estate records might be. They're public information. You can't steal something that's already yours."

Pennegar pointed to a desk. "Over there. Sit down and keep your hands where I can see them. Now you." He motioned Bullock to the wall and I realized we had bigger worries than Pennegar's understanding of the public's right to know—namely the derringer strapped to Bullock's calf. I expected Bullock to volunteer that he had a weapon. But he was silent, and Pennegar's search was cursory as he struggled to pat one of us down with one hand while keeping the pistol trained on the other two at the same time. The derringer went undetected.

Brad was next to face the wall and he tried his best to defuse the situation.

"Olen, why don't we forget this morning ever happened," he said. "We didn't mean to break in. Honest. We won't come back until Miss Patty's here. And we'll only look with her permission."

Pennegar didn't respond but when the frisking was finished, I could see him relax. He holstered his gun.

"Olen," Brad said, "There's been no harm done. Nothing's been stolen. Nothing's missing."

"It's still a crime."

"A misdemeanor," Brad deflected. "How about if we bring Judge Buchan into this? If you arrested us, we'd be entitled to a hearing. Better to find out beforehand if it'll hold up."

As Pennegar wavered, Brad pressed his edge. "He's going to need to know what happened anyway."

"Might be right," Pennegar conceded. "It's his day off but I'll get him down here. You all sit around that desk and keep your hands where I can see them."

I breathed a sigh of relief. Magistrate J. Rutledge Buchan was a good ol' boy who had collected every penny he could from us when we faced him over the speeding violation. But he seemed like someone who could be reasoned with and, better yet, he was unlikely to send Everett Hall's son to jail or charge him with a felony.

Pennegar dialed Buchan's number and turned away. Bullock used the opportunity to take his hands off the table and scratch his nose.

"Huntin'," Pennegar said when he hung up. "Be back directly."

"What's directly?" I wondered.

"'Fore too long," Pennegar said. "Lunchtime at the latest."

I breathed another sigh of relief. It was clear that this day of reporting was going nowhere. The best we could hope to accomplish was to get out of town without being charged with a crime—and to do it in time to beat it back to the newsroom for the night shift. To do that we would need to get this cleared up and be on the road by 12:30 p.m. I hoped Buchan bagged his quota early.

When Bullock asked if we could take our hands off the table, Pennegar said yes. "Stay seated, though. No looking through documents and no trying to get out of here. I'm going to make coffee. You boys want any?"

Bullock and I said yes and a few minutes later Pennegar returned with three cups of coffee.

"Better than the newspaper's," Bullock said. "But then, that don't take much."

Pennegar laughed and took a sip. The conciliatory approach taken by Brad was working. "Let me ask you something, Mr. Hall. You're a nice person. You come from a big rich family. Why are you out to make trouble?"

Brad was taken aback. "Why do you think we're out to make trouble?"

"Well, you *have* been making trouble."

"I don't see how."

"That article in the *Reporter*, to start. Dragging up stuff that don't matter no more. Bringin' them down here, too." He nodded at Bullock and me. "The judge says you're stirrin' up all the blacks."

"All we're trying to do is find out who killed Wallace Sampson," I said. "We're doing the same thing you do. Trying to solve a crime. It's just like police work."

Pennegar looked me in the eye. "I don't go around making sick old men cry."

I winced, embarrassed at the memory of my impudence. "I'm sorry. We just wanted to talk to him. Still do."

"No chance," Pennegar said. "How would you like it if some reporter wanted to write something about your daddy and he didn't want it? Imagine what you would feel like then?"

For the next two hours Bullock leafed through a stack of magazines, trying to find something of interest in *City Manager Monthly* and *Public Works Today*. Brad poked around in his knapsack and compared plant samples to pictures in the pages of *South Carolina Wildflowers*. Pennegar sipped coffee and did paperwork. I counted the tiles in the ceiling while my stomach tightened in a knot. At 11:30 a.m. I suggested that we call the magistrate's house again.

"No point," Pennegar said. "He'll get here when he gets here."

"Officer Pennegar," I said, "Mr. Bullock and I need to be back in Charlotte by 4:00 p.m. We're hoping to get this thing resolved in time to make it back by then."

Pennegar snorted. "You'd best be thinking more about bein' in jail at four o'clock than thinking about bein' at work." He stepped into the bathroom but kept the door open so he could watch the front entrance in case we tried to escape.

"We got to get out of here and get back home," I whispered to Bullock.

"What we do on our own time is our business," Bullock said.

"Yeah, but our ass is grass if we don't show up for work."

"We'll just call Walker and let him know."

By noon, I almost couldn't take it any longer. With no protest from

Pennegar, I left the table and started to pace. I glanced out the window every eight seconds. Even if Buchan showed up now, explaining to him what had happened and hearing Pennegar's side of the story was going to take more than half an hour. There was no way we were going to get back to Charlotte in time for the start of the night shift.

"We need to call Walker," I finally said. "Don't see any way around it."

"Still got a half hour," Bullock said.

"Not enough time," I said. "Officer Pennegar, whether or not we are technically under arrest, I believe we're entitled to make a phone call."

Pennegar looked up from his paperwork. "Go right ahead," he said. Then, thinking about it, he added, "Keep it to three minutes. You can reimburse Patty later."

I dialed the newspaper.

"*Charlotte Times*. Can you hold please?"

"No, I—" But the operator hadn't waited for my answer and I was greeted by a generically sweet voice which explained that the *Charlotte Times* cared deeply about my call. But apparently not enough to actually hire people to answer it, I thought angrily. I twisted the phone cord as I paced, alternately looking out the window in hopes that Buchan might appear and checking back in with the on-hold message which was now telling me to call a different number if I wanted to complain about a delivery problem and yet a different number if I wanted to buy a classified ad.

"Just pick up the damn phone," I swore. But no one did. Not after one minute. Not after two minutes. And not after three.

"Idiots!" I exploded.

Pennegar snickered. Four minutes on hold. Five minutes on hold. My blood pressure was clicking up another notch with each second.

"You're gonna have to wrap it up," Pennegar said.

"Relax, I said we'd pay for it," I hissed.

Finally, "*Charlotte Times*, thank you for holding."

Thank God, I thought. "Newsroom please." I heard the click as the call was transferred. "Circulation."

"Sorry. I was trying to reach Walker Burns in the newsroom."

"This is circulation."

"This is Matt Harper. The switchboard switched me to you but I'm trying to get Walker Burns in the newsroom."

"Just a moment. I'll transfer you." The phone clicked and I heard a dial tone.

I slammed the phone to the cradle. "Damn it!" I picked up to dial again.

"One call's all you get," Pennegar said.

"I didn't get anyone," I protested. "I need to tell my boss we're going to be late."

"You should have thought about that before you broke in."

I put the phone down and returned to the desk with Bullock and Brad.

"Well, we tried," Bullock said. "It ain't our fault if they don't answer."

I looked at the clock. It was now after 1:00 p.m. "We're screwed, " I said, as resignation replaced anxiety and adrenalin gave way to fatigue. Too much tension and too little sleep had drained me. I headed toward the coffee pot.

"Don't," Brad whispered. I sat down.

Pennegar, too, was beginning to nod off. His eyes closed briefly then he suddenly jerked forward in his chair and looked around, as if he didn't know how long he'd been asleep.

He stood unsteadily, drew his pistol and waved it at a large closet. "Y'all get in there."

Before I could say anything Brad poked me in the ribs and whispered, "Go ahead."

We piled into the closet. Pennegar shut the door. I heard the bar latch click. It was pitch dark in the closet until an overhead bulb snapped on.

"What's this all about?" Bullock yelled. "You can't lock us up like this!"

"Just need to rest my eyes," Pennegar slurred. "Need to keep you from goin' anywhere until the judge gets here."

Brad put his finger over his lips, telling us to hush.

We heard Pennegar sit. A moment later we heard a thud that could only be one thing: the officer hitting the floor.

"Well," Brad said. "I guess that did the trick. Now let's get out of here."

Bullock and I looked at him like he was crazy.

"Lady slipper," Brad explained with a smile. "The flower's a natural sedative. Puts you right to sleep. I collected some this morning. Dropped it in the coffee pot while he went to the bathroom."

Bullock and I looked at each other.

"Don't worry," Brad said. "He'll be fine. But for the next two hours, he's going nowhere except dreamland."

Bullock crashed into the door with his shoulder. It wouldn't open, held by the latch on the outside of the door. He tried it again but the closet wasn't big enough for him to get any speed.

Bullock hitched up his pants leg and drew the derringer. "We got one shot," he said. "It has to be a good one." He examined the door to determine the precise location of the latch. He raised the derringer and pressed it against the wood. I closed my eyes and put my hands over my ears but there was no need. The bang when Bullock shot through the latch was barely louder than a cap pistol. Bullock turned the knob and we stepped out of the closet and over the form of Olen Pennegar Jr., who snored away on the floor.

Bullock put the derringer back in the holster. "And you thought this wouldn't come in handy."

"C'mon, Ronnie," I said. "Let's get out of here."

"Hold on," he said. He took out his wallet and left a twenty dollar bill on Patty Paysinger's desk. "That ought to cover the lock and the door repair."

"Don't forget the phone call," I reminded him.

He took out another twenty and left it on the desk.

"Let's go," he said. "I'm driving."

Walker Burns was in the 3:00 p.m. news meeting when I called.

So I left a message with the receptionist that Bullock and I had been unexpectedly detained by authorities in South Carolina but would be in the newsroom by seven o' clock. I could have said six-thirty but we were already so late there was no reason for Bullock to race.

"Did you tell them that we'd been arrested?" Bullock asked when I returned to the Dodge.

"I don't think we ever were. Detained is the right word."

"What do you think Pennegar's gonna do when he wakes up?"

"I'm thinking he says nothing. It ain't gonna look too good if he says he caught three criminals but they got away when he fell asleep."

"He's going to have to explain the lock."

"He just has to face Miss Patty. We got Walker."

Journalists are gossips. We get paid to find out information that people want to know and we delight in telling them. The more shocking the information, the greater the delight. I guess I shouldn't have been surprised that the newsroom receptionist was driven by the same instincts. By the time Bullock and I walked into the newsroom, everyone knew something had happened between Bullock, me, and the authorities in South Carolina, and they were waiting.

"You guys okay?" I heard someone ask as we headed for Walker's desk.

"Free at last!" someone else called and Bullock raised a clenched first. A smattering of applause broke out among some of the reporters in Metro. All they knew is that we had clashed with authority and authority hadn't won. I gave a little wave. The respect felt good.

Wow, I thought. Even the publisher has shown up to herald our return. Tall, tanned, and tailored, Warren Reich stood talking with Walker at the Metro Desk, with his arms folded protectively against his chest, his massive gold cufflinks on display. As we got closer, I could tell that neither was happy.

"What's that asshole doing here?" Bullock whispered.

"I think we're about to find out."

"Howdy, men," Walker greeted us. "Had a little dust-up, did we? Everybody okay? Anybody hurt or facing a felony?" He smiled weakly.

There was no smile from Reich, who made a point of looking at his watch. "Fine. Just a little misunderstanding. It's worked out." I harbored the hope that we could skate through this with just a reprimand, that maybe even Reich's presence was unrelated. "Sorry we're late."

"Carmela tells me you were back in South Carolina," Reich interrupted, his arms still crossed

"Yes, sir," Bullock answered.

Reich turned to Walker. "I thought we had agreed that we would stick closer to home."

"We were on our own time," I volunteered. "We intended to be back to start our shifts."

But Reich had stopped listening. His attention was distracted by an open bottom drawer on one of the metro desks. He reached in and extracted a shiny, almost-new, pair of black men's shoes. "Walker," he asked, "what's this?"

"Shoes, sir. Size ten, if I remember."

"I see they are shoes," Reich said. "What are they doing here?"

"They're staff shoes, sir."

"Staff shoes."

"Yes, sir. We purchased them for use by the staff whenever it might be necessary."

"You bought these shoes with company money?" he exploded. "Who in hell authorized this?"

"You did, sir. Do you remember when Les Becker won first place in the state press association contest and he wanted to go to the awards ceremony and you said he could but only if he wore a decent pair of shoes?"

"I did not want the *Charlotte Times* publicly embarrassed when he walked up on stage to accept the award in his sneakers," Reich said. "With no laces, no less."

"Right. Well, he bought the shoes and wore them to the awards ceremony and then turned in the cost of the shoes on his expense report."

Reich was livid. Livid doesn't mean angry, it means purple. Despite his deep tan, Reich was purple.

"He expensed the shoes," Walker explained. "Claims he was required to buy them by the company, that he wouldn't have bought them otherwise and therefore they were a company-mandated business expense."

"You approved the expense report?" Reich was incredulous.

"Yeah, but if the company paid for the shoes, then they are company shoes. So I made Becker turn them in. We keep them right here."

"In case he wins again," I joked.

Reich was steaming. "This is an abomination. Staff shoes. Reporters wandering around down in South Carolina wasting the company's money and doing things you don't even know about. Getting arrested! Walker, I told you I would not have the *Charlotte Times* embarrassed again. Your people are out of control!"

Ordinarily, the publisher's contact with the newsroom is confined to top editors like Walker. But the high-level pow-wow had caused reporters and copy editors alike to find work that called them to a spot where they could hear what was going on. Reich's outburst marked the first time many of them had been directly exposed to the business-side pressures that good editors fight against. I decided I needed to step in.

"No one got arrested," I said to Reich. "If you're going to get involved in journalism, you ought to learn to get your facts straight."

The crowd behind me murmured. I watched the shock on Reich's face. "Easy," I heard Bullock say. I didn't care. I was tired, cranky and pissed.

"Then what are the facts?" Reich challenged.

"The facts are that we were down in South Carolina doing investigative reporting. We were committing journalism and we were doing it on our own time because apparently the *Charlotte Times* is either no longer willing or able to pay for it."

I paused to see if Reich would take the bait and pronounce there in front of everyone that the newspaper was indeed committed to investigative journalism. He was silent so I summarized what had happened, leaving out the part about Bullock, the lock, and the derringer.

"You missed the first part of your shift," Reich said. It sounded weak and he knew it.

"You're right," I said with all the contempt I could manage. "Tell you what. How about if I just put in an extra three hours on the day that I retire?" Reich turned from an angry purple to an embarrassed red. Someone whooped.

"That's enough," Walker said sternly. "We'll have the rest of this discussion behind closed doors." He started to head off to the conference room, but Reich stopped him short.

"I will brook no more discussion about this," he yelled. "We are done spending this newspaper's resources making fools of ourselves on a story hundreds of miles away that will not sell us one more newspaper or one more ad."

"Making it easy for you to sell an ad is not why I got in the business."

"Selling ads pays your salary. Newspaper people like your father and grandfather understood that when they were in the business," he answered. "What happened to you?"

I thought of Dad stepping off the curb and marching in the streets for civil rights. I thought of him using the editorial page to oppose the Vietnam War. I thought of Glenn Hudson's editorial about Wallace Sampson and his son's smashed bike.

"Newspaper people like my dad also understand that one of the reasons to make a profit is so the newspaper can be used to fight injustice and to right wrongs."

"Enough," Reich barked at Walker. "I command you to end your ceaseless thrall with Wallace Sampson."

I thought of the town of Hirtsboro, of the lynching cross, of the faces of Mrs. Sampson, Reverend Grace, Mary Pell, Vanessa Brown, and Brad Hall. I recalled Delana's words: Someone killed Wallace Sampson and has gotten away with murder.

Walker was silent. I looked at Bullock. He wasn't about to intervene. I looked at my colleagues who stood hushed on the periphery too frozen to act, like they were watching a car wreck in progress. I was on my own.

"You can command our hours and you can command our assignments and you can command what goes in our paychecks," I said, shaking with rage. "You can even command if we get paychecks. But as long as it is on my time, I, not you, will decide when I end my involvement in what you refer to as our ceaseless thrall."

I slammed my fist on the metro desk with such force that the baseball cap flew from the urn containing the ashes of Colonel Sanders, his cigar went cart-wheeling across a stack of old newspapers, and the urn itself did a slow motion topple, spewing the fine dust of what had been the Colonel onto the desk.

My newsroom colleagues stood in stunned silence. Then someone in back began to clap. Someone joined. Soon sustained, dignified applause echoed from around the room. I felt my face redden.

Reich dusted Colonel Sanders from his sleeve. "I'll talk to you later," he said to Walker, before he escaped though the double doors of the newsroom.

Walker grabbed me by the elbow and hustled me in the same direction. "Let's go, pardner," he said. "I'm getting you out of here before you shoot the other foot."

"Sorry, Walker. The son of a bitch made me lose it."

"Yeah, but it was spectacular. I've seen a publisher told off before but seldom have I seen it done better."

Halfway through the door I heard the whine of an unfamiliar newsroom machine. I looked up to see assistant managing editor Bob DeCaprio vacuuming the ashes of Colonel Sanders from the desk and the keyboard, crossing himself and muttering as he did so.

I could not hear what he was saying but I knew it anyway: Thank God it wasn't Coca-Cola.

# Chapter Thirteen

I dreamed strange dreams, dreams that jumbled my past and present, dreams that joined the living and the dead—the publisher marrying Delana; my brother Luke dead on the ground outside De Sto; Dad and me breaking out of the Hirtsboro jail, triggering a ringing alarm bell. The dream ended but the ringing did not. It took me a while to emerge from my fog and realize I'd been asleep for more than fourteen hours. I answered the phone.

"Mr. Harper, this is David Riley. I'm a reporter for *The Daily Collegian* up at the university. I'd like to talk to you about a story I'm doing on your father and his illness."

My stomach flip-flopped. I hadn't begun to make peace with the idea of Dad having a fatal disease and the thought of it being in a story, of it being public, wasn't something I was ready to deal with. Nor was it something Dad should have to deal with.

"People get sick all the time," I said breezily. "What's the story?"

"Well, we understand that it doesn't look so good. We're told his illness is generally . . ."

"Fatal?"

"Yes."

"No one knows," I said hoping to destroy the premise of the story while being reasonably truthful. "Besides, life's fatal."

I figured this kid was just a student and I'd be able to blow him off, but David Riley didn't buy it. Today's Live Toad wouldn't go down easily. "I was hoping you could give me some quotes. And I'd like background on his newspaper days."

"David, you're a good kid and if there's ever a time for a story, I'll let you know. But right now, it's a private matter and we'd like to leave it like that."

"I'm sorry, sir, but it's a public matter," he said firmly. "Your father is a state university professor. He's on the public payroll. He's paid with public money. I'm sorry about his illness but the public has a right to know." Who *was* this arrogant little jerk? I didn't need to be in a story debate at the moment, especially one concerning my own father. I tried to be patient and reasonable.

"A right to know what? How's the public adversely affected?"

"Well, he won't be able to teach next semester. He announced that he's taking a leave." I didn't let on that my father taking a leave of absence was news to me. Dad hadn't mentioned it.

"David, when you've moved beyond the student paper, we'll sit down over a few beers and talk about news judgment. It's a complex thing with many factors involved, not the least of which is timing. On this one, you need to trust me to tell you when the timing is right to do a story about my dad, if it ever is."

David Riley answered, "With all due respect, sir, we at *The Daily Collegian* must be the ones who decide when something is news for our newspaper, not the people we are writing about."

Words I had used myself. Words I had heard growing up. Words from my father, now being used against him.

The best I could do was buy some time. I told David Riley I'd think about his requests for quotes and background from the newspaper days and get back to him.

He said, "Mr. Harper, I'm sorry, it can't wait any longer. I need to write the story."

IT RAINED the day we buried Luke. On the way from the church to the graveyard, I watched from the back seat of the limousine as the drops hit the window and merged into streams that raced like drunken worms to the bottom.

Mom sat beside me and held me, her eyes shut tight and something missing—the enveloping comfort of her perfume. Dad sat at the other window and stared at the back of the driver's head. The stiff collar of my white shirt scratched my neck. We were dressed in the clothes we had worn for the family portrait at Christmas, including Luke in his coffin in the hearse ahead.

It had been just three days since Dad came home and found Luke dead in the garden, a lanky thirteen-year-old sprawled face-up among the red mud and broccoli like a scarecrow blown over by the wind. The rusty pistol Dad kept in the shed for killing gophers was in Luke's hand and a bullet was in his head.

Since then, life had been a whirlwind of relatives, food and attention. What happened at the Harpers' was the talk of the town. At times, it was even exciting and I would want to tell Luke and then I would remember what had happened and only then would I begin to get a hint of the loss I would come to feel so deeply in the months and years ahead.

The question of what happened had been answered quickly for Mom and Dad. Luke had gone into the garden to shoot gophers, my father guessed, just as Luke had seen him do. The gun was old, rusty, and had misfired. Thinking the gun broken, Luke had gotten careless and accidentally shot himself. "This terrible accident," the minister had called it at the funeral. "This tragic mistake." But I had heard the talk among my relatives. Apparently there were questions. Not everyone was so sure.

At the graveside my mother's knees buckled when the dirt hit Luke's coffin. My father held her up and did something I had never seen him do. He wept.

When we got back in the limousine for the ride home, there was a tap at my father's window. I recognized one of the reporters from the newspaper. Dad rolled down the window.

"Mr. Harper, I'm sorry, but it can't wait any longer. I need to write the story."

MY ATTENTION SHIFTED from the memory to David Riley.

"What do you mean, 'Can't wait any longer?'" I challenged.

The delay was uncomfortably long. Finally Riley said, "Have you seen your father recently? I'm afraid we're running out of time."

I knew the story that Riley wanted to write. It was a good story, one I could see being assigned by Walker Burns. Famous professor won't teach next semester as he battles a vicious disease that is almost always fatal. Friends, relatives and colleagues recall the great man's days in a living tribute. It was an early obituary.

But my father is a private man, a man uncomfortable being the focus of attention, especially if it involves emotion. So even though he had spoken about the prospect of his own death with a maddening journalistic detachment the last time I'd seen him, a decision about whether to make public the news of his condition needed to be his decision, not mine.

"I need to talk with my father. I'll call you back," I said.

"Harper here," Dad answered when I reached him, as if he were still at his editor's desk. His voice sounded high and thin.

"It's me, Dad. I'm planning to be up your way today. I thought I'd check in."

"It's a chemo day," he rasped. "And radiation. I'll be at the hospital."

"Everything okay?"

"Considering the circumstances."

"Can I see you there?"

"Suit yourself."

There is no security in hospitals. I've found that if I wear a coat and tie and act like I know where I'm going, I can go anywhere I want. Once, in search of an interview with a wounded survivor of a motorcycle gang shootout, I walked right past police guards and into a surgery preparation room where the victim surprised everyone by pulling a gun from beneath the sheets, just to make sure I understood that comment would not be forthcoming.

Security in the Oncology Department at the University Hospital was no different. In my rep tie, blue shirt, blue blazer, shined loafers, and khaki pants, I looked like a doctor as I breezed past the receptionist, past a private security guard, down the tan tile corridor and into the room marked "Outpatient Chemotherapy."

I saw a pair of immaculately shined loafers before I saw his face and I knew that it was Dad, tilted back in a lounge chair, a cane propped against the arm. An IV tube ran from a bag on a stand, through the collar of his shirt and into the port implanted in his chest. His sport jacket hung on the stand next to the bag. His eyes were closed, his head tilted toward me. Drool ran from his mouth. In the artificial blue-tinged fluorescent light, he looked dead.

But he was only dozing. His eyes fluttered awake and he tried to get up before he remembered he was hooked up to the IV. He fell back on the recliner, looking small, shrunken, and weak. And then his eyes found me. "Hey," I said gently. I was shocked at how much he had deteriorated.

He reached out his left hand and I squeezed it. "Hey," he smiled.

My shock must have shown. "Don't worry," he croaked.

"I'm not," I lied. "How are you feeling?"

He nodded to the IV bag. "Stuff really zaps me. Must have dozed off."

"Good. It's supposed to zap you. It's doing its thing."

"I suppose. After this, I go to radiation. That's no sweat. Five minutes and no side effects. They gave me a tattoo. Want to see?" He struggled to unbuckle his trousers. Looking around to make sure no one was looking he modestly pushed down his gray slacks so I could see the blue bulls-eye on his side, just below his waist.

"What's that for?"

"It's so they can aim the radiation beam," he said, rearranging himself. "It's spread to my hip."

Maybe I shouldn't bring this up at all, I thought. Maybe there will be a better time to tell him about the Riley story, a time when the chemo hasn't make Dad so weak. But I knew there would probably be no such time. Dad was getting worse, not better. I heard the voice of Walker Burns tell me to "Stick your hand into the wound" and I decided to listen to it.

"Dad, do you remember David Riley? Used to be one of your students?"

"Bright kid."

"He wants to do a story about you. For the campus paper."

"Really? What's the peg?"

"This," I said, motioning around the room. "Your disease."

"No." He was quick and firm and it caught me a bit off guard.

"How come?"

"Well, in the first place, what would the lede be? What's the key paragraph?" Dad pulled the recliner upright and his eyes blazed. Nothing like an argument to bring out the life in him.

"Apparently you're taking a leave of absence next semester. Unplanned. Because of the multiple myeloma. He thinks it's a story. Called me for quotes, background on your career, that sort of thing."

"The leave is no big deal." He waved his hand as if shooing away a pesky fly. "The thing with the hip makes it tough to get to class, is all. But as soon as we get that cleared up, I'll be ready to go. Might not even miss the whole semester."

The effort had exhausted him. He lay back in the recliner, shut his eyes and turned his head away. I surveyed the rest of the room's IV population—a healthy looking woman my age, her head wrapped in a brightly colored turban, who read *Vanity Fair* as chemo dripped into her arm; a child of no more than five who looked at me with silver-dollar eyes as she sucked her thumb and clutched her teddy bear; four men in flannel shirts who played hearts; and several barely living, jaundiced hairless skeletons of indeterminate age, people who I reckoned to be only days from death, hooked up to the drip.

I've read about the stages people go through when they're facing their own imminent demise, from denial to acceptance. Dad must be going through them in reverse. Starting out, facing death had been no problem. It was something of academic interest. Now, it was something he didn't want to consider. I should have been happy he was still in the fight. Instead, I was angry. I'd already dealt with the idea of him dying and he needed to, too. I moved around to the other side of the recliner so I could look him in the eye.

"Dad, all he wants to do is write a story about you and the illness. About the leave. It's nothing that isn't true."

"He's going to make it sound like I'm dying. You'd think I was about to die."

I reached out and took his hand. "Dad, do you remember when we left the graveyard? When the reporter asked you about writing the story about Luke? Do you remember what you said? You said, 'Go ahead and write it.' And you told Mom, 'Writing stories is what we do.' You said, 'The truth may be painful but it's never wrong.'"

"There's a difference." He strained to pull himself up to a sitting position. "The truth is that I'm not going to die. The truth is, I'm getting better. The truth is," he said loudly, "THERE IS NO STORY. I AM GOING TO BEAT THIS THING."

Around the room, a few patients began to applaud. Dad slumped back into the chair.

"No story," he begged. "Please. I need your help."

I suppose bravery is easy when you think the worst is never really going to happen. All around us was the evidence that the worst sometimes does. I could feel the fear and I knew that Dad felt it, too.

I sat down on the edge of the chair and held Dad's hand.

"Whatever you need, Dad."

When the bag was nearly empty, Dad surprised me again. "So, where are you with that story you're working on?"

"The publisher shut us down. I believe the phrase was, 'End your ceaseless thrall.'"

I told him about our clandestine trips to Hirtsboro, about our emerging theory that the shooting of Wallace Sampson was linked to De Sto's firebombing which itself stemmed from the prostitution ring run out of the back of the building. He shook his head in amazement when I told him about our "arrest" at the hands of Olen Pennegar Jr. and about our escape, thanks to the botanical knowledge of Brad Hall and Bullock's derringer. He relished the details of the very public confrontation with the publisher in the middle of the newsroom, chuckling out loud at the staff shoes. I was enjoying telling the tale and watching his reaction so much that I forgot that I was telling a tale about a low point in my professional life to a dying man.

"I'm amazed I still have a job. But so far, there's been no fallout."

"You owe that to the fact the fight was public. No way he can fire you for a good journalistic discussion in front of the staff. He'd look like a small-minded bureaucrat. But that doesn't mean you're out of the woods. They'll figure out some way to make life tough for you. You've burned the bridge."

"I shouldn't have done it. I was tired, stressed out. But sometimes you feel like you just have to make a stand."

My father propped himself up on his elbows. "Do you believe in the story? Is it important?"

"Yes. It is to Mrs. Sampson. And to a lot of people in Hirtsboro. And it ought to be to people in Charlotte. There's a wrong to be righted. What does it matter where it is?"

"Do you believe you can get it?"

"If we keep at it."

"Then do it and screw the consequences. You did the right thing."

And then Dad said something that wasn't "I love you" but it was close. He took my hand and looked me in the eye and said, "I'm proud of you, son."

My eyes welled up and I looked away.

"So what do I do now?"

"Get back down there. Get the story done."

"But how?" I was going down a largely untraveled path—asking my father for help. "I assume—"

"Assume something and it makes an ass out of you and me. You said the publisher has an obsession with obits, right? When he saw your bylines in the paper on obits he believed you were writing daily stories, not working on some project. Do you have to be in Charlotte to write a Charlotte obit?"

"No. It's phone work. The dead don't interview well."

"Exactly. This is what you do."

I took out my notebook in case I needed to make notes of Dad's advice, the first I'd ever gotten beyond the best way to mow the lawn. Driving back and forth took too much time, so we needed to set up shop in Hirtsboro. We could report on the Sampson story during the day. Then, when the night shift started, we could make calls on obits and write them from there.

"The next morning, the publisher picks up the paper, you and Bullock are all over the obits, and the publisher's happy."

"It works if Walker buys into it."

"Try him. He's a good editor. I'm betting he wants this story just as much as you. One more thing. On your key interviews, put that thing away."

"What thing?"

"The notebook. It intimidates people. They see that 'Reporter's Notebook' on the cover and they start thinking about how they're going to be quoted. They clam up. Put the thing away and just remember what they say. You can always confirm the quotes later."

He fell back on the recliner out of breath. The bag was empty. Dad unhooked the IV and looked at his watch. "Let's get out of here. I'm due in radiation and then my teaching assistant is coming to get me. Get that wheelchair and push me. It's just down the hall."

I grabbed an empty wheelchair and helped him into it. He felt like a bag of sticks. Then I rolled him slowly down the hallway to a room marked "Radiation Therapy" and turned him over to a nurse.

"Thank you, son."

"Sure thing, Dad. Thanks for the help with the story." I bent down and hugged him. "Take care."

Before I left the hospital I called David Riley. He wasn't in so I left a message. "Any story you propose to write would be wrong. I've just been visiting with my father and he's fine. He's going to be okay."

# Chapter Fourteen

Ilived the next four days as a condemned man. My outburst against the publisher—in full view of the staff—would demand the death penalty, I was sure. But the date of execution was uncertain because Walker, mysteriously, was absent from the newsroom and I knew he would be the one to pull the trigger.

So I dragged myself into my cubicle each day with a fear of losing my job that was only equaled by my loathing for it. Without journalism, I'd have a hard time defining myself. But if journalism had gotten to the point where a good-size daily newspaper wouldn't pursue a Wallace Sampson story, I wanted no part of it.

My colleagues played both sides of the street. Supportive in private, they avoided me in the newsroom. No one wanted to get to close to a man whose days were numbered. But Walker's assistants took pity on me and I picked up a couple of good assignments, including one about a postal worker who simply decided, without telling anyone, to stop delivering to one neighborhood because it was infested with fleas. The editors knew my favorite kind of story was one about Official Stupidity. The flea story was akin to a gourmet last meal provided to the prisoner on Death Row.

Walker returned on Friday. Several times he appeared headed toward my cubicle and I braced for the inevitable. But each time he was on his way to somewhere else. I felt like a man strapped to the electric chair waiting for the switch to be pulled, then realizing the power wasn't on and that I was still alive.

I was still skittish at the end of the night when Walker Burns stood up at his desk and announced, "I'm thirsty."

The newsroom of today was a long way from the newsrooms of old when reporters like Ronnie Bullock kept gin bottles in their bottom drawers and nearly everyone could recall a great story they'd written while hung over. But Friday nights, when the last of the weekend copy had been edited and the final high school football scores were in, many staffers still made a habit of finishing up their shifts and heading across the street to The Depot to drink, rehash the news, and do what they did best—tell stories.

The signal that it was time to head to The Depot always came with Walker's announcement that he was thirsty and by the time he'd reached my cubicle, he was being trailed like the Pied Piper.

"C'mon, Big Shooter," he said as he passed. "We need to talk."

"At The Depot?" I couldn't believe the execution was going to be in public.

"I've got a powerful thirst."

In the era of passenger trains, The Depot had been just that. But now just two freight trains a day traveled on the tracks through our side of town, plus an occasional special trip by locomotives hauling boxcars of newsprint to the *Times* warehouse. The Depot had been converted into a restaurant and bar, with a turn-of-the-century railroad theme inside and clusters of tables on the platform outside, covered by the huge overhanging roof.

It was near midnight but The Depot was crowded with more than three dozen patrons. A quick head count revealed more than half of them were *Charlotte Times* staffers, a few of them dayside reporters who had gotten off earlier, started drinking and were still at it by the time the night shift rolled in. Country songs played on the jukebox and the place smelled of sawdust and beer. Walker had seated himself at a corner table, back to the wall. The two Lone Star longnecks had already been delivered and one of them was almost empty. He waved me over.

"Get yourself a Texas tea and come sit down," he shouted above the din.

I did as he said, sipped my beer, and waited for the axe to fall. Walker picked at the label of his Lone Star and said nothing. Finally, I couldn't stand the tension.

"You wanted to talk to me about the other day. I already know I blew it."

"I wanted to tell you that I'm proud of you. You took a stand. It had to be done."

I was stunned. "You mean I'm not going to get fired?"

"Not over this, pardner. Now, long-term, I ain't holdin' all the cards. I am saying it ain't gonna happen as long as I'm the dealer."

"And you've talked with Reich about this?"

Walker drained his first Lone Star and swallowed a belch. "Yup."

"Good God, what did you tell him?"

"Same thing I always tell him. Reporters are crazy. The truth is always the best defense. It's good you nailed him in public. There's no way he could retaliate without looking like the jerk he is."

"That's what my father said. Problem is, we may have won the battle but lost the war. I don't get fired. But the Sampson story's a loss. You didn't change the publisher's mind about that, did you?"

"Didn't even try." He burped. "Would have been like tryin' to talk sense to an Oklahoma fan. Besides, if I convinced him it was a good story, he'd probably want the E.B. assigned to it."

Walker put down his second Lone Star and leaned toward me. "You know you're right about it being a war. And it's more than a war for the Wallace Sampson story. It's a war for people we write about and the people we write for. Reich calls 'em customers. I call 'em citizens. It's a war for journalism. And you know what? If we don't win, it's not worth being here. So as long as I'm the trail boss we're gonna keep ridin' that story no matter how wild it gets. Reich told me to 'end this ceaseless thrall' but he didn't say it to you. So I'm checking out. I'm hooking you up with another editor until you bring this thing in."

Reich's command had indeed been directed to Walker but I had no doubt he meant it for the whole newsroom.

"Isn't that stretching it? He meant the newspaper should end its ceaseless thrall."

"We are a business that depends on precise language. It's not my fault he's a cretin. I intend to follow his instructions precisely. My ceaseless thrall is over. But yours isn't. The only thing I haven't figured out is how to cover for you guys while you're doing it." He sat back in his seat and took a long pull on the Lone Star.

I told Walker about Dad's point about obits—that it didn't matter where you were when you wrote them. We could do them just as well from Hirtsboro, South Carolina as we could from the newsroom of the *Charlotte Times*, leaving the daytime hours free for pursuing the story of who killed Wallace Sampson.

"Your dad always was a sly bastard," Walker said when I had finished. "How is the old boy?"

"Lousy." I told him about the cancer but I talked a lot about the upbeat parts. New strides in treatment. A relatively good quality of life. As I repeated them, I began to feel stronger, better, like maybe we could lick this thing.

Walker has no tolerance for anything false, including self-deception. "Pardner, sounds like he's cooked. You know, this may not be the best time for you to be doing this investigation."

I thought of my dad and I thought about Delana. "Maybe. Maybe not. But I know one thing. I'm not waiting. This murder has gone unpunished for far too long."

Suddenly, my feet began to vibrate. The table began to move and the railroad memorabilia on the walls began to rattle. Soon the whole building was shaking as a slow freight train rumbled by on the tracks beside the passenger platform. Conversation stopped. It was a tradition at The Depot that when the train rolled through you chugged whatever drink you were holding and immediately ordered another. Walker finished his second beer, I finished my first and a waitress quickly appeared with replacements.

The Depot was becoming even more crowded as the stragglers from the copy desk and sports rolled in. Someone pushed some tables together and soon, Walker and I were surrounded by a half dozen loud conversations.

"So, what's this I hear about you being in Minneapolis?" one of the copy editors asked Walker. Walker just shook his head and smiled.

"What do you know?" a dayside reporter demanded of the copy editor.

"You remember Alex Tift? Guy who used to be on our national desk and went up to *The Star-Tribune*? He called yesterday. Said he saw Walker in the *Star-Tribune* building. Am I right, Walker?"

Walker said nothing.

"Said Walker was wearing the biggest thickest winter coat anyone had ever seen."

Even Walker laughed.

I left The Depot feeling almost buoyant. I still had my job. And miraculously, we were going to get to resume work on the Wallace Sampson story. I called Delana who was happy but not surprised.

But the unease that I felt when I learned Walker was in the job market was still with me two days later when Bullock and I loaded up the Dodge and headed for Hirtsboro.

"Do you think Walker's history?" I asked Bullock as he drove.

"One way or the other. He can't take the publisher and the publisher can't take him. So either he leaves or he'll be fired." Bullock lit a cigarette, noticed my grimace, grunted and cracked the window. "I've seen it a million times."

"What about us?"

"Hell, I'm the oldest rat in the barn. I'll outlast 'em all. Besides, they can't do anything to me they haven't already done."

"What about me?"

"I'd say if Walker goes, you're screwed."

Tasha and Maybelle sniffed the tires of the Dodge and greeted us with tails that wagged like wiper blades in a downpour when we parked in front of Windrow. A note on the door from Brad told us to make ourselves at home. It was 3:30 p.m., almost time to start the obituary shift. We dumped our clothes in our rooms and moved a phone, a couple of chairs, and a small table into the nook off the kitchen.

"There," Bullock said, emerging from underneath the table where he had been plugging in the phone and a fax machine. "Our office away from the office."

"Yeah, all we need is a publisher to walk through here twice a day and demoralize us."

At 4:00 p.m., Bullock called the news desk and got the obituary listings for the next day. Obituaries at the *Times* took three forms. The first were the simple six-line listings that merely provided name, profession, date of birth, date of death, hometown, survivors, and funeral arrangements. These were phoned in to the newspaper by the funeral homes each afternoon and were printed free, as a public service.

For a price, these obituaries could be lengthened to include as much information as the family was willing to pay for, told in whatever way the family saw fit. It was advertising, not news, and had nothing to do with the newsroom. But it was a popular way of honoring the departed and, for the newspaper, a very lucrative one, with no ads to be designed, no sales commission to be paid, and no writer to be employed.

The third kind of obituary, the kind that had become the publisher's obsession, was known as the headed obit because it carried a headline. These obituaries were real news stories, objectively reported by journalists like Bullock, me, and almost everyone else who's ever passed through the profession. Many newspapers ran three or four a week and confined them to the noteworthy. But at the *Charlotte Times*, obituaries were a beat unto themselves and then some. To keep the publisher off track, Bullock and I had committed to producing at least one headed obituary apiece every day we were in Hirtsboro.

Our starting place was the free listings provided by the funeral homes. From these scant facts came the clues about who might make an interesting headed obit. The most obvious clue was the name. Whether it was in the newsroom in Charlotte or in the Halls' breakfast nook in Hirtsboro, the technique was the same: scan the listings for the famous or simply well-known—not just the names of the deceased themselves but the names of the survivors. The death of a relative of the famous can be almost as newsworthy as the death of the famous person himself. Then look at professions. An interesting job can make good copy. So can a top position in a company people might recognize. Anyone who'd ever worked in the newsroom was guaranteed a nice write-up. Treat your departed colleagues kindly, was the rule, because when it is your turn . . .

Look at the age of the decedent and pay particular interest to the young and the very old. By publisher's decree, everyone in the circulation area who made it to one hundred was honored with a headed obit in the *Charlotte Times*. And the young. What can you say about a kid who died? A lot, it turns out. Look at the dates of death—for spouses who might have died together or for someone who might have gone out on their birthday.

I scanned the faxed listings and settled on the founder of an electrical supply firm whom I knew was a member of Warren Reich's country club.

"Jesus, Gene Roy died," Bullock said in amazement when he reached a listing for a retired lieutenant from the Charlotte police department vice squad. "I can write this off the top of my head."

There was only one phone so as Bullock made his calls to the police department and to the Roy family, I wandered around Brad and Lindsay's plantation home. The earthy smell of slow-cooking collards drew me to the kitchen. A collection of bright gourds filled a carved wooden bowl on an antique table in a bay-windowed alcove. From a certain angle—an angle that left out the stainless steel refrigerator built into an adjacent wall—the bowl and gourds looked like a still life by one of the old masters. Outside the window, the bare fields of the plantation stretched to the Savannah. Stripped of vegetation, the land showed more contour, more hills and ravines than when the crops were high. I listened to Bullock on the phone, a familiar newsroom event, and looked back out the window. The view was much better than the one from my cubicle.

Down the hall, I poked my head into Brad's study. A photograph of his Harvard fencing team hung above his desk, which was buried beneath plastic baggies of vegetable matter, photographs and drawings of plants, and pages of text that I imagined were for his book on Windrow's botanicals.

A few minutes later I found myself in the Halls' living room, studying the books they had on their shelves. I can tell a lot about people from the kinds of books they keep. Sometimes I will pull them down and open them to look for an inscription or to see if they've actually been read. I browsed the titles: *An American Dilemma* by Gunnar Myrdahl; *The Obedient Dog* by Benjamin Broad; the complete report of the 1967 Commission of U.S. Civil Disorders; *The Joy of Sex* by Alex Comfort; *The Orangeburg Massacre* by Jack Bass; and book after book about plants.

The front door opened and Lindsay Hall walked in. I jumped back as embarrassed as if I'd been caught peeking in her medicine chest or spying in her boudoir.

"Sorry. Didn't mean to frighten you." She reached behind her neck with one hand and removed the band that held her short pony-tail. She shook her blonde hair out to collar length. She wore jeans, a white blouse, an old blue blazer, and knee-high riding boots. Her outing had given her cheeks color and her casual dress helped soften the reserved, patrician image I had of her.

"You didn't. I mean you did," I stumbled. "Brad left us a note and said it was okay to come in."

"She knows," said Brad, piling through the door with his arms loaded with groceries. "I'm glad you made it back," he said as he headed into the kitchen.

I felt my stomach returning to its normal position. "I hope we're not imposing," I told Lindsay.

"Brad's an impulsive man," she sighed. "I've learned to live with it." She caught herself and brightened. "It will be good to have you here. It's always nice to have visitors. Not many people to talk to in Hirtsboro. Brad can take it for long stretches at a time. I can't. Not without company."

She walked into the kitchen and I followed. When she saw the nook, the office set-up and Bullock on the phone, she stopped short.

"How long do you expect to be here?" she asked.

I was the invited guest. I wasn't sure what to say. But Brad saved me. "Until we're done," he answered.

"What constitutes done?" Lindsay asked with a touch of impatience.

"Done is finding the killers of Wallace Sampson," Brad said.

At that moment, there was an explosion of profanity from the nook where Bullock was on the phone. "Cut the shit," he yelled. "I don't need that goddamned department crap about all comment's gotta come from the damn chief. I'm trying to do an obit, dammit, and I need some asshole to talk to!"

Lindsay sighed. "Brad, I wish I didn't have my doubts about the likelihood of your success. But I think we can all agree it will be best if that happens sooner rather than later."

"Sorry about that." I waved to get Bullock's attention in the nook so I could prevent any further outbursts.

Together, the Halls unloaded their groceries. Bullock and I stayed in the nook and went about our assignments. When he was done reporting, Bullock began the Gene Roy obituary, writing long-hand in his reporter's notebook. I took up the phone. First I called the library and asked Nancy Atkinson to check the clips to see if my electrical supply owner had ever made the news. I called the photo morgue to see if we had a mug shot. Employees at his company provided background and anecdotes. I remembered the publisher's country club connection. It was almost 6:00 p.m. but I had a brainstorm and I took a chance.

"Warren Reich, please," I said when his secretary answered. "Matt Harper calling."

Bullock looked up from his story wide-eyed. "What the hell are you doing?"

I put my hand over the receiver. "I'm reporting an obit. The publisher knew this guy. Besides, what better way for the publisher to learn how I'm spending my time?"

Bullock shrugged. The publisher came on and I told him why I was calling. I got the quotes I needed. We both played it straight, with no mention of the recent flare-up in the newsroom. At the end, he thanked me for calling.

"You see," I said. "The publisher's not such a bad guy after all."

Bullock snorted.

We broke for a dinner of cornbread and collard greens, wrote the obituaries, and phoned them in without trouble.

The next morning, Bullock dressed in his usual uniform, but today, it just felt wrong. I swallowed my instinct to say something. At breakfast at the Hungry Tummy, he wolfed down side orders of ham and sausage as well as a regular order of three eggs over with bacon. Our favorite blonde, heavy-hipped waitress looked on with respect.

I stuck to coffee and grits while I thought about the best way to approach Vanessa Brown. She'd haltingly answered our questions when Bradford Hall and I had interviewed her the first time. But I'd left feeling that she'd been scared, that she was holding back.

I thought about my father's advice to put away the notebook so the subject would feel at ease.

"Ronnie, we need to change course," I said as he mopped his plate with a piece of toast. "We need to talk to Vanessa but it can't be here and it can't be you."

He stopped in mid-wipe. "Why not?"

"Because this is where she works. Her boss is here. She's not going to be relaxed. If she has something to say, she's sure as hell not going to say it here."

"And what's the problem with me?"

"You haven't met her before. When I interviewed her the first time, it was with Brad. For another, you look like a cop The last thing we need is for her to be intimidated by some stranger in a quasi-uniform."

Bullock looked hurt. "Well, that's just fine. But what about you? You're the only guy in the whole town of Hirtsboro and probably all of South Carolina in a friggin' tie. What do you figure she thinks you are? The plantation owner?"

I looked at myself in a mirror that ran the length of the wall above the grill. Blue blazer with brass buttons. Blue Oxford shirt. Rep tie in the colors of my alma mater. If not the plantation owner then certainly the Princeton Club.

I took off my tie and unfastened my top button. "Let's drop back and punt until we figure out exactly what we need to do."

We ordered a second cup of coffee and then a third before we finally agreed on a plan. I'd talk to Vanessa Brown here at the Hungry Tummy but only to set up a time and a place when we all could talk later. When and where would be her choice but it would be someplace away from work.

Bullock paid the bill and went to the Dodge to wait, taking my tie and jacket with him. I sat at the picnic table for nearly an hour before she appeared, laughing as she spilled out of the door with the rest of the kitchen crew and dressed in the same Brown Family Reunion T-shirt and blue bandanna she'd been wearing when we first met. As the rest of the workers drifted a discreet distance away, Vanessa Brown approached me.

"Wanda said you was back."

"Who's Wanda?"

"The girl that waited on you."

"I wanted to talk with you a little more about Wallace." I traced my finger through a set of initials carved deeply into the picnic table.

She looked down and kicked a stone with her sneaker. "I done told you what I know." She looked up and exchanged glances with the knot of workers. Her brown eyes looked enormous through the lenses of her over-sized glasses.

"Not here. Somewhere else. You pick when and where."

"Why you were with the po-lice?"

"What?"

"The man you were with at breakfast. The one that ate all the pork."

"Ronnie? He's my partner. A reporter just like I am. He just dresses like the police."

Vanessa Brown shrugged.

"There are some questions I didn't ask. Please," I pleaded.

"Mac-Donald's," she mumbled, swallowing the last part of the word.

"Huh?"

"How about at Mac-Donalds? Mickey D's. By the interstate."

She glanced at the workers, who were starting to snuff out their ciga-

rettes in preparation for their return to work. "I'll have to get someone
to carry me out there," she said and after some discussion we agreed to
meet at 8:00 p.m. that night. "Just you," she said.

Bullock was understanding when I got back to the Dodge and told
him about the conditions of the meeting. He agreed there was no reason
to introduce a fresh face into the equation, someone new Vanessa Brown
would have to learn to trust. He did not agree with my initial assessment
that the timing of the meeting meant that he would have to handle both
of our obit assignments that day.

That afternoon, I took the path of least resistance when the day's
obituary listings from the funeral homes arrived by fax. I selected a former Charlotte City Council member who died at eighty-five. He was
long-retired and nearly forgotten but I guessed the clips would be full of
background. They were. The reporting went easily and I wrote quickly
that afternoon, despite being distracted at one point by Lindsay, who
strolled into the kitchen, her hair wet after showering, apparently dressed
only in an oversized men's shirt.

"Panties?" Bullock questioned when she had retreated to her bedroom.
He answered his own question. "It'll be easier to work if I think yes."

By 7:00 p.m., my obit was done. An almost-full moon rose over the
Georgia hills in the distance and pockets of fog filled in low spots in the
barren fields as the Dodge crunched down the sand and gravel road of
Window and out to the highway. I wasn't sure why Vanessa Brown had
agreed to see me. I reminded myself that almost one hundred years after
the Civil War, black people in Hirtsboro still weren't all that accustomed
to saying "no" to a white man.

I could see her as I drove up to the McDonald's, alone in a booth,
framed by a section of the plate glass window that wasn't covered by a
poster touting a value meal, and dressed as she had been that morning.
I was starving but I just ordered a soft drink. You can't eat and ask questions at the same time. I slid into the seat across from her just as a table
of white teenagers in backwards hats and cutoff shirtsleeves pushed out
of their booth and swaggered out. I looked around the restaurant. Except

for the boy behind the counter and a cook in back, Vanessa Brown and I were alone.

She pulled a small gun out of her purse and set it on the table between us. I took a sip of my drink and tried to pretend that placing a pistol next to the fries was normal behavior.

"Thanks for meeting me. I know you told me once but tell me again about what happened the night Wallace got shot. Take me through the whole evening, everything that happened."

She picked up a straw, removed the wrapper and began tying the straw into knots. "Like what?"

"Well, what time did he come over that night?"

"Maybe around nine o'clock."

"What did ya'all do?"

"Sat on the porch swing. Talked. Held hands."

"That all?"

"Kissed." She giggled, as if she were still a schoolgirl and tied another knot.

"You told me your mom made him leave at around midnight that night. You told me that you walked him part of the way home. Take me on that walk."

She dropped her straw and tucked her legs underneath her on the booth's bench so she could sit up taller. "Wallace," she called to the boy behind the counter, "bring me another suicide." The boy put a cup under the nozzle that dispensed soft drinks and pressed all the buttons. He brought the mixture to the table and I made a connection.

"Vanessa, are you married?"

"No."

"Kids?"

She smiled. "Two."

"How old?"

"Latetia is twelve." She nodded at the counter. "Wallace is sixteen."

"Named after Wallace Sampson?"

She shrugged. "It's a beautiful name so I gave it to him."

"What do you remember most about Wallace Sampson?"

"How smart he was. He was the smartest boy in the class. Too smart to stay in Hirtsboro."

"What'd you see in him?"

"He loved me. That's the thing. He loved me."

"You still miss him."

I expected tears and I got them, tears that splashed on the Formica counter and soaked the wrapper of the straw that Vanessa Brown had tied into knots. But I also got anger. "Why do you care so much about Wallace? No one cared when it happened."

I don't know what led me. I'd never made the connection before. But I reached into my pocket and pulled out my wallet. I took a picture from it that I have kept with me every day of my life since the day it happened—a school picture of Luke. I put it on the table.

"He was my brother. He died at thirteen from a bullet in the head. No one still knows what happened."

Vanessa Brown took the pistol from the table and returned it to her purse. She pulled out a photo—the class photo of Wallace Sampson, a wallet version of the one on Mrs. Sampson's wall, and placed it on the table right next to Luke's. She took my hands in hers and then she began to pray, "Our father, who art in heaven, hallowed be thy name . . ."

She kept hold of my hands after we had finished. She looked into my eyes. "I walked down our street, out to the corner by the church. He kissed me good-night. He told me he loved me. I stood there in the street and watched him walk toward home. He got to the front of De Sto. The lights were on so I could still see him. He turned back to look where I was standing and then he waved."

She took a deep breath and let it out with a sigh. "And then I heard a shot. And then I saw him fall. And then . . . and then I saw Billy Bascom running away from where it happened."

It took a moment for the words from the killing's only known eyewitness to sink in.

"You saw someone running away? Who is this Billy Bascom?"

"An old redneck. Hasn't been in Hirtsboro in years. Worked on cars back then."

"When you saw him that night, was he carrying a gun?"

"No."

"And no gun was ever found. Do you think he's the one who shot Wallace?"

"Don't know. Like I say, he wasn't carrying a gun."

"Vanessa, why didn't you tell anybody about this before?"

"Scared, I guess. Plus, nobody ever asked."

Over the next hour, as patrons came and went, I asked her every question I could think of. I was determined to leave no stone unturned. I got a few more details but the guts of the interview came down to the Billy Bascom revelation.

"Thank you," I told Vanessa Brown when I got up to leave.

"We've shared the same pain," she said and hugged me.

I told Wallace Brown behind the counter to take care of his mother and ordered six cheeseburgers and three orders of fries to go.

The sodium lights had come on in the parking lot and as I walked back to the car I thought what I was seeing was just an odd reflection. But as I got closer, and then when I rubbed the paint, I realized the truth: Someone had scratched "Nigger Lover" onto the hood of the Dodge.

Back at Windrow, the takeout food and the Billy Bascom revelation almost soothed Bullock's anger—that, and the news unearthed by Brad's continued digging at Town Hall: J. Rutledge Buchan, the Hirtsboro magistrate who'd presided over our speeding case, was the current owner of the building that housed De Sto.

# Chapter Fifteen

We embarked on a frenzy of reporting—the stories of the recently dead by night, the story of a long-dead thirteen-year-old by day.

Bullock suggested sending Bradford Hall to search for any official records that might help us find Billy Bascom, the man Vanessa Brown had spotted running away from the scene. "Ol' Brad's two for two," he pointed out. "He found the police report about the firebomb and he found out that Buchan owns the building that housed De Sto."

"And that housed de hookers," I agreed.

"And de hookers. I say we stick with him while he's hot."

"I do rather like it," Brad confessed.

"Property tax records might be able to tell you where he lived," Bullock said. "We can see if anyone remembers him there. And see if Miss Patty will let you check the death certificates, too. No point in looking for the guy if he's croaked."

Bullock and I decided to scour Hirtsboro—door to door, if that's what it took. "Hell, the whole town ain't that large," he said. "We could gather 'em all right there on Jefferson Davis Avenue and ask 'em all at once."

"That, or on Sunday, we could go church-to-church."

Our efforts were a study in contrasts. The obituaries were a snap, the facts easy to come by, the whereabouts of the subjects well known. We were getting good at them. And fast.

"I'm gonna do two tonight," Bullock announced one evening and he did. Of course, I had no choice but to follow suit. For days, we kept that killer pace.

The object of our dayside investigations was more difficult to pin down.

Each day, we'd park the Dodge at the railroad tracks and go about our rounds: the Farmers & Mechanics Insurance Agency, Classen's Clothes, and the Great Southern Auto Supply and Appliance Store where I figured we had one of our best shots. If Bascom had worked on cars for a living, I reasoned, maybe he had come in for parts. But to the people at each of those places and others, Billy Bascom was a stranger.

At *The Hirtsboro Reporter,* editor Glenn Hudson said he had never heard of Bascom and reminded us that the Sampson killing had happened well before his time. When I asked if we could look through *The Reporter's* clip files, he laughed.

"There's your library and photo morgue all rolled into one," he said, pointing to shelves of oversized volumes holding actual copies of past editions classified by year. "You're welcome to it."

I gave silent thanks for electronics and for librarian Nancy Atkinson. Even the old system of clips in envelopes was light years ahead of this. Reading each story in each copy of *The Hirtsboro Reporter* for the last twenty years in hopes that we might run across a reference to Billy Bascom was simply out of the question.

At Town Hall, Brad found an old property tax listing from a William J. Bascom at a rural route address. The address turned out to be an empty slash pine red clay country lot, its broken concrete trailer pad overgrown with weeds.

"No neighbors," Bullock observed as we drove away in the Dodge.

By the end of the week, I was getting frustrated. Our big new lead was leading nowhere. We had traces, but no hard truth. More than anything else, I wished we could consult with Walker.

"Maybe I should call him," I suggested during our dinner break as I stirred a bowl of noodles into a sizzling wok. Brad had joined Lindsay for a few days in New York and with both gone, the cooking had fallen to me. "What harm can one phone call do?"

"It'd cost him his damn job, that's what it'd do," Bullock said, pluck-ing a chunk of chopped chestnut from a bowl and popping it into his mouth. "Direct violation of a superior's order." He swallowed. "It's just the opportunity the publisher would be looking for. We've got to keep him clean."

"Well, if we did call him, what do you think he'd say?"

"He'd say, 'When you guys finish this story, would you mind sending a copy to the old folks home because that's where I'll be living by then.'"

We laughed but it got me thinking about something I'd heard Walker tell the projects staff: every day you have to make two lists—what you want to know and who you need to talk to. Every day you work both lists until one of them has nothing left on it. When either of the lists ends, that's when you know you're done. You have the story or you don't.

The list of what we wanted to know was plenty long—starting with who shot Wallace Sampson and why. The list of who we needed to talk to was getting shorter. We needed to take another run at Olen Pennegar but, given our prior experience, that task seemed best left for last. We needed to find Billy Bascom, for sure. But, at least for now, that effort had run into a dead end. And there was one new name on the list—Magistrate J. Rutledge Buchan.

"Ronnie, what do we know about the magistrate?" I asked.

"Brad says he's a decent guy. Shoots birds with his old man. Been here forever. Appointed to his job by the governor. His daddy was the magistrate before him."

I lifted the cover of the wok, releasing a steamy billow of soy and ginger. "What about him being the owner of the building?"

"We don't know if he owned it back then. Plus, if his family goes way back, he probably owns a good bit of property around town." He dipped a fork into the wok and extracted some noodles.

"I thought you didn't like this stuff."

"It's not bad as long as I get a big ol' burger for lunch every day at the Hungry Tummy. Anyway, Buchan is worth interviewing if only because he was the magistrate."

I removed the wok from the stove and dished out dinner.

SOMETIMES, two people is one too many to take on an interview, an un-necessary show of force. But neither Bullock nor I were willing to stay at Windrow where there was nothing but obits to work on and nothing but work to do. So the next day we piled into the Dodge and headed in search of Judge Buchan.

Patty Paysinger told us when we checked in at Town Hall, "He hasn't been here today and I don't expect to see him. You might try up at the house." And then, "Where you been, Ronnie? I told you not to be a stranger."

"I think she's got her eye on you, Ronnie," I said as we walked the few blocks toward the magistrate's two-story brick Victorian home.

He ignored me.

No one answered the door at Buchan's.

"Who knows where he is or when he'll be back. Let's just leave a note," Bullock suggested. "He knows what we're doing. It won't exactly catch him by surprise."

I took my notebook and scribbled a note for Judge Buchan to call us in connection with the Wallace Sampson killing.

"It dodges the point about whether he owned the building back then," Bullock observed. "Good."

We both signed it and I added Brad's name, hoping the associa-tion with the Hall family might help. Then I slipped the note into the magistrate's mail slot.

When we hadn't heard from him by the next morning, we drove in a pouring rain back into town and left a duplicate note with Patty Pay-singer. "I'll tell him you've been looking for him." She smiled at Bullock. "Thanks for coming by again."

"Thanks for coming by again," I sing-songed when we got out-side.

"Screw you," Bullock said, hunching down into his trench coat.

For good measure, we dropped another copy of the note in the U.S. Mail.

The rain slacked by dusk. By the time Bullock and I had finished our first obits of the evening and had eaten another veggie dinner, the sky had cleared. Bullock stepped out on the deck overlooking the swamp and lit a cigarette. I went out with him.

The night had turned crisp. Moisture rose from the land and the swamp, forming a low fog that hovered just above the fields, trapping the smell of cold, rich earth. Light lingered in the Georgia hills on the western horizon where a quarter moon was rising bright and clear.

Bullock extracted his miniature expandable telescope from his shirt pocket and squinted into it, scanning the sky. "Jesus, look at Venus." He handed the telescope to me just as the phone in the kitchen alcove rang. Bullock went in to answer it and returned a minute later, shaking his head,

"I'll be goddammed. That was the metro desk. The latest edition of *Saints & Sinners* is just out and guess what? Because of our extraordinary work on obituaries, we've been named *Saints & Sinners'* Co-Employees of the Week!" We exploded into laughter.

"What in hell do you imagine crazy Carmela was thinking?"

Bullock sniffed. "Probably just sucking up to the publisher. *S&S* said it was the kind of stories local should be doing more of. Sounds just like something Reich would say."

"I've never been Employee of the Week. Do we get some kind of prize?"

"In the great *Charlotte Times* tradition, we get the satisfaction of a job well done."

"Well, at the very least, this deserves a toast." I went inside and returned with the bourbon and tumblers that had become a fixture of what he called our B&B (bourbon and bullshit) sessions on the deck.

"To Ronnie and Matt," I said lifting my glass. "Never were they more valuable to the newspaper than when they were away."

We laughed. Bullock draped a white napkin over his left forearm and, doing his best imitation of a steward, poured us another stiff round. I looked at my watch. It was after 8:00 p.m. "What about the rest of the obits?"

"Just one obit tonight." He took a big swig, swallowed hard and wheezed. "We don't need to be ratcheting up expectations on any permanent basis. It'll just make life tougher for the next generation."

After another drink, Bullock hopped off the deck, walked to the Dodge and returned with his 30.06 and an infrared scope. "I've been looking for a good time to see how this baby works," he said, screwing on the scope and attaching his miniature tripod. He aimed at the swamp and peered through the eyepiece. "Damn," he said. "Check this out."

I squatted and looked through the red lens. A grainy raccoon sauntered unaware of our surveillance along the top of a fallen cypress in the swamp.

"No need to kill him," I said hopefully.

"Hadn't planned on it."

To the left of the swamp, a light—yellow and diffuse through the low-hanging fog—moved slowly across the horizon. I couldn't tell if it was traveling on the ground or through the sky.

Bullock spotted it, too. "UFO. Maybe swamp gas."

"Then it's swamp gas movin' at sixty miles an hour."

The light moved toward us and soon diverged into two beams, a car bouncing up the road toward Brad Hall's modern plantation home. A white Range Rover emerged from the mist and stopped in the driveway.

The headlights snapped off. Two doors of the Rover opened and slammed shut, one right after the other. Everett Hall and J. Rutledge Buchan crunched double time across the gravel driveway. They wore identical uniforms of camouflage pants tucked into boots and khaki field jackets cinched tight at the waist. Beyond their hunting clothes, I was amazed at how much alike they looked—tall, tan, mid-sixties, silver hair glinting in the moonlight. Hall wore glasses. Buchan carried his crop.

"What is the meaning of this?" Everett Hall bellowed, waving one of the notes we had left.

"Mr. Hall, I'd like you to meet Ronnie Bullock," I said, ignoring his question and his anger. "Mr. Bullock is my colleague at the *Charlotte Times*. Ronnie, this is Brad's father, Everett Hall."

Bullock stepped forward smartly and thrust out his hand. "Pleased to meet you, sir."

Hall ignored Bullock and glared at me. "I said what is the meaning of this?"

"The note was not intended for you, sir," I said evenly. "It was intended for Judge Buchan." I turned to Buchan. "Judge, I'm Matt Harper and this is Ronnie Bullock. We met several weeks ago."

Before I could finish, Everett Hall lunged forward, grabbed my tie, and pulled me close to his face. "You'll talk with me and you'll talk now, you little prick." I could smell liquor on his breath.

I jerked my tie out of his hand. "Keep your hands off me!"

"What in hell do you mean bringing Rut Buchan into this cockamamie investigation of some dead nigger kid?" Everett Hall snapped.

"Easy, Everett," Buchan said. "I'll handle this." Buchan turned to me. "We must do things a little different down here than they do up in Charlotte. If we have business with a man, around here, we go see him. We don't write him a note. Mr. Hall was a bit offended by you leaving notes for me all over town."

"A bit offended, hell!" Hall yelled. "I've never been so pissed off. Where the hell is my son?"

I felt the sting of a father's anger, as painful as if it had been from my own. I didn't need another fight with Everett Hall. "New York," I answered. "He told us we could stay."

"I'm sorry," I said to Buchan, particularly regretting the copy of the note we'd left with Patty Paysinger at Town Hall. "We looked all over for you. We've been on this story a long time. We were just trying to move things along."

Buchan relaxed. "We've been bird huntin' all day. We're tired. We got skunked so we were already upset, even before we got your note. And we're thirsty. Now go fetch two more glasses and let's sit down. I don't know what I can tell you about whatever it is ya'll are looking into but I'll try."

For the next hour, the four of us sat on the deck and talked. Mostly,

Bullock, Buchan, and I did the talking. Everett Hall got drunker.

"I know we own that building," Buchan acknowledged when I asked about the place that housed De Sto. "I don't know how long we've owned it. I think if you'll check, you'll find we own a lot of the property around town."

"Your family has been here a long time," Bullock offered.

"We have. But it's not so much that. You see, my daddy was the magistrate before me and his daddy was the magistrate before him. And my daddy got in the habit, maybe it was his granddaddy's, too, of buyin' up a piece of property if it went into auction after foreclosure. If he could rent it out, well, that was good business. But he also felt it was good for Hirtsboro. Kept property on the tax rolls. So we own a lot of little things here and there. None of it has ever amounted to much."

From where he slouched in his deck chair, Everett Hall jolted to life. "I'll tell you boys this. I've known Rut Buchan and his family . . . How many years is it, Rut? All my life. Done more for Hirtsboro than any man alive. And I mean for everybody. Especially the blacks." He pulled himself up and walked unsteadily over to where Bullock had left the 30.06. He hefted it, sighted through the scope, tested its balance. "Damn fine weapon. Whose is it?"

"Mine," said Bullock.

"You a sportsman?"

"All my life."

"You should go with us sometime." He stumbled back to his deck chair still holding the 30.06.

"You leased the building to Raeford Watson for De Sto," I said to Buchan.

"We did. Ol' 'Do What.' That's what we used to call him. No matter what you said, he'd always say, 'Do what?' He ran it until he got sick. Then it was more trouble than it was worth. Watson was the only one willing to go in there and sell those people groceries. He was doing them a favor. The thing is, they didn't always seem to appreciate that fact. There were cuttings, shootings, holdups. All that stuff that comes from being in that side of town. Wasn't hardly worth it."

"I understand someone threw a firebomb at the building one time," I said.

"Buncha hot heads. That's what I'm talking about. Probably all hopped up on dope."

"Judge, did you ever hear about any prostitution going on in the back of the building, the part behind the store?" Bullock asked.

"Never had a case like that."

It was an obvious dodge. I sensed it and Bullock did, too. "I'm not talking about a case," Bullock said, his tone just a touch tougher. "I'm talking about whether it was happening."

Buchan stiffened. "Mr. Bullock, I don't believe I appreciate your tone."

So, I thought, it's true.

"And I don't believe you've answered my question," Bullock pressed.

Everett Hall stood up and staggered from his chair, still holding the 30.06.

"I've about goddam heard enough," he said. He raised the gun to his shoulder, squinted through the scope, aimed at the swamp, and then swung the rifle so it pointed directly at me. My heart stuck in my throat. My eyes wouldn't leave the trigger.

"Put the gun down, Everett," Buchan said calmly.

"I've heard enough of this bullshit. You boys need to get gone," he said. The barrel of the gun traced small circles. I couldn't seem to avoid it.

From nowhere Bullock sprang like a panther, applying a headlock to Everett Hall with his left arm while grabbing the barrel of the rifle with his right hand. Bullock wrenched the rifle away and released Everett Hall from the headlock. Hall stumbled backwards into Buchan who grabbed him by the elbow and steered him toward the Land Rover. "C'mon, Everett," He said. "Time to go."

Hall shook him off and stepped in front of Bullock.

"What the hell are you doin' stickin up for the goddam niggers? You've been around long enough to know better. What kind of a Southern boy are you, anyway?"

"One who doesn't care about the color of murder victims."

"You're a goddam traitor to the South."

Drunk as he was, Everett Hall was a sitting duck for Ronnie Bullock's powerful right uppercut, which struck him squarely in the gut. Hall pitched forward, his glasses flying, and he melted to the ground like a snowman in a heat wave.

"Nobody calls me a traitor," Bullock said evenly.

We helped Buchan load Everett Hall into the backseat of the Range Rover.

"I think it would be good if you boys were gone in the morning," Buchan said stiffly.

In my mind I heard Walker say, "Stick your hand into the wound."

"Judge, there are people in this town who believe Wallace Sampson was killed in retaliation for the firebombing or maybe because someone thought he was the one who had tried it the first time and was coming back to try it again."

He looked me dead in the eye. "There are people in this town who believe in voodoo. When one of them gets shot, ninety-nine percent of the time, it's by their own kind."

"Judge, we're trying to find Billy Bascom—used to live in Hirtsboro."

"Can't help you," he said. He started the engine and nodded at Everett Hall lying in the backseat. "I need to get this ol' boy to bed. Mr. Bullock, I want you to know I'll do everything I can to keep him from pressing charges. Like I said, I think it would be good if you boys were gone in the morning."

"Nobody calls me a traitor," Bullock repeated as we watched the red taillights of the Range Rover snake through the fog.

With Brad Hall in New York, Bullock and I decided there was no practical way to appeal our eviction. The next morning we loaded up our Dodge and went in search of the nearest, cheapest motel.

"This is coming out of our own pocket," Bullock pointed out. "I suggest we share a room."

"The good news is, we're running out of stuff we can do down here."

"Right. With any luck, we'll only need to stay a few more days."

"With any luck, we would have been done already."

"We won the Employee of the Month Award. Our luck's starting to change." And maybe it was. In our search for a place to stay, Bullock and I stopped for gas at Ray's Amoco on the outskirts of town.

"Ray here?" I asked a gangly teenage boy who rolled a tire from the station's double-bay garage.

"Ain't no Ray here," he grunted, hoisting the tire into the back of a pickup. "Owner's Larry."

"Larry here?"

"In there," he said, motioning to a pair of legs in overalls that stretched from beneath a blue 1965 Impala SuperSport in one of the garage bays. While Bullock pumped, I walked into the garage's atmosphere of oil, hot rubber, and exhaust. A light cord stretched from the ceiling into the open hood of the Impala. A Snap-On toolbox lay open on the floor nearby. I heard the chug of a compressor out back. The legs in the coveralls, attached to a torso that was lying on a creeper, whipped around like those of an overturned insect trying to right itself.

"Yo. I was wondering if I could talk to you for a minute. I'm trying to find a guy who used to live around here, maybe twenty years ago. He worked on cars. Maybe you know him. How long have you owned this place?"

"Longer than that." I waited for him to push himself out from under the Impala but the creeper didn't move.

"Ever know a guy named Billy Bascom?"

The creeper shot out from underneath the Impala and an old man appeared. He deposited a wrench in the toolbox, brushed a strand of sweaty hair from his forehead, and looked up at me from the crawler. "Possum?" he asked.

"Maybe. I didn't know he was called that."

"Who's looking for him?"

"Matt Harper. I'm a reporter with the *Charlotte Times*." I stuck out my hand. Larry stood up, looked at his grease-covered hands and shrugged. We shook and I nodded in the direction of Bullock at the pumps. "We're working on a newspaper story and someone told us Mr. Bascom might be able to help us with it."

"The story must be about huntin' or women or cars. Because that's about all Possum was ever interested in. 'Cept drinkin'. Lord, it has to be twenty years since he worked here. Good mechanic. He knew his way around a car."

"What happened to him?"

He chuckled. "Possum had a habit of ramblin'. Just take off and disappear for days at a time. One day, he just picked up and moved on. Never did come back. Haven't seen or heard of him since."

Instinctively, I reached for my notebook but thought better of it. Instead, I made mental notes that I could recall and write down as soon as I was alone. Bullock walked into the garage and I introduced him. Finished pumping gas, he started pumping Larry for more information. But together we got no further than I had alone.

"Why'd they call him Possum?" Bullock asked.

"You obviously ain't never seen him." He led us into the office and pointed to a framed picture on the wall. In the photo, a crowd of people stood around a race car. In front of the car, a young man in a driver's uniform was accepting a huge trophy from a scantily clad blonde with a sash that read Miss Summerville Speedway.

"That's him," Larry said pointing with a bony finger to a thin-faced man with a shock of black hair and a dark tan who stood in the crowd beside the race car. A cigarette dangled from his lips. His head pointed away. But his eyes stared directly at the camera, dark and beady over his sharp-pointed nose, and his smile stretched back on just the left side of his face so that he looked guilty, like a kid caught in a lie about missing homework, and, unmistakably, like a possum.

# Chapter Sixteen

Night was falling by the time Bullock pulled the Dodge into the dirt and gravel lot of the Travelers Rest Motel, just off U.S. 301, once a major north-south tourist highway that had been bypassed by the interstate.

I surveyed the single-story, twelve-unit cinderblock building with a red neon Office sign on one end and a half-dozen run-down cabins in back. "Nineteen dollars and ninety-five cents a night and it's only a forty-five minute drive to Hirtsboro," Bullock said. "We're on our own dime."

I agreed. But when I walked into our tiny room, I wished I hadn't. Twin beds sagged beneath thin and faded brown and orange checked bedspreads. Matching curtains covered a window so filthy that curtains were superfluous. I ran my finger through a coating of dust on a shaky brown desk and a beige rotary phone. A dozen cigarette burns pocked the brown plastic indoor/outdoor carpeting. A crinkled stalk of aluminum foil allowed the black and white TV to pull in one station, from Augusta. The place reeked of dust and disinfectant. I saw myself in the mirror and figured I was the first guy ever in the room wearing a tie.

"We shouldn't be here long," Bullock said hopefully.

"We won't be here long," I said with certainty.

"We've already paid. Let's settle in."

I agreed and again wished I hadn't, especially when Bullock raised the possibility that the sheets in the twin beds hadn't been changed since the last occupant. I spent a fitful night fully clothed atop the bedspreads, turning over my body and my situation, the dim surroundings an expression of my inner gloom.

Walker Burns, one of the few good things about the *Charlotte Times*, was looking for a job elsewhere and was surely gone. When I'd called New York to tell Brad about our eviction, I learned the sad news that he and Lindsay were having serious problems and had decided to seek counseling. I was missing Delana more than I had imagined. Phone calls between us weren't getting it done. Dad sounded okay when I called to check on him but no matter how hard I worked, I couldn't escape the fact that he was dying. I was getting tired of spending so much time with Bullock.

And, we still didn't have enough to write a decent story. We could write that Wallace Sampson's girlfriend had seen a man named Billy Bascom running from the killing. But we didn't know if he was the killer or simply a man running from gunfire. Bullock and I both believed that Buchan knew about the hookers in the back of his building and we had Mary Pell's word that the firebomb was thrown to protest them. But the link between the firebomb and the killing of Wallace Sampson was speculative.

My depression didn't lift until just after dawn when the bathroom door burst open and Ronnie Bullock, khaki pants around his ankles, hopped out shrieking.

"Holy shit! Holy shit! Look at this!" he shouted, waving newspaper clippings that I could see were from the *Times*. "Bascom's right here in the damn clips!" He spread the clips out on the dresser and stooped to pull up his trousers. "Look at this. Unbelievable. We've had it all the time, right there under our noses!"

Sure enough, in the last paragraph of a story about Raeford Watson's trial for beating civil rights marchers in Columbia was the following sentence:

"Watson will be sentenced next month along with Leroy Hord, O.O. Mayhew and William J. Bascom, who pleaded guilty before the trial."

"Jesus, Ronnie, how'd you find that?"

"You can't buy a newspaper in this God-forsaken place and I gotta have something to read when I'm in the can. I grabbed the file of the clips that Miss Nancy saved for us . . ."

"And which you promised to return."

"And there it was. I'll return them once we've read every word."

Thirty minutes later we left the Travelers Rest Motel in a cloud of dust, headed toward Columbia, on the trail of the Possum.

"We might be able to track him through the Department of Corrections," Bullock said. "Hell, if he served time, he might still be on probation."

"Ronnie, here's the low-end story, the story we can write if we get nothing else." I kept my eyes peeled for cops as Bullock nursed the speedometer up to eighty miles an hour. "Here's the lede: A man who later pleaded guilty to civil rights charges was seen at the site of an unsolved killing that followed racial unrest in Hirtsboro, South Carolina."

"Make it 'was spotted fleeing from the scene of an unsolved killing.' 'Spotted' and 'fleeing' are stronger."

"I'm not sure we can say 'fleeing.' It goes too far."

"What the girl said was that she saw him running away. That's fleeing. The lede is: 'A man later convicted of civil rights charges was spotted fleeing from the site of an unsolved killing that occurred during racial unrest in Hirtsboro, South Carolina.' And I bet no one interviewed him, either. But that's not the story we want to write. We want to write what happened and why. We still need to find the Possum." He reached into his shirt pocket and pulled out a photograph. It was Bascom's face, enlarged and grainy like those photos of robbers taken by bank security cameras.

"How'd you get that?"

Bullock extracted his camera from his pocket. "I took a picture of the picture at the gas station while you were talking to Larry. I have a mini-darkroom in the trunk."

The Possum proved almost as elusive in Columbia as he had been in Hirtsboro. The Department of Corrections had no record of a William J. Bascom ever having been an inmate. Clip files at the *Charlotte Times* and at *The Columbia State* failed to include any stories on the sentencing of Watson, Bascom, Mayhew, and Hord. None of the earlier stories mentioned the name of Bascom's defense attorney. As shots in the dark, we searched records at the S.C. Department of Revenue and the Division of Motor Vehicles. None hit the mark.

The pale winter sun had dropped low in the sky as we left the DMV. Bullock looked at his watch. "Seventeen hundred hours," he said. "We're going to have to find another hotel room soon. Got to crank out a few obits."

I wasn't looking forward to it. I read the clip about the trial that I carried in the pocket of my sports coat. "Prosecutor was named Red McCallum," I said. "Maybe someone there knows something."

Bullock shrugged. "It's right down the street. We have time."

We took an elevator to the third floor of a converted federal post office, which housed the administrative offices of the Richland County Courts. I knocked on the door where gold letters read "Solicitor's Office." When no one answered, we walked in.

In the outer room, a man in a gray suit bent over an open drawer of files. When he stood up and faced us, I was struck immediately by the contrast between his age—over seventy I guessed—and his youthful shock of red hair. Beyond that, he was chubby, his cheeks almost cherubic—Howdy Doody as a senior citizen. I figured there was a good chance we had just found Red McCallum.

"Can I help you?"

"Ron Bullock and Matt Harper from the *Charlotte Times*," Bullock said. "We were looking for someone who might help us with a story we're working on."

"*Charlotte Times*? Did something happen to ol' Henry?"

Henry Ashley was the *Charlotte Times* reporter who'd been stationed in Columbia since Sherman's March, as Walker liked to say. He knew everyone and still carried the title of Bureau Chief, a relic of the days when the *Times* had actually employed more than one person in the bureau.

"No, sir," I said quickly. "Henry's still here. We're on another kind of story. I'm sorry. I should probably know this. But do you happen to be Red McCallum?"

"All my life. Unless you happen to be from the IRS." He laughed and we all shook hands. Bullock and I gave him business cards. He studied them. "In my thirty years in office, I've always tried to have a good relationship with the press. I like Henry. What can I help you with?"

I handed him the clip about the Watson. He put on a pair of wire-rimmed glasses and read it. "We're trying to find Bascom," Bullock said.

"Ol' Possum and I got to know each other quite well. I'm surprised he's back in the news."

"He isn't yet. We want to interview him. We're hoping you can help."

Bullock produced another print of the photo from Ray's Amoco. "Just to make sure we're talking about the same guy . . ."

"That's him." McCallum put his reading glasses back in his front pocket. "Come into my office." He turned and I took the opportunity to glance at my watch. There wouldn't be much chance for writing any obits. I prayed that no one important—or known to the publisher—had died in Charlotte.

McCallum's walls were a memorial to his life and career—photos with every celebrity who'd ever passed through Columbia; countless civic awards; a corn liquor jug with a cartoon of a Confederate flag, a drawing of a defiant Rebel soldier with the caption "Fergit, Hell!"; an autographed football from Clemson's national champion football team; an autographed South Carolina Gamecock basketball jersey; a framed bumper sticker with the Gamecock logo and the words, "You Can't Lick Our Cocks."

McCallum laughed when he noticed that the bumper sticker had caught my attention. "We had some interesting free speech versus contemporary community standards litigation over that one a few years back." He sat down on a red leather chair and pointed Bullock and me toward a matching couch.

"So you need to track down Possum . . ."

We started at the beginning, with the civil unrest in Hirtsboro and the firebomb directed at the building that housed De Sto. We told him about the life and shooting of Wallace Sampson, about the lack of police investigation into the killing, about the new information that we had developed—but not where it came from—that Billy Bascom had been seen fleeing just after the shots were fired.

Sometimes I talked. Sometimes Bullock did. For the most part Mc-Callum listened quietly and without expression.

"When we learned that Bascom had been convicted in another case of civil rights violence, it all kind of came together," I explained.

"So you think he was involved in the Wallace Sampson killing."

"We have fresh eyewitness testimony that he was on the scene. We know that you had him in court up here for beating those civil rights marchers and that he was found guilty. We know that one of his co-defendants was Raeford Watson, the Klansman who owned the store where the Wallace Sampson shooting happened. There's got to be a connection."

"You're wrong about at least one thing," McCallum said. "Bascom wasn't convicted."

"He pleaded guilty," I corrected myself. "Same thing. The point is, he did it. He committed other civil rights violations in addition to anything that happened in Hirtsboro."

"Interesting but circumstantial," McCallum said.

"Circumstantial is good enough for a newspaper story," Bullock said. "We don't have to convict. We know that when Possum Bascom is around, bad things happen."

"You know, Ronnie, that's not a half-bad lede," I said. I took out my notebook and wrote it down.

"So you're prepared to write a story that ties Billy Bascom to the unsolved murder of Wallace Sampson?"

"We could write that story now," I confirmed.

"Blacks get uppity and firebomb the building housing De Sto as well as a hated whorehouse," Bullock said. "Next night, someone shoots a black teenager at the site. Friend of the man who runs De Sto is spotted fleeing from the scene. Later, the friend and the guy who runs the store are found guilty of beating up some blacks who are agitating for civil rights. It seems pretty clear to me. I think it would be to our readers."

McCallum sighed and slumped back in his chair. He pressed his palms and fingers together. For a moment, I thought he was going to pray.

"You could write that story and it would be accurate," he said. He leaned forward. "But if you write that story you would be making a terrible, terrible mistake."

"Facts are never a mistake," I said.

"Son, I've lived a long time. I've been in a lot of courtrooms. I've heard a lot of stories. Here is what I know for sure. Facts and the truth are *not* the same thing. The fact is, Billy Bascom might have been at the site of that young man's killing. But the truth is, when it comes to advancing the cause of civil rights in South Carolina, Billy Bascom isn't the bad guy. Billy Bascom is a hero." He looked us up and down. Finally, he said, "You know Henry and I have a deal. Everything I say is off the record unless we agree upfront otherwise. Do you boys work like that?"

"We can," Bullock answered.

"This is off the record and not for attribution or for publication unless you get it from someone else."

"Agreed," we both answered.

"Billy Bascom was an informer for the State Law Enforcement Division. Never did know how they flipped him but he became an informer once he'd risen pretty high up in the South Carolina Klan. Billy Bascom was SLED's best source of information about what the Klan was up to. Billy Bascom probably headed off more civil rights violence and sent more Klan to prison than anyone in this state. And that's the truth."

"Then what happened up here in the case you prosecuted, when he got convicted along with Watson, Hord, and Mayhew?" I asked.

"Like I told you, he wasn't convicted. He pleaded guilty. There's a big difference. That was how they'd work it. He'd tell the SLED agents what was coming down, they'd show up and all the Klan would get arrested, including Billy. When trial came, he'd plead guilty. It preserved his cover. When it came time for sentencing, we'd make sure he walked away with no active time. Or maybe just time served."

"Which explains why there's no record of him at the Department of Corrections," Bullock said.

I couldn't have been more stunned. For the second time, Bullock and I had zeroed in on a Wallace Sampson angle only to have our central thesis destroyed. But this time, the story had gotten even better.

"A government informer inside the Ku Klux Klan was spotted at the scene of an unsolved civil rights murder, the *Charlotte Times* has learned," I said sounding out a new lede.

McCallum looked horrified. "You can't write that story!"

"Why not?"

"Because it would get Billy killed. There are people in prison today because of him. And believe me, if they knew he was the cause of their being there, they *would* have him killed. No question."

Something nagged at me. "So if Bascom was an informer, how come he never informed about the shooting of Wallace Sampson, either in time to head it off or even afterward, after the shooting happened?"

"I don't know the answer to that," McCallum said. "He dealt directly with the agents. Maybe he told them and they decided not to pursue it. Maybe it would have jeopardized something bigger."

Images of Etta Mae Sampson, weeping in the rain at her son's grave, flashed through my head. "Try telling Wallace Sampson's mother there was something bigger," I said.

"Or maybe he just didn't tell the agents everything he was involved in," McCallum offered. "I said Billy Bascom was a civil rights hero. But he wasn't all good. He wouldn't be the first informer to walk both sides of the street. Don't forget. To catch the devil, sometimes you have to visit hell."

"If Billy Bascom is a hero, that's a story we need to write," Bullock said firmly. "I'm asking you to let us put what you said on the record. All this happened a long time ago. Things have changed. There is no Klan anymore, at least not one that counts."

"You'd be betting his life on that."

"Then let it be our decision," I argued.

"If anything, it's got to be Billy's." McCallum closed his eyes and placed his palms and fingers back together. "You'd scare hell out of him if you showed up."

"How about this," I said. "How about you ask him for us. Ask him if we could interview him about the killing of Wallace Sampson."

McCallum took the business cards we'd given him from his pocket. "Is this where to contact you? At the paper in Charlotte?"

"Let's make the call now," I said.

"Can't happen," said McCallum. "I don't know where he is but I believe I can find him. So should I call you in Charlotte?"

"Uh, we're on the move a lot," I said. "How about if you call this number and leave a message." I ripped a page from my notebook and wrote down Brad Hall's number.

Outside, our run of luck continued. I called Brad and learned that he and Lindsay were back at Windrow and that his father was out of town. Bullock and I were welcome back at the plantation, at least for a while.

"Screw the obits," Bullock said. "Right now I'm just thinking about a clean bed. I might even have a nice serving of tofu when we get there. On second thought, let's grab a steak on the way back."

It was after midnight by the time we rolled into Savannah County. Thick fog hung low in the road as we neared the river and the entrance to Windrow. Squinting and hunched over the steering wheel, Bullock slowed the Dodge to a crawl. A pair of headlights snapped on to our right and a car swung into the road behind us. It quickly closed to within inches of our bumper.

Bullock speeded up a little and muttered, "What makes you think I know what I'm doing, pal? I got no better idea where the road goes than you." The car stayed glued to the Dodge. Bullock speeded up some more.

I turned around and squinted into the trailing headlights. The car switched on its high beams. I couldn't see a thing. Bullock accelerated but the car closed the space again.

I was about to tell Bullock to just move over when the car slammed into the back of the Dodge, causing us to fishtail wildly.

"Bastard!" Bullock shouted. He resisted the instinct to brake and instead let the wheels roll free. The Dodge swerved then straightened. The car rammed us again. I was thrown back into the seat. My leg hit the glove box and the .38 rolled onto the floor.

"Grab it!" Bullock yelled. The Dodge jolted forward with another crash. The .38 slid just out of my grasp. Bullock punched the gas and the Dodge leapt forward. "Give me the damn gun!"

I found the pistol but Bullock had his hands full. We were careening blind down the road door-to-door at eighty miles an hour. A curve or a vehicle ahead and we were dead. The car—an aging Plymouth—swerved to the right. The Dodge took a hard hit in the quarter-panel. Bullock cursed and fought for control.

I stole a glance inside the Plymouth. A man in a baseball hat wrestled with the steering wheel. Bullock notched the Dodge up to ninety. Our pursuer kept pace and we traded paint again.

Bullock pushed the accelerator to the floor. The Dodge surged ahead. Bullock pulled into the on-coming lane. "Shoot his radiator out!"

I leaned out the passenger window, clicked off the safety, aimed at the massive grill of the Plymouth and pulled the trigger again and again, my arm jumping from the recoil. The Plymouth rolled on unimpaired.

"Reload!" Bullock yelled

But before I could, steam began pouring from the hood of the Plymouth and it pulled to the side of the road. We raced on.

"I got him, Ronnie!" I yelled.

"Damn. You have the makins' of a good ol' boy after all."

We inspected the damage to the car when we finally arrived at Windrow.

"Ronnie, we need to wrap this story up. It's time to get out of Dodge."

"No," he said, giving the smashed rear bumper a kick. "It's time to get the Dodge out of here."

We crept past Maybelle, who didn't budge from her bed by the door. Tasha opened one eye, stretched, yawned and went back to sleep. Brad Hall appeared in a bathrobe in the hallway and held his finger to his lips.

"Lindsay's asleep. Sorry about my old man. Judge Buchan told me what happened."

Friday, we slept late, wrote enough obits to make up for the ones we'd missed the day before and waited for McCallum. Instead we got a call from one of the *Times* assistant editors. *Charlotte Times* newsroom raises for the year would be limited to two and one-half percent.

"The eagle flies on Friday," Bullock said happily when I passed along the news.

"Ronnie, how can you be happy about two and one-half percent? That's barely a cost-of-living increase."

"Beats what I got last year by a long shot."

I made a vow not to grow old in the daily newspaper business.

When Saturday arrived with still no word from Red McCallum, Bullock decided to go out and play.

"I can't stand just sitting around here waiting for the damn phone to ring." He laced up a pair of hunting boots. "Brad's gonna take me and the dogs on a flora and fauna tour of Windrow. Too bad you can't come along."

"What do you mean?"

"Someone needs to man the phone."

"Oh, yeah." And then I realized I'd forgotten about Lindsay. Since our return, signs of strain between her and Brad hadn't been evident. But then, mostly she had stayed in her room. "Can't Lindsay take a message?"

He snorted. "Lindsay isn't good for much beyond spending money, if you ask me."

As had become my practice with many of Bullock's offensive remarks, I chose to ignore him. But I agreed to stay.

I went to the library when they left and scanned the shelves—volume after volume on botany, a surprising number on fencing. I pulled down several, leafed through them and put them back. I was lost in my solitude, absorbed by someone else's interests. I pulled two volumes that had caught my eye earlier—Jack Bass's *Orangeburg Massacre*, because it was a true story of civil rights violence in South Carolina and, for no particular reason—other than maybe being without female companionships for weeks—Alex Comfort's *The Joy of Sex*.

I had stretched out on a leather couch, had put down Bass and had just opened Comfort when I realized I wasn't alone.

"I thought you'd gone," said Lindsay.

I sat up. "Jesus, you surprised me." I put the book on the coffee table. My heart beat wildly and my stomach was in my throat. "I'm sorry. What did you say?"

"I said I thought you'd gone."

I saw her look at the book on the table. It happened to be open to a section on oral sex. I felt like a fifteen-year-old caught by mom with a dirty magazine. "I just picked it up," I laughed nervously. "It opened there."

"Not likely in this house."

I felt myself flush. I looked at her and for the first time I became aware of how she was dressed—heeled blue slippers and a matching blue silk robe tied loosely at the waist. She bent over to pick up the book and I was enveloped by her blond hair and surrounded by her smell. Her robe opened slightly and I caught a glimpse of the top of her lacy blue bra. My mouth was dry. My heart rate doubled. I found myself calculating. We'd be alone for at least an hour. Lindsay and Brad were having troubles. If I pushed things and she was willing, no one would ever know. *But I would. I would know.*

I was unaware that I had actually spoken until Lindsay asked, "Would know what?"

"Sorry," I stammered. "I'm a little distracted."

At that moment, the telephone in Brad Hall's study began to ring. I answered it.

"Red McCallum, here," said the voice on the line. "What's the matter? You sound out of breath."

"Had to run to get the phone."

"Too bad. I thought maybe you were havin' sex." He laughed. "Beats me why, but Possum says he'll do it Monday. Got a pencil?"

I took down the directions, read them back to McCallum and reaffirmed our promise not to write that Bascom was an informer without Bascom's okay. When I looked up, Lindsay was gone.

Mary Pell came in through the back door. And less than a half hour later, Bullock and Brad showed up, their tour cut short by a flat tire.

I replayed the scene with Lindsay as I lay in bed that night but my thoughts kept turning to Delana. I thought of her gathering the berries for the crisp, swinging a wicker basket as she walked past the black-dirt garden that once grew lima beans and lettuce for me and tomatoes for her, past the hillock where we sat when I asked her to marry me and on to the patch of low-hanging fruit—quarter-sized blackberries that hung on thorny branches that tangled from thick stalks spiking from the ground. Delana was willing to have her hands stained purple if it meant doing the right thing for someone else.

Delana has always believed in me. She has always been my rock. The greatest mistake in my life had been running away from her. I knew that now. She was right. My fling with the garden writer had nothing to do with her and everything to do with me. I felt ashamed.

Early the next morning I found myself alone in the kitchen with Mary Pell.

"Could I ask you for a favor?" she said. "I need a ride to church tomorrow."

"Sure. I've got the whole day free."

"Good. Mr. Matt, it just might be a good idea for you to come, too."

# Chapter Seventeen

On the front lawn of the Mt. Moriah House of Prayer choir members chatted and helped each other with their robes as Mary Pell and I arrived in the Dodge. I parked on the sandy street and walked around to open the passenger door.

"Nice ride. I hate that it got tore up." She wore a bright red suit, matching shoes, and a red pillbox hat with a black feather so long that she had to twist her head to get out of the car. In her right hand, she carried a well-worn Bible. I took her left elbow and guided her into the sanctuary where the piano had started. "Showtime," I heard one of the choir members say.

In a moment, my eyes adjusted to the dim light and I beheld the most visible difference, other than the skin color of the congregants, between this church and the one I grew up in—hats. In the Mt. Moriah House of Prayer, every woman of every age wore a hat—not simple hats, but huge, flamboyant hats in red and purple and black and white, hats with wide brims, hats with tall feathers, hats that seemed to increase in audacity with the age of the wearer.

Mary Pell led me down the aisle to her pew near the front and I squeezed in beside her.

The service was a replay of the one Bullock and I had attended earlier: prayers with feeling, music with conviction; joys and concerns from the congregation, including Etta Mae Sampson's continuing plea for "justice for my loving son Wallace." And then Reverend Grace rose from one of the two red velvet chairs placed in front of the altar and began to talk.

He started with church announcements and tidbits of news from the congregation—the fish dinner fund-raiser would be next Thursday; the youth basketball team would practice Tuesday; special prayers were needed for Miss Lottie Moore who was ill; we mourn the passing of Brother Smith. Grace dropped his chin to his chest and shut his eyes. He massaged his forehead. He was silent so long I began to feel uncomfortable. The place stood still.

"No," he said quietly, slowly looking up. A long pause. "We do *not* mourn the passing of Brother Smith. I have got it wrong, my brothers and sisters. We do not mourn the passing of Brother Smith. Instead, we *celebrate* the passing of Brother Smith!"

Scattered "amens" from the congregation.

Grace turned to face the choir, which sat behind the altar. Several members worked their fans.

"You see," he said, "You must live today as if you were going to die tomorrow. I still believe that. But those words have a different meaning for me now."

"Tell it, preacher!" someone shouted.

"When I was a young, I took it as a challenge. Live today like you are going to die tomorrow." Pause. "So I drank the liquor."

"Lord have mercy!"

Louder. "And I ran the streets."

"Lord have mercy!"

Louder. "And chased the women." Pause. Then softly, "Caught a few, too." Grace grinned. A few of the men smothered chuckles. Mary Pell elbowed me in the ribs.

"But I've changed all that now," Grace shouted.

"Praise, Jesus!"

"I've changed the way I feel about death."

"Praise, Jesus!"

"I still live today like I am going to die tomorrow." Pause. "But it has a different meaning for me now. Today, I don't drink and chase women because I'm worried I might die tomorrow and run out of time. No, sir. Today, I live in a state of grace because I might die tomorrow. Today, I stand ready to meet my Maker because that could happen tomorrow.

Today, I live my life like I'm ready for the Judgment Day because tomorrow, the Judgment Day might come."

"Amen!"

When it comes to praying, I'm a little out of practice. But the bond I felt with Mary Pell and the people of Hirtsboro, the struggle I shared with them in some small way, made me set aside my self-consciousness when Revered Grace asked us to pray. I prayed for Mary Pell. I prayed for Bullock. I prayed for Brad and Lindsay. I prayed for Wallace and Mrs. Sampson. I prayed for my father. I prayed for Luke and my mother. I prayed for Delana. I prayed for my soul.

THE NEXT MORNING, we awoke to wind and a cold, hard rain.

"Stormy Monday," Bullock said as he strapped on his derringer.

"I hope Tuesday's not as bad," I mumbled from beneath the sheets, but Bullock missed the reference.

I was excited. We'd been fooled before but at last we were closing in. At the very least, Billy Bascom was an eyewitness to the Wallace Sampson murder.

We decided to break the rule about too many people on an interview and take Brad with us. Without him, we would never have been on the story in the first place. It was something he deserved.

"The only difference between Brad and an investigative reporter is that he isn't getting paid," I said.

"He doesn't need to be," Bullock added.

Bullock drove. I navigated from the directions provided by Red McCallum.

"We're not far from Pennegar's," Brad said as we made a turn.

"That's it," I said, pointing to the right.

Ahead, a small red brick ranch house with black shutters sat in a tired yard surrounded by a picked-over cotton field. A green and white mobile home rested one hundred feet behind the house. In a grove of tall trees, behind the mobile home, a weathered wooden house with shattered windows and a rusting tin roof sagged into the leaves.

"That's how it works," Bullock said. "First generation builds a nice house. Next generation moves out, but not too far away. They get a trailer and put it right by momma and daddy's. Later, they can afford to build a regular house. So they put it right in front of the trailer. Momma and daddy pass on. The original house is used for storage and then abandoned. Reminds me of home."

The wind whipped the rain into torrents. Bullock guided the battered Dodge down the driveway, doing his best to avoid the potholes brimming with muddy water. He parked beside the house, got out, knocked on the door, and returned dripping to the car.

"He's got to be here somewhere," he said. "No tire tracks on the driveway. No one's left here since the rain started."

We eased further down the drive, past a yard of tall brown grass and a crop of two dozen rusting oil drums, each with a square opening cut at ground level and surrounded by chicken wire fencing. Outside several drums, brightly colored roosters, each with a leg attached to a tether, pecked at the ground in the rain.

"Gamecocks," Bullock said. "Fighting chickens."

"Isn't that illegal?"

"Only fighting them," Brad said. "People around here still breed them."

I made a mental note about yet another South Carolina story for Walker.

Bullock saw Bascom first, smoking a cigarette beneath the tin roof overhanging the abandoned house in back. He wore jeans, a denim jacket, and brown work boots covered in mud. His hair had turned completely white. He looked small and hunched. But when I compared him to the picture over the sun visor, there was no doubt we were looking at the Possum.

We parked the Dodge and splashed through puddles to the porch, where we took shelter from the sheeting rain. Bascom's eyes tracked us but his head faced a different direction, as if he were perpetually in the process of sneaking a glance and quickly looking away. Even his grin was lopsided, stretched long and narrow on one side of his face, revealing a row of tiny brown teeth.

"Bill Bascom," he said, sticking out his hand. "I've been expecting you."

Bullock and I gave him our cards. Brad thanked him for seeing us.

"Red said you could be trusted. He told me what you're after." Bascom lit another cigarette and motioned for us to sit down on some empty apple crates.

We talked for the next three and a half hours as the wind blew and the rain played on the tin roof like a snare drum. Bascom answered every question Bullock and I threw at him and seemed to light a fresh cigarette for each one, alternating between a pack of menthols in his right jacket pocket and a pack of regulars in his left. I took fifteen pages of notes. Brad listened intently.

When we could think of no more questions, Bullock asked Bascom to pose for a picture.

"I don't mind," he said, striking a pose almost exactly like the one in the photo we carried.

"I need to ask it one more time," I said as we prepared to leave. "There's no question you told your contacts in state law enforcement what happened in Hirtsboro?"

Bascom sucked in a lung-full of smoke, dropped his cigarette and ground it out. "I told them everything. That wasn't the only case they never followed up on. Why they followed up on some and not on others is not for me to know. But I told them, all right. And they wrote it all down."

"Just one more," Bullock said. "Red McCallum said he never did know how they flipped you."

The Possum gave me a sidewise glance. "Had me by the balls," he shrugged. "Had pictures of me havin' sex with a black woman. Threatened to go public with 'em or give 'em to the boys in the Klan. I'd have been strung up for sure. By my first wife or the Grand Dragon, depending on who got me first." His hearty laugh turned into a hacking cough.

"What happened to the woman?" Brad asked.

He glanced at his watch. "She works nights. Ought to be up in a minute."

Brad seemed stunned. "You're married to a black woman?"

"Common law. Been together almost fifteen years."

"Why on earth were you ever a member of the Klan?"

Bascom shrugged his shoulders. "At the time, I believed in it. 'Course, liquor might have had something to do with it, too."

I had one other question. "Billy, Red McCallum said you'd be in danger if we wrote that you'd been an informer."

He lit another cigarette. "Hell, I don't care. Cancer's eatin' me up anyway."

The rain had stopped by the time we left the porch. Intervals of sun had warmed the interior of the Dodge. It felt good when I climbed in. I sorted through my thoughts and emotions—a deep and burning anger at the appalling story we'd just been told, relief at finally getting what we had come for, excitement about the splash we were about to make, happiness for Mrs. Sampson and Brad, anxiety about the list of things that still needed to be done.

"I never imagined," Brad said.

"I did," Bullock said. "I've already got the lede."

A vision of Walker Burns and the questions he'd ask us flashed through my mind.

"One more stop before we write," I said.

We could see old man Pennegar from almost a half-mile off, sitting in his lawn chair by the side of the road, his right hand raised, his left hand limp, a floppy straw hat shielding his face from the sun which was now out in full force.

We parked the car and approached. He nodded and I could tell that he remembered us.

"Sorry to trouble you again, sir," I said. "We won't take much of your time."

For the next half hour he listened while Brad, Bullock and I talked. We told him what we had learned about the night Wallace Sampson was shot and what had and hadn't happened later. When I got to the part about the actual shooting, the eyes of former Hirtsboro policeman filled with tears.

At every point in our story, he perceptibly nodded his head "yes."

We had almost finished when I heard the roar of an engine. I looked up to see the Hirtsboro town police car fish-tailing down the narrow road. It skidded to a stop and Olen Pennegar Jr. jumped out, gun drawn.

"I told you to stay the hell away from here," he yelled. "You've got ten seconds." Olen Pennegar Jr. leveled his gun and began to count. "One, two, three . . ."

Before I could speak, a loud, long moan, half cry, half wail came from Pennegar Sr. The young policeman walked over to his father, knelt on the wet ground, and held his face close. "What is it, Daddy?"

His father grunted. Pennegar holstered his pistol.

Another sound came from the old man. He was trying to speak but I couldn't understand.

"One more time, Daddy," urged his son.

Then he made the same sound that he had made when we had first come to question him. Suddenly, I knew what it was.

"Bluffing," I said. "Your dad is trying to say the word 'bluffing.'"

Pennegar Sr. nodded "yes."

Back at Windrow, we called Walker. He was in a meeting so Bullock left a message with the receptionist. "Tell him to get ready," he said. "Harper and Bullock are coming in."

# Chapter Eighteen

We had just finished packing the Dodge the next morning when Mary Pell burst from the house, waving. "It's a Mr. Burns," she shouted. "He wants to talk to Mr. Matt."

I picked up the phone, feeling cocky. "Walker, we've got the story. We're comin' home to nail the coonskin to the wall."

"Matt, your father's oncologist has been trying to reach you. It's not looking so good."

One thing about Walker, he doesn't mess around. He gave me the details. When he was done, I felt nauseous and scared. This was all happening much faster than I had expected.

I called Delana and told her the news.

"I know. I'll meet you at your place. We'll drive over this afternoon together."

Bullock and I hashed out the Wallace Sampson story lede and the first ten paragraphs on the way back to Charlotte. He drove and I wrote.

"Holy shit," he said when I read the paragraphs back aloud.

"Holy shit, *Mabel*," I corrected. As powerful as the story was, I loved the process just as much. It was exhilarating, consuming. It was why I had become a reporter in the first place. And it gave me something to focus on other than my father's sudden deterioration.

"I'll take the first draft the rest of the way," Bullock said as we neared town. "We can still get it done for the weekend."

It's not how I would have preferred it, but I knew I had no choice.

Bullock dropped me off at my place. I shook his hand and wished him luck. He bear-hugged me and gave me a slap on the back. Delana arrived in the Honda looking more beautiful than I'd ever seen her. I told her so.

Sad as I was about my father, the trip gave me an opportunity I'd been aching for—the chance to share the news about the Wallace Sampson story with Delana. I replayed the interview with Bascom and the confirmation from Olen Pennegar Sr.—developments that made it certain we could write the story of our lives. She wanted every detail.

"I knew it would happen, Matt!"

"I was never so sure. When I think of all the luck we had . . ."

"You make your own luck. You wouldn't have been lucky if you hadn't believed. You saw something no one else saw. You took a chance no one else would."

"I'm just happy for Brad and Mrs. Sampson. And for Wallace."

"Matt, I've never been prouder of anyone." She touched me tenderly on the arm.

Delana's words—her steadfast belief in me—meant more to me than anything else I could have heard.

Less than two hours later, we pulled into the parking deck at University Hospital. Delana freshened her lipstick and checked her makeup in the rearview mirror before we hurried toward the main entrance, her heels clicking hollowly on the concrete walk.

We passed a row of newspaper racks that huddled, along with a half dozen smokers, just outside the sliding glass doors. Out of habit, I paused to scan the front pages—not so much for news as for insight into what other editors were thinking, what headlines they imagined might cause a passerby to part with a quarter or fifty cents. A headline in *The Collegian*, the student-run paper, stopped me cold. "Famous Journalism Professor Nears Death," it read. I looked at the byline: David Riley. I took a copy and stuck it in my pocket without reading it. There's no point in getting information second-hand if you can check it out yourself.

Delana and I hurried past the receptionist. A security guard stopped us before we entered the elevators.

"We're here to visit a patient," she explained.

"You'll need to wait until I can get you a pass."

I was in no mood for delay or small-minded bureaucrats. "Not gonna happen," I said. I took Delana by the arm and we walked on.

The elevator doors slid open and we stepped into a world where the promise and peril of humanity had been captured in a small stainless steel box. Smiling grandparents laden with balloons, teddy bears and a camera, beamed all the way to the Newborn Nursery. A woman, face pinched with tension, handkerchief twisted tightly in her hand, exited at Oncology. I pushed the button for the floor marked "Intensive Care." From Maternity to Eternity in less than a minute.

Green-shirted orderlies pushing carts of hospital food, linens, and medication wheeled by as Delana and I stepped from the elevator into the bright glare and antiseptic odor of Intensive Care. A nurse sat low behind a semi-circular desk, her eyes occasionally scanning eight monitors that showed each patient's pulse, temperature, and respiration.

"Your father's stable today," she said, glancing at one of the monitors which had started to beep. "He's in Room 388. The doctor'll be by later."

I walked down the hall and knocked softly, pushed the door open, and made way for Delana, who walked in and flinched.

A tiny figure in a thin gown lay on his back in the hospital bed. Blue veins mapped his skin, which hung from his bones as transparent as parchment. His head was propped on a pillow—eyes sunk deep and unnaturally blue; flesh retreating so that his jaw and teeth protruded; bald so that he did not look so much like my father as my father's skull. I was shocked.

Dad tried to pull himself up and get out of bed, the result of never-forgotten breeding that dictated that a gentleman stands when a lady enters the room.

"Sit down, Colonel," Delana said.

He slumped back. I bent down and cradled his neck in my arms. He seemed so fragile he would break if I really hugged him.

"It's good to see you," he said flatly. "What brings you here?"

A nurse knocked and told Dad it was time for his medication. She propped him up while he swallowed some pills. A minute later his eyelids fluttered and he slumped and started to snore lightly.

I heard a page in the hallway for Dr. Heart and I knew that somewhere on the floor someone had stopped breathing. A few seconds later a crash team rushed by.

"I hope he wakes up soon," I told Delana. "I still have things I want to talk to him about."

"We'll be here as long as you need."

Night descended outside the window and the doctor arrived, a woman about our age dressed in a pantsuit, her brown hair pulled back in a bun. She took Delana and me to a room down the hallway where a small sign read, "Reserved for Grieving Families." We sat on the edge of stuffed chairs, Delana's and my hands intertwined, the doctor across from us.

"I'm sorry," she said. "I've never seen a case like this. Nothing has worked. Multiple myeloma has no cure but generally we can keep it at bay for eight or ten years or more. In your father's case, nothing we've done has had any real effect." The doctor's face showed genuine despair.

"What about experimental therapies like interferon?" Delana asked.

"I don't believe he's a candidate for that. We're not treating him to make him better now. We're just trying to make him comfortable with pain medication. There's nothing we can do anymore."

"What about a bone marrow transplant?" I asked. "I could be a donor."

She shook her head. "I'm afraid your father's situation doesn't lend itself to that."

Delana sobbed. I didn't. I was out of tears.

"So what happens now?" I asked.

"We'll stabilize him. Then hospice is the right thing."

"Stabilize him?" Delana asked.

"We almost lost him the other day. His red blood cell count had dropped so low." She looked at me. "We're bringing him back with transfusions. But it's a short-term fix."

"How long does he have?" I asked.

She sighed. "It's hard to say. His heart's strong. Could be weeks. Could be a few months. No more than that. I'm sorry."

When we returned to his room my father looked even smaller. Delana and I sat holding hands until Dad began to stir.

"Would you mind affording me a little privacy, cutie?" he said to Delana when his eyes opened.

"Not at all, Colonel," she smiled.

"Need to take a piss," Dad grunted when she had gone. "Help me out of this coffin, will you?"

I reached for his arm and started to pull him up.

He shouted and fell back into the sheets. "The stuff's in my bones," he panted. Sweat slicked his forehead. "Here. Do it this way."

He gritted his teeth and groaned as I lifted him to a sitting position. I held him steady while he caught his breath. "Now, hand me that," he said, pointing to a urinal.

I turned my head until he called me to take away the bottle and help lower him into bed. When I bent over, the copy of *The Chronicle* fell out of my jacket pocket and onto the bed. The headline "Famous Journalism Professor Nears Death" stared us in the face. I knew Dad would be angry. "I'm sorry," I said. "I did my best to talk him out of it."

"I know it. He did a good job."

"I thought you'd be pissed . . ."

"He got his facts right."

"I haven't read it. The headline certainly looks overblown," I lied. "You're looking okay to me."

"Actually, it's accurate. However, it happens to apply to everyone on the planet. We're all nearing death. Therefore, it is not a very good headline." Ever the critic, I thought. He rested for a minute then asked, "How's your Wallace Sampson story going?"

"We got it. We're going to write it for the weekend."

Energized, he pulled himself up. "Tell me all about it."

When I had finished he said, "Son, that's a damn fine job of reporting."

"Thanks for your help." I knew that we were past pretending. We

were almost out of time. I knew it. He knew it. Everybody knew it.
Hell, it was a headline in the damn paper. In the face of such evidence, it
would have been unlike a Harper to let the obvious question hang there,
unasked. So I asked it. "Dad, how come it took so long? How come you
never helped me before?"

"Luke," he said simply.

"Luke? What's Luke got to do with it?"

"Luke was going to be the next great journalist. He had the name
and he had the talent. We had great dreams for him. Luke was going
to be the ultimate Lucas Harper. The new and improved version. What
happened was hard on us, son. Your mother never recovered."

"Dad, do you remember in eighth grade, when I got the writing
award?"

"What award?"

"Doesn't matter. So Luke died. And you just quit. You just stayed in
that study while Mom drank herself to death. You quit on her and you
quit on me. I didn't have the talent. I didn't have the name. Hence, the
vise grips and work-with-my hands thing."

"No. That wasn't it. What vise grips thing?"

"The vise grips I got for my birthday so I could get a job working
with my hands."

"I don't remember that. You had all the promise that Luke ever
had."

"Then why didn't you want for me what you wanted for him?"

"I didn't want to screw you up," he said, as if it was a question he'd
thought about all his life. "Like what happened to Luke."

I knew I might never get another chance, that if I never asked, a key
mystery of my childhood might never be understood. "Dad, at Luke's
funeral the reporter came up to the car and told you he was running out
of time. That he needed to go ahead and write the story."

"Yes."

"You told him to do it. You told him he had to write the truth as
best as he could determine it."

"Yes. I did."

"Dad, I thought Luke's dying was an accident. I thought he was in the garden killing gophers and the gun was old and it misfired. Is that what the story said?"

"It did say that could have happened. But it said police also found evidence that Luke's shooting might not have been accidental."

"Evidence?"

"A note in his diary that said, 'Sometimes at night fear comes to me that I will be the first Lucas Harper not to be famous.'" He began to weep.

I knelt beside my father's bed. I lay my head on his chest and held him as gently as I could. We lay there together just breathing for I don't know how long until Delana came in. She bent over and wrapped us in her arms.

"I love you, Dad," I said.

"I love you too, son."

# Chapter Nineteen

For months I had compartmentalized—Dad here, Delana there, Wallace Sampson over here, with a general worry about the direction of my life and career overlaying it all. In the midst of tumult, the Sampson story had been a refuge, a place I had been before, a place where I knew what to do.

But as I drove to work the next morning, my feelings respected no boundaries. When I thought about Delana's love for me, I felt Mrs. Sampson's love for her dead child. When I thought about Dad, I committed myself to the fight for the journalistic ideals he'd taught and practiced, the importance of crusading and of righting wrongs. When I thought about Luke, my anger raged over the casual murder of thirteen-year-old Wallace Sampson. I swore again there would be justice.

By the time I pushed though the swinging doors into the newsroom, I was angry, fearless and ready to write.

Bullock was already in my cubicle. Walker Burns was sprawled in my chair, his feet on my desk. He looked worried and that unnerved me until I found out he was worried for me.

"How's your dad?"

"Bad. We need to finish the story."

I had been thinking that Bullock and I would be writing for the upcoming Sunday edition but Walker quickly quashed that notion.

"Before it ever sees print this story's gonna get picked at like a pan of stale cornbread in the chicken yard. Lawyers are gonna be all over it, not to mention the copy desk."

"It's Wednesday morning," I argued. "We're probably half done. We can finish by quitting time tomorrow."

Walker shook his head. "Lawyers get paid by the hour. I ain't countin' on them being in a big hurry."

"We can work Saturday," Bullock volunteered.

"The publisher cut out the overtime budget," Walker said. "There's no money. Extra hours can't be authorized."

"How about we just retire a day early?" I said.

He laughed. "Sorry. There's just not enough time. You'll be lucky if the thing's ready next week."

Walker was right. I'd forgotten about meetings, bureaucracy, and the schedules of people other than myself. For weeks we'd been able to concentrate solely on reporting and writing. I'd been living on Windrow time too long.

Just as I organized my notes, we were subjected to an hour-long meeting where the publisher and personnel director explained why reductions were required in the company benefits plan. Later, every employee cycled through the company auditorium to watch a movie about the importance of a local charity campaign sponsored by the newspaper.

By the end of the day, we hadn't made much progress.

"We need to head back to Windrow," Bullock said. "We can't write here."

In self-defense, we went with what had worked before. I sat at the computer while Bullock guarded the perimeter of my cubicle growling at would-be intruders. Word had spread that we'd nailed a big story and the interruptions were coming in increasing numbers—from the proud, from the jealous, from the genuinely helpful, and, because it is a newsroom, from the simply curious. Occasionally, someone had real business.

Bob DeCaprio, the perpetually gray-suited assistant managing editor, came by to ask how much space the story might take. But first he had to tell us about the latest glitch with the newsroom hyphenation system. "Every time we wrote about the Super Bowl in last Sunday's paper," he grumbled, "the damn computer changed it to Superb Owl." We howled.

A meeting with Walker and the photo editor took another hour. The photo department wanted to reshoot Bullock's pictures for reasons that had nothing to do with quality and everything to do with turf.

"With the exception of bothering Mrs. Sampson, be my guest," Walker told the photo editor. "But Ronnie's pictures are the ones we'll be publishing."

After another meeting, Walker gave the art department permission to go to Hirtsboro so artists could produce a diagram of the shooting scene.

"The *Charlotte Times* is about to publish a blockbuster. Everybody wants a piece of it," Bullock griped.

We spent an hour briefing Elaine Heitman so she could prepare an editorial on the Wallace Sampson case.

Carmela Cruz came by, her voice dripping with false helpfulness, to assure us that the national desk would be prepared with an excellent newsworthy package should a similar shortcoming befall our efforts this time as it had the last.

"Oh, yeah? What's the package this time?" Bullock snorted. "Discrimination against Puerto Rican lesbians? Spic chicks who wish they had dicks?"

"Ronnie!" I gasped. "I'm sorry, Carmela."

"Hardly his worst. What I find endearing about Ronald is that he is so consistently inappropriate." Then, with a flip of her hair she said, "Bandage your knuckles, Bullock. You've been dragging them again."

It was a measure of our current standing that Bullock's comments weren't immediately reported to the Discipline Committee even though the eyes of the newsroom were on us. News was about to break out. In terms of time and freedom, we'd been given much. Now, much was expected. Glory for everyone awaited.

I knew the word had really gotten around when the garden writer slithered up to me one morning.

"I hear you've got a big one," she said. "Story."

From time to time, I'd emerge from the cubicle to walk around, think, and check in with the outside world. At the hospital, transfusions were making Dad stronger, if only temporarily. Despite Walker's instructions, we worked through the weekend, each of us driven by our own demons and the need to find justice for a long-dead thirteen-year-old.

Sunday night, Henry Garrows, the sports writer, dropped by with an offer to lend us the shroud and noise-canceling headphones he used to shut out the outside world when he was writing. I declined, but sympathized with him about the need.

Late Monday afternoon we finished. I read our story through one more time and pushed myself away from the computer.

"That's it," I said to Bullock. "Tell Walker it's ready for the first read."

Bullock paced and I tweaked until after first-edition deadline when Walker finally moseyed over to the cubicle, commandeered my chair, put his feet on my file cabinet and settled in.

"Pardner, you look as nervous as a long-tailed cat in a room full of rocking chairs," he grinned. "Relax. This won't hurt a bit."

But it was hard to relax. Bullock and I both knew that of all the hoops we would have to jump through over the next four days—Walker, the lawyers, the copy desk—Walker would be the toughest. I hovered as he read, wondering why he paused so long on this paragraph, why he grunted when he read that.

When he got to the end of a sidebar I had written about Wallace Sampson, he just stared at the screen.

"Goddam son of a bitches," he said finally. "This really pisses me off."

"Holy Shit, Mabel?" Bullock asked.

"Yeah," he said, "At least that."

Bullock and I slapped each other on the back. But Walker was far from done. He ordered up a timeline, plus a sidebar on Brad Hall. Over the next day and a half, he continued to pick at our copy, challenging our reporting and asking the same question six different ways.

"How do you know?" was his most frequent question.

The only answers that ever satisfied him were "because we saw it" or "because he told us."

Wednesday, we decided to send Columbia bureau chief Henry Ashley back to Hirtsboro for one final piece of reporting.

"It won't do any good," I told Walker.

"Yeah, but we have to do it anyway."

I yowled at Walker's rewrites, his moving and even cutting of whole paragraphs—what he called "just polishing." But when he was done Bullock and I agreed that, as usual, Walker had improved the story.

Friday, we held our breaths while the *Times* lawyers reviewed the story in detail. Just to show they were paying attention they asked one or two questions that weren't half as difficult to answer as Walker's. And just because everyone thinks he's an editor, they also suggested a few changes in wording.

Saturday, both Bullock and I showed up to nurse the story through the copy desk. By the end of the day, only one question had surfaced. We had written that Hirtsboro was one hundred and eighty miles south of Charlotte. The copy desk atlas said it was one hundred and sixty-five.

"Where'd we get one eighty?" I asked Bullock.

"My expense reports. Go with one hundred sixty-five."

At dinnertime Walker checked in with Carmela just to make sure the latest dust-up in Uruguay hadn't bumped us off the top spot on the front page.

At 10:00 p.m. precisely, Bullock and I took the stairwell to the bottom of the building and slipped into the pressroom where a low rumble was becoming a roar as the huge Goss offsets spooled up to full speed, thickening the air with a fine mist of black ink droplets.

Copy after copy of the next day's first edition flew through rollers and a web of folders and emerged at the end of a line in a stack. Even from twenty-five feet away, I saw the Wallace Sampson story with a sixty point headline splashed across the top of the front page.

A blue-suited member of the press crew spotted us, pulled two copies from the stack, gave us a big grin and a thumbs-up.

"Thanks," I mouthed.

Bullock and I walked together to the parking lot carrying our hot-off-the-press copies. It seemed like such a strange way for it to end. The moment for which we had worked so hard and so long and there was no one around with whom to share it. Bullock dodged me when I tried to give him a hug. He saluted instead.

I thrashed in bed that night too exhausted to think clearly, too excited to sleep. I mentally reviewed every paragraph of the story and re-examined the evidence we'd amassed to back it up. I thought of all the things that could go wrong. I imagined all the possible outcomes.

I was still awake at 5:30 a.m. Sunday morning when I heard the thud of the Sunday *Charlotte Times* on my doorstep. I went to the door, got the paper, saw the headline, saw our story, fixed myself a cup of coffee, and sat down to read.

### Three Named in Unsolved Killing of 13-Year-Old
**By Matt Harper and Ronald L. Bullock**
*Charlotte Times* Staff Writers

Hirtsboro, S.C.—For more than 20 years, the killing of 13-year-old Wallace Sampson during civil rights unrest in this small Savannah River town has gone uninvestigated, unsolved and unpunished.

But after a three-month inquiry, the *Charlotte Times* has located two men who say they and a third person were involved in the killing. The three are:

• O. P. Pennegar Sr., the sole Hirtsboro town policeman at the time of the shooting who has since retired.

• William Bascom, a Ku Klux Klan member who became an informer for the South Carolina Law Enforcement Division (SLED).

• J. Rutledge Buchan, the magistrate at the time of the killing and now in Hirtsboro, a town of three thousand people 165 miles south of Charlotte.

Pennegar and Bascom have confirmed their role in the killing to reporters for the *Times*. Both said independently that Buchan was also involved.

To date, the *Times* has been unable to determine which of the three fired the fatal shot or why Wallace Sampson was selected as a victim.

Bascom told the *Times* he would supply that information and other details of the killing to authorities if he were granted immunity from prosecution. He said he was speaking now because he has a fatal disease and wants to die with a clear conscience. "It's been on my heart all these years," he said.

Pennegar has had a stroke and has difficulty speaking. But he also confirmed his involvement and expressed remorse.

Buchan is aware of the *Times* investigation but said he would not meet with reporters or respond to attempts by the *Times* to interview him for this story.

There is no statute of limitations on state charges involving murder. South Carolina judicial officials would not comment on whether they would reopen an investigation into the Sampson case based on the *Times* investigation.

Murder is not a federal crime and there is a statute of limitations on an 1879 law that makes it a federal crime for police or anyone else "acting under color of law" to deprive anyone of their civil rights. For that reason, U.S Justice Department officials told the *Times* they expected to take no action as a result of the *Times*'s investigation.

Wallace Sampson, a 13-year-old middle school student, was shot in the head shortly after midnight as he was walking home after spending the evening visiting his girlfriend, Vanessa Brown. Sampson was taken by Hirtsboro ambulance to the Medical University of South Carolina in Charleston where he was pronounced dead. An autopsy disclosed that he had been shot in the head with a deer rifle.

The killing followed a night of racial unrest in Hirtsboro, a poor rural community where all town officials are white but the population is 80 percent black. The unrest included a firebomb thrown at a building near where the shooting of Wallace Sampson occurred the next night.

Hirtsboro town records show that Magistrate Buchan owned the building.

Bascom said the killing was in retaliation for the firebombing but the *Times* found no indication that Wallace Sampson had any role in the firebombing or in the previous evening's racial unrest. He had no police record. "He was a sweet boy," said his mother, Etta Mae Sampson. "A sweet, sweet boy." *(Editor's Note: For a profile of Wallace Sampson, see Page 6.)*

Based on interviews and an extensive review of Hirtsboro town records, the *Times* found no evidence of any investigation into the killing by city, county or state officials. Pennegar, now disabled, has been succeeded by his son, who initially resisted the *Times*'s attempt to conduct an investigation.

As magistrate, Buchan was and is the town's top judicial officer.

Reached Saturday, Hirtsboro town clerk Patty Paysinger declined comment.

The *Charlotte Times* began looking into the killing of Wallace Sampson after it was contacted by Bradford Hall, 35. Hall is a Harvard-educated botanist whose family owns homes and a hunting preserve known as Windrow Plantation on the Savannah River near Hirtsboro. He had grown curious after hearing about the unsolved killing.

"It had poisoned Hirtsboro," Hall said when he met with the *Times*. "The knowledge of the crime hung over everything."

*Times* reporters found that more than 20 years after the shooting, the incident still polarizes the town, with many blacks convinced that whites were responsible and many whites convinced that Sampson had been killed "by one of his own," the result of black-on-black violence.

The events that led to the shooting of Wallace Sampson began the night before with civil unrest that swept through Hirtsboro, a no-stoplight town bisected by the Southern Railway Tracks. Before six squad cars carrying 24 county deputies intervened, a crowd of black youths threw rocks at the Hirtsboro town police cruiser and smashed a half dozen store windows.

Later, someone threw a firebomb against a single-story, tin-roofed building. The bomb burst into flames. Soot and charring still mark the spot on the building where it hit but the building failed to ignite. The person who threw the firebomb remains unknown.

The building housed a gas station/grocery store called De Sto which several Hirtsboro residents said had the reputation of taking unfair advantage of the black community.

"The community knew De Sto was ripping them off," the Reverend Clifford Grace told the *Times*. Grace is the pastor of the Mt. Moriah House of Prayer in Hirtsboro. "They just didn't have the ability to shop elsewhere."

But according to two Hirtsboro sources who asked that their

names not be used, the building also housed a secret second business, a brothel featuring black prostitutes who catered to temporary workers at the nearby Savannah River nuclear plant. One source said the brothel was a particular irritant to Hirtsboro's black community.

"It hurt to know what was going on," the source said about the brothel, adding that if gouging by De Sto had been the issue, "it'd have been firebombed long before."

*Times* reporters, along with Bradford Hall, examined the building in question and found indications of the secret brothel business.

Both businesses were apparently operated by Raeford Watson, a Ku Klux Klan member who was later convicted in state court of beating up civil rights marchers in Columbia. Watson suffered a heart attack the day following the firebombing and is known to have been in the hospital when the shooting of Wallace Sampson occurred. He has since died.

Bascom told the *Times* that he, Pennegar and Buchan talked about the shooting as a way to "keep the blacks in their place" and to retaliate for the firebombing which they believed caused Raeford Watson's heart attack.

He said that while he had been involved in the incident, he didn't fire the rifle that killed Sampson and hadn't expected anyone to die.

The *Times* learned about Bascom from a witness who saw him fleeing from the scene of the killing. Bascom lived near Hirtsboro at the time and worked at Ray's Amoco station.

According to South Carolina Solicitor Red McCallum, Bascom was a high-ranking official in South Carolina's Ku Klux Klan who was persuaded to become an informer for the South Carolina Law Enforcement Division (SLED).

"Billy Bascom was SLED's best source of information about what the Klan was up to," McCallum said. He said Bascom would alert officials to planned illegal Klan activities and then get arrested along with other Klansmen. Later, he would provide testimony at trial and receive leniency. In the case of the Klansmen who beat civil rights marchers in Columbia, Bascom provided testimony that helped convict Watson and two others.

Bascom "isn't the bad guy," McCallum said.

Bascom confirmed that he served as an informer while in the Klan. He said he told officials about his involvement in the Wallace Sampson killing but doesn't know why they never pursued the information.

"I told them everything," he said. "That wasn't the only case they never followed up on. Why they followed up on some and not on others is not for me to know. But I told them, all right. And they wrote it all down."

SLED officials told the *Times* the agency would not comment on Bascom's allegations or even confirm that he had been an informer.

The *Times* interviewed Bascom at his home not far from Hirtsboro. He said he consented to be interviewed because he no longer feared retaliation from former fellow Klansmen who would learn about his past as an informer. He told the *Times* he expected to die soon from cancer.

"I want to get right with Jesus," he said. "I've reached the point where I'm starting to think about cramming for the final exam."

The *Times* also interviewed O.P. Pennegar Sr., the Hirtsboro town police officer at the time of the Sampson shooting, who recently retired from the force. Though Pennegar has difficulty speaking, he was able to indicate his agreement when presented with Bascom's version of the Wallace Sampson killing.

Pennegar wept during the recounting of it.

The *Times* spoke with Magistrate Buchan during the course of its investigation into the shooting but *Times* reporters did not know about allegations of his involvement at the time.

Contacted last week by *Times* Columbia Bureau chief Henry Ashley and informed of the details of the upcoming story, Buchan said he was outraged by the *Times* conduct and would not meet with a reporter or respond to questions.

The decision about whether to pursue charges in the killing falls to South Carolina Solicitor McCallum who said he would read the story and then decide whether to conduct his own investigation.

I breathed a sigh of relief that no typographical gremlins had worked their way into our wording. The story was straightforward, dry, and emotionless. That's how the lawyers wanted it—with no hint of judgment. I had resisted but they were right. We had named the killers of Wallace Sampson. The facts of the story were damning enough.

I took the paper inside and spread it out on the table so I could examine the entire package—the timeline of events prepared by the art department, the diagram of the scene, the sidebar on Bradford Hall, Bullock's photos of De Sto and of Mrs. Sampson at Wallace's grave, a sidebar I was particularly proud of headlined "Wallace Sampson: Never Forgotten" and a box Walker had insisted on titled, "These Questions Remain Unanswered." In the box were two bullets:

• Who pulled the trigger?
• Why Wallace Sampson?

The box and the bullets were reminders that these and other questions still needed to be answered, along with the most important question: what happens next? But for the most part, I was pleased. We had done what we set out to do.

I turned to the short story I had written to try to tell readers something that would make them see Wallace Sampson not just as a victim of a civil rights murder or the subject of a newspaper's crusade but as a thirteen-year-old boy, as a mother's son.

## Wallace Sampson: Never Forgotten
### By Matt Harper and Ronald L. Bullock
*Charlotte Times* Staff Writers

Every day, Wallace Sampson's mother visits his grave.

Etta Mae Sampson leaves flowers and thinks about the copy of *Charlotte's Web* that she placed in Wallace's coffin, the book she had intended to give him for his birthday, before a slug from a deer rifle tore through his brain and killed him a few days before he turned 14.

And she prays, always the same prayer: "Lord, give me strength to trust that there will be justice in heaven."

At night Etta Mae Sampson goes to Wallace's room. She's kept it just the way it was when he died. Two pairs of pants and two shirts hung on nails. A baseball bat, its broken handle nailed and taped back together, in a corner. School pictures of puppy-love girlfriends tucked into a small mirror above his dresser. A poster of Hank Aaron. A basketball trophy inscribed "Wallace Sampson–Mr. Rebound" on a small table. Wallace was starting to grow tall like his daddy, she remembers.

Sometimes she awakes from dreams scared she will forget him. So she comes to this room and lies on his bed and picks up his shirt and she smells him.

"Each child has their own smell," she tells a visitor. "My worst time is when I become afraid that I will forget what he looked like and what he smelled like. I think that no one will remember him. So I look at his picture and I smell his shirt and I hold the trophy and I think to myself, I am holding the very thing that he held. And I tell him, 'You will never, ever, ever be forgotten.'"

I re-read the story and I stared at Wallace's picture—the picture of the Saran-wrapped photo on Mrs. Sampson's wall—until his eyes stared back through me, demanding that I not confuse his story with my complicated feelings involving Dad, Luke and Delana.

This isn't about them, his eyes told me. It is about me.

I held the newspaper up to the sky as if it were an offering. "Here it is, Wallace. This is for you."

# Chapter Twenty

For the next two weeks, I lived in two worlds, working in the newsroom until mid-afternoon, burning up the highway to the university to sit for a few hours with Dad each evening, driving home late to get ready to do it all over again. The best and the worst in one day.

Dad slept a lot while I just watched him. When he was awake, he was mostly lucid. But not always. One afternoon his eyes fluttered open. He pulled himself up and stared out of his window. "Who's that sitting in the tree?"

I followed his eyes to dark bare limbs of a water oak swaying in the wind outside. "I don't think there's anyone there. Do you see someone?"

"Yes, it appears to be Strom Thurmond," he croaked. Then he slid back down and fell asleep.

Each day, he seemed to grow smaller, to sink deeper into his pillows. Each day I told him I loved him and he said I love you back. Each day I told Delana death could not be far away. In contrast, the newsroom had never been more lively. News had broken out. Reporters and editors seemed to move more crisply, aware that the *Charlotte Times* itself was the center of attention. Something new developed almost every day.

Monday, the day after our investigation ran, *The Columbia News* published a story the general tone of which was that Judge Rutledge Buchan was a respected jurist who'd been blind-sided by long-disproved rumors dredged up by liberal, big-city reporters twisting the word of admitted deceivers and the mentally disabled.

The centerpiece was an exclusive interview in which Buchan denied any involvement in the Wallace Sampson killing and called the allegations the result of *Times* reporters "trying to be Woodward and Bernstein."

"I ought to be mad, but I'm sad," Buchan told *The News*. "They took advantage of a misguided young man from a fine family, a poor retired policeman who developed a mental problem and can't even talk, bless his heart, and an admitted liar."

He said in the story he planned to sue the *Charlotte Times* because the newspaper had libeled him and the whole town of Hirtsboro. "No one in Hirtsboro," he added, "has done more for the Negro race than I have."

"This is a damned outrage," Bullock roared when he read it.

"Yeah. You'd think in this day and time even Buchan'd be aware of his language."

Bullock looked puzzled. "I'm talking about the sons of bitches at *The News*. They didn't even ask us for comment."

Walker tried to calm him. "We just took a big South Carolina story from right under their noses. Of course, they're gonna try to knock us down."

"How about some basic journalistic integrity?" Bullock shot back.

Walker's unconcern didn't head off a long meeting with the *Times* lawyers. In the corner conference room with the Famous Front Pages, we plowed old ground about our sources while I occasionally amused myself by watching the parade of the paranoid and the curious passing by outside. I paid closer attention when the lawyers opened up a new line of inquiry to see if we had committed any acts during our reporting that might be construed as showing malice toward Judge Buchan.

"We can make a good case that as a judge, Buchan is a public figure," one of the lawyers explained. "So the only way we could be guilty of libel is if the story is wrong and we knew when we wrote it that it was wrong but we wrote it anyway out of malice."

"Did you do anything that would indicate malice?" Walker asked.

"No," Bullock said. "We're in good shape on that. I had to knock the lights out of one ol' boy down there, but I don't recall it being the judge."

"It was Brad's dad," I pitched in.

"Right," Bullock said as the lawyers looked on slack-jawed. "And it wasn't malice. I was defending my honor as a Southerner."

"I think we should move on," one of the lawyers said.

By the time we left the conference room an hour later, we had decided that fairness required that we record Buchan's denial, even though he would still not submit to an interview by any *Charlotte Times* staffer, including Columbia Bureau Chief Henry Ashley. Tuesday, despite our misgivings, we published the full version of what appeared in *The News*. But the story also included a statement from Walker saying that the *Charlotte Times* stood by its reporting and a quote from Reverend Grace expressing the community's thanks that Wallace Sampson's murder had not been forgotten.

With all the distractions and with me working half days, our efforts to answer the unanswered questions weren't making much headway. We didn't know who pulled the trigger and we didn't know how Wallace Sampson became the victim. Those were details that likely would come out only if a grand jury was impaneled and Billy Bascom were granted immunity.

Our best shot for a story, we figured, was one that pinned down what state officials had been told about the Wallace Sampson killing and when they had been told it. And once they had information, why had they never pursued it?

But officials from the State Law Enforcement Division said it would be days before they could tell us if they could even respond to inquiries relating to possible informants, and Solicitor Red McCallum's office said he would have no comment about whether he would initiate an investigation into the Wallace Sampson shooting.

"Usually, Red will trust me with most anything," Ashley, the Columbia Bureau chief who'd been assigned to dog McCallum, told me. "On this one, he won't even acknowledge that he's read your story."

The best we could do in terms of a quick follow-up was a piece that ran Wednesday saying that the South Carolina Judicial Standards Commission would investigate Buchan if it received a formal complaint about his conduct as a magistrate. The story went on to point out that, to date, no such complaint had been received.

The next day we caught a big break. *The Associated Press* bureau in Atlanta produced a version of the Sampson story for southeastern newspapers, television and radio stations, crediting the *Charlotte Times* for the investigation and incorporating Buchan's denial. Then, an editor on the *AP*'s general desk in New York decided to boil the Wallace Sampson story down to fifteen paragraphs and put it on the *AP*'s national wire. Because the story used Buchan's "Woodward and Bernstein" quote, the story mentioned Bullock and me by name. By Thursday evening, the Wallace Sampson story and Buchan's denial had gone nationwide.

Friday morning I was awakened by a call from Brad Hall saying that the *AP* version, with an additional paragraph highlighting his local connection, had appeared in the *New York Times*.

"You're going to be famous!" Delana said when I called her.

I enjoyed that thought for maybe thirty seconds—until the phone rang again. It was Marjorie Stark, the British-accented secretary to Warren Reich, the publisher.

"Matthew, I'm sorry to trouble you so early but Warren would like to meet with you, Ronald, and Walker immediately. Can you be available by nine?"

So the hammer falls, I thought. We'd flown successfully below Reich's radar for so long that I'd almost forgotten about him. But not quite. I understood from the beginning that our defiance of his orders to abandon the Wallace Sampson story was not likely to be overlooked, that our Judgment Day would come. Now, it had.

"Not famous," I told Delana when I called her back. "Fired."

WE GATHERED AT NINE in the anteroom outside Reich's office on the third floor, right next to the advertising department, the department that brought in the money, the place where most publishers feel most at home.

I searched the expression of the prim and proper Miss Stark for a clue to our fate. She betrayed nothing. "Mr. Reich will see you now."

We trudged in like schoolboys summoned to the principal's office after being caught smoking in the bathroom. The silver-haired Reich, dressed in a yellow tie, blue pinstripe shirt with a white collar, and the usual gold cufflinks, sat at his desk, studying spreadsheets. He didn't look up until Walker cleared his throat.

"Ah, yes," he said, as if he had suddenly remembered why we were there. With the back of his hand, he waved us to his couch. "Gentlemen, we have a problem. This Sampson story is getting quite a bit of attention. It's in this morning's *Washington Post*."

"The *New York Times*, too," I added.

"I'm assuming it's accurate," Reich said.

"Bullet proof," Walker answered.

"It had better be. *People* magazine called this morning. They want to do a story. I am disinclined to cooperate."

Bullock and I exchanged surprised glances. I could read his shrug: *People* magazine? Why them?

"I wish it were *Time* or *Newsweek* but I'm not sure I see what the problem is," Walker said.

Reich pulled his chair closer. "I'll tell you what the problem is. I will not be the black hat in this thing. I can see where this *People* story is going. Courageous reporters pursue the truth against the orders of their publisher. Murder is solved and justice prevails. I will not have it. I will not be the black hat." He stared hard at Walker.

"I don't believe that's the story," Walker said. "The fact is, whatever was said internally, the story got done. The right thing happened. Debates over the worth of stories happen all the time."

Bullock and I sat forward, surprised by Walker's uncharacteristic diplomacy.

Reich's jaw unclenched. "If asked, what would you say about my role in this Sampson thing?"

"That we're the kind of newspaper where this sort of journalism can happen." Walker looked at Bullock and me for confirmation. I followed Walker's lead and nodded. Bullock remained stone-faced.

The look of relief on Reich's face told me what I'd failed to perceive earlier. The national attention the Wallace Sampson story was receiving was protecting us. Reich no longer had the power either to prevent us from pursuing the Sampson story or to punish us for disobeying his orders to end our "ceaseless thrall." Not only that, we now had the ability to do serious damage to him by portraying him in the press as an impediment to the investigation. The balance of power had shifted.

"Do you think if we let *People* do the story, that I could be the one to be quoted saying that?" Reich asked.

"I think you're just the right person to say it," Walker said.

"Jesus, Walker, what a damn hypocrite," Bullock spat when we were outside the office. "You should have hammered him."

"Pardner," Walker smiled, "When you're holdin' the cards you want everyone to stay at the table. I walked in there thinking we're gonna get told to stop by and pick up our final paychecks. Instead, we're walking out with the publisher beggin' to be quoted in the national press supporting investigative journalism. We don't need to be hammerin' anyone. Besides, he's still the trail boss and I'm on the ride."

THE PEOPLE REPORTER and a photographer came a day earlier than scheduled, a day I'd taken off to visit Dad. Bullock drove them down to Hirtsboro and they spent the day shooting pictures and interviewing Brad at Windrow. Later that day, they flew back to New York. The next day, the *People* reporter interviewed me by phone.

At the University Hospital, Dad was still keeping up with the daily papers, although what used to take forty-five minutes now took all day. Friends and colleagues dropped by from time to time to visit and to pay their respects. He was awake to talk with fewer and fewer.

But more than once he surprised me. He was snoring as two visiting colleagues from the law school fell into a bedside discussion of English Common Law and its relationship to the Magna Carta, which was, one of them said, written and agreed to in 1216.

"1215," my father corrected, suddenly awake. "June. Runnymede." He closed his eyes and was soon snoring again.

When I got to work the next Friday, an advance copy of *People* was already circulating. I joined Carmela Cruz and her colleagues on the news desk as they dissected the four-page spread.

"Justice on Trial in South Carolina" read the main headline. "Yankee Blueblood and Investigative Reporters Say They've Cracked Old Civil Rights Case."

I scanned the photos as Carmela turned the page: black children at play on Jefferson Davis Boulevard in downtown Hirtsboro; Brad Hall in a hunting jacket with Tasha and Maybelle beside the fireplace at his home at Windrow; the widely-circulated photo of the photo of Wallace Sampson; a head shot from the church directory of Rutledge Buchan; a photo of Bullock looking tough in a trench coat posed at the site of the shooting in front of De Sto; a simple mugshot of me, the one from my press pass.

"*People* magazine!" sighed Carmela. "The depths to which we have sunk!"

I took a minute to read the story and captions. The writer, Gerry Hostetler, had done a good job. She got the facts right. She quoted the publisher. She was generous in her praise of me. "He's carrying on the tradition," she wrote, describing me as "the third generation of a great family of journalists."

But clearly, Bullock had made the biggest impression. "His voice comes from the bottom of a pit all the way up through the gravel, and by the time it hits your ears it has settled into a growl," Hostetler wrote of him. Indeed, one of her main angles was the unlikely partnership between the Yankee, Harvard-educated, botanist, patrician Bradford Hall and the washed up (she wrote "throwback") street-wise, pistol-packing, redneck (she wrote "Southern") reporter Ronnie Bullock.

Even among the pictures, Bullock's was the biggest of all.

Of course, when a producer for Ted Koppel and *Nightline* called the following Monday, Bullock was who they wanted on the air.

The next day Reich was quoted in a story for *The Columbia Journalism Review* saying that Ronnie Bullock "was one of the finest investigative reporters ever to walk through the doors of the *Charlotte Times*."

"Can you believe that?" Bullock said when he read the quote. "Two months ago I was a politically incorrect has-been stuck on the night shift and qualified only to write obits. Now, I'm the best journalist on the planet, not to mention a damn TV star. Matt, I gotta thank you."

Late in the week, Walker announced that once the Wallace Sampson investigation was over, Bullock would become a permanent member of the dayside projects team.

"Let the fancy pants journalism school graduates chomp on that," Bullock gloated.

I couldn't have been happier for journalism or for Bullock. His rehabilitation was complete.

As for me, it was another week of travel back and forth over the river Styx. Though unconscious most of the time, Dad was still hanging on to dear life.

ON A BRIGHT and sunny Monday afternoon in March, the first day of the year that it felt and smelled like spring, Dad let go.

I reached his hospital room just as two orderlies showed up pushing the gurney to take him away.

"Give us a minute," the hospice nurse told them. As Dad would have wanted, I held the door and followed her in. A sheet on the bed outlined his impossibly withered body. Even though I knew it was coming, even though I'd gotten to the point where I had wished for his death, and even as difficult as it had been sometimes, I couldn't imagine life without him. I pulled the sheet back.

One last time, I buried my face in his chest. I took his cold, stiff hand, already turning purple and blue, lifted it to my face, and wiped the tears from my eyes.

I called Walker from a phone in the room reserved for grieving relatives.

"He's gone."

"I'm sorry, Big Shooter. He was one of the all-time greats. You and a lot of other people are going to miss him."

"I know."

"It was thoughtful of him to go out on our news cycle."

I laughed. "He probably planned it that way." I thought for a moment. "If there's going to be an obit, I'd like to write it."

I could sense his unease. "Too much of a conflict. You can't be objective. I've asked Ronnie to do it."

I thought of Bullock and me cranking out obit after obit in the nook of Brad and Lindsay's kitchen.

"He'll do a good job," Walker said.

"I'll tell you what. He can write it. Let me edit it."

Back in the office later that day, that's just what I did. When I was done, we gave the story to *The Associated Press* which deemed it worthy of the national wire. The next day *The Detroit Free Press* and the other papers where Dad had worked played the story on the front page. Even the *New York Times* ran fifteen paragraphs on their famous obituary page. In Charlotte, the *Times* played the story and a mugshot on the front of the local section, just below the fold. It was the right call, given that my father hadn't ever worked at the *Times*.

And as it turns out, Bullock was the right choice. He got all the facts right and he put in a paragraph that I would never have felt comfortable writing.

"As the son of the late respected publisher Lucas Harper Sr., Lucas Harper Jr. was the heir to a superb journalistic tradition," the second paragraph of the obit said. "As the father of *Charlotte Times* reporter Matt Harper, he died having successfully passed on that great legacy."

For the first time together in the newspaper, grandfather, father and son.

The university's memorial service—"A Celebration of the Life of Lucas Harper Jr."—took place at noon a week later in University Chapel, a huge on-campus stone cathedral with gargoyles and stained glass meant to recall a time when churches were as much the center of academic inquiry as of worship.

Instead of waiting in the back and making an entrance after everyone was seated, Delana and I stood on the chapel steps and greeted the parade of people who came to pay their respects and to say good-bye—scores of colleagues from his newspaper days, dozens of fellow faculty members,

students present and past, friends of Dad's, and friends of mine and
Delana's. A brisk breeze sent bilious white clouds scudding across the sky,
plunging us from light into shade in an instant and causing the arrivals
to alternately don and remove their sunglasses.

Walker and Bullock led a delegation from the paper. David Riley, the
reporter from the student paper, made it a point to shake my hand.

"He was the best teacher I ever had," he said. "He made me pas-
sionate about reporting."

"He had that effect."

"I hope you're not upset about my story. I thought long and hard
about how your father would have handled the situation. He trusted in
the truth."

I smiled. "You learned well. He said you did a great job."

I was surprised to see Glenn Hudson, the editor of *The Hirtsboro
Reporter*, arrive with his son Jimmy.

"I appreciate it, but you didn't need to come," I told him.

"How could I *not* come? I took your father's media law course. He's
the reason I went into this business."

I watched Brad and Lindsay park their Volvo and cross the street
holding hands. Delana hugged them both.

"I've heard so much about you," she said to Lindsay. "Thank you
for everything you've done for Matt."

Lindsay blushed and said, "I'm so sorry for the occasion but I'm so
glad to meet you. I want you to know, we think Matt is a hero."

"I think so, too. And you're married to one."

The chapel bell rang the first five notes of the university fight song
and then began the slow toll of noon. A long blue Buick pulled to the
curb. Reverend Clifford Grace unfolded himself from the driver's seat
and opened the rear door. Mary Pell emerged wearing a lavender dress
and matching broad-brimmed lavender hat festooned with fabric irises.
With one hand on the rail and one arm supported by Reverend Grace
she struggled up the stone chapel steps.

I hugged them both and introduced them to Delana. "Let's go in,"
I said. "Sit up front with Delana and me."

An unlikely foursome, we walked up the aisle as the packed congregation rose in unison. I looked from face to face, overwhelmed by the number of people who seemed to have been touched one way or another by my father. As the organist finished Bach's ethereal "Adagio in A Minor," we entered the first pew and sat down—first Reverend Grace, then Mary Pell, then Delana and me.

The chancellor of the university, a vigorous, long-strided, sixty-year-old whose habitual bowtie accentuated his height, ascended the pulpit.

"Lucas Harper Jr. was a man accustomed to letting people know what he wanted," he began. "He was also a man who did not fear the truth. So it will come as no surprise to you that he faced what was coming and made his wishes known." Scattered chuckles.

"At Lucas's request, this service will consist of a few great hymns and some brief words about his life from his dear friend and colleague Dr. Archibald Murphy. Since Lucas is not here to edit me, I will also add a few words of my own."

More chuckles. The chancellor adjusted his glasses. "Lucas knew that the world was too dangerous a place for anything but the truth. He exemplified the *sine qua non* of teachers: it is not what they teach, but what they are. Let us join together in praising God for the life of Lucas Harper Jr."

The great hymns followed: "A Mighty Fortress Is Our God," by Martin Luther. "The Battle Hymn of the Republic," the anthem from the Civil War. When we got to the pause before the "Glory, Glory, Hallelujah" chorus, I heard someone in the pew behind me say, "Hit it!" It was a Dad trademark and it buckled Delana and me over in laughter.

When the chaplain announced "O God Our Help in Ages Past," I could almost hear Dad say, "Isaac Watts. Probably better known for inventing the steam engine."

I was fine until we got to the lines: *Time like an ever-rolling stream bears all her sons away./ They die forgotten as the dream flies at break of day.*

Then I sobbed. Delana squeezed my hand.

Then Archibald Murphy ascended the pulpit. A tall, red-haired Southerner with a booming voice that commanded attention, Murphy had joined the journalism faculty the same year as my father. The editor of *The Saturday Evening Post* in the days when its weekly arrival was eagerly awaited in hundreds of thousands of households across America, he was a magazine editor's editor, equally comfortable with news and fashion, with journalists and celebrities. He and Dad had bonded at the university, two giants retired from the day-to-day fray but delighted to be paid to tell war stories and to find and nurture the heirs to the traditions in which they believed.

Murphy stood at the pulpit until the congregation grew silent. He put on his reading glasses, withdrew a sheaf of papers from his pocket, and carefully arranged them. Then he put his glasses away and began to speak, never looking at the papers again.

"Lucas Harper Jr. edited our lives and attitudes and made them crisper, clearer, more logical and more worthwhile," he began. He recalled Dad working with students on the university newspaper, "a wreath of cigarette smoke around his head, his tie loosened, cutting, shaping, chopping, flicking out ideas, concepts—using his mind like a blade, like a gimlet.

"You could see him on his feet, tracking a point. He could be oblivious to everything but getting at the truth. It was as simple and unacceptable as that, he was a fool for the truth. Needless to say, he never worked in very heavy traffic." The congregation roared.

Murphy reminded us that Dad had no patience with individuals or institutions that "were violating the rightness of things."

"Lucas could always find the clear and the sound reason for doing the right thing," he said. "At Christmastime, he turned his newspapers' readers into a community and a family. Yet he always seemed slightly startled by the good things that he did. I think there is no more fitting place to honor his memory than in the chapel of a university. Good-bye."

At that, the congregation rose as one for two solid minutes of applause.

In the sunlight outside, Delana and I fought through the crowd of people who wanted to talk and caught up with Brad and Lindsay just as they reached their Volvo.

"It's good to see you together," I said.

Lindsay offered a somewhat sheepish smile. "Funny how the things that drive you crazy about a person become endearing when they're gone. We seem to take for granted the ones we love the most."

"There are always bumps in the road," Brad said. Then he invited me down to Windrow just to get away when I was ready.

I hesitated but like a good fencer, Brad didn't wait for my counter. "No reporting. We're just going to float down the river and see the sights. It'll do you good."

I promised to take him up on it.

Delana and I stayed on the steps until all the mourners had drifted away. A woman who was familiar but whom I couldn't place was one of the last.

"Thank you for coming," I said.

"I'm Mary, your dad's hospice nurse. He was a wonderful man. So smart. I really enjoyed him." She reached into her purse and pulled out a folded piece of paper. "He kept this in the pocket of his pajamas. I wanted you to have it."

I took the piece of paper and unfolded it. It was a section of the *People* magazine article, the part where it mentioned me.

"He was so proud of you," she said.

On the way home, Delana asked if I'd spend the night at The Farmlet. The next morning, after the sun had burned off the dew, we walked hand-in-hand to a thicket of blackberry bushes, near a spot brightened by a clump of daffodils and sheltered by tall pines.

I opened the plastic bag I carried and scattered Dad's ashes among the small shoots of new green growth that pushed through the brown straw thatch, forever tying him and us to that place.

I picked four daffodils and arranged them in a cross on the ground— one flower each from Mom, from Delana, from Luke and from me.

# Chapter Twenty-One

The day before Palm Sunday I drove the Honda through light traffic at well below the posted speed limit on the familiar route to Hirtsboro and reached the white-frame Mt. Moriah House of Prayer just before 9:00 a.m.

I parked off the sandy street a half block away and watched from my car as a handful of people knelt on the ground creating signs with stakes, poster board and paint. A charter bus pulled up, its diesel engine rumbling as dozens of people filed out.

I pulled out my reporter's notebook and jotted an entry, "Charter Bus. 44 blacks. 11 whites."

It wasn't how I'd planned to spend the weekend. But on my first day back in the office after we'd scattered Dad's ashes, Nancy Atkinson had brought me a Manila envelope labeled *Murders–Wallace Sampson*.

"I decided to make him his own clip file so there's a record of the real stories," she'd explained. "Real clips as they appeared in the newspaper, not computer printouts. Just like the old days. Remember? The way the story started out."

The most recent clips were Ronnie Bullock pieces documenting the growing calls for an official investigation into the killing of Wallace Sampson. One in particular, a four-paragraph brief, had caught my attention. Reverend Clifford Grace had announced a "Justice for Wallace Sampson March" from Hirtsboro to the Savannah County Courthouse ten miles away. The march would undoubtedly be the first organized civil rights protest in the history of Hirtsboro. I knew immediately that I had to be there.

Across the street, the front door of the Mt. Moriah House of Prayer swung open and three men led by Reverend Grace descended the steps carrying a large wooden cross on their shoulders. I recognized it as the cross behind the altar, the Lynching Cross. They carried it to a wooden shed behind the church, moved it inside and propped it upright against a wall. When they were done, Grace locked the shed door.

I got out of the Honda and walked through the crowd that had swelled to more than one hundred. I spotted Columbia bureau chief Henry Ashley interviewing someone from the NAACP bus. He saw me and waved me over.

"Walker told me you were coming," he said. "He said it's fine to double-cover it. But only one of us gets a byline. He says he can't have the publisher thinking we have so many reporters that we can send two of them to a South Carolina civil rights march. Even if it is this one."

I caught up with Reverend Grace who was with Brad Hall.

"Good of you to come," Grace said.

Brad asked, "You reporting or marching?"

"Reporting. Journalistic objectivity and all that." I nodded to the shed. "What's with the cross?"

"Church has a plaster problem," Grace said. "The cross needs to come down for a couple weeks while repairs are made."

"Too bad it had to happen at Easter."

"Oh," he grinned. "I imagine we'll get by."

The march got underway an hour later. Walking under a banner which read "JUSTICE FOR WALLACE SAMPSON" and held on either side by the men who had helped Grace carry the cross, Reverend Grace, Brad Hall, and Etta Mae Sampson led one hundred fifty participants up the street toward the middle of Hirtsboro.

I copied some of the signs: *SC NAACP March for Justice; Justice for Wallace Sampson; No Justice No Peace.* A black youth I judged to be no more than thirteen, the age Wallace had been, carried one with a more defiant message: *Indict the Killers.*

I got in the Honda, zipped up a side street to the center of town, and parked by the railroad tracks as the marchers turned onto Jefferson

Davis Boulevard. White faces stared unblinking from the windows of the Farmers & Mechanics Insurance Agency, the Great Southern Auto Supply and Appliance Store, the International Feed & Seed, Second Time Around, Classen's Clothes, in fact from the windows of almost every business except the First Bank of Hirtsboro which was only open Monday, Wednesday, and Friday. The door to the offices of *The Hirtsboro Reporter* opened. Glenn Hudson and his son emerged to the marchers' cheers. They fell in at the end of the line.

A truck from a TV station in Columbia parked beside me. A cameraman hopped out, shot sixty seconds of tape, and sped away.

I drove a mile down the highway, got out of the Honda, and waited for the march to catch up. Cars whizzed past, spawning whirlwinds of dust and grit that stung my skin and irritated my eyes. Henry Ashley parked beside me and we retreated to the edge of a ditch further away from the road. I studied the debris while we waited—beer cans, a hubcap, shotgun shells, a golf ball, a road sign, cancelled checks, and other paper in various stages reverting to pulp.

With the long-legged Reverend Grace setting the pace, the marchers stretched more than a quarter mile by the time the first group reached us. I studied their faces and made notes as they passed—Grace looking confident, even light-hearted through his salt-and-pepper beard; the NAACP marchers from Columbia looking like determined veterans; the members of the congregation of the Mt. Moriah House of Prayer, energized, less tentative than when they had started.

A faded red pickup slowed. "Go back to Africa!" the driver, an angry-faced middle-aged white man, shouted.

"Damn South Carolina," I said to Ashley.

"You know, you're as bad as the racists," he scolded. "Don't stereotype South Carolina. Reverend Grace. Mrs. Sampson. Glenn Hudson. All these marchers. These people are South Carolina, too."

"Thank you for what you did," Mrs. Sampson shouted.

All my reportorial instincts told me marching was wrong. Reporters are compelled to demonstrate objectivity, to never betray a particular point of view even though they usually have them. A reporter does not participate.

But my human instincts and the lessons of my father told me something else—that the world is too dangerous a place for anything but the truth.

This march wasn't about politics or race or points of view or anything that ought to worry a reporter. It was about the pursuit of the truth. Truth does not have two sides. Truth does not keep to itself. Truth does not frown on commitment.

I believed in the truth of what we had written and I was willing to be a fool for it.

I tucked my notebook into my pocket and joined the crowd in the street.

# Chapter Twenty-Two

At a Friday afternoon press conference in Columbia almost three weeks later, Solicitor Red McCallum announced that a South Carolina grand jury had indicted Magistrate J. Rutledge Buchan and former police chief Olen Pennegar Sr. for first degree murder in the killing of Wallace Sampson.

The indictment named William A. "Possum" Bascom as an unindicted co-conspirator.

Tipped by Henry Ashley who had gotten an off-the-record call from McCallum, Bullock and I drove down the night before. We arrived early at the South Carolina Department of Justice and claimed folding chairs in the front row as reporters and cameramen from outlets ranging from the *New York Times* to *The Hirtsboro Recorder* jostled for space behind us.

"The actions of this grand jury bring an end to a painful chapter in the history of South Carolina," McCallum read from a statement as cameras clicked and automatic film advances whirred. "We hope this provides closure for the family and serves notice that the state of South Carolina is committed to the redress of grievances and to justice for all of its citizens."

McCallum paused to wipe sweat from his forehead with a red bandana. "I'd like to say a special thanks to Hirtsboro's own Bradford Hall, and especially to the *Charlotte Times*. Without their investigative efforts, this case would not have been solved and we would not be here today."

"Have the defendants been arrested?" the *New York Times* reporter asked.

"Agents from the State Law Enforcement Division served warrants at the defendants' respective homes and took both men into custody within the last hour."

"Where are they now?" the *Times* reporter followed up.

"Because of his position, we believe it would be unsafe for Judge Buchan to be housed in the general prison or jail population. In addition, Mr. Pennegar has medical needs. Because of those factors, both men will be housed in the state prison hospital at least until their bond hearing on Monday."

Bullock stood up. "Mr. Solicitor, can you tell us what was the connection between Wallace Sampson and the defendants? What was the motive? Also, who pulled the trigger?"

"That will come out at trial."

Working from Henry Ashley's office, Bullock and I produced the indictment story for the *Charlotte Times's* first edition with less than an hour to spare.

Walker congratulated us on a job well done. "You got all the key stuff up high. Carmela's taking it for the main story on the front page in every edition. We're ridin' this hoss all the way to the barn!"

For later editions, we added mini-profiles of Buchan, Pennegar, Bascom and of Wallace Sampson. For the weekend, we cranked out a recap—known in the trade as a situationer—that brought occasional readers up to date and pointed out two of the questions that still remained unanswered: Who actually fired the deer rifle? Why was Wallace Sampson selected as the victim?

"We're not done until we get that stuff figured out," Walker said as he edited the story. "Maybe you'll learn something at the bond hearing."

Just like old times, Bullock arrived before dawn Monday morning. The Dodge had been repaired and sparkled with a new paint job. An invoice for the work sat on the front seat. "I figured I'd give the bill to Rut Buchan," he explained. "I'll bet he knows how to get it to the guy who rammed us."

I called Delana before we left.

"Why so early?" she mumbled. "The hearing's not until 10:00 a.m."

"Ronnie. His stomach has an appointment at the Hungry Tum-my."

After breakfast, we drove to the courthouse and followed the freshly waxed pink marble hallways to the courtroom of The Honorable R. Horace Williams.

Nine heads turned to face us: Reverend Grace, Mrs. Sampson, Brad Hall, and Vanessa Brown in the front row; Glenn Hudson and a reporter from the *Associated Press* one row back; three beefy deputy sheriffs in folding chairs near the jury box. Bullock and I slid in beside the report-ers. As I prepared to take notes Red McCallum entered and set up shop at a wide table on the left. Two men in suits followed, unclicking thick briefcases on a table to the right.

"The defense," Bullock whispered.

J. Rutledge Buchan, wearing an orange jumpsuit, was escorted in by a deputy. Another deputy pushed a wheelchair holding Olen Pennegar Sr. Dressed in his Hirtsboro police uniform, Olen Pennegar Jr. followed close behind.

"All rise!" a bailiff commanded. "This court is now in session. The Honorable R. Horace Williams presiding." All rose except Pennegar who sat in his wheelchair, swallowed by an oversize jumpsuit.

Judge Williams, a black man in his forties with gold wire-rimmed glasses, breezed through the side door in black robes and sat down at the bench.

"Be seated. Counsel, please identify yourselves for the record."

McCallum introduced himself, followed by the defense lawyers—sil-ver-haired and distinguished Lewis Gasque for Judge Buchan and the much younger Ed Williams representing Olen Pennegar.

"Let the record show there is no relation," Judge Williams noted to chuckles. "At least so far as Brother Williams and I know." The lawyer blushed.

The judge began by noting that this was not a trial, merely a hearing on a defense motion to free the defendants on bail. Only two questions were relevant, whether the defendant was a flight risk and whether releas-ing the defendant posed a threat to the safety of the community.

Pennegar's young lawyer argued that Pennegar was physically unable to be a flight risk or a danger to anyone. The courtroom stirred when he added, "Solicitor McCallum will confirm that he and I are in discussions about a possible plea bargain for Mr. Pennegar in exchange for his future testimony at any trial. We ask that he be released on his own recognizance."

Gasque shifted in his chair and whispered to Buchan who shook his head. I inferred that Pennegar's potential deal with the state was news to them.

Then the fireworks began. McCallum stood and said he wouldn't oppose the motion to free Pennegar on bail or on his own recognizance. However, he said, "The state takes a very different position on the other defendant. In Judge Buchan's case, we will be seeking capital punishment."

A murmur went through the courtroom. "Damn!" the *Associated Press* reporter whispered. He scrambled out of our row and raced out the back doors to file a bulletin.

Vanessa Brown turned to Mrs. Sampson. "What's that mean?"

"The death penalty," she said.

Wide-eyed, Vanessa Brown clasped her hand to her mouth.

"Order!" Judge Williams commanded.

A red-faced Gasque jumped to his feet. "Your honor, that's preposterous! These charges are the result of a fanciful collaboration between a known liar and reporters trying to sell newspapers. You know Judge Buchan. I know Judge Buchan. Everything he has is tied up in this community. He is innocent. He is hardly a flight risk."

The judge turned to McCallum. "Is the state alleging the defendant's involvement in any other criminal activities?"

"No, your honor."

Judge Williams looked skeptical. "And the state opposes any bail?"

"The state does."

"That's outrageous!" Gasque interjected.

"Sit down!" Judge Williams commanded.

"Solicitor, I'm going to have to ask you to provide some support for your allegations. Is the state prepared to offer evidence?"

"Yes, your honor."

"Proceed."

"Your honor, the state would like to present testimony from William A. Bascom."

The bailiff opened the side door. Vanessa Brown shifted nervously. The white-haired Billy Bascom entered, his sharp nose pointed down and to the left, his beady black eyes staring sideways. He stuck close to the rail separating the spectators from the business end of the courtroom, like a possum trying to avoid the light, as he climbed to the witness stand.

McCallum began by leading Bascom through his career in the Klan and his decision to become an informant.

"Did there come a time when during your activities with the Klan that you got to know Olen Pennegar and Rutledge Buchan?"

"Yes. They were members. And I also knew them because Judge Buchan was a judge and he owned De Sto that Raeford Watson ran. Olen Pennegar was the police chief."

"And you were all in the Klan?"

Gasque stood up. "Objection your honor. They are not charged with being members of the Klan."

"Sustained," Judge Williams said. "Mr. McCallum, where are you headed?"

McCallum ignored the question but hurried up. "Mr. Bascom, on the night in question did you have the occasion to be playing poker with any of the defendants?"

"Yes, sir. With both of them."

"Where?"

Bascom reached for his shirt pocket and pulled out a cigarette. He was groping in his suit jacket pocket for his lighter when he realized where he was.

"In Town Hall. We was drinking and playing poker while we was standing guard against the blacks. They'd about tore up the town the night before. Broke some windows. Somebody threw a firebomb at

De Sto. Judge Buchan was pretty upset about it."

"Objection!" Gasque shouted. "He couldn't know Buchan's mental state."

"Sustained."

McCallum plowed ahead. "Mr. Bascom, did Judge Buchan say anything about the firebomb?"

"He said he was pissed off about it. He said he was losing a lot of money because the blacks were scaring away the jumpers."

"Jumpers?"

"The boys from the bomb plant who'd come for the hookers Raeford kept in the back. Raeford said that's where the big money was. He ran the hookers and De Sto for Rut Buchan."

"Sustained," Judge Williams said, not waiting for the objection. "Mr. McCallum, please get to the point."

McCallum continued, "The judge told you he was upset because the activities of the blacks had cut his revenue from the grocery and from the prostitution operation, is that correct?"

Bascom pressed his hands together. "Yes. That and he said the firebomb had caused Raeford Watson to have a heart attack. He said he was angry about that, too."

"Mr. Bascom, did the defendant say anything else about the firebomb?"

"Yes. He said, 'Just like a damn nigger to build one that don't go off.'"

Judge Williams cleared his throat.

"During the poker game, did the defendant offer an opinion about what should be done about the firebomb?"

"He said we needed to keep the niggers in their place, that we couldn't let them think they could get away with something like that. He said it threatened the whole town, not just him."

"Did he suggest a method—" McCallum made a show of consulting his notes– "for 'keeping the niggers in their place'?"

"He said there needed to be a killing."

"Did he say who needed to be killed?"

"No. He said we should just kill the first nigger to walk past De Sto after midnight."

Mrs. Sampson wept.

Reverend Grace took her hands. There was a look of rage on his face I had never seen before. Angry murmurs rolled through the back of the room.

"Get that quote exactly," Bullock whispered to me.

"Order!" said Judge Williams.

"And how did you decide who would do the killing?"

"We played a hand of poker. Me, Pennegar, and Buchan. To decide who would be the shooter and who would be lookouts."

"And the loser would be the one to pull the trigger."

"No. The winner."

The air went out of the courtroom. A chorus of groans and an outraged "No!" erupted from behind us. Even Judge Williams seemed staggered.

"Order!" the judge commanded.

McCallum took a deep breath and asked, "And who won the hand?"

Bascom looked surprised. "Why, Judge Buchan. Four of a kind beat a full house."

More murmurs from the crowd.

"Then what happened?"

"Midnight came and Rut got his deer rifle from the trunk of his car. Olen said he wanted to go home. He said he thought Rut had been bluffing."

"That's what he was trying to say," I whispered to Bullock. "Bluffing.'"

McCallum said, "Please continue, Mr. Bascom."

"Rut said it was fine by him, just as long as Olen kept his mouth shut. Then the judge set up in the woods across the road. I hid in some bushes down the street. I waited until midnight. I saw someone walking down the road. I could tell it was a black. I whistled, like we'd planned. A minute later, I heard the shot from where Rut was standing. The person fell. I took off running." He reached into his pocket for another cigarette then put it back. "I didn't know it was a kid until the next day."

"On a subsequent occasion, did you talk to Buchan about that?"

"I did."

"What was his response?"

"He said, 'Just another nigger we won't have to worry about growing up.' "

Sobs exploded from the front row. This time, there was no gavel.

When the courtroom quieted, McCallum said, "We have no other witnesses, your honor."

Judge Williams cleared his throat. After a pause, he said, "Before I rule I would like to hear from Mrs. Sampson on the question of whether the defendants pose a threat if released on bail. Please direct Mrs. Sampson to the stand."

All eyes followed Etta Mae Sampson. Clutching a white handkerchief and wearing her purple Sunday dress, she walked to the front of the courtroom, her heels clicking on the marble floor. She placed her hand on the Bible, took the oath, and sat straight-backed in the witness chair. "Mrs. Sampson, I have only one question," Judge Williams said kindly. "Judge Buchan has been charged with killing your son. Would you be in fear if he were free on bail?"

"No, sir."

"You're not afraid he might kill you?"

"He might. But I do not fear man. Only God."

The Judge smiled. "Mrs. Sampson, you're a trusting woman. How does Wallace's father feel about the question?"

"I have no way of knowing."

"Is he here today?"

"No, sir."

"Where is he?"

I waited for her to say that Wallace's father was dead. Instead she twisted her handkerchief and stared at the judge.

Judge Williams leaned toward the witness box. "Mrs. Sampson . . ."

"I . . . don't wish to say . . ." she whispered. Her eyes pleaded for help.

Bullock shot me a look that asked, "What the hell is going on?" I was starting to have an idea but this wasn't the time to tell him.

"Let me remind you, Mrs. Sampson, that you swore to tell the truth," the judge said. "Where is Wallace's father?"

Mrs. Sampson looked at the spectators, then at the judge, then at the Bible on the corner of the witness stand.

"At Windrow . . ."

"He works there?" the judge asked.

She took a deep breath and I could see her strengthen. "No. He lives there."

"So Wallace's father is . . ."

"Mr. Everett Hall."

"What the hell!" the *Associated Press* reporter said as he vaulted out of his seat for the second time. "I'll be damned," Bullock whispered. In the front row, Brad Hall sat stunned. Vanessa Brown wrapped her arms around him. At the defense table, Rut Buchan paled and slumped in his chair, deflating like a punctured blow-up toy.

The courtroom roar quieted when the spectators realized Mrs. Sampson was continuing. She uncrumpled her handkerchief and smoothed it across her lap, carefully adjusting the corners so that it was even on all sides. She looked straight ahead, as if she were staring into the past.

"He raped me," she said evenly. "We didn't call it that then. But that's what it was. He'd been shooting birds and drinking. He came to the Big House where I was working. I remember what he said. He said, 'Why pay for brown sugar at De Sto when you can get it in the kitchen for free?' I never told anyone, even when I found I was pregnant. It made no matter. I never loved my Wallace any less. God wouldn't have given him to me in the way that He did unless Wallace was something special."

Less than an hour after the hearing ended, Judge Williams ordered

Pennegar released on his own recognizance.

In the matter of Buchan, Judge Williams ruled that, "The heinousness of the crime and the fact that the state is seeking the death penalty implies a flight risk. However, given Judge Buchan's history and ties to the community, a very high bail and electronic monitoring is not unreasonable." He set the bond at one million dollars.

Late that afternoon, having put up one hundred thousand dollars cash and assigning title to some of his real estate to cover the rest, Buchan emerged from the courthouse, his orange prison jump suit replaced by gray slacks, white shirt, red silk tie, and blue blazer. He seemed to have recovered his poise. I wrote the words "unruffled," "taciturn," and "military bearing" in my notebook as he walked quickly toward his car. Bullock and I fell in behind him, followed by a gaggle of other reporters.

Bullock asked, "Judge Buchan, do you have any comment?" Buchan ignored the question, climbed into his car and started the engine. He lowered the driver's side window. "My comment," he said calmly, "is that I hope you gentlemen have a pleasant evening."

We filed our story from a phone at the courthouse. Learning who had pulled the trigger and how Wallace Sampson had become the victim answered the biggest remaining questions about the case. But the biggest news was the allegation that Everett Hall had committed rape as a young man—and that Wallace Sampson was the result. Our story devoted as much space to that as it did to the outcome of the bail hearing.

"It explains a lot of things," Bullock observed. "Everett Hall rapes a black woman and has an illegitimate son—a problem he thought was conveniently buried when Wallace Sampson happened to get shot. Then we come along and he does everything he can to stop us, including calling in his chips with the governor. Make a note to check if there's a statute of limitation on rape."

"More South Carolina stories," I said as I wrote. "Reich will be thrilled."

I had just finished when a deputy ran breathless into the courthouse.

"Holy shit!" he yelled. "Holy shit! Holy shit! Buchan shot himself.

Put the gun in his mouth at his family plot at the cemetery and pulled the trigger. One of the cemetery attendants found him."

"My God, how awful!" a woman said.

"And there's a fire at the church. All hell's breaking loose!"

We sprinted to the Dodge. With Bullock driving, we made Hirtsboro in record time and pushed through the crowd that had gathered on the street by the Mt. Moriah House of Prayer.

The flames didn't come from the church but from the shed behind it. We watched for a few minutes as the fire roared higher. Then, the shed's roof fell in, sending a cascade of sparks to the sky. A wall collapsed. The shed's interior boiled in flames and in a few minutes most of its contents were consumed– all except the Lynching Cross, which remained propped against one wall, bright flames eating away at each of its sections.

I walked over to where Mary Pell and Reverend Grace were standing.

"Praise God," Reverend Grace said.

Mary Pell smiled. "This time it worked."

# Epilogue

Assistant Managing Editor Bob DeCaprio took the call when the Pulitzer Prize committee phoned with the word that the *Charlotte Times* had won the Gold Medal for Public Service for the Wallace Sampson investigation.

A roar went up from all corners following his announcement over the newsroom public address system. Ronnie Bullock, I, and everyone else at the *Charlotte Times* had just achieved the pinnacle of journalism.

Bullock ran over to my desk and jumped into my arms, like Yogi Berra after Don Larsen's no-hitter. "I can't believe it," he roared. "We won the big one!" Before I could answer, we were surrounded by a cheering mob of reporters, editors and photographers. Other *Charlotte Times* employees—press operators, ad sales people, secretaries—flooded into the newsroom from their offices in the building. Out of the corner of my eye, I saw Fred Drake snapping pictures.

Walker Burns climbed atop his desk and raised his hands for quiet. "All I want to say is thank you. Thank you to Ronnie and to Matt. Thank you for giving us one of the greatest days of our lives."

Another roar went up from the crowd and then, "Ron-nie! Ron-nie! Ron-nie" until Bullock climbed to the top of the desk and waved. More cheers. Then, "Har-per! Har-per! Har-per!" until I climbed up, too. Even more cheers.

"Speech!" the crowd demanded. "Speech!"

Bullock shrugged. Walker stepped back. At that moment I saw Warren Reich and the E.B. pulling a wagon of bottles of champagne packed in ice into the newsroom.

Champagne corks began to pop. Someone handed me a bottle. I caught the E.B.'s eye. From across the room, she lifted her glass to me in a silent salute.

"I don't want champagne on the carpeting," DeCaprio, the assistant managing editor, shouted into the din.

It wouldn't have mattered, even if everyone could have heard him. I, for one, was determined that champagne was going everywhere, including the carpeting. I popped the cork and bubbles spewed out in a torrent. I took what was left and poured it on Bullock's head.

"Lemme have one of those!" Bullock demanded. Someone handed him a bottle. He hopped off the desk and sought out Carmela Cruz.

"I've always wanted to see what you look like wet," he said, drenching her.

"Too sweet," she laughed, licking her lips. "I prefer something drier."

The celebration went on until far too close to deadline. When it came time to take the official Pulitzer Prize pictures, Bullock and I were feeling magnanimous enough to accept the suggestion of Human Resources Director John Hafer that we make everyone part of the team—from the publisher, to the printers, to the delivery people.

"Why not?" Bullock said.

With Walker, Bullock, and me up front—the "bell cows" as Walker put it—all the newspaper's employees gathered in front of the *Charlotte Times* building while Drake set up a remote control camera on the roof.

"You know what the best part about this is?" Bullock whispered as Drake hustled down to join the group.

"What?"

"When they write our obits, it'll say 'Pulitzer Prize-winner.'"

THE PULITZER PRIZES are presented each spring in a special ceremony at Columbia University in New York. The publisher registered only a mild objection when Walker told him all three of us intended to go.

On the day of the ceremony, Walker took us to the *New York Times* for a tour. We saw editors on the phone with correspondents in Peking, a sports department that occupied almost an entire floor, an elaborate test kitchen for the food writers.

We dined on poached salmon, asparagus, and a chilled New York State white wine in a private dining room with one of the editors that Walker knew.

"It must be incredible to work here," I said to the editor. "Foreign correspondents, huge travel budgets, unlimited staff . . ."

"It's not bad," she said. "But the *New York Times* could be really good if we had sufficient resources."

I stole a glance at Bullock who rolled his eyes. In the cab on the way to the ceremony, I asked Walker if he was still looking for another job.

"Pardner, I was until that lunch. I got to figure if they don't have enough cowboys on the roundup at the damn *New York Times*, maybe there ain't no such thing."

A FEW DAYS after I got home, I called Brad and told him I was sorry about his father.

"He's up north now and if anything comes of this—there's no statute of limitations for rape in South Carolina—he'll have the best lawyers. I'm just sorry for all the hurt he's caused."

"Be proud of what you've done to make it right."

"It's strange to think of Wallace as my half brother. It makes his death even tougher."

"I know."

"You need to come down to Windrow. I still owe you and Reverend Grace a botany tour."

Two days later I took Brad up on his offer. It was still dark when he tapped me on the shoulder Saturday morning. I rubbed my eyes and looked at my watch. Just after five o' clock, I heard the clanging of pans and the sing-song voice of Mary Pell from the kitchen.

The sky was lightening to morning gray and it was cold enough that we could see our breath when we climbed into the pickup thirty minutes later. I lifted the napkin covering the basket Mary Pell had handed me and the cab filled with the smell of warm biscuits—sausage biscuits for

me, plain for Brad. I looked back at Tasha and Maybelle riding happily
in the truck bed.

"I don't recall them being vegetarians."

"Go ahead," Brad said.

I took patties from two biscuits and tossed them to the dogs.

We followed a sandy dirt road until it ended by a grove of trees at
the edge of the Savannah River.

"Live oaks," Brad said. "See how those low-hanging branches end
up growing almost parallel to the ground? You can see why they'd be so
good for ship planks."

I saw what he meant but my attention was diverted by the fact that
a long blue Buick was already parked at the grove, its driver's-side door
open and its driver lounging half in the car and half out. As we got closer
I could see that it was the lanky Reverend Grace dressed in jeans, high-top
black sneakers and a blue satin LA Dodgers baseball jacket.

It was the first time I had seen Grace since the Sampson story broke.
I hugged him and thanked him for his belief.

"Truth finds a way," he said.

"Eventually," I said.

"In the long run, truth doesn't need help. But in the short run,
sometimes it uses people like you and me to speed itself along."

Brad pulled a green fourteen-foot jonboat from a grove of bushes,
slid it into the river and maneuvered it to a short dock that stretched into
the river just inches above the water. He took a five-horsepower Evinrude
from the back of the pickup and bolted it to the stern of the jonboat as
Tasha and Maybelle scrambled in. Grace and I followed.

The sun was poking over the horizon. Brad started the quiet Evinrude and steered us away from the dock as small waves slapped the front
of the boat.

"Botanically, half of South Carolina's in the inner coastal plain and
half is in the outer coastal plain," Brad said above the outboard. "We're
right at the northern limit for plants that thrive in the tropics and right
at the southern limit for the mid-Atlantic species. So we have an incredible variety of vascular flora—three thousand, one hundred and sixty

different kinds, if you count native and naturalized."

Brad turned the tiller on the engine. The nose of the boat swung around so that we were heading upriver. "The thing about plants is that every one of them has something interesting about them," Brad said. "Did you see the Yaupon Holly?"

"Maybe," said Grace, stroking his salt-and-pepper beard.

"The bushes where we stashed the boat. Pointed leaves and little green berries. The leaf has the highest caffeine content of any plant there is. Much higher than tea or coffee. Used to be a very popular tea."

We were beating against the current with the wind at our backs. The sun was rising higher and it was starting to get warm. I peeled off my sweatshirt.

"Oleander," Brad said, pointing to the bank. "Also known as Southern Belle Suicide."

"Why?" I asked.

"It's a deadly poison but virtually undetectable in the human body. Legend is that it was the favorite of Southern belles who married rich men for their money, then killed them off with Oleander and set the death up to look like suicide. No muss. No fuss. No evidence."

A low growl emanated from Maybelle and in a moment both dogs were pointing in front of the bow, barking. Twenty feet in front of the boat a curious wet head with cat-like ears popped out of the water and watched us intently.

"Beaver," said Grace.

"River otter," corrected Brad. "Look at the skinny tail." For the next hundred yards the otter swam with us, popping up on one side of the boat, disappearing under water and then popping up on the other side. The dogs were invariably caught looking the wrong way and I began to feel the otter was enjoying the game, that he knew exactly what he was doing. In the next few miles we heard the calls of gulls and saw egrets, herons, osprey, and the nest of a bald eagle.

I found myself totally absorbed and relaxed, as if this life on the river was the only one I was living. I had almost forgotten about my father, Wallace Sampson, or why I had come to Windrow in the first place until we pulled to the bank to let the dogs run.

"That Pulitzer was a pretty good lick for you," Reverend Grace said as we sat on a log by the riverbank eating a biscuit. He picked up a cypress branch and began drawing crosses in the mud, releasing a musky smell of decomposition and decay. "That's journalism's highest award. And *People* magazine, you're right there with Oprah Winfrey and Rod Stewart."

"Matt, you ought to be pleased with yourself," Brad agreed.

I was, but for a different reason. I've learned it's not wise to depend on other people to define one's worth. I'd spent the better part of my life seeking approval from someone else and I'd found the search frustrating and never-ending. It turns out I'd been looking in the wrong places, outside, instead of in.

It was getting close to midday as we loaded back in the jonboat. Brad used the Evinrude to move us to the middle of the river and then cut the engine, letting the current take us where it wanted as we drifted downstream toward the dock. The breeze had vanished. Grace stripped off his jacket, draped his arms over one side of the boat and legs over the other, closed his eyes, and tilted his face to the sun.

I was alone with my thoughts until Grace said, "You're awfully quiet."

I told him I missed my father. "We were just starting to get to the good part," I said.

In one of those moments where everyone happens to be focused on the same thing, we were all watching when a dead tree suddenly toppled from the bank and splashed loudly into the river, flushing a flock of egrets.

"Tupelo gum," Brad said.

"If a tree falls in the forest and there's no one around to hear it, does it make a sound?" I asked.

We drifted on a ways before Grace spoke up. "You know your relationship with your father is like that tree making a sound because we were around to hear it. Let's say your father died but you didn't know it. You'd continue to think of him just the way you did when he was alive. You wouldn't know he had died so as far as you're concerned, the relationship is unchanged."

"I know. We're all going to meet on fluffy clouds one day in heaven."

"I'm not talking about that," Grace said. "My momma died when I was eight. Years later, I felt I'd been called by God to enter the seminary but I prayed for clarification. When I had finished a vision of my mother appeared to me. She told me something she always used to say when I was a young boy. 'Son, whatever your path, do something nice for someone along the way.' In other words, years after she was gone, my momma still spoke to me. Your father will always be in your heart and in your head. You will talk to him and you will know what he would say and what he would do. He will always exist for you. Death won't end that relationship. "

We rounded a turn and pulled up to the dock where we had put in. Tasha and Maybelle scampered down the dock, waded into the water up to their bellies and lapped up the river. Brad unhooked the Evinrude and loaded it into the pickup while Grace and I pulled the jonboat into a holly grove.

I arrived home Sunday to find a beaming Delana in a slinky dress— sexy and silly at the same time—doing her best Vanna White imitation with a fully restored green TR 3 in the driveway.

I was stunned. "It's just like the one Dad had when I was growing up," I marveled.

"It *is* the one your dad had when you were growing up. I tracked it down through the Triumph club six months ago and had it restored."

The next morning I drove the Triumph back to The Farmlet and surprised Delana in her pottery studio. She took off her clay-spattered apron and we walked to our favorite spot, the old dock at the pond. I knelt, took her hand, and proposed to her then and there. I barely got the words out before she pulled me up and clutched me tight. I reached into my pocket, took out the ring I had bought months ago and slipped it on her finger.

"It's beautiful," she said. I smiled. My father had always told me, don't scrimp. It's the one thing you'll give her that she'll show off the rest of her life.

We were married with Reverend Grace presiding and Ronnie Bullock serving as best man. Brad and Lindsay arrived in the Volvo along with Tasha and Maybelle and a wedding gift—an autographed copy of Brad's Windrow book, just published by the University of South Carolina Press. The ceremony took place in The Farmlet's pasture, not ten feet from where I had scattered my father's ashes just six months before.

We were having dinner two months later when Delana announced that we were expecting a son on July twenty-ninth.

"Luke's birthday," I said.

"Then that's his name."

I said I wasn't so sure.

"It honors your brother and your father," she said. "Plus it's a beautiful name."

The date was right but Lucy Harper, not Lucas, arrived on the twenty-ninth of July. As my dad taught me, never assume anything.